Linwood Barclay is an international bestselling crime and thriller author with over twenty critically acclaimed novels to his name, including the phenomenal number one bestseller *No Time For Goodbye*, and most recently the *Sunday Times* bestseller *Take Your Breath Away*. Every Linwood Barclay book is a masterclass in characterisation, plot and the killer twist, and with sales of over seven million copies globally, his books have been sold in more than 39 countries around the world and he can count Stephen King, Shari Lapena and Peter James among his many fans.

Many of his books have been optioned for film and TV, and Linwood wrote the screenplay for the film based on his bestselling novel *Never Saw It Coming*. Born in the US, his parents moved to Canada just as he was turning four, and he's lived there ever since. He lives in Toronto with his wife, Neetha. They have two grown children. Visit Linwood Barclay at www.linwoodbarclay.com or find him on Twitter at @linwood_barclay.

Linwood
BARCLAY

THE
LIE
MAKER

ONE PLACE. MANY STORIES

HQ
An imprint of HarperCollins*Publishers* Ltd
1 London Bridge Street
London SE1 9GF

www.harpercollins.co.uk

HarperCollins*Publishers*
Macken House, 39/40 Mayor Street Upper,
Dublin 1, D01 C9W8, Ireland

This edition 2023

1

First published in Great Britain by
HQ, an imprint of HarperCollins*Publishers* Ltd 2023

ISBN: HB: 978-0-00-855569-6
TPB: 978-0-00-855570-2

This book is produced from independently certified FSC™ paper to ensure responsible forest management.

For more information visit: www.harpercollins.co.uk/green

This book is set in 11/16 pt. Sabon by Type-it AS, Norway

Printed and Bound in the UK using 100% Renewable Electricity at CPI Group (UK) Ltd, Croydon, CR0 4YY

For Neetha

ONE

"**H**e could have someone out there," the man said, pulling back the front-window curtains a tentative inch. "Watching the house right now."

He was careful not to step directly in front of the glass as he peeked outside. It was raining. Streetlights reflected in the puddles. He ran his fingers nervously through his thick, dark hair. His handsome features were undercut by the fear in his eyes.

He wasn't used to being afraid. He was unaccustomed to the role of prey.

"He'll have found someone else to do his dirty work," he said. "Jesus, when are they going to get here?" He looked at his watch. "They're ten minutes late. What the hell's keeping them?"

He'd been directing his comments to his wife, a reedy, auburn-haired twig of a woman who looked ready to break into several pieces. She'd made several trips back and forth to the kitchen, trying to keep busy.

"Do you think they'll want coffee?" she asked.

"They're not going to want any goddamn coffee," he snapped.

She took a seat on the flowered couch, crossed her right leg over her left, then her left over her right. Some movement on the stairs caught her eye, and she spotted the nine-year-old boy sitting on one of the upper steps, watching from between the railings. A tear running down his cheek.

"Go upstairs," she told the boy.

"I want to say good—"

"Go to your room and close the door," she said, flinging her arm, pointing up. As she brought her arm back, she wiped a tear from her cheek.

The boy sniffed and retreated from view, waited until his mother was no longer looking his way, then resumed his position. From where he sat, he could see the front door, the three suitcases sitting there, his father still watching the street. His mother was up again, walking around the couch, going into the kitchen. He could hear the rattling of cups, silverware.

When she reappeared, her husband was still standing near the window.

"Get away from there," she said.

He let the curtain fall and stepped away.

"It's not too late, Rose," he said. "The two of you can still come. They've prepared the documents, in case you change your mind."

She stood behind the couch, her hands resting atop the cushions, as though using it as a barrier. Her jaw hardened and her eyes moistened.

"If you're desperate for company, why don't you take your father?" she said. "Maybe he'd like to start all over again with you. *He's* all alone."

"I can live without ever seeing him again. It's been years. But the three of us, we belong together. Once I walk out that door, once they put me in the car, that's it. It's not safe, staying behind. If he can't get to me, he'll come after you."

"And what would be the point of that?" she asked. "To get back at you? You've already washed your hands of us. And we certainly won't be able to tell him anything. You could be in Timbuktu for all we know. They can pull out all my toenails if they want, but I won't be able to tell them a thing. We'll take our chances. Your new friends, they'll keep an eye on us."

He took a step toward her, his face pleading. "I know I fucked up, that it's my fault, but we could start over. You, me, our son."

"He has his friends."

"He'll make *new* friends!" the man said. "They're not moving me to Mars."

"No, more likely Butthole, Nebraska, running a bowling alley or picking up trash."

"It's better than being dead."

She bit her lip. "Is it?"

"And I don't have to take some menial, mindless job. I'll find something . . . challenging. Meaningful."

She rolled her eyes as he took another look at his watch. "Christ, where the hell are they? What if—"

The lights went out.

"Oh, shit," the man said. "Shit shit shit." He rushed to the window again, peeked out. "Looks like the whole street."

With the streetlights out of commission, the living room was plunged into darkness.

"What's happening?" the boy sitting on the stairs asked.

"Go to your room!" his mother shouted, unable to hide the fear in her voice. "Get under the bed!"

"It's him," her husband whispered. "Jesus Christ, it's him. He's killed the power. He's here." He scurried through the unlit room, rounding the corner to the front door, banging his hip on the wainscoting. He checked that the door was locked, slipped the dangling chain into place, shouting to his wife, "The back door!"

She ran blindly from the living room into the kitchen. Seconds later, she called out: "It's locked!"

And then, as suddenly as they'd gone off, the lights came back on. The man froze, listening. All he could hear was the sound of the rain outside.

His wife stepped silently back into the living room. She whispered, "It's the storm. It's just the storm."

He looked through the diamond-shaped window in the door, saw that the streetlights were back on, too.

"Maybe," he said uncertainly.

He turned, looked at his wife, his eyes pleading, but no words came.

"I'm sorry," she said, shaking her head slowly. "I've nothing left to give." She looked toward the stairs, saw the boy sitting there.

Outside, sounds. Car doors opening and closing.

The man pulled back the curtain. "Finally." The woman went to the window to see for herself. A long, black sedan sat at the curb, lights on, windshield wipers flapping back and forth. A woman opened the front passenger door and got out, glanced up for half a second at the light rain coming down. The driver stayed behind the wheel. A second, identical car pulled up behind the first. Two men in black suits got out, took up watchful positions. If they were aware of the rain, they didn't show it.

Backup.

The woman who'd emerged from the first car walked toward the front door. She was clearly the agent in charge. The man turned back the dead bolt, undid the chain, and opened the door before she had a chance to ring the bell, swinging it wide, eyeing her accusingly.

"You're late," he said. "The power just out. It could have been him."

The woman stepped past him and into the front hall, glanced down at the three suitcases sitting there.

"Is this everything?" she asked.

"You said that was all I could take," he said. "Why are you late?"

The woman, stone-faced, ignored the question. "Sir, you need to get in the car, quickly."

His face cracked. "Why? What's going on?"

4

The woman hesitated, then said, "Our pickup plans may be compromised."

"Jesus Christ," the man said. Without thinking, he put his hand to the back of his neck, as though warding off an invisible dart.

"It may be nothing. But we've taken precautions. We have cars at each end of the street, blocking it off. That said, you need to get moving."

The agent looked at the wife. "Ma'am? Any change of heart?"

She did a slow head shake.

The agent spotted the boy at the top of the stairs, then said to his mother, "We'll have someone watching the house for the foreseeable future. They know there's nothing to be gained by intimidating or threatening you. They think things can't get worse for them, but they can."

The woman said nothing.

"It's time," the agent said, standing clear of the open door.

The man turned to pick up his bags and saw that his son, dressed in pale-blue pajamas, had reached the bottom of the stairs and was standing there mournfully. The boy's cheeks were wet with tears and his arms hung limply at his sides.

"Hey," the father said, ignoring the bags and kneeling down in front of the boy.

"Sir," the agent said, "we need to move."

"Just . . . a minute," he said over his shoulder, then turned back to the boy and gripped him by the shoulders. "So, you're going to be okay, you know?"

The boy sniffed.

"I need you to be strong for your mom. You're the new man of the house, you realize that, right?" He forced a smile. "I know you can do it. Because you're tough."

The boy said something, his voice no more than a whisper.

"What's that?"

5

"I want to come with you," the boy said.

"You can't, sport. Your mom doesn't want to come, and if that's the way it has to be, you're better off with her."

"When will you come back?" the boy asked.

The man felt something swell in his throat. "Just know that I'll be thinking about you, all the time, every minute of every day. That's a promise." He smiled ruefully, brought his voice down to a whisper. "Maybe I'll check in on you from time to time."

The boy sniffed, looked his father in the eye and asked, "Why can't you just tell them you're sorry?"

He smiled. "I wish it was that simple." Still on one knee, he said, "Let me give you a little going-away gift. Something to remember me by." He reached around into his back pocket and pulled out his wallet. A simple billfold made of brown leather. He opened it up briefly, exposing a couple of bills. A ten and a five.

"There's a few bucks in there," he said. "Enough for some comics or ice cream or something."

He took his son's hand and placed the wallet in it. The boy studied it, like it was some strange, unidentifiable artifact.

"What about your driver's license?" the boy asked.

"They'll get me a new one of those. New Social Security card, too, probably even a library card. Along with my new name, whatever it turns out to be."

"You won't be Dad anymore?"

The man looked as though he might crumble. He took a moment.

"I'll always be Dad," he said. He folded the child's fingers around the wallet. "You hold on tight to it, just in case. You never know, maybe one day I'll come back for it."

"Sir." The agent was getting antsy.

"Gotta run," the man said, pulling the boy into his arms and giving him a squeeze. "I love you, sport." He held the boy in his arms for a good ten seconds before standing. He tousled the boy's hair, gave him a thumbs-up, and turned to face the agent.

His voice breaking, he said, "Let's do this."

His wife remained by the window and made no move to give him a farewell embrace. She mouthed, "Goodbye."

"Okay, then," he said, grabbing one bag with each hand, which left one on the floor. He looked at the agent, as though expecting a hand. When she didn't move, he managed to tuck the third under his arm.

"So, anyway," he said to no one in particular, and stepped out into the rain. The agent followed, and the wife closed the door.

She looked at her son. "Off you go. I'll come up and see you in a minute." She went into the kitchen, where she could be heard opening and closing the fridge, followed by the sound of ice cubes being dropped into a glass.

Instead of heading for the stairs, he went to the front door, quietly opened it, and ran out into the rain. He caught up to his father just as he was about to get into the back seat of the lead car.

"Wait!" he cried.

He threw his arms around his father. The man knelt and went to wipe tears from the boy's cheeks, but they were indistinguishable from the raindrops.

"Son, I have to—"

"You have to tell me," the boy said. "You have to tell me why you can't tell them you're sorry."

"Sorry isn't good enough sometimes," his father said.

"What did you do?"

The father hesitated. The agent had settled into the front passenger seat to avoid the rain, but powered down her window to listen.

"You'll find out eventually," he said. "Your dad's not a good

7

person. Your dad killed people, son. That's what I did. I killed people. Sorry just doesn't cut it."

He gave the boy a final hug, got in the car, and closed the door. The boy watched him through the glass and stood there in the rain until the car had reached the end of the street and turned the corner.

TWO

Jack

I should have been more excited, first day at a new job.

It wasn't as if I didn't care. I was glad to have found some-thing. I told myself it was temporary. Didn't mention that in the interview, of course. No prospective employer wants to think you're viewing a position with them as a stopgap, although I think the guy who interviewed me, Terry, probably suspected it.

Like when he asked me, point-blank, "So, Mr. Givins, why on earth would you want to work for us?"

It was a good question.

Terry Crawford was the managing editor for a stable of trade magazines: *Contractor Life* (aimed at the construction industry), *RV Life* (for recreational vehicle manufacturers and enthusiasts), *Plumbing Life* (no explanation necessary), and so on. When I had observed, in the interview, the recurring theme in his magazines' titles, he had grinned and said, "We're high on life here."

He'd added, "Doesn't strike me that this would be the kind of place where you'd want to put your skills to work. Not that you aren't qualified. Getting two books written up in the *New York Times*? That's pretty impressive."

So he had done a bit of internet sleuthing. The books had been written under a pseudonym, but I'd been revealed as the author in one of those reviews. Someone at the publishing house must have leaked it at some point, although it created little buzz in the literary world. Good reviews in the *Times* had not led to a spot on the paper's bestseller lists. My first book, *Avoidably Inevitable*, had sunk like a stone. My second, *A Life Discontinued*, also garnered some praise, but the sales were only marginally better than the first book. My third, *Lost and Unfounded*, had yet to find a home despite the efforts of my literary agent, Harry Breedlove. I'd told him just before I interviewed with Terry that if he couldn't sell that book I was putting the full-time novelist thing aside indefinitely.

I could live with that if I had to. I'd only been out of the conventional workforce a couple of years. I'd spent a few at a medium-sized daily Massachusetts newspaper, writing as well as working on the desk, editing stories, writing headlines, assigning reporters. I liked that world, and was lucky to have worked in it, given that I had no journalistic background. I'd arrived at the right time, when the paper was short-staffed and the editor wasn't fussy.

But the timing wasn't entirely fortuitous. The industry, fighting a losing battle with the internet for readers and advertisers, was already in decline, and in the short time since I'd left, had contracted even further. Even before I left the *Worcester Tribune*, it had gone through two rounds of layoffs. The pandemic had made things even worse. Reporters had been working from home for so long, several papers dispensed with their newsrooms altogether and sold the buildings. The publishers were so encouraged by how much money that saved them that they started to look for more ways to make a profit, so they slashed their reporting staffs. It was like trying to save money at a restaurant by firing the cooks.

Anyway, getting a job at a paper again was out of the question, so here I was looking to work for a publisher of trade magazines. But I didn't feel I could tell Terry he was my last hope, even if he was. I was running out of money.

"The books are kind of a side thing," I said. "I'm looking for something steady."

"Gotta keep the paycheck coming in, right?" Terry said. "Married? Got kids?"

"No," I said after a second's hesitation. "Not married. No kids."

"You'd oversee production of five magazines," he said. "Each comes out six times a year."

"Sounds manageable," I said. "I can turn things around in a hurry. I'm pretty meticulous about getting things right."

Terry smiled. "Well, that's great, although to be honest, it's not that big a deal since I don't even know how many of our subscribers read these things, unless it's an actual story about them. The way we work it is, with a lot of our publications, we assign stories based on who buys ads."

The dreaded "advertorial." Content based on what someone was willing to pay. So much for objective journalism. I wasn't going to let that worry me today.

Terry's operation was based in Everett, one of Boston's suburban so-called cities, just across the line from Charlestown. I already had an apartment there, so there wouldn't be much of a commute. I'd moved closer to the city not long after I'd left the Worcester paper to have more of a cultural life—movies, theater, music—as well as to be nearer to Lana Wilshire.

Well, almost nearer. Lana was no suburban girl. She lived in the heart of the city, in a fancy condo that overlooked the harbor and, on the other side of the bay, Logan Airport. She was one of the *Boston Star* newspaper's senior reporters, and we'd met a few years earlier when she was covering a winter plane crash near Rutland, northwest of Worcester. I was on that story, too, and while we were waiting for a press briefing I offered to share a warm car with her while her photographer was elsewhere with the vehicle they'd driven up in. An hour and a half later we had each other's phone numbers and email addresses and had arranged to meet for dinner the next weekend in Boston.

We'd seen each other off and on for a few months. The relationship went quiet for a while, and then we picked things up again. Things had been semi-serious for the better part of a year. Neither of us had proposed any kind of major step, but it was in the back of my mind.

I'd just parked my car to go in for my first day on the new job when she sent me a text, which I only noticed when I took my phone out to check the time. I'd muted my phone the night before and forgotten to flip it back on that morning. I'd missed a call from the place I was about to walk into.

Lana had texted: **Got your Funk & Wagnalls?**

An inside joke, referencing a long-extinct American dictionary and encyclopedia publisher. I grinned, and thought about composing some witty retort before I headed into the building, but settled on:

Talk soon.

Once the phone was tucked into my pocket and before I went into the building, I did something I'd done out of habit for as long as I could remember. I did a visual sweep of my surroundings. Scanned the parking lot and the street in both directions. It was second nature to me, and I did it without really thinking about it.

I didn't know where my office was supposed to be, so I went straight to Terry's.

He was behind his desk when I rapped on the jamb of his open door. "Jack Givins, reporting for duty."

It was far from glamorous, his office. This wasn't *The New Yorker* or *Vanity Fair*, although, for all I know, they're a mess, too. His desk was littered with papers and folders, all crowded around a desktop and a laptop. Gray filing cabinets lined the walls, and half a dozen calendars from companies his magazines had done stories on decorated the walls, hanging from pushpins, not one of them turned to the right month. It was the kind of office that, forty years ago, someone would have plastered with centerfolds from *Playboy*, but even *Contractor Life* had moved on from those days.

Terry was a small guy, maybe five-four. Slight, with a receding hairline. His thick-rimmed glasses were his dominant facial feature.

"Oh, hey, Jack," Terry said. "Tried to call you." He didn't look well. Like he'd had a bad chili dog the night before and it was just now catching up with him. "Have a seat."

"Everything okay?" I asked.

A nervous laugh. He glanced at his desktop monitor, then the laptop, not looking for anything in particular. Killing time. "The thing is, there have been some developments."

"Developments," I said.

"I've been thinking, and I don't believe this is a good fit for you. I mean, it's great for us, because you've got the skills, you know, but with your background, I think we'd be holding you back."

"Shit, Terry, you firing me before I've even started?"

He kept trying to avoid eye contact. "I mean, if you were to be honest with me, you'd only be taking this job until something better came along."

"If I gave you that impression," I said, "then I apologize. It was never my intention. The truth is, Terry, I need this job."

His face went grim. "Then that makes this even harder. We were doing a review, and we've lost a lot of subscriptions post-pandemic. That wouldn't be so bad, but that corresponded with a significant drop in advertising. Everyone's pulling back. Take *Screener Life*, for example. That one's gone off a cliff."

That was their magazine for projectionists and movie theater owners. It made sense that that one would take a hit, given that film lovers had been fearful, for a couple of years, of going to a movie and catching something from the somebody sitting next to them.

"Only one we got making any money is *RV Life*. During the pandemic, so many people were hesitant to fly or leave the country, they went out and bought Winnebagos. And with the way gas prices are, that one's probably gonna be on life support soon. Anyway, what I'm getting around to saying is, I've got no money in the budget for your position anymore."

I sat there, numb. Surprised, for sure, but also, at some level, relieved. I hadn't been lying when I told him I needed this job. I had under five grand in my checking and savings. I wasn't looking forward to writing and editing stories about drywall and advances in water-saving toilet technology and peel-and-stick tile, but life is full of compromises, of making decisions we don't want to make.

"Sorry," he said.

I stood.

"Okay, then," I said. I was holding a quick debate in my head about whether I wanted to make this difficult for him. "I'm not sure this is legal, Terry."

"Yeah, well, I looked into that, Jack, and in this state, unless you're fired because of your gender or race or a disability, or you're pregnant, an employer can pretty much fire anyone for any reason and there's nothing you can do about it, even on the first day." He tried to lighten the mood in the room. "You're not pregnant, are you?"

I headed for the door.

"Funny thing," Terry said, and I stopped and slowly turned. "I guess you figured out I googled you, which is how I found out about those two books you wrote. And some stuff came up about when you worked at that paper up in Worcester. But there's not much online from before that."

"Is there a question?" I asked.

"Were you, like, living off the grid or something?"

"Maybe I was just minding my own business," I said. "You might want to give it a try."

I left. I was just getting into the car when I got another text from Lana:

Where should we go to celebrate tonight?

THREE

The dog was at the door, whining and scratching.

"Jesus Christ, didn't we just go out?" asked Willard Bentley. Only moments earlier, he'd settled into the overstuffed leather chair in his study with his evening brandy, about to resume reading *A Tale of Two Cities*. Bentley had promised himself that when he retired, he would take his wife, Audrey, on a round-the-world trip, and finally get to reading some of the classics he'd always intended to conquer but never managed to. For the trip, he'd bought one of those devices you could download books into so he wouldn't have to lug a bunch of heavy tomes from country to country.

But that trip never happened. The flights had all been arranged, the hotels booked, new luggage purchased. They were going to stay a week in each location, starting in London, then on to Paris, then Mumbai, followed by Hong Kong, Sydney, Christchurch, Hawaii, and then back home to Boston.

A week before their planned departure, Audrey got sick. Audrey did not get better. Around the time they would have been in Hong Kong, she was gone.

There was a period of mourning, of course, during which Willard found he could not focus on the printed word. It wasn't just Dickens he couldn't tackle. It was his daily newspaper. He could barely take in the headlines.

One day, his daughter and son-in-law showed up with a surprise by the name of Oliver, a feisty terrier pup who took no time at all to win Willard over, despite the man's protests that he wasn't up to looking after a dog. But it was Oliver who got him up and moving several times a day, going about the neighborhood to do his business.

(Oliver was not, by the way, named for Dickens's Oliver Twist, but for Oliver Wendell Holmes Jr., the onetime Supreme Court justice who had also served two decades as a justice on the Supreme Judicial Court of Massachusetts. Willard had always been a fan, and his daughter knew it.)

Willard credited Oliver with dragging him out of his doldrums and allowing him to resume his interests. He'd plowed through the works of Charles Dickens in the order in which they were published—actual hold-in-your-hand books now, since he wasn't going to be traveling—which meant starting with 1837's *The Pickwick Papers*. But there were eighteen works between that one and *A Tale of Two Cities*, published in 1859, and it had taken him only nine months to get through them.

It had been worth the wait. That first sentence resonated as strongly today as it had when Dickens had written it.

It was the best of times, it was the worst of times.

No shit, Willard thought.

What a world he was living in. Technological advances beyond anyone's imagining. A wired, connected world. Ordinary citizens able to buy tickets for trips to space. Homes that could be made from 3-D printers. And yet, at the same time, widespread belief in baseless conspiracy theories. Rejection of cures to serious health threats because some brain-dead radio host railed against them. The human race ran the gamut from unparalleled genius to total idiocy.

And yet, weren't people still basically good? The ones who misbehaved got all the attention, but there were small acts of kindness happening all the time, like when his next-door neigh-bors, Sylvia and Martin, came by unexpectedly the other day with a bag of three croissants, still hot from the bakery. Didn't that make it the best of times?

Oliver whined again.

As much as Willard hated to have to put his book aside and take Oliver for a walk around the block, having to clean up one of his messes from the carpet was even more objectionable.

"Okay, okay," he said. He felt his hips whimper in pain as he stood. He always had to take a few steps to get his joints operating smoothly.

He went to the front hall, found a light jacket in the closet and slipped it on, then snapped the lead that was hanging from the front door onto Oliver's collar. Willard grabbed the house keys, opened the door, and, once out on the front step, locked up. Oliver strained at the leash, desperate to begin his sniffing of the neighborhood.

A young woman emerging from the Beacon Hill residence next to Willard's glanced his way and waved. It was Sylvia, a backpack slung over her shoulder.

"Evening, Judge!" she called out.

They all still called him that, even though he hadn't presided over a case in years. He smiled and gave a half-hearted wave in return. "Hello, Sylvia," he said. "Off to the gym?"

"Gotta stay in shape to keep up with you," she said, springing down the few steps to the sidewalk. "Hey, there, Oliver! How's it going?"

Oliver was too busy sniffing a wet mark on the curb to respond. As Sylvia waved a second time and walked briskly up the street, Willard noticed that there weren't too many people out and about tonight.

That was fine. That meant he wasn't going to run into anyone he knew, wouldn't feel obliged to make small talk. Chitchat exhausted Willard. He wanted Oliver to do his business so he could get back to his reading and his brandy.

Oliver picked up the pace, trotting his way down the sidewalk, the leash taut. He had forgone sniffing every fence post and fire hydrant, and appeared to be on a mission. Maybe he had picked up some faraway scent that demanded investigating.

As they were passing a dark gap between houses, Willard heard something. A scuffle, a trash can being knocked over.

Rats, he thought. No, a raccoon, maybe. A rat couldn't make that much noise.

But then a voice. Someone whimpering. Willard couldn't tell whether it was a man or a woman. He stopped, listened, Oliver still straining at the lead, wanting to move forward.

It occurred to Willard at that moment that he had left the house without his cell phone. If someone was hurt, and if that person did not have a phone, Willard would have to start knocking on doors to summon assistance.

"Hello?" he said, standing at the mouth of the alley. Shadows, snatches of light. The old man squinted, trying to see into the darkness more clearly. He thought he could make out a shape, someone struggling to stand.

"Judge, is that you?"

A man's voice. And clearly, someone who recognized him. Maybe one of his neighbors.

"Yes, yes," Willard said. "Who is it?"

"I'm hurt," the man said weakly. The retired judge could see someone raising an arm to the wall, supporting himself.

Willard entered the alley, pulling Oliver along with him.

"What's wrong? Who is it? Are you injured?"

Willard took several more steps into the alley, until he was close enough to make out the face of the person who had called out to him.

"Do I—do I know you?" Willard asked as the man took his

hand off the wall, and Willard saw that it had been holding something. Something that looked like a club, like a short baseball bat.

"Someone would like to have a word with you," the man said before bringing the club down.

Moments later, Oliver came wandering out of the alley, not quite sure what to do or where to go, dragging his leash behind him, feeling, as much as a dog is able to, that it was the worst of times.

FOUR

Jack

"Looks like I won't be doing any road tests of the new John Deere for *Lawnmower Life*," I said.

"That's a joke, right?" Lana Wilshire said. "There's not really a *Lawnmower Life*."

"Honestly, it wouldn't surprise me."

We were in her tenth-floor condo in the Harbor Towers. Her place faced the harbor, with a view of the New England Aquarium to the north, and across the water, we could see the planes coming in and taking off at Logan. Her digs were only about five thousand times better than my small second-floor apartment in what was once a large, two-story Everett home. Lana's place was a short walk to a dozen five-star Boston restaurants. Mine was a stone's throw from a strip mall whose main attractions were a bagel place and a Dunkin' Donuts.

Lana was probably as well paid as anyone in the *Boston Star* newsroom, but that still wouldn't be enough to afford a place like this. Lana could make it on her own, without question, but she hadn't said no when her parents, both retired lawyers living in Beacon Hill splendor, offered to help her buy this place. I wouldn't have said no, either, but what family I had would have been hard-pressed to come up with a Christmas bonus for Lana's doorman.

While her parents had helped her buy it, she had definitely made it her own, with big, puffy couches and chairs that managed to be stylish as well as comfortable. The walls were adorned with several enlarged black-and-white journalistic photographs with a common theme: famous and not-so-famous people raising their hands to the camera, desperately trying not to have their picture taken. The photos had a blurry, urgent immediacy to them, and they sent a message that was central to Lana's approach to her craft:

You can run but you can't hide, you son of a bitch.

I wasn't so sure. The first time I was here, as I went from picture to picture, studying them, Lana had asked, "See anyone you know?"

"Don't think so," I'd said.

On another wall, hung more subtly between some pictures of friends and family, was another black-and-white shot, this one of the late writer Joan Didion leaning up against her Corvette Stingray. It had been taken back in the late sixties, shot by Julian Wasser for a *Vogue* profile. Didion's novels and journalism were an inspiration to Lana. And these two women had something in common beyond a dedication to exposing people to truths they might prefer to avoid. They were diminutive in stature, which meant their subjects often underestimated how formidable they could be until they read what they'd written.

Lana, just over five feet tall in her stockinged feet but partial to four-inch heels so she wouldn't be overlooked when she waved her hand in the air at news conferences, was as fearless as anyone I knew. She'd walk into a mob of people chanting "Fake news!" with her notepad in hand and shout back, "Then set me straight." She'd grab that orange vest and hard hat she kept in the trunk of her aging BMW and walk right under that yellow caution tape to get up close to an accident scene.

I loved her.

Instead of going out to celebrate—I'd texted Lana earlier to suggest more modest plans, and intended to wait until I actually saw her to explain that morning's disappointing developments—we brought back to her place a couple of tuna tacos and a sausage and cherry-pepper pizza from Fin Point. Just as well, because as it turned out Lana had been handed a last-minute evening assignment and we hadn't connected until almost ten.

We had forgone plates and fine cutlery for standing at the counter and eating out of the box.

"I'm so sorry," she said. "How could he do that?"

I shook my head. "Doesn't matter. Hell with it. I wasn't very excited about the job anyway. Sometimes I think I should never have left Worcester, but if I'd stayed, I'd probably have been laid off by now."

"You can't drive yourself crazy second-guessing the things you should or shouldn't have done. You have to— Hello."

Something had caught Lana's eye. Her wall-mounted flat-screen TV was on and tuned to the local eleven o'clock newscast. Lana always had some news station running in the background. The set was on mute, but now she wanted to hear what was going on.

Carrying a slice, she went over to the coffee table, grabbed the remote, and upped the volume.

"—and after the break, the latest on that missing judge," the female anchor said.

"Want to see what they've got on this," she said, putting the set back on mute.

"A missing judge?"

She waved the question away. "And nothing from Harry?"

"If he'd had any nibbles on the book he'd have let me know."

"You need a new agent."

We'd been over this before. Just because Harry wasn't with one of the big literary agencies, she thought he wasn't up to much. Granted, he hadn't represented a lot of big names, but at least he'd managed to sell my first two novels.

I walked to the window to get a better look at the planes taking off and landing, but then found my gaze drawn to the street, watching people going about their business. It was late, and there weren't that many. Someone stopped to look up at the building, then kept on walking.

"You've got that look," Lana said.

"What look?" I asked, turning to face her.

"You get it all the time. We'll be sitting in a restaurant and it's like you're looking over my shoulder, or turning around to look over your own. Like you're expecting somebody."

"I don't think I do that."

"Well, you do."

I didn't want to admit she was right. It was a hard habit to break.

She unmuted the set once again. "Here it is."

A news correspondent for the local NBC affiliate was standing on a street in Boston's Beacon Hill neighborhood. Behind him, a stately looking two-story home that had no doubt been updated several times since it was built a couple of centuries ago. At the curb, a couple of unmarked police cars. Across the bottom of the screen, the words RETIRED JUDGE MISSING.

"This is why I was late," Lana said. "It's around the corner from my parents' place. Got sent to cover it."

The reporter was talking about some elderly gentleman who'd taken his dog out for a walk early that evening and never returned. They'd found the dog. The missing man, whose name I did not catch, had a long judicial career.

"Wouldn't normally cover an old guy who'd wandered off

from home, but he was a big deal once. Just wondered if they had anything new."

"His family's got to be worried sick."

"Might be Alzheimer's or something, although everyone I talked to said he still had all his marbles. He was out walking his dog, Oliver. The mutt showed up later, leash still attached to his collar." She sighed, hit the mute again, and said, "Anyway. I'll probably be doing a proper follow-up on him tomorrow that may turn into an obit if they find his body."

And then, suddenly, she sneezed.

"Oh, shit," she said. "I nearly blew pizza through my nose."

She walked back over to the island. I handed her a napkin, which she used to first wipe her nose, then her chin. Another sneeze followed.

"That time of year," she said, and went rooting about in her purse for some allergy pills. This was September, when the ragweed was in full bloom, and Lana took various over-the-counter antihistamines to hold the symptoms in check.

She sniffed a couple of times, took a shot from some nasal inhaler, tossed it back into her purse, and dabbed her watery eyes with a tissue. Allergy attack over, she reached into the fridge for another bottle of wine and was about to open it when she stopped and asked, "You staying over or are you driving?"

Part of me wanted very much to stay over, and I told her so.

"But I want to get an early start tomorrow on what I'm going to do next," I said. Not that I had a plan, but I had to do something.

"Maybe your dad would have some leads?" she suggested.

"Earl's not exactly my go-to guy when I have a problem."

Lana believed parents were referred to as "Mom" and "Dad," but she was used to my use of "Earl."

"Funny you should mention him, though," I said. "He called

me a couple of days ago. Wants to see me. Set it up for tomorrow. Told him it would have to be quick. Couldn't exactly take a long break from work my second day on the job. Don't have to worry about that now."

"You almost never talk about him. Or your mom."

I shrugged. "Not much to talk about. She passed away a long time ago. Earl and I kind of drifted apart after that. See him maybe once a year. If he didn't live around here I probably never would. He's probably got some pyramid scheme he wants me to invest in."

Lana slipped her arms around me, came in close, and offered her lips to mine.

"You're sure about not staying over?" She smiled slyly. "How about . . . five more minutes?"

"I'd like to think I'd take just a little longer than that."

I was back on the street fifteen minutes later. As I walked away from her building to where I had left my car on the street, a couple of blocks from Quincy Market, I could hear sirens. Hardly surprising in the heart of the city.

Moments later, a fire truck went screaming past me, heading the same direction I was going. As I turned a corner to walk down the street where I'd left my aging Nissan, I saw that this was the fire truck's destination. Something was ablaze near where I had parked.

I'd only run about twenty yards when I realized that it wasn't that my car was close to the fire's location. My car *was* the fire's location.

The firefighters were already training their hoses on it, dousing the vehicle with water. Steam and black smoke billowed into the night air. They were working quickly to keep the blaze from spreading to other vehicles or nearby buildings. For now, the Nissan was the only thing in flames.

"That's my car!" I shouted, running toward one of the fire-fighters stationed by the truck.

The firefighter turned my way and shrugged.

"Lucky you weren't in it," he said.

Yeah, I was having a real run of good luck lately.

FIVE

"Sit down, sit down, I need to talk to you."

"What is it, Dad? Am I in trouble?"

"Of course not. Don't be silly. I guess you've probably heard your mother and me talking."

"I might have heard . . . something. About you being in trouble."

"Yeah, that's right. I'm going to have to go away."

"Where?"

"Don't know exactly. That's still being sorted out."

"Is Mom going with you? Are you guys leaving me all by myself?"

"No, no, nothing like that. It's going to be just me going."

"For how long?"

"Okay, so this is the hard part."

SIX

Jack

I grabbed an Uber from home to meet someone from my insurance company the next morning at a garage where the charred remains of my car had been taken.

His name was Arnold, and he was a thin, short man who wasn't much bigger than your average twelve-year-old. He made little clicking noises with his tongue as he walked around the car, taking photos with his phone, making notes.

"Looks like it caught on fire," he said.

Sharpest knife in the drawer, this one. "Yeah," I said.

"They have any idea why?"

If the police and firefighters who responded to the call knew, they hadn't passed the information on to me. Electrical fault, arson, it was anybody's guess at the moment. "I don't know," I said. "The car'd been parked, the engine was off."

"I'll be getting a copy of the report," Arnold said.

"So what'll I get for it?" I asked. I wasn't expecting much. That year's model, with nearly a hundred thousand miles on it, could be found online for less than four grand. Whatever the insurance company decided it was worth, I wanted it sooner rather than later. My monthly rent of nineteen hundred dollars was due in ten days. I had about nine hundred bucks on my Visa.

"I'll be in touch," he said.

I got out my phone to get an Uber back to my place, but it rang before I could call up the app. The caller ID said EARL. I'd remembered, the night before, that I was supposed to see him today, but the business with the car had pushed it to the back of my mind again.

I took the call.

"Hey, Earl."

"Where are you?" he asked in his raspy voice. "I went inside, they said you don't even work there?"

Shit. When we'd arranged this, I'd told him to drop by my new place of employment. "Yeah, that didn't work out." I told him the location of the garage.

"Okay," he said. "I'll come to you."

It was a strange relationship I had with the man. I was twenty when my mother died, and out of the house, for the most part, at college. I'd always had the feeling that rather than causing him to wallow in grief, my mother's death and my departure had given my father a sense of liberation, a freedom from responsibility, although responsibility was never his strong suit to begin with. But after Mom died, Earl didn't have to worry about her, and her stern judgments of him, and he didn't have to worry about me. I was off to college at that point and had indicated, even before Mom passed, that it wasn't my intention to return.

Earl sold the house shortly after her death, and he hadn't bothered to ask me what I thought of the idea. This wasn't the house I'd grown up in as a kid, but the one I'd lived in since I was twelve. It wasn't so much that Earl wanted to start over or live somewhere that wasn't haunted with memories of my mom. He just needed the money.

Earl wasn't particularly talented when it came to finances. Maybe that's not fair. He was very good at spending it, at throwing it away. He was less skilled at hanging on to it, investing it, making it work for him. He wasn't a gambler in the strictest sense of the word. He didn't frequent casinos or play cards or bet on the horses. But he was big on get-rich-quick schemes, things that would bring huge rewards in a short time with a minimum of effort.

"*This* is the one," he would tell my mother, and you could almost see her deflate as she imagined more of their savings—actually, more of *her* savings—evaporating. Among the things he'd sunk money into while I was still at home were a housing project that was built on a sinkhole, a window that opened and closed through voice activation (ahead of its time, not totally unheard of now with some wired houses), and a drive-through fast-food operation with a totally vegan menu. Well intentioned, maybe, but situated as it was between a McDonald's and a Burger King, it never stood a chance against the airborne aromas of Big Macs and Whoppers.

And yet, somehow he skated through these financial misadventures, always confident that one of them would pay off. Borrowing from friends—soon to be *ex*-friends—to pay off previous debts, selling off anything he could, including, at one point, Mom's 1995 Eldorado while she was visiting her mother, and doing the occasional wise real-estate flip. That was one thing he'd had some success with. Finding some run-down property, getting it fixed up just enough that it looked presentable, then selling it quickly at a profit. If it weren't for one of those deals every eight to ten months, he'd have been on the street begging for change.

I don't think he could have pulled off any of it if he weren't so charming. He was, at his core, a likable enough guy, and he gave it his best shot where I was concerned. He tried to impart what little wisdom he possessed, and when I was in my teens and getting into shit I shouldn't, he'd either find a way to bail me out—not literally; I never found myself arrested for any of my shenanigans, and they were plentiful—or at least cover it up so my mother didn't find out.

It's only right that I point out here that I was as much a source of stress for my mother as Earl. Starting around age ten. Stealing shit from corner stores, staying out to all hours, worrying my mom to death. Ran away from home repeatedly. Once, when I was eleven, I was gone three days. Had saved up some money— well, had stolen a little from my mom's purse every few days over a couple of months so she wouldn't notice—and bought an Amtrak ticket to Chicago. Had to lie to the ticket taker. Told her I was going to see my uncle. Police finally found me sitting on those steps in Union Station where they filmed the famous baby carriage scene in *The Untouchables*. Mom had to catch a plane to come fetch me and bring me home.

The next year, I took a bus to Providence one day without telling my mother, and another time I hitchhiked to Cape Cod, telling the couple who picked me up that I was on my way to see my aunt in East Sandwich. Both times, Mom had to come and get me. She caught me once while I was on the phone trying to book an airline ticket to Phoenix. Didn't make that flight.

"Why?" she asked me repeatedly. "Why are you doing this to me?"

Like she didn't know.

I became less of an asshole as I progressed into my later teens, and after I finished college, where my interest in writing had been rekindled by an English lit professor, I made my first attempt to get a newspaper job, but it didn't pan out.

Did a bit of this and that for a few years.

Finally ended up getting that journalism job in Worcester. All this time, I kept in touch only sporadically with Earl, who had a small apartment in Quincy. I'd hear from him around my birthday—not every year, but at least every other year, and usually about a week late—and he'd take me out for dinner. I rarely saw him at Christmas. He liked to head down to Florida or Arizona for a month or two, escape Boston's often unbearably cold winters, and, I surmised, find some attractive widow to bunk in with at minimal expense.

My birthday wasn't today, it wasn't last week or the week before, and it wasn't coming up any time soon, so I had no idea what the occasion was, why my father wanted to get together now.

He showed up about fifteen minutes after our phone call, driving a mid-engine, two-seater Porsche Boxster. I knew my cars well enough to know this was one of the early models, and even if I didn't, the pimples of rust around the wheel wells would have been a clue. He pulled up to the curb, the top down, which showed off the cracked leather passenger seat with some of the padding sneaking out. This was pure Earl. Something that looked flashy so long as you didn't look too closely. Like shining the toes of your shoes so you make a good impression when you meet people, but not polishing the backs because you don't care what they think of you when you leave.

"Well," I said, casting my eye across the dash, the stick shift, and then him.

"Just basic transportation," Earl quipped, a smug grin on his face.

I had to admit he was looking pretty good. In his mid-sixties, he could have passed for mid-fifties. Still had most of his hair—albeit silver—and he was trim and tanned, which I was guessing was either sprayed on or maybe he had a friend on the Cape who'd let him flake out on the beach for a few weeks. He had on a pair of knockoff designer jeans and a white, short-sleeve, button-down-collar shirt.

"What happened to your car?" he asked, aiming his thumb over his shoulder as we pulled away from the curb.

"It blew up."

Earl shot me a concerning look. "What?"

I filled him in.

"That why you weren't at this new job of yours?"

"Long story. Let's walk."

He quickly put up the car's convertible top, which had some rips and tears to match the upholstery. Once it was locked up, we strolled down the sidewalk and I told him about the job that was pulled out from under me.

"The son of a bitch," Earl said.

I shrugged. "I'll find something."

"I don't understand why you even wanted that gig, working on magazines you can't even buy at a newsstand. Was it research? You doing a book set in the construction industry? Something like that?"

"No."

Earl looked puzzled. "I thought you were writing another book."

"I did."

"So when does it come out?"

"My agent hasn't found a home for it."

There was something in Earl's look of disappointment that suggested it was more for himself than me.

"But he *will* sell it, right?"

"Hope so."

"And for a lot of money, right? When a writer sells a book, it's usually for a hundred grand or half a million or something like that, right?"

"Some writers, sure."

We'd come to a bench and I motioned to it. We sat facing the street. I watched the people who walked by, the cars that went past.

"Maybe it's this fake name you're using," Earl said. "'Oscar Laidlaw.' Where'd that even come from? The Oscar part sounds a little, I don't know, pompous or something. Off-putting. Jack Givins sounds better. You could finally put your picture on the cover. Readers see you, it's like they make a connection. And I'd stop feeling hurt that you don't want to use my name."

"It's got nothing to do with you. I like keeping a low profile."

"How do you expect to sell books that way? Did you even do *one* TV interview for them when they came out?"

"I might have had I been asked," I said. Neither of my novels had exactly been a *Today* show pick or anything. "Earl, why'd you want to meet up? My birthday's four months away. You're early."

He smiled. "Maybe I'm eight months late." He was kind of right about that, actually. He hadn't been in touch back in January when I'd turned thirty-four. I looked at him, waiting for a straight answer. Finally, he shrugged and said, "I just wanted to, you know, check in."

I was skeptical.

"You still seeing that reporter? Works for the *Star*?"

"Yeah."

"What's her name again?"

"Lana Wilshire."

"Right. I see her byline all the time. Sometimes they run a little headshot with her stories. Pretty girl. Very nice."

I waited. He was working up to whatever it was he wanted to talk about. I watched a blue Corvette rumble past. A red Explorer SUV went the other way. A young woman walked by with four dogs on leashes.

Earl cleared his throat, licked his lips. He was ready.

"There is *something* I wanted to discuss with you."

I waited.

"You probably noticed, over the years, that some of my investments didn't always pan out the way I'd hoped."

I kept a straight face and nodded.

"Lots of ups and downs. Right now I'm in a situation where I'm a little overextended. I guess what you would call a negative liquidity situation." He paused, maybe waiting for me to ask him a question, which I didn't. He sighed. "Basically I'm up to my ass in alligators."

"Sorry to hear."

"Guess you heard about that thing in Florida? That building that went down a few months back? Pancaked? By the beach?"

The story had made news around the world. The apartment tower collapsed in the middle of the night. Nearly a hundred killed. Rusted-out support beams in the underground parking garage blamed.

"I heard."

"I had this opportunity about a year ago to buy into some of those units. Old folks who'd been living there had died, the grown kids didn't want them, wanted to sell. Figured I could flip them pretty fast, make a good buck."

"How many did you buy?"

He raised two fingers.

"Jesus," I said.

He licked his lips again. A few beads of sweat had broken out on his forehead. "There's a big investigation going on, probably gonna take years, and until they settle this, it presents some financial challenges for me, if you get my drift. Meeting the payments, that kind of thing."

"Were people living in those condos? The two you bought? Were you renting them out?"

He nodded slowly. "Nice lady from Brooklyn died in one. A retired couple from Duluth in another. It's a tragedy, a terrible tragedy, no doubt about it. And my heart goes out to their families, for sure. That's my number-one concern. But I'm a victim here, too. Going to sell the car, and my condo in Quincy." Earl sniffed. "I could use a loan."

"I'll bet."

"I'll pay you back. Thing is, I can't go to the banks. They won't lend me a dime. I'm kind of at the point where I might have to approach more unconventional lending services."

Guys with broken noses in the back room of some North End takeout joint, I was betting.

"I'm sorry, Earl. I'm tapped out."

"Yeah, but when you sell this latest book . . . you must have something tucked away."

"What do you need?"

He shrugged. "I don't know. Fifty?"

"Fifty . . ."

"Thousand. Fifty thousand," he said.

It was hard not to laugh. The corner of my mouth went up.

"You think this is funny?" he asked.

"No. It's just . . . you have an inflated sense of what most authors actually make. I could barely lend you fifty *dollars* right now."

"You gotta be kidding me."

I shook my head.

He sat back against the bench, dropped his hands into his lap. "Fuck."

"Sorry," I said. I was about to tell him that even if I had the money, I wouldn't have given it to him, but there was no sense making him feel worse than he already did.

My phone rang. I dug it out of my pocket, saw the name HARRY, and declined the call.

"Who was that?" Earl asked.

"My agent. I'll get back to him."

"That could be *the* call," he said urgently. "That's your fucking ship coming in."

"Or yours," I said.

We were both quiet for a moment. A bus went by. A kid on a skateboard. An elderly woman using a walker.

Earl was the first to speak. "Can't believe my own kid won't help me out."

That one caught me off guard a bit. It wasn't often he used those words to describe me. If he was trying to lay a guilt trip on me, it wasn't going to work.

He put his hand on my knee, gave it a squeeze, and stood. "Anyway, it was worth a shot."

"Hope you can sort it all out," I said.

Earl nodded. "Everyone's got problems, right?" He took a long look at me and suddenly appeared thoughtful. Concerned, even.

"So your car, the fire and everything. You don't think it means anything, do you?"

I'd been wondering the same thing.

"I don't think so," I said.

Earl nodded slowly. "You're probably right. It doesn't make any sense. Been too long. And what would be the point? Why would somebody send a message after all this time?"

"That's what I was thinking," I said.

"Probably just some crossed wires or something like that."

"You take care, Earl."

"You want a lift?"

"That's okay. Think I'll just sit here a minute, get an Uber home in a bit."

Earl nodded, gave me half a wave, and headed back for his car.

SEVEN

When Lana arrived at the *Star* newsroom the following morning she checked in with the Metro editor to confirm that she was to do a more in-depth follow-up on Willard Bentley. The morning edition had carried the news that the esteemed retired judge had gone missing, and there were further updates for the online edition, mostly about how the police were continuing their search, but what the *Star* needed was a more thorough retrospective on the man's career. In all likelihood, a proper obituary on one of the city's more notable citizens.

Lana started with the police to find out whether there was anything new. There wasn't. Then she went to the paper's digital library and looked up stories that mentioned him, which led her to make a list of other prominent Bostonians who had crossed paths with the judge at one time or another. Other judges, politicians, lawyers who had tangled with him but who had nothing but respect, just the same.

Her story was heavy with big names, but what it still needed was comments from average folks who knew him, as well as family members. It was at that point that she decided to head to Beacon Hill and start knocking on doors.

It wasn't long before she connected with Bentley's next-door neighbor, Sylvia Kingston.

"He was the most lovely man," she told Lana after inviting

her into the house. "Oh, my, I shouldn't speak that way. I'm still hoping against hope that they'll find him. Maybe he's just lost, or . . . But he really *is* the most lovely man. Very low key, unassuming. You'd never know, talking to him on the street, that he'd been such a big deal at one time. We moved in eight years ago, around the time he retired, I think. He'd just presided over that case about the two brothers who planted a bomb outside the Paul Revere house, the one they disarmed just before it blew up? You remember that?"

"I do."

"Mr. Bentley went through a rough patch there, after his wife died. Was very down, but he came out of it, I think. They were going to go on this big trip, and then she got sick. It's so sad."

"According to the police, you're the last person known to have seen him."

"He was coming out of his place, with Oliver? His dog? His daughter gave him the dog after his wife died, and he grumbled about it at first, having a pet to look after, but he sure loves that dog. I was heading to the gym when he was coming out."

"How did he seem to you?"

"He was fine."

"Not confused, or unwell in any way?"

Sylvia shook her head. "I don't understand how he could just vanish. They found Oliver. If the judge fell or hit his head or something, you'd think they would have found him by now. Do you know who's looking after the dog?"

"I don't."

"If you find out, would you let me know? I mean, if they've sent him to the pound or something, we'd take him in until he's found or whatever."

"Sure, I can do that."

Willard Bentley's daughter, Katie Ward, was having a difficult time pulling herself together.

"I'm sorry," Katie said. "I keep waiting to hear something, anything, but there's nothing."

Lana, sitting in the living room of the woman's Mission Hill home, said, "I'm sure the police will let you know the moment they know anything."

On the couch with Katie, his head resting on her lap, was a snoozing Oliver.

"Your father's neighbor will be relieved to hear Oliver is with you," Lana said. "She offered to look after him if no one else was."

Katie stroked the dog's head. "My husband and I gave him Oliver after Mom died. He thought it was a stupid idea at first, but then they formed this kind of bond, you know? They just love each other to death."

She winced, realizing she could have chosen her words more carefully.

"I've talked to so many people this morning who are praying that he's found soon and that he's okay," Lana said. "He's so respected."

Katie bit her lip and looked away. "It's been more than eighteen hours now. I don't understand why he hasn't turned up."

"Have you noticed any . . . cognitive issues with your father lately? Confusion?"

Katie shook her head wearily. "I don't . . . think so. I mean, he's more forgetful now. He has a hard time pulling up people's names. At our last lunch a month or two ago, we got talking about some TV shows that we'd been binge-watching, and he had the hardest time trying to remember the titles. But we're all like that once in a while, aren't we?"

"I know I am," Lana said. "When did you last speak with him?"

"I guess it was a week ago. I call him every few days or he calls me, and we get caught up on each other's news. Sometimes we'll take him out for Sunday brunch. He's been working his way through all of Charles Dickens, something he's wanted to do all his life but never had the time. He was on *A Tale of Two Cities*."

Oliver stirred, uttered a barely audible whine, and stayed asleep. Katie ran her hand softly down the dog's spine.

"It's okay," she whispered. "It's going to be okay." Teary-eyed, she looked at Lana and said, "If only he could talk, tell us what he saw? If . . . if . . . And now I feel like, if he hadn't had to take Oliver for a walk, he wouldn't have been on the street at that time, and whatever happened to him . . ."

Lana gave the woman a moment.

"I don't know why anyone would want to hurt him," the daughter said. "I haven't wanted to let my mind go there, but I know . . . there have been incidents where judges have been targeted, their families attacked, out of revenge. And sometimes there doesn't even have to be a real motive. People get it into their head to do something crazy and they do it. I remember there was a case where Dad dismissed charges against a man who'd been charged with a sexual assault, because the evidence was seriously tainted and it looked like police had fabricated some of it, and this talk-radio host went to town on Dad, said he wanted to let all the perverts out of jail, and it was scary there for a week or so, all these threats he received. But he's been retired a long time now. It doesn't make any sense that anyone would want to do him any harm." She wiped away a tear. "So he must have gotten confused, or lost, or fallen."

Lana was inclined to agree with the retired judge's daughter. The man had not presided over a case in nearly a decade. Why would anyone want to exact any revenge at this late date? Still, he could have had a run-in with some common thug. Maybe someone strung out, looking for drug money. Then again, he was an old man, and even if he hadn't been exhibiting any serious signs of dementia, he might have become confused. Wandered off, gotten lost.

Sooner or later, Lana guessed, he'd turn up, one way or another.

EIGHT

Jack

Harry Breedlove lived in Manhattan, but he came to Boston every few weeks to visit an ailing aunt and another author he represented. I'd told him the next time he was in town I wanted a sit-down to talk about where things were with my third book. I'd had a feeling for the last month or so that he was avoiding me. In the past he had almost always responded to emails within the hour. Lately, it took a couple of days or a second email from me to prompt a response. Ditto for texts.

So I was grateful that he had gotten in touch to say he was going to be in the neighborhood the next day. His text was followed up with a phone call.

"All those times I've been to Boston, I've never been to that aquarium," he said. "Do you want to meet there?"

I wanted a serious business meeting, but I supposed it wouldn't hurt to take him for a quick tour of the New England Aquarium. "Sure. It's like this massive four-story goldfish bowl with a descending walkway around it. A Guggenheim full of fish."

Harry's call was only a minor distraction that kept me from thinking about my other problems: my employment situation, my incinerated car, and Earl's financial woes. I was more worried about the first two. Earl was on his own.

After Earl drove away, I Ubered home and put the TV on for background noise. Found a *Law & Order*, my go-to. There was always a station, at any hour of the day, running an episode from one of its twenty seasons (and that wasn't counting all the spin-offs or the reboot) and when I stumbled on one, I often stopped and watched, at least for a few minutes. I got out my laptop and started surfing through job sites, the occasional *thunk thunk* from the TV interrupting my search.

I started with postings that would make some use of my writing skills—public relations, speechwriting, advertising—but there weren't many of those to be found. None, actually. I would have to broaden my search parameters. Not so far, I hoped, as to include "Walmart greeter."

I was having some trouble focusing. In the back of my mind, I could hear Earl saying, *Why would somebody send a message after all this time?*

He was right. Didn't make any sense. Didn't make any sense *at all*.

I folded down the laptop screen. Maybe I should put off my job hunt for one day. If Harry had good news, that he had sold my book, maybe the advance money would keep me afloat for a while. Why meet up with me in person to deliver bad news? He could do that over the phone. When you had good news to share, you wanted to see the expression on the person's face.

Or so I was telling myself. God, it was like waiting to get tests back from the doctor.

The next day, I got to the aquarium a few minutes before eleven, which was when we had agreed to meet. I went in first and bought us tickets. Harry had said he was flying up the night before and had booked a room at the Marriott Long Wharf, about a one-minute walk from the aquarium.

I spotted him heading my way from his hotel. If you have an image in your head of what a literary agent might look like, especially one with a name like Harry—unassuming, glasses, tweed jacket, thinning hair—you wouldn't be picturing Harry Breedlove. Late thirties, black jeans, black jean jacket, longish black hair pulled back into a ponytail. And yes, glasses, but with soft pink lenses. I was never sure whether they were just sunglasses, corrective, or both, but he almost never took them off.

He greeted me with a wide smile and a handshake.

"Jack, Jack, Jack, how are you?" he said. "You're looking good."

That was a pleasure to hear, even if it was most likely bullshit. Recent developments had done nothing to raise my spirits. I felt as though someone had painted a sad clown face on me.

"You, too," I said. We exchanged pleasantries. How was the flight? How's your room? How's your aunt?

I handed him one of the two tickets I'd purchased.

"Oh, you should have let me get these," he said.

I led him into the building. We went to the top floor and began our walk down, and around, the massive tank, a re-creation of a Caribbean coral reef that was home to hundreds of species.

"I want to see Myrtle," Harry said.

Myrtle was a green sea turtle that had lived in this tank for decades and was a star attraction.

"Just keep looking," I said. "I let her know you were coming."

Harry marveled at everything he saw, taking his time, looking deep into the tank to spot the myriad creatures. I was getting to where I couldn't take it anymore.

"Harry," I said, "what the hell is going on?"

"Oh, yeah, sure," he said, managing a chuckle.

"You didn't come up here just to see Myrtle."

"No, that's true," he said sheepishly. Harry took a deep breath, steeling himself. I guess I had my answer.

"Shit," I said. "You've got nothin'."

Looking away from the tank and directly at me for the first

46

time since we'd come in here, Harry said, "I wish that weren't the case. Everyone's looking for sure things. No one wants to gamble on anything."

"Given what I got for the first two books, they weren't exactly taking a huge risk. What did Ann say?"

Ann Finley was my editor on the first two books. She'd nurtured me this far along. I didn't think she would abandon me.

"She feels terrible, turning it down," Harry said. "She thinks it's a good book, too, but the numbers just aren't there."

Whatever the fuck that meant. They were always blaming "the numbers."

"But the thing is," Harry said, "I wouldn't want to meet with you if I didn't have *some* kind of good news."

I waited. An old joke popped into my head, the one where the doctor tells the patient he has good news and bad news. The bad news is that the patient has only six months to live. But the good news is, the doctor is fucking his receptionist.

"Don't look that way," Harry said. "I'm serious. An opportunity's come up."

"What?" I said. "Writing web copy for Nordstrom Rack?"

"Look, I can't tell you much about it," he said. "But they very much want you. They think you're perfect for this. Love your writing. And they hinted that the money's good. Better, frankly, than what you'd get for a book."

"Who's *they*?"

Harry's eyes darted about.

"You looking for someone?" I asked.

"No, I just—look, I'm afraid I can't give you any more detail than that. It's better if you hear it directly from them."

Harry reached into his jacket pocket and pulled out a phone. Nothing fancy, like a brand-new iPhone, but a cheap-looking model. A flip phone from when dinosaurs roamed the earth.

"What the hell's this?" I said as he handed it to me.

"Hang on to it. They'll call you. Oh, I've got a charger for it, too."

He went back into his pocket for a length of cable and small plug-in unit. He put that in my hand with the phone.

"*Who* will call me? Christ, Harry, is this a *burner* phone? Am I ghostwriting El Chapo's life story?"

He shook his head. "No, it's nothing like—I mean, I don't think it's anything like that. But they'll explain it when they call. Come on. Trust me on this."

I was slowly shaking my head as I considered what to do. This felt like some sort of turning point. Where you decide to go for Door Number Two instead of Door Number One, not knowing whether it's a new car or thirty bags of manure.

"When are *they* supposed to call?" I asked.

"Don't know for sure. Probably the next day or so."

"You met these people?"

"I was . . . approached. By a representative. Asked to relay their interest and give you the phone."

"Suppose I just pitch it?" I said, raising the phone in my hand.

"Then you'll never know," Harry said. "You'll never know what the opportunity was, and you'll never stop wondering, either. The road not taken, that kind of thing."

Shit. Like some dime-store-thriller writer, Harry had set the hook.

"Jesus!" Harry said, looking through the thick aquarium glass. On the other side, staring at us, was a massive, prehistoric-looking turtle the size of a Honda.

"It's Myrtle!" Harry said.

NINE

"Okay, stick a fork in me, because I'm done," Dr. Marie Sloan said, peeling off her surgical gloves and mask and pitching them into a plastic-lined waste bin. One gunshot wound (not too serious, nicked the guy's arm), a five-year-old with a high fever, two elderly heart attack patients (lost one, saved the other), a woman who had nearly cut her finger off trying to pry the lid off a tuna tin, and a guy whose seasonal allergies were so bad he couldn't stop sneezing no matter how many over-the-counter meds he took. And that was just the last three hours of a twelve-hour shift in the ER at Boston Community Hospital.

She headed to the doctors' locker room, peeled off her scrubs, tossed them into the laundry basket, and debated whether to have a shower before heading home to Zack, her husband, who would be fast asleep, given that it was midnight and he had to be up at six for his own shift at the local fire station. When he went to work, it would be Marie who was comatose. She wouldn't even feel it when he kissed her forehead on his way out.

One of these days, they might actually see each other. There were times when Marie wondered whether this was any way to live. Could you be burned out at thirty-four? Could she put up with this kind of shit for another three decades? Okay, so maybe she'd switch gears, set herself up as a GP out in the suburbs somewhere, maybe even in a small town, somewhere in the Berkshires, get some regular hours. Zack could probably find a job there, right? There are always forest fires, aren't there? One day, maybe. If she could make it to that point before she self-destructed.

Back during the pandemic, which had gone on for so much longer than anyone could have predicted—Delta, Omicron, just how many Greek letters were there, anyway?—how many times had she nearly packed it in? Pretty much the end of every shift.

Even now, with the worst of it over, Marie was still dealing with the trauma. Nightmares, for sure, but for months now she'd been suffering from a general, debilitating anxiety. It didn't hit her so much when she was at work—she was so busy she didn't have time to think about how fucked up she was. But in the off times, the quiet times, it often overwhelmed her. Like the middle of the night—or the middle of the day, if she'd been working the overnight shift—she'd stare at the ceiling, praying for sleep to come, but terrified that it would, because then the bad dreams would resume.

She compared it to having ants crawling through her veins. She needed to be numbed to make it stop. That was when she started hitting the booze pretty hard when she wasn't at work. Drugs, too, on occasion, and luckily she managed to hide it from her superiors. As if she was the only one. If they started sacking the nurses and doctors who were self-medicating, there wouldn't be anyone left to tend to the afflicted.

She'd engaged in dangerous, risky, random sex with one of the other doctors in the back of his Cayenne in the staff parking lot late one night, and the guilt from that only compounded everything else. Christ, how could she have betrayed Zack that way?

Jesus, those early days. Patient after patient coming to the ER. So many in the hallways you could barely make your way through. Shortness of breath, fever, coughing, diarrhea. At that time, they weren't sure how many ways it was spreading. Was it just airborne? Could you get it from touching someone? What if you ate something that was prepared by someone who might—just *might*—have it?

And because they didn't know, they had to keep the sick separated from their healthy loved ones. It seemed so cruel, so heartless, but did they really have any choice?

One time when she got home from her shift she told Zack about an eighty-two-year-old man who was fading fast, and his grown daughter had demanded to speak to him before he passed.

"So we get hold of her at home and I'm putting the phone right up to her father's ear so they can say goodbye to each other, right, and I can hear what she's saying. That she loves him, that he means more than anything in the world to her, and then she pauses because she's waiting for her dad to say something, and I realize he's dying, that he isn't hearing a thing she's saying, that he's slipping away as she talks to him. And she starts saying, 'Dad? Dad? Did you hear me?' And I have to tell her it's too late, and she just goes nuts on the phone. Should I have lied? Should I have said he whispered that he loved her but she just didn't hear him? That's what I should have done."

Zack took her in his arms and told her she'd done the best she could.

He was, bless him, a good listener. He'd seen his fair share of shit in his line of work, too. Colleagues trapped in a burning building when a ceiling gave way. Children overcome by smoke. Bad stuff, for sure. But it was sporadic. She tried to explain what it was like. Imagine the fires never stopped. Every call you went to led to another, and another, and another, and pretty soon the whole fucking city was on fire, and when you went to hook the hoses to the hydrants, there was no water left.

On this night, Dr. Marie Sloan, sitting on the bench in the locker room, leaned over, put her head in her hands, and had a short cry. Just enough to get it out of her system so she could move on, get in her car, and go home.

"Okay," she said to herself, raising her head. "I got this."

She slipped on a jacket, grabbed her purse, and closed her locker. Skipped the shower. She'd have one when she got home. When she reached the outdoors she inhaled two lungfuls of cool night air, then let them out slowly.

It suddenly hit her that she was starving. The McDonald's drive-through would be open. She'd do that on the way home.

Marie crisscrossed her way through the doctors' parking lot, hit the button on her remote. The lights on a Lexus SUV flashed once. She got to the car, opened the door, and was about to get behind the wheel when she felt something sharp and pointed touch the side of her neck just below her ear.

A man whispered, "Someone would like to have a word with you."

TEN

Jack

"You're shittin' me," Lana said, staring at the phone Harry had given me. "You've had this for two days?"

It sat on the island in her kitchen, and we were gazing upon it as though it were some rare artifact recovered from King Tut's tomb, or a chunk of a meteorite from Mars. A mystery, an enigma made of metal and plastic that was no bigger than a—well, a cell phone, sitting right there before us.

"Yeah," I said. "I carry it around with me wherever I go, plug it in and give it a charge if the battery starts to run down."

"It's like a Tamagotchi," she said.

"A what?"

"Don't you remember those? They were huge about twenty years ago. This little electronic egg you had to take care of and feed and nurture."

Lana picked up the phone, felt its heft in her palm, as though physically examining it would provide some clue as to who was supposed to call me on it. She pressed the "redial" button.

"Nothing on redial," she said. "It's never made a call out, unless the call history was erased. Nothing in contacts. It's never been used to answer a call, either, so far as I can tell."

"I know," I said. "I checked."

"You know what it probably is?" she said. I waited. "Harry was sworn to secrecy, but Steven Spielberg gave him that phone, and he's going to call and tell you he wants to make a movie out of one of your books."

I nodded. "Of course, that must be it. But why can't Spielberg just have one of his people call me? Why go through all this bullshit?"

Lana shrugged. "You know movie people. They have to do everything in a special way. Like when they go to restaurants. They never order anything off the menu."

"How do you know that?"

"I think I read it in an Elmore Leonard book."

"Okay, so, a movie deal. That's one theory. Any others?"

Lana thought. "Someone big wants you to ghostwrite their life story."

"That's what I said to Harry. El Chapo wants to set the record straight. That he's just a misunderstood businessman."

"Doesn't have to be a drug dealer or some other big-time criminal. Could be someone involved in the insurrection. An intelligence guy who gave secrets to the Russians, or a Russian who gave intelligence secrets to us. One of Putin's oligarchs wants to come clean. Could be a big celeb who had a drug problem or a comedian who liked to jerk off in front of people who's trying to rehabilitate his image."

"Yeah, I might give that one a pass."

"Whoever it might be, it's someone who's got a story to tell but doesn't have the writing chops to tell it."

I knew of an Australian writer who had a decent career writing thrillers but had started out ghostwriting books for politicians and pop stars. "Possibly," I said.

"Would you want to do that?"

I thought about that as I went to the fridge for a bottle of already-opened wine. I got two long-stemmed glasses from the cupboard—I'd been here enough times to know where every-thing was—and poured some into each.

Handing a glass to Lana, I said, "Maybe. I could get past the anonymity of it, not getting my name on the cover. And it would depend on who it was. And what kind of money the publisher was ponying up."

"It's come along at the right time," Lana said.

"No shit," I said. "No job, no car, no money in the bank. Who cares if it's El Chapo? I'm sure he has some redeeming qualities."

We clinked glasses and drank.

Changing subjects, I said, "I read your piece this morning on the missing judge. The name rings a bell. Bentley."

"It should. He's a big deal."

"They haven't found him?"

She shook her head and tipped the glass back again. "Nope. Anyway, I've moved on to other stuff. They've got me covering this possible city workers' strike. Contract talks have broken down."

Lana moved in closer to me.

"You know," she said, "there's a silver lining to your car catching itself on fire."

"And that is?"

"You don't have to worry about where you parked it, for one thing. There's no chance it's going to get towed. And seeing as how you have no wheels, you don't really have to worry about how much you have to drink."

"There is that."

Then Lana did something I'd rarely seen her do. She walked over to the muted television, which was, as always, tuned to an all-news station, and turned it off.

"Good God," I said. "What is happening?"

As she walked back over to me, she said, "I am thinking that

55

I would like to get a little drunk. And I would like to encourage you to join me in this venture."

"Hold that thought," I said.

I went to the fridge for another bottle of wine, found a chardonnay, and uncorked it. I topped up her glass. She had a drink and smiled.

I said, "Do you have any ambitions beyond the getting drunk part?"

By way of answering, she grabbed me by the top of my jeans, hooking her fingers into my pants behind the belt.

"I might," she said.

We each took one more drink, then set our glasses on the island. As we slipped into each other's arms she tipped her head back so that I could kiss her, which I did, with more than a little enthusiasm.

I thought about how lucky I was, despite recent setbacks, to have this woman in my life. And how I hoped nothing would come along to sabotage that. There were times when I wondered whether I should tell her all the things I'd kept from her up to now. And then I thought, If it ain't broke, don't fix it.

Lana started to unbuckle my belt.

The cell phone on the island began to ring. We stopped, froze, looked at the phone, and then looked at each other.

I said, "I should probably get that."

ELEVEN

"**M**om, Dad says he's going to be gone for a long time."

"Looks that way."

"Why does he have to go away? Andy said he did some really bad things."

"Who the hell is Andy?"

"He's in my class."

"Andy doesn't know a damn thing, and you can tell him I said so."

"He says Dad hurt people."

"Jesus Christ, I can't deal with your questions right now."

"Can I go with him?"

"What?"

"Can I go with Dad?"

"Is that what you'd like? You want to leave me alone? Would that make you happy?"

"I didn't mean that. Can't we both go with him?"

"No. Don't ask me again."

TWELVE

Jack

I was given the address of a redbrick six-story building on Boylston that was a stone's throw from the Lenox Hotel on the other side of the street. I'd only been in there once, for a friend's wedding reception about five years ago. My meeting was to be held in the fourth-floor offices of Pandora Importing, but when I checked the directory in the lobby I didn't see it posted.

I got into the elevator and pressed 4. The doors opened onto an unadorned, pale-yellow corridor with entrances to offices every thirty feet or so on either side. I passed Delroy Accounting and Kendrick Asset Management and Childers Talent Agency before reaching the door marked, with a narrow, horizontal brass nameplate, PANDORA IMPORTING.

And what the hell was Pandora Importing? What services could I possibly provide for a company that brought goods into the country? Why the secrecy? Maybe I was going to be working for El Chapo after all. Writing a manual on how to import various illegal substances into the United States. That didn't sound like something I wanted to do.

When I turned the handle, I found it locked.

That was when I noticed the small panel mounted on the wall by the door, and the red button. I pressed it.

Seconds later, a male voice crackled over the intercom. "Yes?"

"Uh, Jack Givins? I have an appointment?"

Nothing for several seconds. But then the door buzzed, and before it stopped, I turned the handle and entered.

This was an office that could have been dedicated to just about anything. Half a dozen desks topped with files and computers, two of them in use. A man with a short-cropped, military-style haircut, dressed in a crisp white shirt and tie, sat at the desk closest to me, bobbing his left knee up and down like a rapidly firing piston. Beyond him, a silver-haired woman in a blue business suit sat at another. They could be processing insurance claims, booking customer flights to Tasmania, or monitoring Russian intel sites on the dark web for all I knew. Whatever it was they were doing, it was more interesting than my arrival, given that neither of them gave me a second glance.

What might, or might not, have offered a clue as to who was running this office was the framed portrait of the current president of the United States that hung on the wall, and the American flag that stood in one corner near the door. Beneath the flag were a couple of chairs and a table with magazines, a kind of mini reception area.

From somewhere at the back of this office, a woman appeared, walking my way and flashing a remotely welcoming smile. When she reached me, she extended a hand.

"Mr. Givins," she said.

"Hello," I said. She motioned to the two chairs, inviting me to take a seat, which I did.

She was about my age, maybe a year or two older, which put her in her mid-thirties. Medium height, dark hair that fell just to her shoulders, green eyes, and a build that suggested a kind of solidness, like maybe she worked out, knew how to handle herself. She was dressed in black jeans, a white blouse, and a black jacket. Businesslike, in a laid-back kind of way.

Before she said anything else, I thought back to our brief conversation the night before when I answered the mystery phone.

"Is this Jack?" she'd asked.

"It is. Who's this?"

"Gwen."

"What's this about, Gwen?" I'd asked.

"An opportunity."

"What kind of opportunity?"

"Are you available to meet tomorrow morning at ten?"

I'd hesitated a moment, then said, "Okay."

"Write down this address."

I'd scrambled to find a pen and something to write on. Lana dug a pencil out of a drawer and handed me a takeout menu. I scribbled in the text-free borders. "Pandora what?" I asked.

She told me. When I asked another question—"Ten o'clock, you said?"—and got no reply, I realized she had already ended the call.

"So you're Gwen," I said, now that we were meeting face-to-face.

"I am," she said. "Apologies for taking a couple of days to get in touch after you'd been given the phone. I had a few other things on my plate."

"You have a last name, Gwen?" I asked.

"I do," she said. "Gwen Kaminsky."

"So, what do you folks import?"

"Not a goddamn thing."

She reached into her jacket and brought out a black billfold. She flipped it open, revealing a badge. "Gwen Kaminsky, with the U.S. Marshals Service." She gave me about two seconds to inspect the badge before she snapped the billfold shut and tucked it back into her pocket.

"You're a U.S. marshal?" I asked.

"I think that's what the badge suggests."

"What the hell do you want with me?" I took a second, then smiled. I had it all figured out immediately. "You want to write your memoir. True tales of a U.S. marshal. You need a ghost-writer. My girlfriend was right. I'm flattered, but unless you've already got a publisher behind you with a decent advance on the table, I don't think this is something I'd be interested in."

"If you know everything I'm going to say, then I guess we can wrap this up now. Thanks for coming."

She made like she was going to get up, but I stopped her by saying, "Wait. Sorry. Maybe I jumped the gun a bit there."

"You want to hear what this is about or don't you?"

I nodded. "Sure, go ahead."

Gwen Kaminsky took a breath, shot a quick, withering glance at the man with the bobbing knee at the nearby workstation, and said, "You're a writer."

"I am."

"I had some research done on you. Two novels. Good reviews. Haven't read them myself—had never heard of them—but the people I had read them for me said they weren't bad. They did summations for me."

"Great," I said evenly. I was going to get a swelled head with all this praise.

"You know what they liked about them?" she asked.

Rather than try to guess, I waited for her to tell me.

"The characters, how fully developed they were. How you invented these rich past lives for them, these detailed backstories. I'm told the characters were very authentic, very three dimensional."

"I see."

"So that made you one of our candidates."

"Candidates," I said.

"Do you know what we do here?"

"You mean, like, the U.S. Marshals generally, or in this office specifically?"

"You've heard of the Witness Security Program? A lot of people refer to it as witness protection, or witness relocation."

I blinked. "Of course. Everyone's heard of it. I mean, everyone who's ever seen a movie or read a crime novel or watched the news."

"It hasn't been around forever," she said. "It's not like the post office or something. It was authorized in 1970 by the Organized Crime Control Act. Since then, nearly twenty thousand people have been protected through the program."

"That's a lot of witnesses."

"The U.S. Marshals Service oversees the program. I don't know if you knew that or not."

"I do know that," I said.

"So let's say you have a witness to a serious crime, and it's reasonable to assume that there will be serious retribution against this individual if they testify. We can give that person a new identity, relocate them, set them up with a new life so that they're safe, so that anyone who might seek revenge or to silence them won't be able to. A lot of the people we relocate are themselves facing serious legal consequences, and in exchange for their testimony, those charges will be dropped and we'll set them up with a new life. Not just them, but their family, too, like a spouse, and children."

"I'm aware," I said. "Why are you telling me all this?"

"Getting to that," Gwen Kaminsky said, and smiled. "Just like you, I have to let the story take its course, you know?"

She shot another stern look at the guy with the nervous knee, then turned her attention back to me.

"Here's the thing. We're pretty good at what we do. We get people set up in a new location, we keep tabs on them, we do everything we can to keep them safe. And we have a pretty damn good record in that regard. But I'm going to admit that there's one area in which we fall a bit short."

"What's that?"

"We're not very creative."

"Creative?"

Gwen smiled. "We don't just relocate these individuals, give them a new identity and a new job. We need to give them a backstory. Who they are, where they came from, what makes them tick. They need stories, *new* stories. If they settle into some community and start running off at the mouth about things that really did happen to them, then people might start putting things together. Realize they're someone they read or heard about in the news, and maybe they'd tell a friend, and that friend tells someone else, and before you know it, these stories get to the wrong people, and not only do these relocated witnesses find their covers blown, they may be in very real danger of being found and killed."

"Wouldn't it be smarter for them to just keep their mouths shut?" I offered.

Gwen smiled. "Indeed. In a perfect world."

"But if they're telling stories of things that never happened to them," I said, "someone's going to catch them in a lie. Something won't ring true."

She pursed her lips, considering my point. "Maybe, but think about your own experience. Someone tells you where they went to school or about their first job or the time they got on an elevator with Robert Redford. Do you check out their story? Of course not. And even if you think they're lying, what do you do? You think, what a bullshitter. And let it go at that. But that's better than one of our people telling you legitimate details about themselves that could get them in trouble."

There was some truth in that. I'd known plenty of people over the years who liked to tell stories to puff themselves up that

I knew had to be complete fabrications. Someone I'd gone to school with liked to tell a story about how he once dated a famous supermodel. The truth was, he'd been in line behind her waiting to board a flight to Atlanta and said hello.

So yeah, maybe Gwen had a point. We rarely challenge people on their lies unless there's something big at stake.

"We've got people who do their best at cobbling together fictitious anecdotes, work histories, imagined shenanigans from their school days. But they spend most of their time staring at their computer screens trying to come up with something. We were recently putting together a fictitious biography for a bookkeeper we were relocating. A somewhat nerdy kind of fellow who was keeping the accounts for an embezzler, and one of our so-called writers came up with the idea that at one time he was a rodeo clown."

"You never know," I said. "Someone has to be the rodeo clown."

"It was ridiculous."

I could finally see where this might be going.

Gwen said, "We would like to engage you to write those backstories."

"I see," I said.

"You don't look very excited about the proposal."

"I have questions."

"Shoot."

"First, how did you know I wrote books? They were published under a pseudonym."

"Oscar Laidlaw might be the name on the cover," Gwen said, "but the tax forms you get from your publisher are in your name. You think we don't have friends at the IRS?"

"Okay. Why didn't you just get in touch with me directly? Why go through Harry?"

She smiled slyly. "I thought it best if you were approached by someone you trust. And I won't lie. I thought the way I went about it would pique your interest. Tell me it didn't."

"It did. Does Harry—"

"Just a sec," she said, and then she turned to the guy whose knee hadn't stopped pistoning since I'd sat down and said, "Excuse me."

The guy didn't realize she was talking to him at first. So, raising her voice, she said, "Hey!"

He took his eyes off the screen and looked at Gwen. "Yes?"

"Could you stop doing that?" she said. "With your knee? It's *very* annoying."

He was dumbstruck. "Uh, sorry." He went back to whatever he was doing, and his knee stopped bobbing. Just as well, I thought. This woman was a U.S. marshal. If his knee didn't stop she might shoot him.

"Drives me crazy," she whispered to me. "Sorry, go on."

"I was asking whether Harry knows what this is all about."

"Much less than you do now. What else?"

"Why me?"

"I told you. You're a good candidate."

"There are lots of writers."

"I'm aware. If you wanted to do this, you wouldn't be the only one. We have several published novelists doing this kind of work on the side. Names you'd recognize if I were at liberty to reveal them to you."

"So no other reason," I said.

Her brow furrowed. "Like what?"

"Just wondered."

"No, nothing else. Look, if you don't think this is for you, that's fine. Some authors we approached turned it down. It was an ego thing. They liked to see their name in print. This is, needless to say, uncredited work."

"Of course."

"But seeing as how you already write under an assumed name, I figured that wouldn't be an issue." She eyed me suspiciously. "Why *do* you do that, anyway?"

"I like to keep a low profile," I said.

The suspicious gaze remained. "And why's that?"

I shrugged. "I've never been in the limelight, and don't think I would enjoy it."

She thought about that for a moment while I considered my employment status and my destroyed car and my nearly empty bank account, as the knee bopper left his station to go to the bathroom or maybe find someplace where he could engage in his nervous tic without getting scolded.

Gwen stopped looking at me like I was a suspect in a bank robbery and moved on. "Look, if you're not interested, you probably don't care what it pays."

I said, "I'd at least be interested to know."

"A thousand dollars a day."

I did a very good job at not letting my jaw drop. In ten days I could make more than I got for my first book, which took me a year to write.

She continued. "I don't know how long it will take you to craft these backstories, but we're okay with you working at your own speed. We would want this to be done right." She smiled. "We have the money, and a number of profiles that we would need you to work on. Couple months' work, minimum. Could turn into a permanent arrangement if we like what you do."

Math wasn't my best subject in school, but I was able to do the calculation quickly enough. Based on a five-day work week, that would be a cool forty thousand for eight weeks.

"There are conditions," Gwen said. "Not a word to anyone. You wouldn't even be able to tell your wife."

"I'm not married," I said.

"Girlfriend, then. Or boyfriend?" She raised an eyebrow.

"Girlfriend," I said. So they'd checked me out professionally, but hadn't delved into my love life.

"And you'd deal with me exclusively. I'd be your point person. You'd keep that phone we gave you. You'd use it only to talk to me. And you can work on a computer, but it has to be offline. No internet connection. And you don't email any of your work. You print it out and deliver it, or I'll have an associate pick it up."

She paused, took a breath. "And you absolutely, positively, cannot ever, in the future, write about the people you create backstories for. Anything you might learn about the Witness Security Program cannot be fodder for some novel in the future. Certainly not any of the specifics. If you did decide to write something that was merely inspired by this experience, we'd still have to read it. Clear it."

Okay. So there were some loopholes. I might be able to turn this experience into something sellable one day if I changed all the pertinent details. If it was good enough for the late John le Carré, it was good enough for me.

Gwen was waiting for me to say something. "Understood?"

"Yes," I said.

"I've got something you could work on right away. A witness who's testifying against a criminal enterprise. Setting him up on his own, away from his family."

I nodded. "Why does it say Pandora Importing on the door?"

"You think we should have a big neon sign on the street that this is where we look after relocated witnesses whose lives are at risk? Christ, Jack, maybe this isn't for you."

"Just asking."

"And in case you're wondering, we're a small satellite office. Things work out, you'll see the Washington office one day."

I felt, for the first time, a tingle of excitement. The world of law enforcement. Adventure. Bad guys. Intrigue.

I cracked a smile. "Would I get a gun?"

Gwen stared at me, stone-faced, and said nothing.

"That looks like a no," I said.

"Interested or not? I've got three other writers to talk to today."

I swallowed. "Yes. I'm interested."

THIRTEEN

Way back before the Big Dig, before the city went through sixteen miserable years of chaos as underground roadways were installed through the downtown, and before there was a connecting tunnel from the city out to Logan, Dick Struthers always opted for the water taxi.

Not only was it a hell of a lot faster than going around the bay in a regular taxi, it was fun. You felt the wind in your hair, got a whiff of sea breeze up your nostrils. Going to the airport, or coming home, it was often the part of the trip he liked most. Coming home was better. He liked standing by the railing, watching the skyline grow larger as he got closer.

And now, even years after the dig was done and you could get to the airport in minutes by taking the tunnel that went under the bay, Dick still took the water taxi. Oh, if it was raining, or Boston was in the grip of some terrible snowstorm, he'd reconsider and take a ride with wheels, but today he was on the boat.

He exchanged a few pleasantries with the captain, then, wheeling his carry-on bag behind him, moved toward the bow to take in the city view.

Right away, something caught his eye. Off to the port side, a glimpse of white and black atop the water, rolling with the waves.

"Hey!" Dick called to the captain. "Hey!"

The captain looked his way, shouted back to be heard over the motor and the churning water, "What?"

Dick pointed. "Over there! That way!"

The captain cut the throttle, looked where Dick was pointing, squinted, caught sight of whatever it was that was bobbing in the water.

The water taxi's captain had been doing this job long enough to have seen most everything, and he had a pretty good idea what his rider had spotted. He altered the taxi's course, kept the engine going at a low speed, barely above an idle.

"Yeah!" Dick said. "Almost there. Jesus!"

The captain came out onto the deck, standing by the railing next to Dick. Didn't need a long look to know what it was. Old guy, the captain thought, judging by the few wisps of gray hair. Facedown, like they almost always were. Probably been dead for a few days, he figured. Most likely went to the bottom at first, then the gases would have started to build up in the body, finally bringing it back up to the surface.

As someone who read the Boston papers every day—the real thing, not some online version—the captain wondered if this might be that old judge who'd gone missing. Maybe wandered down to the harbor, fell in.

The captain said to Dick, "I'll call it in."

FOURTEEN

Jack

That night, Lana wanted to know everything.

"Spill it," she said. "It's been driving me crazy all day."

Lana and I had met for a drink at the Granary Tavern. She was working on a Seaglass Riesling. I'd ordered a Jack's Abby House Lager.

"There's not a lot I can tell you," I said.

"Come on," she said. "So where'd you meet this woman?"

"I don't know that I can say."

"Oh, come on."

"An office on Boylston. I can't be any more specific."

Lana hated not knowing things. Whenever I was with her and got a text, if she could get to my phone first she'd read it out to me.

"So who was this woman? Can you tell me that?"

"I can't."

"Can't, or won't?"

"I was kind of sworn to secrecy."

"Okay, well, what was she like?"

"Like?"

"Young? Old? Frumpy? Hot?"

My mouth felt dry. I took a drink of water. "She was . . . businesslike."

Lana rolled her eyes. "Businesslike? Definitely not hot then. Okay, let's talk about the gig. Are you *really* not going to tell me what this is about? Is it some secret government project or something?"

When I didn't say something right away, she said, "Ah, so I'm already warm."

"Okay, all I can say is, yes, it might, just might, have something to do with some level of government. It's totally legit, and that's about it."

"What level of government? What department?"

"Sorry."

"Jesus. This is ridiculous. Why can't you tell me?"

"I was told not to."

"Oh, my God, I think I know what it is," she said.

Lana was good, but could she be this good? Was she able to intuit what it was I'd been hired to do?

"What?" I said.

"Speechwriter," she said, smiling triumphantly. "It makes perfect sense." Now she was scrunching up her face, thinking it through. "The question now is, for whom? You going to write speeches for the mayor? Good luck with that. Or maybe state. You're going to put words into the mouth of our governor. He could certainly use help with that, given how few he seems to know. Or maybe federal? Senator? Huh? Is that it? You're going to write speeches for a senator?"

I had to admit, I was enjoying this. There was a kind of thrill in being drafted to work for the witness relocation program, even in a tangential kind of way. Composing histories for people who were going to be sent off into hiding for the rest of their lives had filled me with a sense of purpose.

God, how I wanted to tell Lana what I was up to. It wasn't that I didn't trust her. But hell, she was in the news business, and even if she did keep my secret, if Gwen ever found out I'd blabbed about what I was up to, I was pretty sure I'd lose this gig before I'd even gotten started. I could kiss that grand a day goodbye.

She rested one elbow on the bar and stared at me so intently, it was like she was trying to see what was in my soul.

"Or maybe not a politician," she said. "Politicians don't usually keep it a secret that they have speechwriters. No one expects them to come up with all that bullshit themselves. So maybe it's something corporate. Big companies are totally paranoid about everything. Is it something in big tech? Or maybe it's what we were talking about the other night. You're ghostwriting a book. No, you already admitted it was government-related. So it's not that." Her eyes narrowed. "Unless it's a bio for some *former* government official, so not technically a government gig but kind of."

I shook my head. Not as an answer, but in exasperation.

"Okay, okay, I know. There was a shake-up recently in the mayor's PR office. That has to be it. You *are* writing speeches for the mayor, but you can't talk about it until they see if you work out."

"If that's what you want to think, then that's what I'm doing," I said.

Lana shook her head disapprovingly. "I don't think this will make you happy."

"I'm sorry?"

"Whoever you're writing speeches for, whether it's the mayor or somebody else or if it's corporate, you won't find it satisfying. It's not what you're meant to do."

"You think I should go back to *RV Life* and see if they'll reconsider?"

"Okay, so whatever you've signed up for is probably better than that, but still. It's just, you won't be able to write what you *want* to write. You'll have to write what they *tell* you to write. Sure, you can get creative up to a point, but you'll have to follow the script. Espouse policy you may think is total bullshit."

"You done?"

"Fine. Whatever it is, I hope it makes you happy. But writing speeches for self-serving shitheads and liars might not be very satisfying."

Lana held a rather low opinion of most elected officials.

"Don't worry about me," I said. Now I was feeling ever so slightly annoyed. Lana had a great job that paid her well, and now that I had an opportunity to turn things around, she was putting it down without even knowing what it was.

"Sorry," she said, as if reading my thoughts. "No more negativity. If you think this is a good fit, then great. And I won't pester you with more questions." She smiled. "But I'm going to be listening to the mayor's speeches more closely now, in case I pick up any of your figures of speech."

"If that's it," I said mischievously.

"I should warn you," she said. "You know what I'm like. You've presented a challenge to me. Finding out what you're up to."

There was already so much she hadn't uncovered about me that I wasn't particularly worried.

We were both finished with our meals. The waiter appeared and said, "Anything else?"

"We're good," Lana said as the waiter put the check on the table. Lana was going for her purse.

"I got this," I said.

Lana raised an eyebrow. She'd been picking up the tab for our more recent lunches and dinners out. But U.S. Marshal Gwen Kaminsky had given me a week's advance—a wired deposit that went straight into my account—and I was more flush than I'd been in a very long time.

I took out my wallet, pulled out my Visa card, and set the wallet on the table. The waiter punched some numbers into the wireless gadget he was holding, then handed it over to me. I inserted the card, added a tip, entered my PIN, withdrew my card, and gave the machine back to the waiter as it printed out a receipt.

"Would you like a copy?" he asked.

"That's okay," I said, and the waiter slipped away.

Throughout the entire transaction, Lana had been looking at my wallet with considerable interest.

She said, "If you're suddenly loaded, might I suggest you finally get a new one of those?"

I slipped the credit card back into my billfold. It was, I had to admit, in tatters. The brown leather was worn and scarred on the outside and inside; the various dividers for bills and cards were in shreds.

"I suppose," I said. "But I'm kind of attached to this one."

FIFTEEN

"Tell me about your wife, Zack," Lana said. "Tell me about Marie."

It was the following morning, and the city was starting to become aware, through news reports and social media, that Dr. Marie Sloan, an emergency-room physician from Boston Community Hospital, had now been missing for nearly two days.

Lana and the doctor's husband, Zack Porter, were sitting on a red bench a stone's throw from the fire station where he worked, a majestic, three-story brick building built nearly a century earlier. It had three bays, with one door raised open, and faced Huntington Avenue in the city's Roxbury neighborhood. Just inside the station, several of Zack's colleagues watched as Lana interviewed the distraught man.

Zack was sitting with his head in his hands as Lana asked her question. He sat up slowly, eyes bloodshot, and said, "She's the most wonderful person in the world."

"Everyone I've talked to has nothing but great things to say about her. Do you have any idea where she could be?"

He shook his head. "No idea. It's not like her. It's not like her at all."

What the police knew so far: Dr. Sloan had finished a twelve-hour shift, walked out of the hospital, and that was the last anyone had seen of her. Her car was still in the parking lot. She wasn't answering her cell phone. Calls went straight to message, suggesting the phone was off. There had been no large cash withdrawals on her bank account. No activity on her various credit cards. She hadn't summoned an Uber to take her anywhere. Surveillance footage from the hospital's camera did show her walking out of the emergency entrance but did not provide a good image of the area where she had left her car.

Lana didn't like conducting these kinds of interviews, writing these kinds of stories. Only a few days after writing about Willard Bentley—whose body had been found floating in Boston Harbor, and who was presumed to have wandered down to the harbor and fallen in—now here she was working a story about a missing doctor.

"She's the love of my life," Zack said, brushing a tear from his eye. "This isn't like her. Except . . ."

"Except what?" Lana asked.

"She's just so dedicated," Zack said. "You can't find a more caring, dedicated doctor. She's the best, you know?" He wiped away another tear. "She cares about all her patients. Someone comes into the ER, she's like, only known them for a few minutes, but she treats them like she's been looking after them for years. That's how she is. Everyone matters. I think . . . I think that's why the last couple of years have hit her so hard."

"Tell me about that," Lana said, holding her phone so that it would pick up everything Zack said.

"Not being able to save everyone. Losing so many patients. How they kept coming and coming and for such a long period, there was no relief. All that heartache. For the people she treated, and her, too. It did something to her. It . . . changed her." He paused. "She's been on a kind of never-ending burnout. You can only deal with something like that for so long."

"Do you think she might have . . ." Lana let the question trail off. He would get her meaning.

"I don't . . . I can't let my mind go there. I could never forgive myself if there've been signs that somehow I've missed."

He leaned back onto the bench and tipped his head back, as though looking for answers in the clouds that hovered overhead. Lana felt a tickle in her nose and thought, Christ, don't let me go into a sneezing fit now.

"The thing is," Zack said, "we hardly even see each other. It's been that way for years. I'm sleeping when she's at work and she's sleeping when I'm here. Sometimes we get shifts that line up. Like planets aligning, you know? So that we're both off at the same time, but it hasn't worked out like that much. Christ, I don't even know why I'm here today. I guess I'm thinking she's going to show up, walk into the station, have some crazy explanation for where she's been. So if she's been upset about anything, if all this work stuff has really been starting to get to her, she's hardly had a chance to talk to me about it."

His mood shifted from despair to anger. "How could she not be upset? How could she not feel unappreciated? The kind of shit that people like her have been taking for so long. Working their asses off trying to save people's lives, trying to get people to do the right thing and take precautions, and being told they didn't know what they were talking about? What the hell is wrong with people these days?"

He leaned over again and put his head in his hands.

Lana gave him a minute.

He sat up, turned to Lana and said, "She's a hero. She's a hero and everyone needs to be looking for her."

"That's what I'll write," Lana said.

"Thank you."

And then she sneezed. She'd held it off as long as she could.

"Bless you," Zack said.

She took a tissue from her purse and wiped her nose before thanking the man for his time. He got to his feet and turned around to head for the open bay, where two of his colleagues were waiting. They put their arms around his shoulders and walked him back into the building.

This will not end well, Lana thought.

SIXTEEN

Jack

I hadn't been given a whole lot to go on. My first subject, according to what Gwen had told me, was male, white, and forty years old.

Where to begin? What kind of life did I want to create for him? And not knowing what he did now—was he a butcher, a baker, a candlestick maker? What if, by chance, I gave him a background that was too similar to his real one? No, that seemed unlikely, against the odds.

Anyway, before I began to consider so much as this man's favorite color or snack, I had to prepare my workstation, also known as my kitchen table. Gwen had sprung for an extra laptop, a base model, that I could use solely for the profiles, and leave unconnected to the internet. When I had something to show her, I could run a cable from it to my printer and arrange a meeting to hand over the material. My other laptop could sit on the table, available for research.

Just as I did at the beginning of any project (we writers have our rituals), I went to a nearby office supply store and loaded up on fine-point pens, spiral notebooks, printer cartridges, paper, sticky notes, and coffee pods for my Keurig, the one and only decadent appliance I owned.

I didn't know where they were going to place this witness, but I supposed that didn't matter. Where was a good place for him to have *come* from? Someplace in upstate New York, perhaps. Albany, or Rochester, or maybe start him off farther west, in Buffalo. A Buffalo suburb. Cheektowaga or Lackawanna, maybe Niagara Falls.

I liked Niagara Falls. That was a place almost everyone had been to, and even if they hadn't, they knew about it. It was a place you could say you hailed from, even describe with some confidence, without ever having seen it. Was our guy born there? Did he go to school there?

This was where the other laptop came in handy. I googled the names of schools in the Niagara Falls area. There was a Niagara Falls High School, a Madonna High School. I liked that second one. Easy to remember. What kind of student was he? What clubs did he belong to? I made him a member of the basketball team. And then, to show that he wasn't a total jock, had him join the chess club.

What did our guy's parents do? His mother didn't have a job outside the home, and his dad worked for . . . okay, they were only a few miles from the Canadian border, so he was a border guard, customs agent, whatever. I gave him an older brother. Much older. Ten years. The way our guy figured it, his parents were done having kids, and then, whoops, a little surprise. Big age difference, so the brothers were never that close. By the time our witness was starting grade school and still playing with Tonka trucks in his sandbox, his older brother was getting his driver's license and trying to be the first among his friends to lose his virginity.

Made a note: *Need good story about the first time our guy gets laid.*

Once I'd scribbled down a few things, I typed them onto the screen. I dreamed up childhood friends for our guy. Since I knew his age, I looked up popular TV shows that would have been on when he was nine, ten years old. *Lois & Clark: The New Adventures of Superman*, *Batman: The Animated Series*, and the Tim Allen sitcom *Home Improvement* would very likely have been shows he would have loved. Who knew, maybe my guy really *did* love those shows.

A couple of times, Lana called to check on my progress.

"How's the speechifying coming?" she asked playfully.

If she wanted to believe I was writing speeches for some politician that was fine with me.

"Just great," I said. "Putting the finishing touches to the governor declaring war on Rhode Island."

"It's about time," she said. "They've been getting away with shit for too long."

I spent five days creating a life for my relocated witness. I hooked the laptop to the printer and found I had twenty double-spaced pages for my new employer's consideration.

I called Gwen. "Got something," I said.

"Put it in an envelope and I'll send someone around to get it later today."

Two hours later, I got a call on the phone Gwen gave me, but this was the first time it came from a number other than hers.

"Out front," a man said.

I already had the papers tucked into a nine-by-twelve manila envelope and had written "Gwen" on the front with one of my new pens. I added "For Your Eyes Only" beneath her name.

When I came out the front of the building, there was a black van with heavily tinted windows at the curb. A guy who looked like an extra from a Martin Scorsese movie—stocky, broad-shouldered, buzz cut—got out.

"Hey," he said as I handed him the envelope.

"Hope she likes it," I said.

That prompted a grin. "She's hard to please. Whatever she

says, don't take it personally. It's just her style. She wouldn't be where she is now if she was happy with work that was 'good enough.'"

"Noted," I said.

He opened the van door, tossed the envelope onto the seat next to him, gave me a little salute, and took off.

Gwen called four hours later.

"I have notes. You'll have them back shortly."

My new friend didn't even get out of the van when he returned. He powered down the passenger-door window, leaned over and handed the manila envelope to me without comment, put the window back up, and was gone.

I glanced at the front of the envelope and saw that Gwen's notes started there. She'd crossed out "For Your Eyes Only" and scribbled, "Don't be cute."

Once upstairs, I took a beer from the fridge, twisted off the cap, and took a seat on my Ikea couch. I slid my pages out of the envelope and had a look at them. She'd taken a red pen to them, circling words, scribbling notations in the margins. Correcting typos, for Christ's sake. On the last page, where my own text only went down to the halfway point, were the real notes.

Among them:

— Why Niagara Falls? Would Chicago be better? Or maybe someplace out west, like Wyoming, that fewer people would be familiar with?
— I don't see our guy having a border guard father. He has no regard for the law, so a parent in any kind of enforcement makes no sense. He's good with tools. Maybe he works at a hardware store.
— You've got TV shows. What about movies? Our witness likes movies.

— Our guy needs a part-time job when he was in his teens. Not a fast-food place. He's kind of a foodie. Play on that.

How the hell was I supposed to know he was a foodie or a movie fan when Gwen had given me virtually no information on him?

Sure, I had a nice profile here, but he was fictional in every possible way. Maybe none of this worked. I had him meeting the love of his life in a chemistry class, but what if that was the one subject he never took? He didn't know cadmium from kryptonite. How would he bluff his way through that if his new identity happened to bring him into contact with a science professor from the local university? Somewhere I'd come up with horseback riding as a hobby, but what if he had a bad back and couldn't do that?

I was a tailor making a suit for a man I hadn't measured.

The entire process was flawed.

I picked up the hotline to Gwen.

"This isn't working," I said when she picked up.

"What's the problem?"

"I need more information about the witness. About who he really is. What makes him tick. I'm flying blind. *Writing* blind." I took a breath. "I want a meeting."

"A meeting."

"With your witness. Before you ship him off to wherever he's going, I'd like to spend some time with him. Even an hour. To get a sense of who he is. Then I can come up with background stories that suit him."

"There are security issues. Look, there are people out there. Bad people who would very much like to find him. Putting you two together could put him, and you, at risk."

"I figure you're good at that sort of thing. Security. It's right in the name of your agency."

"I'll get back to you," she said.

"When?"

"I'll get back to you when I get back to you."

She ended the call. Talk about an attitude. If being a U.S. marshal didn't work out someday, maybe she'd want to consider going into publishing.

SEVENTEEN

Lana Wilshire, by her very nature, was curious. She couldn't help it.

When she was a child, she would, without her parents finding out, search the house for hidden Christmas presents. And when it came to opening gifts on the morning of the twenty-fifth of December, she could feign surprise like a young Meryl Streep. Her snooping for gifts was not something she'd grown out of. One time, at Jack's apartment, a week before her birthday, she had been casually looking around his place while he was out picking up some Chinese food—okay, maybe it was a little more than *casual*—and discovered a signed first edition of Joan Didion's 1979 book of essays, *The White Album*.

She'd started out looking for evidence of possible former romantic involvements, like letters or photos, and had completely struck out on that score. In fact, she found virtually nothing about Jack's life before his days on the paper in Worcester. No family albums, no high-school yearbooks, no old birthday cards.

But the Didion book was an unexpected find. Jack knew her so well. It was the perfect gift. She didn't let on she'd found it, and waited patiently until he gave it to her a week later. Although, if Jack had been more suspicious, he might have wondered why, that evening, she gave him a night to remember in the bedroom unlike any they had had before.

And now, Jack was keeping a secret from her, and it was driving her crazy. Did Jack really think she wouldn't find out? He had no idea who he was dealing with.

After she had filed her story about the missing doctor, she made a call to the communications director for the mayor's office.

"Hey, Sandy, Lana here."

"Hey, Lana," said Sandy Schwartzman. "What's up?"

"Just checking on the mayor's schedule you posted. Looks thin. That tells me he's got some things going on he doesn't want us to know about. I'm looking at between one and four in the afternoon, tomorrow. There's nothing. Come on. No check presentation to the Rotary? No speech at the Chamber of Commerce? No ribbon cutting?"

"It's a light schedule tomorrow," Sandy said. "Not trying to pull anything over on you."

"I've heard that before."

"Seriously. Off the record"—at this point, Sandy's voice dropped to a whisper—"the mayor's got a case of the runs."

"Oh, my," Lana said.

"Intestinal flu, maybe, but it might be food poisoning. Went to a banquet last night and he might have had some bad shrimp. Does *that* satisfy your curiosity?"

"Definitely," Lana said. "Hey, while we're talking, I heard there was some new blood in your section."

"In communications?"

"Yeah. That there was a new guy? Jack somebody? Writing speeches for the mayor?"

"That's a new one on me," Sandy said. "Same old, same old here. We were down one for a while there when Gracie had her baby, but she's back."

"Oh, my God, I totally forgot. What'd she have?"

"A little boy. Named him Gregory. Cute as all fuck."

"Can I quote you on that?" Lana asked.

"Dare ya," Sandy said. "Oh, and we're putting out a statement about Willard Bentley."

"Right. They found him."

"It's what you'd expect him to say. Huge loss, stellar career, that kind of thing."

"I already did a profile, but what you've got could be worked into the funeral coverage, whenever that is. Might not be me who covers it."

"We'll send the statement out to the usual suspects."

Once they had said mutual farewells, Lana ran the same game on the governor's office. Got the public relations office, asked to speak to a Jack Givins.

Jack who?

So then she tried the two senators' offices. Got through to the communications departments and said she was trying to get an email address for a Jack Givins. They said they didn't believe they had anyone working for them by that name, but if Lana wanted to hold, they would check.

When they came back on, they said they didn't have any Givins in their directories. Lana said she must have made a mistake, and offered quick apologies before hanging up.

Hmm, she thought.

So her initial hunch, that Jack had been hired to write speeches for some local politico, appeared to be a nonstarter. That didn't mean he wasn't doing that kind of work for someone at some lower level of government, but there were thousands of those.

Lana only had so much time to devote to this foolishness. But it sure would have been fun, next time she saw Jack, to have been able to say, "So, how's it going putting words into the mouth of so-and-so?" She'd have to dig a little more another day.

EIGHTEEN

Jack

Three days went by before my favorite U.S. marshal, Gwen Kaminsky, got back to me. The cell phone started buzzing a few minutes after ten in the morning.

I picked up.

"Yeah."

Gwen said, "Grab your notebook. Be out front in five." Before I could say anything, she'd ended the call.

One of the pluses of working from home is that there's not what you would call a strict dress code. I was not, at this hour, wearing anything more than a pair of boxers. Nor had I showered or shaved.

I'd stayed up past midnight, watching one talk show after another but not really registering what the hosts and their vapid guests were saying. I was having a hard time getting to sleep.

This whole thing with Gwen was bothering me. When she didn't get back to me within twenty-four hours of our last conversation, I figured the gig was over. She wasn't going to let me talk to her person for whom I was creating a past, and if that was the case, I didn't see how I could proceed. It was like grasping at air. There was nothing to latch on to. And I was still not convinced that Gwen had come to pick me randomly.

I felt there was more to it than she was letting on, and that was making me uneasy.

Maybe, at some point, I'd press the issue.

And as Lana had pointed out the other night, I was always, figuratively or literally, looking over my shoulder. A couple of times that night I'd pulled back the curtain and looked down at the street. Twice I had noticed some low-slung sports car—an older-model Corvette, maybe—with someone behind the wheel. I could tell someone was there by the orange, glowing dot. The driver was having a smoke.

The third time I looked, the car was gone. I finally flopped onto the couch and fell asleep around one in the morning.

I awoke after nine and drank some coffee while I read the news on my laptop at the kitchen table.

And then at ten, my five-minute warning.

Five minutes was more than enough time to get my act together. I showered, skipped shaving, and pulled on jeans, a black T-shirt, and a pair of sneakers. As I was coming out the front door, pushing one arm into my windbreaker, then switching my notebook to my other hand so I could get my other arm in, that familiar black van did a U-turn out front and stopped at the curb.

The side door, its window tinted almost to black, slid open. Gwen, in the center seat, beckoned me with a finger.

I stepped forward, hesitating briefly because I didn't know whether she wanted me next to her, or to take a spot in the back row. She pointed a thumb that way, so that was where I parked myself. I put my notebook on the seat beside me.

"Did you bring a cell phone?" she asked, turning in her seat to face me.

"My own or the one you gave me?"

"Both. Either." When I nodded, she said, "Hand them over."

I dug the two phones out of my jacket pocket. "What's the problem?"

As she took them she glared at me like I was a clueless two-year-old. "Why don't we just *tell* the bad guys where our witness is?"

"Are you saying I'm being tracked?" I asked, a chill running through me.

"I'm saying we have to be careful. Always."

The side door slid shut magically, no doubt at the touch of a button from the guy behind the steering wheel, my friend Scorsese. As the van began to move, Gwen handed me a long strip of black cloth.

"What's this for?" I asked.

"Blindfold yourself."

"You're kidding."

"This is what you asked for," she said. "You want to meet this guy? Put it on."

I took the cloth and tied it around my head. The fabric was thick and completely shrouded my vision, but Gwen wasn't happy with how I'd done it.

"Hang on," she said. I felt her fingers on my face, tugging down on the cloth, pulling out the wrinkles and broadening the blindfold, as if I might see a sliver of light at the bottom. I could smell some scent on her fingers, something nice, and as her fingers brushed my cheeks I had a rush of feelings. Anxiety, anticipation, and—I can't explain it, but I was a little turned on.

"Good?" she asked.

"Just peachy," I said.

The van picked up speed. We made a slew of lefts and rights and then I felt the vehicle climbing, as though we were on a ramp. Then we picked up speed, suggesting we were on the highway, clicking along at sixty, seventy miles per hour. The Mass Pike, maybe. But then I thought, Maybe not. The turnpike was a toll road. Would they want to take a chance that they'd be spotted at one of the tollbooths with a blindfolded dude in the back seat?

Sure, they could flash their government ID and get waved on through, but that might take time or require an explanation. So maybe we were on a different route.

Scorsese, behind the wheel, kept jumping from radio station to radio station until Gwen finally snapped, "Could you just pick one and stick with it?"

He did.

Unable to look at my watch, I was losing track of how much time we'd been traveling. I estimated we'd been on the road for more than thirty minutes but less than an hour when I heard the familiar click of a turn signal, the van decelerating, then turning onto what presumably was an off-ramp. We were making more stops now, more turns, and likely not getting above fifty.

And then I heard gravel crunching under the tires. We were moving at a crawl, and did so for about half a minute. Then, we stopped. The engine died. Even before the side door opened, I could hear some kind of din, as if someone not far away was operating a chain saw. I heard the side door slide open, and the sound became louder.

"You may take off the blindfold," Gwen said. "Leave it on the seat for the trip back."

I untied the cloth and blinked a few times as my eyes adjusted to daylight. It was a cloudy, gray, overcast day. I grabbed my notebook, got out of the van, and took in my surroundings.

Before me was what I guess one would call a cabin. That makes it sound more rustic than it actually was. It was a well-tended, single-story structure, about thirty feet wide, with a porch running along the entire front. The place was painted dark brown, and there were flower boxes mounted under the windows. I didn't know a gladiola from a geranium, but the boxes were filled with colorful plants. If I were guessing, the place had been built back in the forties, maybe even earlier, and been subjected to some restoration work over the years. The cabin was set in a small clearing in the middle of a forested area. Those woods looked dark and thick. If there were any nearby neighbors, I couldn't see them.

The noise I'd heard was coming from the house. It was music, if you could call it that. Some kind of loud techno, like a million electric fingernails scraping down a vibrating blackboard. The cabin's front windows, which from where I stood appeared to be screened, were all open, allowing the music to broadcast far beyond the cabin walls.

"Jesus," Gwen said, getting out of the van behind me. "How many times do I have to tell him . . ."

I glanced back at the van and our driver, who was staying put. Scorsese could scan as many stations as he wanted now, what with Gwen heading for the house. I followed her up the two steps to the porch and stood behind her as she knocked on the door.

The first knock wasn't loud enough to be heard by anyone inside. She made a fist and banged on it half a dozen times.

"It's us!" she shouted.

The music stopped. Seconds later, I could hear the turning of a dead bolt and the release of a chain, neither of which struck me as providing much in the way of protection out here in the middle of the woods. If you were a bad guy, you'd just kick the door in, or blow out the windows with your high-powered rifle. Or, since they were open, kick in the screens. But what the hell did I know. I was just the writer guy. I left security to the experts.

The door opened.

A short man, about forty, looked out at us through wire-rimmed glasses. He was bald on top, but he'd let hair on the sides of his head grow down almost to his shoulders.

"This the guy?" he asked Gwen.

"What have I told you about blasting that fucking awful

noise?" she said. "You're supposed to be in hiding, not broad-casting your presence to the entire goddamn commonwealth. What the hell was that, anyway?"

"Angerfist," he said, looking surprised that she didn't know, like everyone would know a band with that name. "From a few years back." He appraised me. "You gonna tell me if this is the guy?"

She sighed, already looking defeated. "This is the guy."

"Hi," I said, extending a hand. "I'm Jack." The moment I said my name I wondered whether that broke a rule. Gwen didn't say anything, so I guessed I hadn't messed up.

The guy gave my hand a quick, sweaty squeeze. "I don't know what you can call me," he said, and looked at Gwen for guidance.

"For today," she said, "why don't you go by Bill."

"Okay." He looked back at me. "Pleased to meet you. You can call me Bill."

"Bill," I said.

"Why don't you come on in and tell me all about myself."

NINETEEN

"What is the point," Kyle Gartner barked into the phone, "in paying people to look the other way if they aren't going to fucking look the other way?"

"I know, I know," said the voice on the other end of the call. "He's being difficult. I think he's just holding out for a little more. His kid needs braces or something."

"Fuck the kid. It's Daddy who's going to need a new set of teeth if he doesn't see reason."

"I think, if we sweeten the pot just a little, he'll see things our way. This works both ways, you know. If he blows the whistle on us, we've still got him by the nuts for turning a blind eye for so long. His bosses aren't going to like that."

Kyle massaged his forehead with his free hand.

"I don't need this," he said. "Not now. Christ."

The voice said, "It's been a tough year for you."

"Tell me about it."

"Your sister was the best. Must be . . . tough, considering."

"Yeah." Kyle paused. "Look, see what you can do with our greedy friend. How are you coming with the other thing?"

"The documents?"

"Yeah."

"Coming along. Still don't understand what you need them for."

"If you need to know I'll tell you."

Kyle ended the call, then opened his desk drawer and took out a bottle of pills. His head was starting to pound. He shook out two into his hand and washed them down with the last few drops of scotch in the glass in front of him.

His associate was right. It was tough, considering.

It was strange, losing a twin. Kyle Gartner didn't believe it was anything like when someone lost a regular sibling. Sure, it could be devastating to lose an older or younger brother or sister, but losing a twin? Someone to whom you felt more than a familial connection? It bordered more on telepathic.

Kyle's sister, Valerie, wasn't an identical twin, obviously. He was born with XY chromosomes and she entered the world with XX chromosomes. But you didn't spend more than nine months in a womb with someone and not have a bond that was special.

He felt he'd lost part of himself when Valerie died two months earlier. And forty-two was far too young. Had she died from a medical condition, Kyle might have worried he was fated to come down with the same thing. But Valerie had not died of cancer or heart disease or a stroke. It wasn't like that at all.

It was a shock. And yet, it wasn't as if Kyle couldn't have seen it coming.

Her problems had started in her late teens. Too much drinking. Pot. Kyle, no stranger to booze and drugs at that age, believed she would move beyond those pastimes. Sure, Valerie had some underlying issues. She'd suffered a loss, just as Kyle had. But Valerie had taken it much harder.

Losing your father was one thing. But to lose him in such a violent way, and for the person who took his life to face no consequences, well, Valerie couldn't deal with it. That man who killed their father was out there, somewhere, with a new name, a new identity, a new life. Valerie found the only way to handle it was to numb herself. And once she got into the habit, it was hard to break it, no matter how much time passed.

There had been some successes along the way. Stints in rehab. A challenging job that took her mind off her problems. Valerie would get her life together, for a while, but no fix was permanent. The other shoe always dropped.

Two months ago, it had dropped for the last time.

Kyle had lived with a simmering rage, too, for more than two decades, but Valerie's passing had brought that rage to a boil. But there was more than rage to deal with. Valerie's death had brought about a kind of reckoning for Kyle. He was second-guessing everything. Not just whether there was any real justice in the world, but bigger questions.

Like, what was the fucking point of it all?

Was this the life he'd always dreamed of? Running Gartner Linens? A thriving company that supplied sheets and towels to several hundred motels and hotels in the Chicago area and beyond? Was that anything to be proud of? Was this the path he would have chosen had his father not died? Had taking over the family business ever been his ambition when he was young? That's a hard no, my friend. Sure, these days, it provided a good living for him and his family, for his wife, Cecilia, and their daughter, Cherie. It had bought them a nice house here in the Highland Park suburb of Chicago. A Lexus and a Jaguar sat in the driveway. He belonged to the local Rotary Club and had won a couple of distinguished business awards.

But for the love of God, the hassles.

It had been hard enough hiring people before the pandemic. Spending your day in a sweatbox running hundreds of industrial washers and dryers, prepping towels and bedding stained with God knows what from dozens of motels and hotels in the Chicago area for a measly fifteen bucks an hour? *Oh, yes, please, pick me!* And now it was even more difficult to find laborers to put in eight hours a day at his plant.

So what was a boss to do? Look south, that's what.

Turned out there were plenty of people streaming into the country every day willing to do the kinds of jobs the locals wanted no part of. Only problem was, these workers weren't, technically speaking, in the country legally.

So you got them authentic-looking IDs so they could get driver's licenses, bank cards, shit like that. And when your friendly neighborhood immigration inspector came snooping, you put some money in an envelope so he'd look the other way. It was the cost of doing business. And then his kid needs braces.

It was always something.

Kyle had people to handle these things, but some days he wanted all these problems to go away. His discontent, which had been evident before Valerie's death, was growing.

There were two things he wanted:

1. Justice for Valerie, whatever that might be.
2. A new life.

He imagined himself in his eighties, thinking back with regret to his forties, realizing that that was the time he should have made some bold moves. That was the time he should have—

"Kyle?"

He was so deep in thought he hadn't heard his wife enter the home office. She must have tiptoed in. He'd had his back to the door, and slowly turned the plush Eames chair around to face her.

"Yes?" he said.

"You've been in here for an hour," Cecilia said.

"You got a stopwatch or something?"

She spotted the container of pain medication on his desk. "You have a headache?"

"You figured that out?" he asked. "Just by looking at the bottle?"

She looked at him with sadness in her eyes. "I'm going to bed." She turned and left the room, closing the door behind her.

There needed to be so many changes. Things needed to be set right. It was a time for new beginnings. There were scores to be settled.

TWENTY

Jack

"I've put together a lunch," Bill said.

We'd stepped into one large room that was a combined living area and kitchen, more dated than I expected it to be. No woodstove or icebox, but the stove and fridge, in avocado green, dated back to the seventies. The large pine dining table was surrounded by six wooden chairs, not one matching any other. A large quilt hung over the back of the brown couch, and probably the only modern item was the flat-screen TV resting atop an old blanket box shoved up against one wall.

At one end of the kitchen counter was an old fan, the kind you might see on a private detective's desk in a 1940s movie. The blade spun around noisily inside its thick wire enclosure. *Tickety tickety tickety tickety tickety.* It did a not-bad job of moving the air around in here, which was nice, because it was unusually warm for a late-September day, the temperature hovering in the mid-eighties. This place was definitely not equipped with air-conditioning.

"Just a bit of this and that," Bill said, gesturing to the food he'd put out on the table. "Gwen had her people do a grocery run for me in town."

"What town is that?" I said, unsure of my bearings.

Bill smiled. "Now that would be telling, wouldn't it, Gwen?"

She said nothing. She scowled at the noisy fan as she took a seat at the kitchen table. Bill had set out a long cutting board covered with cheeses, various meats, pickles, and pearl onions. I wouldn't have expected charcuterie in a place like this. Venison, maybe.

"Drinks?" he asked.

"Coffee, if you have it," Gwen said. "And can you do anything about that fan?"

"What about it?" Bill said.

"It's incredibly annoying."

"If you want to sweat through lunch I can turn it off," he offered.

"Never mind," she said, accepting defeat with a grimace.

Bill looked at me. "Water's fine," I said.

There was a coffee maker on the counter, the carafe half full. Bill filled a glass from the tap, poured a cup of coffee for Gwen, and returned to the table.

"One always likes to be a good host," he said, sitting down.

From the moment he'd first appeared at the door, there was something about him that seemed familiar.

"Have we ever met?" I asked him.

"Huh?"

"I feel like maybe we've met before," I said.

Bill squinted at me. "I don't think so. You spend a lot of time at Suffolk Downs bettin' on the ponies?"

I shook my head. I had my pen and notebook out and on the table. "You mind?" I asked.

Bill shook his head. "Gwen here says you want to get to know me."

"A sense of you," I said. "She explained to you what I'm doing?"

"Yeah." He speared some slices of prosciutto and lean, rare

roast beef, cut off a couple of slices of crusty bread, and started making a mini sandwich. "You're my lie maker."

"I'm working on a backstory for you. Something for you to learn, to remember, and whenever you're with people in your new life, you know, you can tell those stories instead of things that really happened to you, so as to keep people from figuring out who you are."

"Like that *Seinfeld* episode," Bill said. "The one where Peterman buys Kramer's anecdotes and passes them off as his own when he writes his autobiography." He smiled. "I watch a lot of TV."

I recalled the episode. "Something like that."

"But without the laughs," Bill said, chuckling.

His smile faded almost immediately. "So, what can I tell you about myself? I'm not sure I get the point of this. Whatever I tell you, you gotta change it, right?"

I looked to Gwen for some guidance, then back to Bill. "Not really. I mean, just as an example, if you're into cars, I could work into your background that you once sold them at a dealership. Even if you didn't, that's a story you could probably tell pretty convincingly. Or, your interest in food seems to go beyond eating it. Maybe you were a chef, or ran a restaurant, or were a critic."

He nodded slowly, thinking about it.

"Okay," he said. "Well, I do like fine food and fine wine. But you should get a sense of my personality, too. I'm kind of a dick. Ask Gwen, she'll confirm it." He grinned. "A pain in the ass to live with. I was married. Maybe I still am, technically. Had a kid. But they've gone their way and I've gone mine."

Bill took a breath. "I like biographies. I met Donald Trump in an elevator once. I lost my virginity at thirteen to my second cousin. I once dated a girl who was an extra in a *Star Wars* movie."

Bill recalled another brush with celebrity. "I got Patrick Stewart's autograph one time. He was at the table next to me in a restaurant in Memphis, had this cap on, head down low, trying to keep people from noticing him, but I spotted him right off. Thing is, I like TV. Watched it all the time as a kid."

So I got that part right, too, although inventing someone who liked to watch television was not exactly like getting all the right numbers in the lottery.

"Science fiction, sitcoms, crime shows," Bill said. "Everything. If there's a TV trivia contest, like in a bar or something? I can clean everybody's clock. Like, what was Rose's last name on *The Golden Girls*?"

"I got nothin'," I said, although the name was triggering.

Gwen said, "I don't care."

"Nylund," he said, and smiled briefly.

A guy who liked *The Golden Girls and* techno music? If I'd put that in the profile, Gwen would have said that sounded unlikely.

"I got beat up a lot as a kid because the other kids thought I was weird," he said, shrugging. "I didn't do too bad, although I wasn't great at math. Maybe that explains why I've never been all that good with money. Go right through it, you know? I'm always short. That's probably why I started getting in trouble. You know, I couldn't take the long view, have a plan to make more money. I always needed something *today*, so I'd steal stuff and then sell it."

"You going to be able to live a normal life once you're relocated?" I asked.

"That's not really your area of concern," Gwen said.

"Just curious."

"No, that's an interesting question," Bill said. "The thing is, it's not going to work."

"What's not going to work?" I asked.

Bill gave Gwen an apologetic look. "This is great and all, you giving me a new life in return for me testifying against those guys. I mean, if I hadn't agreed to do that, you'd have sent me to prison, and I'd never have lasted a week in there. They'd always be worried one day I'd talk, so I was kind of up against the wall, you know?"

"Where are you going with this?" Gwen asked.

He smiled wryly, then looked at me. "She knows what the problem is. I mean, sure, even if these witness protection yahoos set me up with a new name in a new town with a new job and maybe I'll find a new girlfriend, none of that matters, because eventually, one of these days, they are going to find me, and when they do, they're not just going to kill me. They're going to take their time. They're going to enjoy themselves. You have any idea who's looking for me?"

"No," I said. "Didn't think I was supposed to ask."

He looked to Gwen for guidance. "Can we tell him?"

She shrugged, glanced again at the ticking fan. "Go ahead."

"Russians," he said. "That's who's fucking looking for me. You know anything about those guys?"

"We don't move in the same circles," I admitted.

"Be grateful. They got this thing they call the elephant. You know that one?"

I shook my head.

"So they put a gas mask on your head, so you look, you know, like you've got an elephant trunk coming off your face. You got your hands cuffed behind your back. You're breathing through the mask and then they close off the breathing tube so you start running out of air pretty fast and you're choking and you think you're gonna die and then they open up the tube and you gasp for air and they shoot a little tear gas into it so it goes right into your lungs."

I was speechless for a moment, then asked, "They did that to you?"

"No. But I've seen it done. Been in the room when it happened."

"Jesus," I said.

"These guys don't fuck around. And they're going to be looking for me."

Gwen said, "We *can* protect you."

"That's what you keep saying," Bill continued. "But the only way you can protect me is if I do what I'm supposed to do, and we all know that's not going to happen. You know why?"

I wasn't sure who that question was intended for, so neither Gwen nor I spoke.

"Because I'm a fucking addict," Bill said. "Let me clarify that for you, Jack. I gamble. Horses, cards, fights, you name it. I can try to control it. I can try to keep a handle on it. But one day, I'm going to find a game somewhere. I'm going to go to the track. I'm going to sneak off for a few days and go to Vegas or Atlantic City. Because I won't be able to stop myself. Am I right?"

The question was for Gwen. "It's all on you," she said.

"You see, the thing is, the Russians? They know that about me. They know my weakness. So they're going to be putting the word out. Keep your eye out for that weaselly guy with the glasses and the weird hair."

"We're going to give you a makeover," Gwen said, "and a hairpiece, if you'll wear it."

"Whatever," he said. "Like I said, they'll be talking to all their people, telling them one of these days, maybe not this week or next, maybe not next month, but sure as shit one of these days he's going to show up, and when he does, give us a call, we'll make it worth your while, believe me, and faster than shit goes through a goose they'll be there and they'll scoop me up and take me someplace and have some fun with me, doing the elephant thing for starters, maybe, and probably finishing off by cutting off my dick and shoving it down my throat." He waved his hands at the food spread out before us. "Come on, help yourself. No one's eating."

Gwen and I exchanged glances. I didn't have much of an appetite, and I was betting she didn't, either.

"So, Mr. Writer Guy," Bill said, "how's that for material?"

TWENTY-ONE

There weren't any new developments on the death of the retired judge, and Lana wasn't expecting any.

The prevailing opinion was that the man had lost hold of the leash that was attached to Oliver and gone running after him. And while Oliver was eventually found close to home, it was entirely possible he had at first run off in the direction of the harbor, and that Willard Bentley, in pursuit, had somehow lost his footing and stumbled. Confused after his fall, he had wandered off in the direction of the harbor, walked out onto a pier and plunged into the dark, cold water.

The Willard Bentley story was, for now, over. The glowing tributes had been written. A funeral was scheduled for the day after tomorrow. Originally planned as a major event, it was now a private, family-only affair.

Lana had turned her attention to the missing doctor.

The story got a mention in all the city papers and on the nightly newscasts, but was quickly fading from view. Dr. Marie Sloan, in all likelihood, had taken her own life, and the media tended to soft-pedal suicides unless it was some big-time celebrity. Sloan's disappearance and possible suicide were, however, a way into a larger story about the stress and persistent trauma experienced by frontline health-care workers. The *Star* was planning a major takeout on the subject—and not for the first time—but Lana's editors had assigned it to the special projects team, and that was fine by her.

More recently, her assignments had been more mundane. A tanker truck rollover that brought traffic on the northbound 93 to a standstill for hours. A two-alarm fire that left a family of four homeless. A fatal motorcycle accident in Bunker Hill.

In her downtime between stories, she worked more of her contacts in an attempt to learn what Jack had been hired to do. Her latest theory was that he had been engaged to ghostwrite someone's memoir.

She knew this was none of her beeswax, as her mother liked to say, but she couldn't keep her curiosity in check. If she did learn what he was up to, she wasn't going to tell a soul. Well, maybe Jack. Just to see the look on his face when he learned how crafty she could be. There were moments—fleeting, admittedly—when she told herself it was wrong to pry into Jack's work life. After all, what if it were the other way around? If she were onto some big story that enlisted the aid of anonymous sources, how would she like it if Jack made it his business to find out who they were?

She'd kill him, that's what she'd do.

So maybe she should put an end to this. *Soon*. Just a couple more calls, and if she struck out she'd call it quits. Respect his privacy. Let him work on whatever it was he was working on without her sticking her nose into it.

Even before Jack's first two books were published, and before she had accompanied him to a few bookstore events, Lana had struck up acquaintances with a few people who worked in publishing. One was a literary agent, another an editor at one of the top houses in New York, and a third worked for one of the websites that kept track of industry news. That person's name was Lawrence Eckhart, and Lana decided to start with him.

She fired off an email, asking if he had time for a chat, and heard back almost immediately. Eckhart's email contained a phone number and an invitation to call her the moment she had a chance. Lana wasn't sure, but the couple of times she'd met Eckhart, she thought he had a thing for her.

"How's it going?" he asked when she called.

"Great," she said. "How's things in New York?"

"Not in the office that much. We worked from home for so long, some of us decided to keep doing it. I go into the office maybe once a week, sit in my chair, spin around, then go home. What's up?"

"You heard of any major deals lately for memoirs, biographies, that kind of thing? A tell-all book?"

"There's always a bunch in the pipe. Political ones, celebs, whatever."

"I'm thinking of ones where the subjects wouldn't have the chops to write it themselves. Ones where they'd need a ghost-writer."

"That could be any number of them," he said. "A lot of these people, they only ever have one book come out, have no skills in that regard, wouldn't know a colon from a comma, and have to find somebody to do the heavy lifting for them."

"And the public never knows, right?"

"Depends. Some subjects are open about it, mention the person who helped them write it. Others, yeah, they want you to think they were smart enough to do it all by their lonesome, even though no one believes it."

"If you were looking for someone to write your story, is there a short list?"

"Lana, you could write your *own* story. You don't need someone to do it for you," Eckhart said. "And I'll tell you right now, I'll be first in line to buy a copy. Just so long as you put in all the juicy bits, like that fling with the CNN guy."

"What are you talking about?"

"Come on, you know the rumor that was going around."

"It's bullshit, Lawrence. Whatever you think happened did not happen."

"Okay. But if you want the book to sell, it's gotta have something like that. Even better if it's true, but not absolutely necessary."

"It's not about me. It's something else altogether. Suppose I said I was asking for a friend? Someone who's looking to tell his or her life story? Who are the top ones out there?"

"Hang on," Eckhart said. "We did a piece on this not long ago. Let me see if I can find it."

Lana heard the tapping of keys, then Eckhart was back. "Here we go. You want to write these down."

"Just read them out to me."

Eckhart read her more than a dozen names. Jack Givins was not among them. That didn't mean he couldn't have been approached, but there were clearly a number of writers out there who would have been ahead of him on a list.

"Okay, thanks," Lana said. "I don't hear the name Jack Givins there."

"Ah, didn't I see you with him at something a year or two ago?"

"It's possible."

"Well, if he's writing someone's story, it's news to me. He looking for that kind of work?"

"He's the kind of guy who's always up for a challenge."

"What he should really do is write his own story."

"He's done that. Two novels. Got some very good reviews."

"I'm not talking about fiction. He should write a memoir or something. Although he probably wouldn't. Seems to be a guy who values his privacy, not even putting out those books under his own name."

Lana paused. "Why do you think he's got a memoir in him?"

"I could be totally wrong. Maybe what I heard isn't true."

"What did you hear?"

"Look, it's not for me to say. He just has . . . an interesting story. You've read his books. The clues are all there. Listen, Lana, I've got another call here. Take care."

And he was gone.

Lana slowly put the phone down. The clues were in Jack's books? She'd read them, of course. What was Lawrence referring to?

Jack wrote about emotional abandonment, about young men trying to find their way in a world where there was no one to count on. Jack wrote about boys and young men who were lost.

Was that what Jack was? *A lost boy?* Whatever major events had shaped him, why hadn't he told her about them? He rarely spoke of his family, other than Earl. She thought back to when she stumbled upon the Joan Didion book he'd bought her. How her search had turned up almost nothing of a personal nature.

She needed to talk to him. If there were things he'd been holding back, things he did not trust her enough to share, well, that was deeply troubling, because she—

Because she loved him.

She picked up her cell, intending to bring up Jack's number, but before she could place the call the phone rang in her hand.

"Yeah?"

"Lana?"

She recognized the voice. One of her contacts with the Boston PD.

"Go ahead."

"They found the doctor."

TWENTY-TWO

Jack

Back in the van, Gwen ordered me to put the blindfold back on for our return to Boston. I put my notebook on the seat next to me, picked up the cloth, and did as I was told. The last thing I saw before putting it into place was Bill standing on the porch of the cabin, giving us a friendly wave goodbye.

Scorsese started up the vehicle and we were off, the sound of gravel crunching under the tires loud enough that it wasn't worthwhile to engage in any conversation. Once we hit the main road, things got quieter, but I didn't feel like talking much.

I was a little shell-shocked, I guess. And Gwen had picked up on it.

"You okay?" she asked.

"I'm fine," I lied.

It had all seemed a bit of a lark up to now. Being asked to imagine past lives for people I didn't know had struck me as a fun idea at the outset. Challenging and mysterious all at once. I got a Walter Mitty-like buzz out of this assignment.

And having to keep it all a secret was, in its own way, part of what made the work all the more tantalizing. I could walk down to the deli for my whole-wheat bagel with chive cream cheese and look at all the other customers and think: None of you have any idea what I am up to. I am working for the government on a very hush-hush project. As if all that weren't enough, I knew it was driving Lana crazy, not knowing what I'd been engaged to do.

But lunch with Bill had left me, at least for the moment, shaken. The reality of what the man was facing hit home. This was no fucking game. This guy's life was on the line. If Gwen didn't hide him well enough, and if I didn't do my part in giving him convincing stories to tell, he was a dead man.

And it got me to thinking about more than just Bill. It was all starting to feel a little too close to home.

"Talk to me," Gwen said about ten minutes into our trip back to the city. We were back on a main highway, judging by how fast it felt that we were traveling. She sounded close, and had evidently turned around in the middle seat so that I could hear her better, even if I couldn't see her.

"About?"

"That meeting with Bill. It made an impact."

"Yeah," I said.

"It seems a little more real than it did before."

"Yeah," I said again.

"Bill—I guess it won't surprise you to know that's not his real name—but Bill can be a little dramatic at times."

"Was he making that up? What they'd do to him if they found him?"

"No," Gwen said.

I went quiet again, thinking.

"Did it help?" she asked. "Did getting to know him, even for that length of time, make it easier for you to craft a history for him?"

I took a moment to answer. "I suppose so."

"But?"

"There's no but." I paused. "Maybe there is, but it's got nothing to do with Bill."

"What's that mean?"

"Nothing. Is Bill's experience pretty representative? Do all relocated witnesses live in that kind of perpetual fear?"

"Depends," she said. "Bottom line, we wouldn't be sending them into hiding if they weren't in real danger. Why?"

I shook my head, figuring she was looking at me and would understand I wasn't ready to answer the question. Finally, I said, "You think Scorsese could find a place to pull over and we could get out of the car and have a talk?"

"Scorsese?" she said.

I forgot she wasn't in on my own private joke. "Can your driver find us a place to stop? I mean, we're far enough away from wherever you're hiding Bill that I'd never be able to figure out how to get back there. You think I could lose the blindfold?"

"Sure. Let me."

I felt her hands on me again as she worked her fingers under the edge of the cloth and lifted it up and over my head.

"Thanks," I said, blinking a couple of times as my eyes adjusted to the light. We were, in fact, on a major highway, moving along with other cars and huge tractor-trailers. I could see that we couldn't pull over just yet.

"There one of those service centers coming up?" I asked.

Gwen asked the driver, who said there was one about five miles ahead.

"We're making a pit stop," she said.

Seven minutes later, we were taking the exit to one of those sprawling roadside centers with a gas station and bathrooms and a food court with a variety of takeout choices. The place was popular with truckers, who had parked their rigs around the back of the building.

The side door slid open and Gwen got out first. I followed.

"You want to go in and freshen up or anything?" she asked.

"No," I said, and nodded to the far reaches of the parking lot, which butted up against some low, rolling, manicured lawns. "Let's take a walk."

Gwen told the driver we were going to be a few minutes, and if he wanted to take a break, he was welcome to. As an afterthought, she asked him to grab her a coffee.

"Want anything?" she asked me.

I shook my head.

"Okay, let's walk."

I led her over to the grassy area, hands in my pockets, thinking about how I was going to broach this. I spotted a couple of picnic tables, went to one, and sat down. Gwen swung her legs over the opposite bench and sat across from me.

"Well?"

"When you asked me to take this on, I asked you if there were any other reasons you picked me, other than that your people considered me a good prospect, based on the characters I'd created in my books."

"That's right," she said.

"Nothing else?"

"Why don't you just tell me what's on your mind," she said, glancing at her watch. "You're not the only one I've got doing this kind of work."

"How thoroughly did you check me out?" I asked.

Gwen cocked her head to one side. "Thoroughly enough," she said. "No criminal record, no associations or affiliations with groups on our watch list. You came up pretty clean. You got into some shit when you were a kid. Found some police reports about you running away from home. They had to put out a missing persons bulletin on you once or twice, but you always came back. Or someone went to get you."

"How far back did you go?"

"I'm guessing not far enough," she said.

"It struck me as one hell of a coincidence that you'd pick

someone like me," I said. "Someone with more than a passing acquaintance with the witness protection program."

Her face fell. "Jesus Christ, what are you saying? That I picked a relocated witness to work for the program? You're fucking kidding me. There's no way in the world that could happen. Unless all that stuff about your teenage years was manufactured. Christ, they'll fucking fire me."

"It's nothing like that," I said, raising a hand to calm her. "It wasn't *me*. It was my father."

"Your father?"

"When I was nine, he went into the witness protection program. He wanted my mother and me to go with him, but she refused."

"Was his name Givins?"

"No," I said. "His last name was Donohue. Michael Donohue. And my name was Jack Donohue. But a couple of years after my dad disappeared, and after my mother had officially divorced him, she fell in love with someone else. A man named Earl Givins. They got married, and he became my father, and I took on his name."

"Fuck," Gwen said. "This should have been on file somewhere. There's no way I shouldn't have known this." She shook her head several times, then said, "Why are you telling me all this?"

"Couple reasons. I wanted to clear the air. I wanted to be sure there wasn't something fishy about you coming to me."

"There isn't. I swear. We fucked up. Plain and simple." She shook her head in dismay. "This kind of thing just can't happen." She took a breath, then asked, "What's the other reason?"

"I want you to set up a meeting. I'd like to see my dad. I don't know how to find him, but I figure you do."

TWENTY-THREE

"*I heard you talking to Mom.*"
"*About what?*"
"*About you going away.*"
"*You shouldn't listen in on people like that.*"
"*You said you could make a run for it. What's that mean?*"
"*Jesus.*"
"*Are you running away to Mexico?*"
"*No.*"
"*So you're not going away?*"
"*I'm still going away. Don't cry, okay? Don't do that.*"
"*I want to come with you.*"
"*Come here. Give me a hug. You know I love you more than anything in the world. You know that, right? Now get the hell out of here.*"

TWENTY-FOUR

The police department's news release on the death of Dr. Marie Sloan was written in a way that allowed one to read between the lines:

"Police today recovered the body of Dr. Marie Sloan, age 34, of Cambridge, from Old Harbor, not far out from Carson Beach and Joe Moakley Park. Our preliminary investigation does not show that Dr. Sloan's death was caused by interaction with any other person or persons, and may have been the result of misadventure. Dr. Sloan was a valuable member of the community, a dedicated professional, and someone who always put her patients first. At this time we wish to pass on our condolences to her family."

The department's chief communications officer, Cathi Chiarelli, had phoned Lana to give her a heads-up that something was coming, and moments later a statement landed in her inbox. The release had gone to all the media outlets in town, and Cathi couldn't be expecting much in the way of follow-up questions, given that suicides were not considered particularly newsworthy.

But Lana was puzzled.

Later, she dropped by the police headquarters and found Cathi in her cubicle, which was in a crowded office with several other members of her department.

"Cathi, got a sec?"

Cathi said, "Sure, what's up?"

"Someplace we can talk?"

Cathi led her to a small break room. There was a table, a fridge, a microwave, and a coffee machine. Cathi pointed to it and asked, "Want some? If I were you, I'd say no, but I feel I should offer."

Lana shook her head as they both pulled out chairs and sat down. "So the doctor killed herself?" she asked.

"You read the statement," Cathi said.

"Okay, but off the record, doesn't it seem kind of strange? And coincidental?"

"Like how?"

"First, that retired judge goes missing and ends up in the harbor. And now this doctor vanishes, and they find her in the water, too."

Cathi shrugged. "It happens. People do take their own lives. And with Mr. Bentley, that might not strictly be a suicide. There may have been cognitive issues there, so you're looking at two different things."

"Maybe," Lana said.

"And look," Cathi continued, "there are six to seven hundred suicides a year in Massachusetts, which works out to about two per day, and you figure, in a large metropolitan area like Boston, we're going to get more than our share."

Lana knew the stats because she had done some quick online research of her own before coming over here. She said, "Yeah, that's right, and you know how most people get it done? One of three ways. They either shoot themselves, they take an overdose of pills or some kind of poison, or they hang themselves."

"Okay," Cathi said. "And some people might drive full speed into a bridge abutment. Or step in front of a bus. You've cited the most likely ways someone might decide to take their own life, but there are plenty of others. Including walking off the end of a pier, which appears to be what Dr. Sloan did."

Lana considered that. "It seems like, if you've decided to end it all, that's a pretty miserable way to go about it. It's not like you're jumping off the Golden Gate. It's not that big a drop. That won't kill you. And if you can swim—do you know whether she knew how to swim?"

Cathi said, "I don't know. That wasn't in the information that was provided to me."

"Okay, forget that for now. But your natural instincts for preservation are going to kick in. Maybe you want to end it all by drowning, but I can't see a person letting themselves slip under the surface without putting up a fight. It doesn't track for me."

"You're looking for a story where there isn't one."

"And what about the fact that she was a doctor?" Lana asked. "So?"

"She'd have any number of pharmaceuticals at her disposal. If she wanted to end it all, she could take something. Something efficient and painless. If she wanted to take her own life, why wouldn't she have done that? I mean, if it were you, wouldn't you want to end it all quickly? Just go to sleep and that'd be it?"

"Is there something I can take right now?" Cathi asked.

"Something about it doesn't seem right, that's all I'm saying."

"What do you want from me?" Cathi said. "The detectives involved fill me in, I put out the release. I don't investigate things."

"So why am I talking to you?" Lana asked. "Who's on this?"

TWENTY-FIVE

arl Givins, sitting on the tiny balcony of his apartment, working on his first early-morning cigarette, figured he had no choice but to walk away from the condos that went down with that building. If he'd had insurance on them, he might have been able to count on that money coming, eventually, although the parties involved would probably be fighting it out in the courts for years. But there was no policy, so no sense worrying about that. He had to look forward.

Not that things looked much better in that direction.

He was behind on his rent. His credit cards were maxed out. He'd posted an ad online to sell his aging Porsche. He'd bought a paint touch-up kit at the local auto supply store, hoping to disguise the rust spots around the wheel wells. If he could unload it for fifteen or twenty grand, he'd count himself lucky.

Too bad about Jack. He should have known better than to hit up the kid—okay, he was hardly a kid anymore—for money. Jack had plenty of reasons to resent him. He had to be pissed that Earl sold his mother's house and kept all the money for himself, even though that had all happened years ago. And Earl shouldn't have been surprised that Jack wasn't swimming in cash from the sales of his two books. It wasn't as though Earl had seen Jack's books in the airport bookshops on his trips to and from Florida.

Earl felt he was at least due a modicum of respect. Didn't he give it his best shot getting that boy through his teen years? Tried to impart whatever wisdom he had. Helped him get his driver's license. Gave him advice on girls. Drove him to college. That had to count for something, right?

But if Jack really had no money to lend him now, none of that much mattered, did it?

Earl glanced at his phone to check the time. It was a little after nine. Someone who'd responded to his ad was coming to look at the Porsche at nine thirty. Only the one nibble so far. If this guy didn't bite, he'd try one of those services that were advertising all the time on TV, inviting you to go onto their site, provide all the details about your vehicle, and they'd make you an offer on the spot. Only trouble was, Earl was betting they'd lowball him. Thought the people behind these sites were probably appealing to car owners who were desperate for cash, would be willing to settle for the first offer they got.

People like Earl, in other words.

He feared that if no reputable lenders were going to help him out, he might have to turn to other sources. Unconventional lenders tended to charge much higher interest rates, and if you were late with a payment, well, they didn't politely change the locks on your place and seize your property. They broke your arm.

God help him if it came to that.

Earl came in off the balcony and opened the fridge. Was it too early to drink? What was it they said? It was five o'clock somewhere, right? He looked longingly at the three cans of Bud and the half bottle of a five-dollar white.

What was the harm.

He was reaching for a beer when his phone rang. "Hello?"

"Mr. Givins?"

"Yeah?"

"Here to look at the car?"

"Be right down."

He met the man out front of the building. Big guy, about six feet, handsome, jet-black hair, the kind of guy who'd look perfect behind the wheel of a sports car, Earl thought. They shook hands and introduced themselves.

"Earl Givins."

"Cayden, Cayden Silver."

"Come on in, we'll take the stairs. Car's underground."

Should have already had it parked on the street, Earl thought. He'd been so preoccupied he hadn't thought to bring the car outside. They went through the lobby and down a hallway behind the elevators and took the stairs down two flights to the lower-level garage.

"It's just over here," Earl said.

He led Cayden down a row of cars until they were into one of the corners. Earl had parked the car between a wall and a pillar. The passenger side was no more than a foot from the wall.

"I like this spot because no one can get close to it, ding your door, you know?" he said, hoping Cayden wouldn't notice that the car had plenty of nicks down the side already. Cayden stood a couple of paces back from the front bumper, taking it all in.

"Nice," he said. "One of the early ones. First generation. A ninety-seven?"

"That's right."

Cayden got close to the car, had a look at the convertible top. "This looks kind of rough in places."

"Still pretty airtight inside. It's not drafty with the top up." Earl laughed nervously. "But a baby like this, you're gonna want to drive it with the top down as much as you can, anyway."

"Hard to get a good look at it in this light. And I'd like to be able to walk around it."

"If you're serious, we'll take it outside. You could take it for a spin. Hope you won't mind if I ride along, point out its features and all."

Earl took the key from his pocket and unlocked the vehicle so that his prospective buyer could examine the interior. Cayden opened the driver's door and leaned in.

"Seats are a little tattered," he said. "Cracked in places."

"But they still give lots of support. When you're sitting in them, you hardly notice."

Cayden stood back, closed the door. "The ad said you're looking for seventeen?"

"That's right." Earl had listed it for seventeen thousand, but the truth was, he'd take less.

Cayden said, "I did some research online and they seem to be going for between eight and fifteen, depending on the condition. And the condition of this one is the shits. Those little bubbles on the fender rust?"

"It's not as bad as it looks. I mean, you might have to put a little money in it, but it's still a Porsche, right? Why don't you make an offer?"

"How about twenty-five?"

Earl thought he'd heard wrong. "I'm sorry, what?"

"Twenty-five thou. Cash."

Earl said, "I don't get it."

"Don't get what?"

"You haven't even driven it. You haven't seen it in the light. And you want to offer me eight thousand more than I'm asking?"

"If you're not interested, just say so."

"No, listen—but I don't get why—"

Cayden smiled and put a hand on Earl's shoulder. "If all I wanted was the car, you'd be right thinking I was crazy."

Earl let that sink in. "What do you mean, if all you wanted was the car?"

"I want your help with something. You're in a unique position to be able to assist the person I represent. I'll give you twenty-five grand now for the car, but if you come through for us, we'd be willing to top that up with another five."

"Come through for you? Who the fuck are you?"

Cayden smiled. "Your guardian angel."

TWENTY-SIX

Jack

I had time, on the way back to being dropped off at my place, to tell Gwen more of the story. Or at least those parts I knew. To this day, there was a lot I did not know about my father's placement in the witness protection program. And even the stuff I thought I had right could be wrong.

"My mom and dad had a lot of fights over it," I said, still in the van's third row, Gwen in the middle, turned sideways, her right arm hanging over the back of the seat. "As a kid, you only picked up bits and pieces, you never quite got the full picture. I mean, I was nine. Not old enough to know the ways of the world, but old enough to be worried sick by them."

"Sure," Gwen said. "So your dad was Michael Donohue—undoubtedly known by another name for the last two and a half decades—and your mother's name is?"

"Was. Rose."

"Okay. So, Michael and Rose were arguing. About what?"

"The thing is, they'd had problems for a while. Although it's hard, as a kid, getting a sense of what it was. They were less attentive to each other, less affectionate. Dad slept on the couch a lot of nights. Sometimes he wouldn't come home at night and my mom had no idea why and she'd try hard not to act worried

126

about it. This was before the shit hit the fan. Before the police showed up one day and arrested my father."

"Go on."

"It was really early. We were all asleep. It was, like, five o'clock. And there's this bang on the door and they came right in. I think it was FBI guys. I remember the letters on the back of their jackets. Anyway, there's, like, a team of them, and they came into the house like storm troopers. I was a big *Star Wars* nut back then, had all the action figures, and that was what they reminded me of. Imperial storm troopers, except they weren't all dressed in white. So they come in, march up the stairs, and go straight for my parents' bedroom. Well, all the bedrooms, because they wouldn't have known which one was theirs. Because they came into my room, flicked on the lights, and there's this guy with a gun and I start screaming and I can hear my mom screaming, too, and my dad yelling at them. And I get out of bed, but the guy tells me to stay in the room, but I look out in the hallway and there's my mom in her nightgown and my dad in his boxers being ushered out of the bedroom and taken downstairs, and it's just a huge fucking commotion, you know?"

"Must have been horrible for you," Gwen said. "Traumatizing."

"You think?" I said. "All the yelling and screaming seems to go on forever. I hear someone reading my dad his rights and then they allow him to come back upstairs and get dressed, my mom swearing at them the whole time that they have no business being there, that she's going to sue their asses off, all that shit. My dad gets dressed, and to this day I can remember what he wore. He put on his best suit, a dark navy one, with a crisp white shirt and a blue tie with these little diamonds on it, and the capper was a folded handkerchief peeking out of his jacket pocket, you know? Like, if they were going to haul him out of the house, he was going out looking like a man. Looking professional."

Gwen managed a wry smile. I wondered, in her career, how many times she might have been part of such a scene. Maybe not in her current role, but I had no idea what she'd done before joining the witness protection service. I could picture her barging into houses before sunup, upending people's lives, throwing her weight around.

"The last thing my dad does before they take him out is he shouts at Mom: 'Call Abner!' I thought, Who the hell's that? but learned quickly, because that was the beginning of a lot of calls with Abner Bronklin, who was my dad's lawyer, at least at the beginning. Anyway, even after they took my dad away, they weren't done. They went through the entire house, looking for things. Documents, evidence, whatever they could find. This was around the time people were all getting home computers. Those big monitors and those huge towers with all the guts inside, the slots you put discs into. We had a couple of those, and they took them away. They even searched my room, figuring it would be the perfect place to hide something. I mean, who'd hide stuff in their kid's room, you know?"

"Did they find anything in there?"

I shrugged. "Honestly, I have no idea. I don't know what they found, in my room, the rest of the house, in those computer towers. But they found something."

"How do you know?"

I smiled. "Because they had leverage."

"Okay."

"For a while, I didn't see him at all. They had him in custody, and his lawyer—it was a woman later, Dad switched—was doing what she could to get him out. She came to the house a few times, and I'd hear my mom on the phone with her, hearing words like 'deal' and 'testify' and 'life.' Sometimes, she'd actually talk to me about it, when she'd had too much to drink. I think that's when my mom's drinking really started to become a problem, but that's another story. No matter how many times I asked, she wouldn't tell me what Dad had done, just that he was in a lot of trouble, that he could go away for a long time. But one day she said there was some kind of deal, that if my father agreed to cooperate he might not have to go to prison."

I felt my chin quiver at the memory. I'd been doing pretty well, telling this story without getting emotional, but there was something about that moment, when my mother talked about how my father was being offered a way out. I speculated that the reason it got to me, after all this time, was because that was when I convinced myself Dad would come home and everything would return to normal, that we'd be a family again.

I could not have been more wrong.

"Mom said it all hinged on Dad telling the police things they really wanted to know. I remember saying that it was like *telling*. Remember when you were a kid, and you'd threaten to get one of your friends in trouble, you'd say 'I'm telling!' You know, a tattletale."

"I remember."

"And Mom said, yes, it was like that, but it was different this time because he'd be telling on a very bad person. I thought, Okay, if that's what it takes. But there was a catch. He wouldn't go to jail, but he wouldn't be safe. The people he was testifying against, they'd want to get even. I was familiar with that concept, too. Like, when you were a kid and you tattled on someone, the next day, walking to school, watch out, right? You were likely to get the shit beat out of you. Except, as my mom explained, in Dad's case it would be much worse. If they could, they'd do it before he testified, but they'd still do it after, to send a message. That scared me, knowing there were people out there who wanted to kill my dad."

"When did you hear about the plan to give him a new identity, relocate him?"

"Not sure," I said. I glanced out the window. We were almost back to my place. "Soon enough, I guess. I had mixed feelings about it when I found out what was involved. I was glad there was a plan to keep my dad alive, but we'd have to move. I'd lose all my friends and never be able to see them again. But as time passed, that seemed less important. Other kids stopped having anything to do with me. Their parents read the papers, watched the news. And the morning the house was raided, well, the whole street took notice. All those flashing lights on the street woke people up. I was the kid whose dad was in deep shit. My friends were forbidden to have anything to do with me. And my enemies, if you could call them that, were emboldened. I was teased, bullied, beat up. So I was coming around to the idea. Starting over somewhere else, where nobody would know what trouble my dad had been in, where nobody knew me, that might not be so bad after all." I sighed. "But there was a problem."

"Your mother."

Scorsese had turned the van down my street.

"She wanted no part of it. She had extended family she wasn't about to walk away from. Her parents were still alive, although not in the greatest health, and she refused to abandon them in their later years. The way she saw it, this was my father's mess, and his alone. I think she loved him, in spite of everything, but this was a sacrifice she wasn't prepared to make. He kept pressuring her to change her mind. How would she survive? What if the guys who wanted him dead settled on her and me? Mom said she wasn't worried about that. Although maybe she should have been."

"What do you mean?"

"There were a few scares after Dad left. Threatening phone calls. Anonymous letters. Notes left under the windshield wiper on Mom's car when she went to the market. Saying something would happen to me if she didn't tell where Dad was."

"Christ," Gwen said. "Did they ever actually hurt you or your mother?"

I shook my head. "But the threat hung over us for a long time. I still . . . I still look over my shoulder, wondering." I paused, wondering whether to bring it up. "My car got torched the other night. Probably just bad wiring, or worst case, some random act of vandalism. But you always wonder whether someone is sending a message."

"It's always there," she said.

"After I finished college, I kind of just disappeared for several years. Hitchhiked around the country, did random jobs for cash, wasn't online at all. I needed a break. I needed to go for a period of feeling invisible until I felt it was safe to poke my head up above the parapet. That was when I got a newspaper job. And it's why, when I wrote those two books, I did them under another name."

"I get it."

"So can you do it?"

"Do it?"

"Connect me with my father."

"I don't know. Why's it important?"

"I'd like to know if he's okay. For all I know, the pandemic got him. There are things going on in my life I'd like to tell him about." I paused. "He's my dad. I'd like to see him."

Gwen considered what I'd had to say. "I don't know that I can deliver," she said. "We have strict protocols. We get a hundred requests like yours every day. And in only the rarest of circumstances do we grant them. Let me give you an example. We had an incident not too long ago. Kid needed a liver transplant. Best possible outcome involved a liver donation from the father, who, like your dad, had been relocated and didn't take the family with him. We reached out, presented the situation to him, asked if he was willing to be part of the procedure."

"What'd he say?" I asked.

"He passed."

I let that sink in a moment. I wondered what my own father might have done, presented with that scenario. I couldn't imagine he'd have said no.

Scorsese hit a button and the side door slid open. I got out of my seat, squeezed my way around the middle one where Gwen had spent the trip, and stepped out onto the street.

"One thing," Gwen said. "You've been dancing around this from the beginning of your story. What'd your dad do? Why'd they arrest him?"

"Oh, that," I said. "I finally got him to tell me before they drove off with him. He killed some people."

"Killed people?"

I nodded. "I guess he was what you'd call a hit man."

TWENTY-SEVEN

June 1996

Michael Donohue's beeper went off.

He kept it clipped to his belt. Not much bigger than a box of matches, it had a digital readout on the upper edge that showed the number of the person trying to reach him. All Michael had to do was glance down to know who it was.

Not that there were that many people it could be. His wife, Rose, had the number. A few other senior people in the Frohm organization. And, of course, the president and CEO himself, Galen Frohm.

Sure enough, that's who it was.

Michael had been strolling through the Faneuil Hall marketplace, having slipped out of the office to grab something for lunch. Once a week, duties permitting, he treated himself to an order of deep-fried oysters, tartar sauce, and a Coke from one of the vendors in the food colonnade, found an outside bench, and ate them leisurely while watching tourists and locals shopping, eating, exploring.

He was only halfway through his lunch when he was summoned. That's what it was when you heard from Galen Frohm. You weren't being asked to drop by when you had a chance. You weren't being asked to give him a call at your earliest convenience. You were being told to drop whatever you were doing and get your ass up to his office immediately. You were being *summoned*.

And you absolutely moved your ass when you were Galen Frohm's personal adviser and number-one problem-solver. It didn't matter whether you were having lunch a block away, in the middle of dinner with your in-laws, or having sex at seven o'clock on a Saturday morning. If Galen sought your presence, you went.

It was the nature of the job, and Michael knew it when he signed on. He'd learned, the hard way, what happened when you didn't play by Galen Frohm's rules.

Once—and only once—he'd ignored the page. He had bought his young son, Jack, a radio-controlled speedboat, a sleek, beautiful model about two feet long, and early on a Sunday morning they'd gone to the Boston Public Garden lagoon to try it out. Jack was just getting the hang of it, managing graceful turns with the boat, careful not to hit any swans, when Michael's beeper sounded.

"Shit," he'd said under his breath. A mere nine hours earlier he'd been to the boss's house to discuss some troublesome workers attempting to form a union at seventy of the four hundred cut-rate motels the company owned across the country. If they were successful, employees at the chain's remaining operations would become emboldened. This situation had to be dealt with before it got out of hand.

"This thing is a fucking brush fire waiting to happen," Frohm had said.

Michael did not disagree, and said he would consider some options and bring them to Frohm on Monday morning because, although he did not tell Frohm this, he had promised Jack he would spend Sunday with him.

So when the beeper sounded, Michael ignored it. *I left it*

at home, he would tell the boss later. *The battery was dead.* Something like that. Fuck him.

Big mistake.

When he and Jack got home, Rose told him Frohm had called the house four times looking for him.

"Didn't you take your damn beeper?" she'd asked him.

Frohm had grown angrier with each call, she said, and it was hard to tell whether Rose was more annoyed with her husband or the man for whom he worked. "There are three of us in this marriage," she'd said more than once, echoing comments made by Princess Diana around that time. But the third party in Michael and Rose's marriage wasn't a lover, but a childlike tyrant who believed the world revolved around him.

Michael went straight to the Frohm residence, where he was shown by one of the staff to the man's office. As he entered, he found Frohm was not alone. His daughter, about ten years old, Michael guessed, was demonstrating some high-kick moves she'd learned in a dance class and Frohm was putting his hands together in soft applause. But when he saw Michael, dance time was over, and his mood immediately turned sour.

"Get out of here, you little witch," he told the girl. "I have to talk to Michael here."

The child ran from the room, and the moment she was gone and the door was closed, Frohm lit into him.

"You are mine!" he bellowed. "Every fucking minute of every fucking day, you are mine, and you will make yourself available to me regardless of whether you are in the middle of an epic shit, a blow job from Miss America, or fucking open-heart surgery! You get that?"

He got it.

He got it, and he took it, because as despicable a man as Galen Frohm was, he was Michael's paycheck, the perks were plentiful, and working for the man was like living in some rarefied atmosphere where the rules didn't matter, where you were part of some special class of people who got to look down on everybody else and do whatever the fuck they wanted. Galen knew people. Judges, politicians, lawyers, leaders of industry. The kind of people you needed in your back pocket when you strayed outside the legal and ethical lines.

It was horrible and intoxicating at the same time.

On top of that, Michael had always felt in Frohm's debt. Frohm had taken Michael on as a favor to the boy's father, one of Frohm's employees, just as he was turning seventeen. He'd been a difficult teenager, been running with a rough crowd in Southie, and was rumored to have done some very bad shit, and Michael's father, divorced from a woman no longer on the scene, had given up trying to get him back on the right track.

"Let me see what I can do," Frohm had said, and offered the kid a low-level job at one of his businesses. Loading trucks, hauling bags of laundry. Checked in on him regularly, mentored him, administered some tough love when it was appropriate. Gave him better jobs with increased responsibility. The kid caught on quickly, excelled at whatever task he was assigned.

Then, one day, Frohm offered Michael the position of his personal assistant.

"There's no one I trust more," Frohm told him. "You're the man I need at my side moving forward. There are challenging times ahead, tough decisions to be made. I want you there with me."

How could Michael possibly say no?

He soon learned that being Frohm's assistant was more than a job. It was a way of life. It was a 100 percent commitment.

So he wasn't going to be able to eat the last of these oysters while he sat on that bench. He tossed them into a nearby trash bin and hoofed it back to the office. It wasn't even a five-minute walk back to Frohm International's offices in the high-rise complex at 75 State Street. Before entering the building, Michael used a napkin to wipe any tartar sauce that might be left in the corners of his mouth. He boarded the elevator and hit the button for one of the upper floors.

Frohm International took up three of them. The lowest was dedicated to overseeing the Sleep Tight Tonite chain of cheapo motels. More than four hundred of them around the continental United States, usually situated where one interstate highway criss-crossed with another. Aimed at families and business travelers on limited budgets, Sleep Tight Tonite promised clean, basic accommodation without the frills, and according to customer reports, often fell short of even that.

The middle-floor offices oversaw Frohm's other business inter-ests. A chain of fast-food chicken outlets and several hundred dollar stores where the employees' wages were so poor, they could barely afford the products they stocked on their own outlets' shelves.

The top floor consisted of upper-management offices, confer-ence rooms, and what Michael thought of as Frohm's lair—a mas-sive office that overlooked the city of Boston, the walls lined with photos of the CEO posing with politicians of all stripes, leaders both foreign and domestic, framed honors from various chari-table organizations Frohm had strong-armed to take some cash from him so as to temper his reputation as a money-grubbing shit. There were framed newspaper clippings—so long as they were flattering—and even a *BusinessWeek* cover. The story inside had been actionable, in Frohm's opinion, but still, when you make the cover of a national magazine, that's a moment worth memorial-izing. Frohm might not have been the wealthiest businessman in the country, but he certainly wanted you to think he was.

Michael went straight through the double doors into the office without knocking. When you were summoned, it was understood you were to come straight in. What surprised people meeting

Frohm for the first time was that his physical stature was no match for his public persona. He was a small man, barely five-five, and topped the scales at no more than one hundred and forty. But one sensed a considerable energy, even menace, within him.

"About time," Frohm said.

Michael let it roll off him. If he'd been in the next room and been there in ten seconds, Frohm would have said the same thing. He waited for the boss to proceed.

"We have a problem in Illinois," he said.

"Gartner?" Michael said.

Frohm nodded. Abel Gartner ran a large linen-supply company that serviced seventeen Sleep Tight Tonites in the greater Chicago area.

"He's still a hair in our soup," he said.

Abel Gartner had been trouble for a few months. He didn't want to adhere to Frohm's business practices anymore.

The uninitiated might have thought a company like Gartner's won a contract by offering an excellent service for a reasonable price that undercut competing bids. And while there was an element of that, Frohm tended to go into business with those who were willing to make large, ongoing under-the-table payments to get the job. Gartner was not only tired of doing that, he was talking to other firms that did work with Frohm International, urging them to band together against such corrupt practices.

"We've tried speaking to him several times, get him to see reason," Michael said. "That he could lose the contract altogether. And we tried . . . other ways."

Those had included trying to lure him into a compromising position at one of Chicago's finest hotels, the Drake, get some pics, threaten to show them to his wife. But the girl they hired to try to get him up to the room struck out. Gartner wouldn't take the bait.

"He's already talked to people in Cleveland and Charleston," Frohm said. "This has to stop."

Michael nodded. "I'll fly out tonight. Take one last shot at talking some sense into him."

Frohm slowly shook his head from side to side. "We're past that."

Time to use more persuasive methods, Michael thought. Break a finger. Dangle him from a window. Handcuff him in a locked garage with a car belching exhaust until he came to his senses.

"I can move things to the next level," Michael said.

"We're past that, too," Frohm said.

Michael didn't like the coldness he saw in Frohm's face. "Family?" he asked tentatively.

Meaning, of course, that Gartner be made to understand his obstinance might be putting his wife and children at risk. Subtle insinuations as opposed to direct threats. Let Gartner's imagination do the work. The strategy made Michael uncomfortable. He didn't like bringing family into things.

But Frohm was shaking his head. "This cocksucker Gartner doesn't scare as easy as others we've had trouble with. We need to solve our Illinois problem in a way that sends a message to Cleveland and Charleston."

Frohm leaned back in his chair and looked Michael in the eye, as if he were trying to communicate with him telepathically. Michael felt the room tilt a little. Frohm had never taken matters to this level before.

"Galen, are you—"

The boss shot him a look.

"Mr. Frohm," Michael continued, "I believe there are still other options on the table. Some kind of . . . carrot, instead of a stick." He paused. "Or a club."

"I've run out of patience, Michael. We let these issues drag on for far too long." He started shuffling some papers on his desk, as though looking for something. "Handle it," he said.

"You want *me* to do this. This *kind* of approach."

Frohm glanced up from the desk. "Who else would I ask? I'm sure you'd figure this out on your own, but don't fly to Chicago. There will be a record of your trip. It's too far to drive, but fly to Indianapolis. Rent a car from there."

"Mr. Frohm, there's nothing I wouldn't do for you, but—"

"I know. That's why I'm asking. Because there's nothing you wouldn't do for me. And please don't tell me you're not up to it, that you don't have it in you."

Michael said, "Sir?"

"I know more about the shit that went down in Southie than you think. What was his name? That kid you shot in the head when you were sixteen years old? Anthony, was it? When you were running with that group, engaged in your little turf wars?"

Michael didn't know how he knew, and didn't see the point in asking him how he'd found out. It was clearly an ace card Frohm had been holding for years.

"I'm not that person anymore," Michael said evenly.

Frohm smiled. "Of course you are. People don't change, Michael. We are what we are. Go on. Get it done."

Michael was dismissed.

TWENTY-EIGHT

Jack

I went back to work.

Sitting at my small kitchen table, the two laptops up and running, I scribbled some thoughts onto my notepad.

What had I learned in the short time I'd spent with Bill? He wasn't easy to typecast. He liked loud techno music, but could be charmed by a situation comedy about four retired women in Florida. I thought maybe that gave me some latitude to have some fun with his backstory, or as much fun as one can have when imagining a past for a man who feared he would one day end up dead with his severed member in his throat.

I made some notes about the things I knew he liked and/or was familiar with. He liked to gamble, bet on horses. Maybe I could give him an agricultural background. And a lot of gambling and betting involved sports, so I could pepper his background with all things athletic. Could he have worked behind the scenes in the NFL or NBA? Played baseball in the minor leagues? Maybe he was a high-school football coach. Oversaw a hockey team in one of the northern states. He might have lived and worked north of the border for a while, maybe he was Canadian. No, bad idea. To be convincing, Bill would have to perfect a very subtle accent, make his vowel sounds slightly different, and he'd need to know that Canadians called a restroom a washroom, that an electric bill was a hydro bill, and God help him if he bumped into a real Canadian and had no idea what a Timmies double-double was.

Thinking back to my brief time with Bill, it was hard to peg just where he might be from. It was easier to tell where he was *not* from. Certainly not the South. No hint of a Southern drawl. He didn't even have much of a Boston or New England accent. You wouldn't hear him say, "I just pahhked my cahh in the yahhd." His voice had an almost generic quality about it. What would that mean? Midwest? California? Northeast? It might make sense to have him tell people he hailed from New York. Any accent was possible if you came from the New York melting pot.

Bill claimed to be a whiz at television trivia. Did that interest in any way translate into an occupation? Had he spent time out in L.A. writing for television, but abandoned that when he couldn't make a go of it? Writers for television aren't well known the way actors are. I was betting Bill could bluff his way through something like that.

I scribbled some more notes.

And then I found myself staring off into space. I couldn't stop thinking about my discussion with Gwen about my father.

He wasn't one of those cold, distant paternal figures, although he almost never talked about his childhood or his teenage years. I had the sense he'd run with a bad crowd before Galen Frohm took him under his wing. Dad and I did things together. Red Sox games. Boston Bruins. Dad had connections, so sometimes we'd get into the locker room, kibitz with these athletes who were household names.

Didn't mean much to me. I was a bookish kid, not particularly athletic, but Dad never belittled my interests. If I wanted another Hardy Boys adventure, he'd pick one up at the Barnes & Noble on his way home, surprise me with it. When I showed an interest in writing stories when I was eight, he provided a basic typing lesson on the computer keyboard, showed me which fingers to use to hit which keys, so I wouldn't be a hunt-and-peck writer using my index fingers.

When I wrote a story—usually no more than three hundred words and almost always about space aliens—he would read it and say, "I like it. Write me another one."

We watched movies together, and he saw more of them with me than with my mother, who didn't share our taste for thrills and violence. He let me watch films no responsible parent should, given my young age, and I loved him for that. *Terminator* flicks, James Bond, the *Alien* franchise. One of his favorites was the crime thriller *The Untouchables*, directed by Brian De Palma. He watched it over and over for that shoot-out scene where the baby carriage is rolling down the train station stairs.

No wonder that was one of the places I went looking for him.

He was the reason I ran away so often as a kid. I'd get it into my head that Dad was hiding out in Chicago, or Providence, somewhere out on the Cape. I'd interpret something found around the house as a clue, a message he'd left for me. A picture of a family vacation on Cape Cod would make me think he was there. I'd watch, for the fiftieth time on a faded VHS cassette, that baby carriage scene and know, with absolute certainty, that Dad was in Chicago. I'd stuff some food and a change of underwear into a backpack and off I'd go.

Once, my vanishing coincided with one of those threatening phone calls. Mom was convinced I'd been abducted, and that I'd be killed if she didn't come up with some clue as to where my father was. Turned out I was enjoying the view from an Amtrak train.

And as much as I wanted to find my father, I hated him for abandoning us. I hated him for involving himself in things that he had to have known were going to bring him down someday.

He had to know that doing Galen Frohm's dirty work was never going to end well, that his luck would run out eventually.

Sure, my mother could have chosen for us to disappear with him, and I had come to understand, over time, her reasons for choosing not to. And while I had loved her very much, too, I deeply resented her, as well, for her decision. Maybe we all should have gone with Dad. If we had, I wouldn't have been drawn to themes of abandonment and emptiness in the stories I wrote. Although what do they say? A fucked-up childhood is a writer's best friend.

Hardly a day went by that I didn't wonder where they placed my father. Wisconsin or Wyoming? Arizona or Arkansas? New Jersey or New Mexico? What sort of work did they find for him? Was he stocking shelves in a Walgreens? Working on a road crew, flipping the sign from SLOW to STOP? A short-order cook at a truck stop, maybe? Bad as those jobs might be, they were better than prison, or worse, being buried in the woods after Galen Frohm found someone else to do his bidding.

Had he met someone new? Gotten married? If so, did his new wife know about his background, know that whatever past he alluded to when among friends was a total fiction?

Did they have kids?

Did my father have another son? Did I have stepbrothers or stepsisters I knew nothing about?

Had anyone done for him what I was now trying to do for Bill? Did anyone write Dad's backstory? If so, was there any mention of a son, someone he took to baseball games, someone he took to a pond to run a remote-control boat? Or had I ceased to exist in his fictional history?

Within a few months of my father's departure, he had ceased to be a subject of conversation between my mother and me. She didn't want to talk about him, so we didn't. My musings about where he might be and what he might be doing went unacknowledged. So we pretended to have moved on. (Except, of course, for my occasional, unannounced treks to find him.)

When I was eleven, Mom tried to persuade me that Dad was dead. One night, while eating dinner, there was a story on the evening news about some big-time CEO getting nailed for fraud, and that his conviction had been made possible by underlings testifying against him. I blurted out: "Just like Dad did to that piece of shit Frohm."

I was expecting Mom to reprimand me for foul language, send me to my room without dessert, but instead she said, casually, "He's dead." Then she picked up her wineglass and had a sip of merlot, as if she'd told me it was going to rain tomorrow and I'd better wear my boots.

"What?" I said. "What are you talking about?"

"He's dead," she said again.

"When? What happened? Did Mr. Frohm find him?"

She shook her head. "Mr. Frohm could hardly find anyone. He'll be in jail until his dying day."

"But his people?"

Another shake of the head. "No. Your father had a heart attack. It happened about five months ago."

That was when I knew she wasn't telling the truth. But I played along.

"Why didn't you say anything?"

"I didn't want to upset you. Like you are now."

"How do you know? It might not be true."

"They told me," she said. "The government. It hardly matters. He's been as good as dead to us since the night he walked out the door."

I had walked away from the table, gone to my room, and barely spoken to her for a week. Not because I was upset that my father might be dead, but because she would tell me such an outrageous lie.

I had seen my father within the last five months.

I'll get to that.

I wondered, later, whether my mother was practicing her lie with me so that she'd be able to say it with a straight face to a man she'd met and was starting to become serious about.

Earl Givins.

These thoughts, and the new backstory I was trying to write for Bill, were interrupted by a phone call, on my own cell. I was hoping it would be Lana. We hadn't talked in a day or two, and a text of mine to her, a simple question mark, had gone unanswered. I assumed—I *hoped*—that she was just busy.

But the call was not from her.

"Hello?"

"Mr. Givins?"

"Speaking."

"It's Elaine at Consolidated Insurance. It's about your car. I wanted to let you know the investigation is ongoing."

"Ongoing?"

"There's evidence of an accelerant."

"I'm sorry, a what?"

"An accelerant. Most likely gasoline. Traces were found throughout the vehicle. The vehicle was doused with a flammable liquid, inside and out, and then set ablaze. It was arson, not some manufacturer's electrical fault. We're awaiting a police report before we issue any check."

An accelerant.

Could Earl have been right? Was someone sending a message? But who? And why? And if that was the case, did it even have anything to do with what happened years ago?

"Have there been other incidents?" I asked. "Other cars set on fire like that?"

"Not that I'm aware of. Have a nice day, Mr. Givins."

I walked over to the window and looked out onto the street.

Something was not right.

I went back to the kitchen table and sat, intending to get back to work, but I had my doubts I'd be able to focus. My phone buzzed. It was a text.

Got a minute? It's Dad, and I'm outside.

TWENTY-NINE

June 1996

H e'd decided he wouldn't do it. Fuck Frohm.

There was no way, Michael Donohue told himself, that he was going to Chicago to kill Abel Gartner. Oh, sure, he'd go to Chicago, and he would take another run at persuading Gartner to see reason. But kill the man? No.

I am not that person anymore.

Over the years, Michael'd done many things for Galen Frohm that crossed the line. Immoral and unethical at best, illegal at worst, but they were what Michael had come to see as crimes of little significance. They fell into the category of "doing business" or "process crimes."

The ugly truth was that, in America, if you wanted to get things done, you had to bend the rules, or fucking ignore them altogether. So you cut corners, you had a second set of books, you overpromised and underdelivered, you made secret deals where you had to, you hired the best accountant money could buy so that you paid no taxes even though you were making a fortune.

Sure, occasionally you had to threaten someone to make them fall in line. Which was what Michael had tried with Abel Gartner. He was just going to have to try a little harder.

Michael knew Frohm wouldn't he happy. Certainly not at first, when he returned to Boston without Gartner's head. (A little artistic license here, Michael thought. The man's metaphorical head, of course.) But he was confident he could persuade the boss that this time, Gartner would come around, cease to be an issue. And they wouldn't have to worry about the authorities sniffing around a homicide.

Still, some precautions were worth following.

Michael did take Frohm's suggestion and fly into Indianapolis instead of Chicago. He then rented a car and drove the rest of the way, conducting transactions with bogus identification. Why take such precautions if he did not intend to carry out Frohm's orders? Michael told himself it paid to be careful. He did not want it known by anyone—not by the airlines, not by the police, not by anyone—that he was making this trip.

It was a three-hour drive from Indianapolis to Chicago, which gave Michael plenty of time to think about his approach. He'd done some further research on Gartner, looking for avenues of leverage. What was precious to him? What did he love, outside of his own family?

Gartner collected so-called Detroit muscle cars from the late sixties and early seventies. A 1979 Chevrolet Chevelle SS 454, a 1969 Dodge Charger SE, a 1970 Ford Mustang Boss 302. Michael didn't care all that much about cars, but he knew these were classics for their time and highly desirable automobiles. Once Michael learned where these vehicles were stored, he could arrange to have one or all of them stolen or set ablaze.

Too bad Gartner didn't have a prizewinning racehorse whose head could be chopped off and slipped into his bed, Michael mused. Perhaps a totaled muscle car would do just as well.

But he had something else in mind. Something that was, at least for the Frohm organization, a departure. Not a threat, but an inducement. Something money couldn't buy.

The man had a couple of kids, a boy and a girl, both in their late teens. And from what Michael knew, they'd soon be applying to various Ivy League colleges. There was no guarantee that they would get in. Their grades were good, but were they good enough? All Michael would have to do was pick up the phone, and those kids would be able to get into the school of their father's choice.

Don't threaten. Entice. What father wouldn't want his children to have the best opportunities possible?

Gartner Linens was housed in an aging two-story brick building on Chicago's South Side. Built, Michael estimated, in the early twentieth century, 1920 or so. Thinking back to a previous meeting with Abel Gartner, Michael recalled the man telling him that the building had housed, over the years, a dog biscuit factory and a toy company before he converted it in the 1990s to a linen-supply business.

Michael was waiting in the parking lot when Gartner walked out of the building at four in the afternoon. The man wasn't more than five-six, but packed a good two hundred pounds on that short frame, giving him the look of a fire hydrant. His daily drive was a bland, brown, twenty-year-old Ford LTD, and Michael was leaning against the front fender, having a smoke, when Gartner spotted him.

"God, no," Gartner said. "Not you. Get out of here or I'll call the police."

Michael tossed the cigarette, took his weight off the car, smiled warmly, and extended a hand. "Mr. Gartner, I come in peace." Gartner looked at the hand but did not take it.

"Say what?"

"Mr. Frohm has sent me to patch things up, and that's what I intend to do."

"I've got nothing to say to you. Who are you again?"

"Michael. Michael Donohue." Even though there wasn't so much as a library card on him that carried that name.

"Frohm's errand boy," Gartner said.

Michael maintained the smile. "That's not an unfair characterization, Mr. Gartner, but I do more than run errands. I deliver opportunities. All I am asking from you today is to let me make my pitch, and if you don't like what I'm selling, then I'll be on my way back to Boston. But I think you'll like what I have to say."

"Come to threaten me?"

Michael shook his head. "No, sir. I have not."

Gartner eyed him suspiciously. "I have things to do."

"Wherever you're going, I could ride with you and make my case."

"I'm going to my stable."

Stable? *Did* the man have racehorses after all?

"I didn't know you kept horses."

"Not horses, but plenty of horsepower," he said. "I have some cars."

"I've heard. Some American classics."

"You a gearhead?" Gartner asked.

"Indeed," he lied. "And one of Detroit's grandest periods was the late sixties and early seventies."

Gartner appeared to be considering. "Okay," he said. "Get in."

Michael accepted the invitation, walked around to the passenger side, and got in. Soon they were heading through a different industrial area of low-rise buildings.

"I rent a garage where I keep them," he said. "Just had my guy tune up the Charger, and I want to see how it's running. It was stalling on me. You tromp on it and there was a hesitation. About a second, which, when you're taking off from a standing start, is an eternity."

"Of course."

"Think it was a carburetor issue. Thing is, while I love these cars, I'm no genius at fixing them myself."

"Best to call in an expert when it's something you treasure," Michael said.

The trip didn't take more than five minutes, and Michael decided the business he had come to discuss could wait. Ease into things.

Gartner turned into an alley and came around the back of a nondescript brick building. He parked in front of a set of double garage doors, killed the engine, and said, "We go in around the side."

Gartner flipped up a bank of light switches that turned on several rows of overhead fluorescents.

"Wow," Michael said, and he wasn't faking it.

The three cars sparkled under the lights. The Chevelle was a deep bloodred with two broad black stripes down the hood, over the roof and down the trunk. The Mustang was an electric blue, also boldly striped. And the Charger was jet black with a red stripe that wrapped around the ass end of the car, up the fender, across the trunk, and down the other side. What they called, Michael remembered, a bumblebee stripe. The Chevelle and Mustang were parked nose to tail in front of one garage door, the Charger on its own in front of the other.

Gartner unlocked the passenger door of the Charger for Michael and, before he got behind the wheel, hit a button to open the garage. Then he slipped into the driver's seat and keyed the ignition. The engine roared to life, then rumbled aggressively even before Gartner put it into reverse.

"Sounds impressive," Michael said.

"So far," he said, then looked over his shoulder and backed the car out. Once clear of the door, he hit a remote clipped to the visor and watched to make sure the door went down all the way.

"It'll need to warm up before I can really know," he said, getting the car to the street, putting it in drive, and easing his foot down on the gas.

"Let me make my case," Michael said, raising his voice to be heard above the rumble of the engine and the wind. Gartner had powered down all the windows.

Gartner nodded. "I know Frohm's pissed. But he needs to understand that we're pissed, too. Me and the others. We don't like the arrangement. We want to run our businesses without all the bullshit. We don't like being pushed around. Unless you can tell me that's over, we've got nothing to talk about."

"I didn't come here to threaten you," Michael said. "I came to see whether I could help you with something."

"Yeah?" he said, casting Michael a wary glance. "Another hooker at the Drake? That bullshit doesn't work with me."

"I wanted to talk to you about your children's education."

"You want to what?"

"They're finishing high school, am I right? Your daughter, Valerie? She's seventeen now?"

"Jesus, don't you start bringing my kids into—"

"It's not like that. Let me explain. And your son, Kyle? Am I right that he's the same age? That they're twins?"

"Yeah."

"Not that common, is it? Twins, where one is a boy and the other a girl?"

"It happens," Gartner said.

"Even for a man with your resources, it might be something of a challenge, both of them heading off to institutions of higher learning at the same time."

"We'll manage," he said. "I don't need any help from you."

"Perhaps not financial," Michael conceded, "but how high are you setting your sights?"

Gartner ignored the question and gave the car a shot of gas.

The engine roared and the car moved forward like it was being launched from a slingshot.

"No hesitation there," he said, nodding with satisfaction.

"Have your children chosen what schools they want to go to?"

"We're looking at a few."

"Yale, perhaps? Harvard?"

"You got a point you want to make?"

"Pick a school," Michael said. "Make your choice, and we can make it happen."

"How the hell can you do that?" Gartner asked.

Michael smiled. "All we would ask in return is that you end this organized effort with your friends in other jurisdictions."

"Stop making waves," Gartner said.

Michael smiled again. "Yes. Mr. Gartner, we currently have a mutually beneficial relationship. You supply linens to all our businesses in this area. It is a lucrative contract and, knowing what you pay your employees, which is not all that much, we know that you're making a substantial profit."

"You're not counting the money I slide under the table to your boss."

"That's a fee that is in no way unusual in the business world, and for a man of your experience it's naïve to think otherwise. But that's all immaterial. What I came here to discuss with you today is your children's future."

"You're *bribing* me with my children's future," Gartner said, raising his chin, tilting his head, as though listening to something Michael could not hear.

"If you like," Michael said.

"You hear that?"

"Hear what?"

"Some kind of rattle. I hate rattles. Anyway, okay, listen." Gartner took a long, surrendering breath. "You can really make it happen? These college admissions people, you have some sway with them?"

"We do," Michael said. "Mr. Frohm has more people in his debt, in a wide variety of fields, than you could imagine."

Gartner was nodding slowly. Michael was afraid to feel hopeful, but things appeared to be turning his way.

"Are you sure you don't hear that?" Gartner asked.

Michael tried to pick up what Gartner was hearing. "I don't think so, but it's your car and you're more attuned to it than I am."

"It might not even be the car," he said. "Maybe my guy left something loose in the trunk. Gonna pull over for a second."

At that moment, they were driving through a desolate area, what was probably once a thriving industrial district but was now home to abandoned buildings and debris-strewn sidewalks, with not a soul in sight.

Gartner brought the car to a stop, killed the engine, and took out the key. He needed the other key on the ring to open the trunk. No remote releases on a car this old. Michael sat in the passenger seat while Gartner got out and went around to the back of the Charger.

"Oh, shit," Gartner said, looking down into the trunk, now open.

His curiosity piqued, Michael got out of the car, leaving the door open, and was walking toward the back of the car when Gartner appeared from behind the trunk lid, tire iron in hand.

He took a wild swing at Michael. Caught by surprise, he did not have time to deflect the first blow, which hit him on the left forearm, striking bone.

"Fuck!" Michael shouted, staggering back several steps, clamping a hand over where he'd been hit.

Gartner advanced, wild-eyed. "Tell your fucking boss I don't care if he offers to send my kids to the fucking moon, I'm not backing down. I'm talking to my associates tomorrow. We're going to the FBI or the anti-rackets squad or whoever the hell it is who'll take that son of a bitch down."

"Abel, listen to me, you can't—"

Gartner closed the distance and swung again, but this time Michael ducked and lunged forward, tackling the man around the waist and throwing him down to the cracked pavement. As Gartner's hand hit the asphalt, the tire iron slipped from his grasp. Michael, crablike, scrambled for it, Gartner clutching at his legs, trying to stop him.

But Michael got his hand on the angled metal rod and rolled onto his back, readying himself to get onto his feet, but now Gartner was over him, getting ready to pounce.

Michael swung.

The tire iron caught Gartner across his right temple, and he went down, falling off to the right. He landed on his back, moaned, put a hand to the wound, blood already matting his hair and trickling through his fingers.

Michael got to his knees.

"You motherfucker," Gartner said. "I'm going to ruin you and—"

Michael swung the tire iron across Gartner's face, pulled back, swung again, and again, and again, denting the man's skull, breaking all his teeth, crushing his nose. His face couldn't have looked worse if the Charger had backed over it.

Slowly, Michael got to his feet and struggled to catch his breath. He was shaking. His clothes, his hands, his face were all splattered with Gartner's blood.

Michael nudged the man with his foot, got no response. He walked back to the car, looked in the open trunk, spotted a rag. He used it to wipe down the tire iron, then threw it as hard as he could into a nearby vacant lot.

With the same rag, he wiped the handles of the passenger door and slammed it shut, then closed the trunk and took the set of keys that were dangling from the trunk lock.

He got behind the wheel, brought the engine to a rumble, and drove off.

Maybe Frohm was right. People don't change.

THIRTY

Jack

I did a double-take when I saw the text.

Got a minute? It's Dad, and I'm outside.

Maybe, if I hadn't been thinking of my missing father at that moment, I wouldn't have been so taken aback by the words on the screen. I would have noticed, before I read the message, who it was from.

Earl.

He usually signed his emails or texts with his name—even though, with a text, you really didn't have to identify yourself—but when he was feeling his neck, when he was trying to ingratiate himself with me, he used "Dad." And there was a time, during my teens, when that was what I called him, often grudgingly and mostly at my mother's insistence, so that he would feel accepted, really believe he was the new father figure in my life, that he had effectively displaced the man who had gone out of our lives that rainy night when I was nine.

Rather than reply, I left the apartment, descended the stairs, and went outside. There was Earl, leaning up against some shitbox foreign economy car that was probably worth even less than my torched Nissan. So he'd had to give up the Porsche. Whether he'd sold it or had it repossessed, I didn't know.

"Hey," he said. "Catch you at a bad time?"

"What's up?" I said.

Seeing Earl again, this soon, was setting off alarms.

Looking sheepish, he said, "Can I . . . can I come up?"

I had to give that a moment's thought. After a few seconds, I nodded and turned away, a wordless invitation to follow me.

Once upstairs, I said, "You want a coffee or anything?"

"Maybe something cooler?" he asked. "And stronger?"

I went to the fridge, found a can of beer, and tossed it to him. He almost fumbled the catch.

"Thanks," he said.

He was looking at the two open laptops and my notepad. I'd filled about half the page with scribbles.

"What's all this?" he asked.

I walked over, closed both laptops, and flipped the notepad over.

"I get it," he said. "The great author doesn't want anyone looking at his novel until it's ready."

"It's not a novel," I said, immediately regretting it. I was only inviting more questions.

"Not a novel? So what, then?"

"Why are you here, Earl?"

"I wanted to . . . the other day, I'm not proud of myself, how I handled that. Leaning on you for a loan. That's what I wanted to say."

"You mean, like, you're sorry?"

"Yeah, I guess so. I'm sorry."

I was still standing and had not invited him to take a seat. As if he'd noticed, he said, "Mind if I take a seat?"

I supposed it was only fair to let him sit down while he had his beer. I pointed to my cheap couch, and he dropped onto it, but I stayed on my feet, looking down at him.

"I got rid of the Porsche," he said.

"I noticed."

"That's a rental. One of those rent-a-wreck places."

Did he want me to express some sympathy? At least no one had set fire to it.

"As I kind of mentioned, I've got a negative cash flow situation at the moment and I've had to make some adjustments."

"Like I already told you, I don't have any money, Earl."

Which wasn't, strictly speaking, as true as it had been at our last encounter. Gwen had paid me for eight days' work, which meant a cool eight grand in my account. But even if I gave it all to Earl, it wouldn't be enough to solve his financial difficulties.

"That's not why I'm here," he said. "I've been doing a lot of thinking lately. About you, and your mom, and the situation I came into when we got married."

I didn't know why he would be focused on this now, after all these years, but I supposed he would tell me.

"The time I had with your mother was special, you know, and yeah, it had its ups and downs."

"She wanted stability when she married you," I said. "She didn't get it."

"I was always true to your mother. I never strayed."

"I'm not talking about that. I'm talking about all your get-rich-quick schemes. Every day she wondered what crazy thing you were going to do next."

Earl sighed. "Yeah, but at least I never killed anybody."

Mom had decided not to hide her past from Earl. She'd figured that if she didn't tell him, one day I'd blurt it out. Which I would have.

"That's not setting the bar very high," I said.

He nodded, acknowledging my point. "The thing is, it always felt like your father was there, with us, in that marriage. I always felt this presence. It was hard for me at times. Because I got this sense that there was part of her that still loved him. She believed that in his heart, he was a good man, despite the bad things he'd done."

I had no idea why he was telling me this but figured maybe it was going to take a while, so I took a seat.

"I always expected he was going to come walking through the door. One day, he'd return, figuring, what the hell, I'll take my chances, I'm leaving the relocation program. And then what would Rose do? Would she dump me and take up with him again? Or would that be too risky? Or would his reappearance put us all at risk? I asked myself those questions every day."

He took a sip from the can. "I think sometimes she regretted her decision. She'd get very . . . melancholy. I really believe there were times when she wished the two of you had gone with him. Was he a good father to you?"

Without hesitation, I said, "Yes."

Earl's face fell. "I knew I could never replace him. But I gave it my best shot."

I forced the words out. "I know."

"A real father . . . would have been better at staying in touch after your mom passed. I wonder where he ended up."

"I don't know."

"It's kind of hard for me to believe he wouldn't have contacted you over the years, directly or indirectly," Earl said. "I mean, you say he was a good father. You'd think it would have just killed him to have to give up his son, to never see him again. I don't get how anyone could do that. If it was the other way around, and you knew where he was, and he didn't know where you were, wouldn't you have gotten in touch? Arranged some kind of secret meeting? Something like that?"

"Hard to say."

"But seriously, he's never been in touch? One way or another? Didn't he send messages through the witness protection program? Couldn't they act as an intermediary?"

"Never heard a word," I said, keeping a straight face.

He reached into his pocket and brought out a pack of cigarettes and a cheap lighter. I thought he'd given up smoking years ago.

"You mind?" Earl asked.

"Go ahead," I said, and as he lit up, I thought back to the other night, and the glow of a cigarette I'd seen in the window of a low-slung car across the street. Before, I was guessing, Earl had unloaded his Porsche.

"Were you thinking of dropping by the other night? Parked out front, maybe?"

Earl looked puzzled. "Huh? No. Why would I do a thing like that?"

THIRTY-ONE

It had taken Lana two days to track down Florence Knight, a Boston PD homicide detective who, Lana had been told, investigated the drowning deaths of Dr. Marie Sloan and retired judge Willard Bentley.

Detective Knight was something of a legend in the department, not so much for her investigative skills, although no one was in any way discounting those, but because of her name. She was Florence Straight before she got married to Ronald Knight, and given that this was back in the late 1970s, when not all women were hanging on to their own names, she became Florence Knight.

She wasn't even out of the academy before she was given the nickname "Nightingale."

And it had stuck for her entire career. Years ago, she'd debated whether to go back to the name Straight to avoid the nickname, but instead decided to embrace it. Now, two years away from retirement, she was known simply as Nightingale, most people not even aware that wasn't her actual name.

Lana caught up with her coming out of a chowder place on Atlantic Avenue, a takeout container in her hand, about to get back behind the wheel of her unmarked car. Lana, across the street, called out, catching the woman's attention before she settled in behind the wheel.

Knight sighed as Lana ran across the street, but the truth was, Knight saw a lot of herself in Lana. When she was Lana's age—and oh, it was a long time ago, she thought—she was hustling to prove herself each and every day in a profession dominated by men. One might have thought things had progressed since then, but not nearly as much as they should. Newer, male detectives who did not know her well assumed she would be the one to get the coffees, or grab some notepads and pens if they were having a meeting, like she was some fucking secretary. The older detectives would smile and wait for the newbies to learn their lesson, which came in the form of something that had come to be known as the "Nightinglare," a look Knight had perfected that, without a single word, said, "Who the fuck do you think you're talking to?"

In their off-duty hours, usually over cosmos, Knight and Lana had shared a few war stories, and Knight had passed on whatever wisdom she could. It usually amounted to "Don't take shit from nobody."

Also, be prepared.

Two years earlier, while Lana was covering an angry demonstration at the Massachusetts State House, a burly man waving a crudely painted sign proclaiming LIES! had gone after her when he realized she was with the newspaper. It had started with the screaming of obscenities, including multiple uses of the C-word, and then the man had thrown down his sign and appeared ready to punch Lana in the face.

Knight, who happened to be heading into the building at the time, spotted what was happening and intervened. She flashed her badge, pulled back her jacket far enough for the man to see the gun strapped to her hip, and shouted at him to back the fuck off.

To Lana's relief, he did, running off to join his fellow protesters, no doubt bragging about how he'd put that bitch from the *Star* in her place.

Lana was shaken, and Knight took her for a drink the following afternoon. Said she needed to give some serious thought to better protecting herself. Take up karate. Carry a few surprises in her purse.

"If you're going to suggest I carry a gun, that's not happening," Lana said. "And I think brass knuckles would kind of weigh down my handbag."

"I'm not talking about anything like that." She produced a couple of gifts: a pepper spray about the size of a lighter, and a small knife disguised as a lipstick.

"Are these even legal?" Lana had asked, unsure about whether to accept them.

"When you're in a tight spot, you won't give a shit," Knight replied.

"I don't know," she said. "I'll think about it."

So, today, while Knight would have preferred to have gotten into her car and had some chowder on the run before she went to her next stop, she was willing to make time for Lana.

"Hey," she said.

"Got a sec?"

"Get in. I want to eat this while it's hot."

Lana circled to the passenger side as Knight got behind the wheel, resting the chowder atop the dash while she took a plastic spoon, some napkins, and a small packet of oyster crackers from a paper bag. She pried the lid off the chowder, poured the crackers in, stirred them around with the spoon. Lana didn't say a word during the process. Knight appeared to be involved in a kind of sacred ritual.

Once she had put the first spoonful into her mouth, she looked at Lana and said, "Shoot."

"You got called in on both of those drownings, right?" Lana asked. "The judge and the doctor."

Knight had another bite of chowder. "Mm."

"Your media people are giving the impression that those cases are officially closed. Suicide or misadventure in both cases. Am I right about that?"

Knight didn't say anything for a moment, then gave a noncommittal shrug. "More or less."

"More or less?"

"Yeah, more or less."

"You don't think it's a coincidence? Two prominent people like that, both going into the harbor within a few days?"

"Happens." Knight paused.

Suddenly, Lana sneezed.

"Shit, you nearly napalmed my chowder," Knight said.

"Sorry, allergies. Anything about those two deaths seem strange to you? With Bentley, he had to stray a long way from his neighborhood to end up in the water. And if that doctor wanted to kill herself, there were plenty of ways for her to do it that would have been a lot less painful."

"I should have got more crackers. They never give you enough crackers."

"I admit, it's not much," Lana said. "I hate coincidences, that's all."

"They happen all the time."

"If there's anyone I know who hates coincidences, it's you."

Knight shrugged.

"So you'd go on the record as saying there's nothing in common about those two incidents."

Knight shot her a look. "Is this an actual interview?"

"It is, starting now. You're saying there's nothing that links these two deaths?"

"No comment."

Lana's eyebrows popped up. "That sounds like a yes."

"No, that sounds like a no comment."

"So if I write a story, when I get to the part where I ask the police if they're looking into this, the answer is no comment, which sounds like the police *are* looking into this."

"Look, investigations take time to wrap up, that's all."

"Okay, well, if that's that, have a great day," Lana said, reaching for the door handle.

"Wait."

Lana took her hand off the door.

"Don't do a story," Knight said.

"Why not?"

"We've known each other awhile, and I'm asking you, as a favor, not to run any story at this time."

Lana smiled. "Yeah, we've known each other for a while, so you know that when you make a request like that, alarm bells start going off in my head. Something's going on that you don't want me to know. At least not yet."

Knight looked down into her paper bowl, spooned out the last few drops of her chowder.

"Okay, we've always played fair with each other. If you hold off writing anything now, I'll tell you why I want you to sit on this."

"And?"

"And when I have it nailed down, you're my first call."

Lana thought about that. Slowly, she said, "Okay."

Knight balled up her napkin and the cracker wrapper, tucked them into the empty bowl, put the lid back on, and slipped it, and the plastic spoon, back into the paper bag.

"There might be a connection," she said.

"Are you saying they might not have drowned?"

"Oh, they drowned," she said. "The question is *how* they drowned. Whether they had help. Drownings are tricky. A lot of possible evidence is washed away. There's no real crime scene to search because they're out in the middle of the fucking water."

"So what makes you think they might have had some help?"

Knight went quiet, clearly debating how much to reveal. After a few seconds, she said, "We didn't notice this at first, but there was something in common between the two incidents."

Now it was Lana who was quiet. Waiting.

"Both of them had some minor bruising on their wrists."

"What, like they'd been tied?" Lana asked. "Wouldn't that be pretty obvious?"

"Yeah, it would be, if they'd been tied. But like I said, this was more subtle. More like someone was *gripping* their wrists."

Lana tried to picture what the detective was describing.

"The bruising was consistent on both wrists, on both people. As if someone was maybe straddled over them, holding on to their wrists to keep them down."

"Down? Down where?"

"Under the water," Knight said.

THIRTY-TWO

Jack

The next day I printed out a new backstory for Bill. Five thousand words of an imagined life for the guy that I thought would be easy enough for him to get into. Nothing so technical that he couldn't bluff his way through it. I called Gwen on the hotline and she said she would send her guy around to pick it up.

"How's an hour from now?" she said.

"Fine," I said, and then decided I had given her enough time to bring up our subject from the other day. "Another thing."

"Yes, Jack," Gwen said.

"You given any more thought to my request?"

"Your request?"

Like she'd forgotten. What did she think I'd asked her for? More pens? New printer cartridges? A package of Post-it notes?

"About my father," I said. "About setting up a meeting with him."

"I need more time."

"Why?"

"There's a lot of red tape to cut through to get the information you want. Let me read what you've done, and when we meet to discuss it I'll bring you up to speed on your father."

Not long after our chat, her driver came and picked up my latest attempt at Bill's backstory. This time, we actually had a conversation when he got out of the van.

"How's it going?" Scorsese asked as I handed him the envelope.

"Same old, same old," I said.

"Hope there aren't too many typos. She loses her shit over those."

She'd already marked those up the last time. "A lot of things seem to irritate her."

He grinned as he took a package of cigarettes from his pocket, tapped one out, and lit it. "She's like the princess and the pea. You know that one?" I nodded. "But typos and me fiddling with the radio dial are nothing compared to how pissed she was about you."

"Pissed about me?"

"Sorry, not *with* you. But pissed that she didn't know your background, about your dad. She carved out new assholes on the people who were supposed to have done a thorough check on you. She can't believe something like that fell through the cracks. I'm just glad that wasn't my job. I'd be on the street."

"What is your job?" I asked. As soon as I'd said it I was worried it might have sounded insulting. "Like, are you involved in relocating witnesses? Protection?"

"General dogsbody," he said. "I do whatever needs doing. Often, that's the shit no one else wants to do. Drive, deliver, sometimes protect. Was a cop. Took a bullet in the leg, gave it up. Fully recovered, but didn't need that kind of shit anymore."

"I get it."

He leaned up against the van and drew on his cigarette. "She would never say it out loud, but she's very impressed."

"Oh?"

"First of all, she thinks your work is good. But also that you came forward with that information. If she'd found that

170

out before you told her, she'd have cut you loose, no question. You wouldn't be doing this. And not that it's any of my business, but it must have been tough. Your dad not taking you with him."

I nodded. "Yeah."

He grinned. "My dad left us, too, but he didn't go into witness protection. He fucked off with a bartender he met in Jersey."

That made me laugh. "Everybody's got a story, right?"

"You got that right." He gave me another two-finger salute. "Later."

He tucked the cigarette between his lips, got back in the van, and took off.

At least until Gwen passed judgment on my latest effort, I was idle. That was fine, because I had shit to do. I changed the sheets, did a load of laundry. There were emails to deal with that I'd ignored, bills I hadn't gotten around to paying. I had an email from a friend in Montana who was always telling me what he'd binge-watched lately. I didn't usually have much to tell him in return, given that I didn't watch much other than repeats of legal dramas. It was Lana who liked to dive into some new series that everyone was talking about, watch several episodes in a row about the royal family or some guy who'd gone down to the Ozarks to launder money.

Speaking of Lana.

I hadn't heard from her in a while and was starting to wonder whether something was wrong. I put in a call, got her voice mail, and left a message.

"It's me. Seems like ages. Give me a call."

I went back to clearing out emails and saw that one had just landed from Ann Finley, the editor on my two published novels, who had taken a pass on my third.

It read:

Dear Jack:

Hope this finds you well. I miss our lunches at the Beekman! Just wanted to let you know, in case you want to spread the word on your socials, that both books are going to be daily deals on Amazon next week. Randy will send you the links, if interested.

Sorry we couldn't work a deal on your new one, which I very much enjoyed. I don't know where you ended up placing it—I wish we'd been given a chance to beat whoever made the winning offer—but I wish you every success with it. Who knows, this might be the one.

Best
Ann

I read the email a second time, and then a third. Ann had *liked* my third book? Ann had made an *offer* on my third book? Ann was under the impression another publishing house had *bought* the book?

I picked up my phone, brought up Harry Breedlove's number, tapped it, and put the phone to my ear. My former agent's phone rang five times before sending me to voice mail.

"You've reached Harry Breedlove. I'm sorry I can't take your call right now. Please leave a message."

And then the beep.

"Harry, Jack here. Just got an interesting email from Ann Finley I'd like to discuss with you. When you get a moment, maybe you could get back to me and tell me what the fuck is going on?"

If Harry couldn't be reached by phone, I'd try an email. I banged one off on the laptop and sent it.

The son of a bitch.

Why would Harry say Ann had turned the book down? Was it because he thought the other opportunity—the one that came by way of that phone he handed me—was better? Even if that were true, wasn't it my choice to make?

And then it hit me.

I picked up the hotline to Gwen.

"Give me time," she said without saying hello. "I only just started reading it."

"Was it you?" I asked.

"Was what me?"

"Did you pressure Harry to tell me he couldn't sell my book so I'd have no choice but to accept your offer?"

Silence on the other end for a couple of seconds, and then, "What?"

"You heard me. I know you talked to Harry. You, or one of your people. You gave him this fucking phone. Is that when you leaned on him to sabotage my book?"

"Jack, listen to me, and listen very carefully. I don't know what you're talking about. I told you, I had plenty of other authors I was considering for this job, plenty who are already doing it. If you'd said no, I had plenty of other talent to turn to. You're not as special as you think you are."

I went quiet for a moment, then said, "Something doesn't add up."

"What did Harry say?"

"I left a message. I'll go to New York and hunt him down if I have to."

"Fine, but if you do, not a word about the work you're doing for us. Is that clear? We gave Harry the phone to give to you, but we didn't go into detail about what we had in mind for you."

"Fine."

"And don't go hunting him down tonight. I'm coming by your place at seven." A pause. "I have some news about your father."

For a second there, the room seemed to spin.

"I'll see you then," I said.

She showed up fifteen minutes early. She had the envelope in her hand and dropped it on the kitchen table.

"It's good. I have a couple notes in there, but it's something we can work with."

I didn't really care what she thought about what I'd done.

"Did you hear from your agent?"

"No," I said. "I think he's avoiding me."

Gwen said, "I looked into why your history escaped our attention. When we did a search on your name, we were looking for 'Givins,' not 'Donohue.' 'Jack Donohue' is in our files. We were sloppy. It shouldn't have happened. Someone's going to get fired."

"Not you, I hope."

She shrugged. "Time will tell."

"What did you find out about my father?"

"Can I sit?"

I nodded and she took a kitchen chair. I sat opposite her. "I made some calls," she said. "A lot of the people who worked for the program back when your father was relocated are no longer with us."

"But you keep files."

"Of course," she said. "I'm just saying, that's why it took a little longer for me to track down who might have handled his case."

"It was a woman who came that night," I said. "The one who took my dad away."

Gwen nodded. "Yes, right. She retired a few years ago, moved to Scottsdale. And within a month of her retirement, she died. Cancer."

"Shit."

"Your father's file was passed on to someone else, and he was attached to that person for another few years, and then that guy retired, and then there was one more person who became your father's liaison with the witsec program."

"And you were able to talk to that person?"

"I was."

"And?"

She sighed, looked at the table before meeting my eyes. "Jack, there's still a lot I can't tell you. I can't tell you where they placed your father. I can't tell you what kind of job they got him, or whether he found someone else, whether he was living with someone. I mean, it's all in the file, but I can't reveal it."

"I don't have to know all that. I just want to be able to talk to him."

"I know, I know. And if it were in my power to arrange that, I would. I feel like I owe you that."

"But?"

"But the bottom line is, I can't do it."

I reared back in my chair. "For fuck's sake, why not?"

"They don't know where he is," she said plainly.

"What?"

"They've lost him. Whatever life they built for him, he's walked away from it. He's out there somewhere, doing God knows what, and we have no idea where he is."

THIRTY-THREE

Things were starting to come together. Kyle Gartner had almost everything in place.

The fake passport. The phone. The money. A significant sum had been transferred to a new account. So many precautions had to be taken. One small slip and it would all come crashing down around him.

He knew he had to act as though nothing was out of the ordinary. He didn't want his wife or daughter to suspect anything. It was important to maintain his usual routine. Off to work in the morning, back home in time for dinner.

He knew that Cecilia had noticed he'd been especially on edge the last few months. She'd been willing to make allowances. She knew how troubled he was about his sister's death, how his anger over an injustice from years past had not faded. She tried to be understanding when he lost his temper. Rather than engage, she would walk away, let him cool off.

She didn't know the half of it. The things he had planned.

It was critical that over the next couple of days he hold it together. Dial back the anger. He needed to be agreeable, he needed to be . . . nice. That was perhaps the biggest challenge. Acting as though he was interested in the lives of his wife and daughter when his mind was actually on something else, something much bigger than they could ever have imagined. The seeds had already been planted. The upcoming business trip. How he would be away for a few days.

"You seem . . . better," his teenage daughter, Cherie, had said tentatively just that morning.

"Oh," he'd said casually, like he hadn't even been aware of it.

"I'm glad," she said. "It's good."

Cecilia, who had been hounding him ever since Valerie's death that maybe he should *talk* to somebody, a therapist or a grief counselor or even their family doctor—*anybody*—had abandoned that line of badgering.

Kyle thought he'd been careful, but evidently not quite careful enough.

He was back in his home office and had carelessly left the door open an inch. He was on the phone, talking in hushed tones.

Cecilia had been passing by when she heard his whispers. She stopped, turned her ear to the gap in the door, and held her breath.

"Yes, yes," her husband said. "I'll be coming out there."

This business trip he'd been talking about, she assumed.

"You're being careful?" he asked. A pause, and then, "Yes, we have to be careful. Don't want anyone getting wind of this. It's going to happen. I've waited this long. I can wait a little longer."

Cecilia wondered whether she should go to another phone in the house, pick up the extension, and listen in. But Kyle might not be on the home's landline. He could be on his cell.

At one point, she heard: "We're going to find . . ."

And a moment later, ". . . get this done."

Find what? Or who? Get what done?

"Okay, okay, I'll be in touch," Kyle Gartner said. "It's really going to happen."

He ended the call.

She wondered whether she should enter the room now, pretend to have heard nothing. Or maybe she should face this head on.

Go in and ask what that was about. Because whatever it was, it was clearly something he didn't want her to know—

The door suddenly opened. Kyle was as startled to find his wife there as she was to have been discovered.

"What are you doing?" he asked.

"Nothing. I was just coming in to see you."

"What do you want?" There was an edge to his voice, and he struggled to rein it in.

She hesitated. "I wondered if you wanted a cup of coffee."

He thought about that for a moment. "That would be lovely," he said, leaning in to give her a light kiss on the forehead. "What would I do without you?"

As she headed for the kitchen, he wondered how much she had heard.

THIRTY-FOUR

May 1997

Michael thought it would take him a long time to get over what he'd done. He didn't know whether to be pleased, or distressed, that it didn't.

Sure, he was on edge on the way back from Chicago. If he'd planned, from the outset, to kill Gartner, and hadn't floated that idea of helping him get his twins into an Ivy League college, he would have had everything worked out, been far more methodical. It wouldn't have gone down the way it had, in a mad panic trying to save his own life when that dumb bastard came at him with the tire iron.

When things happened spur of the moment, there were too many ways for it to go south. Too many variables. Too many things you couldn't control.

At least Gartner had stopped his treasured Charger in an area of disused buildings. While it was possible there'd been someone lurking somewhere who'd seen what happened, Michael did not think so. He put up all the windows in the Charger because they were tinted, reducing the likelihood that an individual or a surveillance camera might see him behind the wheel. He wiped down the car and abandoned it in an alley a few blocks away from where he had left his rental. Drove back to Indianapolis, flew home.

He got lucky.

And not for the first time.

On the flight home he thought back to when he was sixteen, the guys he used to run with, the shit they got into. Petty thefts, small-time drug dealing, turf wars, always trying to prove you were tougher than the other guy. Fights over nothing that spiraled out of control.

A kid could get killed. And Michael was the one who'd killed him. He and his buddies had slipped into the back of a liquor store, hauled out into the alley half a dozen cases of hooch. Too much to carry by hand. In the time it took to bring the car around, some other guys, part of a gang from a few blocks over, were running off with their haul.

Had to teach them a lesson.

Within a week, Michael and his friends met up with them one dark night out back of a Wendy's. Someone handed Michael a gun. What happened after that remained, even to this day, a blur in Michael's mind. Lots of shouting, a tussle. Michael felt someone jump him from behind. The gun fired. A kid from the other gang went down. Blood all over his head. Everybody ran.

Michael at least had the presence of mind to throw the gun into the Charles.

He was scared shitless and figured he'd be arrested. Every day that went by he imagined the police were getting closer to solving the murder and coming to get him, but it never happened.

In the subsequent months, during which Michael's own father sussed out what his son had done and gave up trying to set him straight, Galen Frohm took an interest. Michael was smart enough to know he needed to find another path, get off the street, make something of himself, and allowed himself to be taken into Frohm's care. The man could be his ticket out of an early prison sentence, or worse.

All these years later, Michael couldn't help but wonder what Frohm had known from the outset. His father must have told Frohm what he'd done. Had Frohm interceded on his behalf somehow? Paid off some detective to look the other way? And did he see in Michael someone he could mold to do his dirty work in the future?

Once he was back in Boston, Michael went to see his boss.

"It's done," he said.

Frohm smiled. "Good."

"I wasn't going to do it. I thought I could persuade him. But I couldn't make that work."

Frohm frowned. "Never second-guess me, Michael. Next time you'll know better."

Next time.

"It was always the plan, wasn't it?" Michael asked. "Here I thought you were taking me in, rescuing me, helping me get on a straight path. It wasn't that at all, was it? You brought me into the fold because you knew I had it in me. But you needed time to develop it, nurture it, build a sense of loyalty. Because you knew there would be times when you needed someone to do what I just did."

Frohm smiled. "If I am anything, Michael, I am a good judge of character."

It was hard to know whether to take that as a compliment or an insult, but Michael knew it to be the truth. Frohm did know who he was, and the sooner Michael accepted it, the easier it would be to move on.

Michael had come to terms with the kind of man he was. An emboldened one. A man to whom the conventional rules did not apply. He'd learned it was possible to kill a man in America and get away with it. Not just once, but now twice. Michael began to absorb Galen Frohm's worldview as if by osmosis, to believe in his own entitlement. There were givers, and there were takers. You had to choose which you wanted to be.

And yet, somewhere, buried inside him, in a place that was not always easy to find, Michael wanted to be good, to believe he was not a bad man. He loved his wife, was devoted to his son, helped little old ladies cross the street, for Christ's sake.

But he was in too deep now to walk away from Frohm. They were each other's prisoner, had too much on one another.

So when that *next time* came, Michael was ready.

The manager of three dollar stores in the Milwaukee area, part of the Frohm empire, was found to be stealing from the company. Michael dealt with it.

Three months after that, a man who oversaw nine Frohm fast-food franchises in Nebraska was known to be selling DVDs and VHS tapes of child porn. That alone, Frohm said, was reason to have him dispatched, but if the man were arrested, he might try to get a shorter jail sentence by telling all he knew about Frohm's kickback schemes and other illegal practices.

Michael dealt with him, too.

Things were going along fairly well. And then, nearly a year after the Gartner incident in Chicago, came the assignment that would change Michael's life forever.

Len says he's retiring, but he's not," Frohm said.

He was speaking of Len Klay, a top executive in Frohm's empire. A senior vice president who knew every aspect of the company's operations, from the cheapo motels to the dollar stores to the fast-food chicken outlets. Sixty-five years old on his last birthday, which happened to be in March. They had a celebration in the office. There was cake, streamers were hung. There was booze. Lots and lots of booze. Klay announced, to everyone's surprise, that he was winding down his work schedule, and within a few weeks would be out the door and spending a lot of time at his house in Vermont, fishing three seasons of the year, cross-country skiing in the winter. "At least as long as my knees hold out," he said, and everyone laughed.

Klay, since buying the place a decade ago, had spent much of his free time there, and since his wife's passing two years earlier, had made the place more of a primary residence, having sold the family home in Boston, and was renting a modest condo for when he was in the city.

Not only was Klay going to spend time sitting on the end of his dock come summer, dropping that line into the water, he was intending to dedicate himself to a new hobby—painting. Not the house, he said when someone at the party made a joke, but landscapes. Watercolors. Didn't expect to sell any of them or have some gallery beg him to do a show, but he found it satisfying, something to nurture the soul.

"He's fucked us over," Frohm had told Michael a few weeks later. "He's taking a consulting job with Agamemnon."

Frohm's nickname for Agamom Inc., which also just happened to own a chain of discount motels, restaurants, and other assorted entities. One of Frohm's biggest competitors.

"He can't," Michael said. "There's a noncompete clause in his contract. And it goes for at least ten years once he no longer works for us."

"It's off the books."

"Your source is solid on this?"

"Don't need a source," Frohm said. "I have the recordings."

Frohm said that Klay's working for the opposition had the potential to be devastating. Klay knew all of Frohm's marketing and financial strategies, and would know how to undermine them on behalf of a competitor.

"It's the ultimate betrayal."

"Why would he do this?" Michael asked, but he knew the answer. There was hardly anyone in Frohm's employ who hadn't been victimized, humiliated, or manipulated by the man. Michael knew that as well as anyone. He'd allowed himself to be bullied by Frohm, to be molded into a different kind of person. Why should Klay be any different? Frohm had dressed him down in meetings, mocked him behind his back. (The man had a stutter, and Frohm liked to mimic it, sometimes to Klay's face.)

What made Klay different from Michael, evidently, was that he was going to get even. Or at least try.

"You know what to do," Frohm said.

Michael understood. And when he left Frohm's office, he turned off the mini tape recorder he kept in his pocket.

He drove to Vermont.

Len Klay's place was near the small town of Salisbury, just like the steak, on a small body of water called Lake Dunmore. It was about a four-hour drive from Boston, less if the traffic wasn't bad.

Michael left before dawn, hoping to get to Len's place before eleven. He'd thought about calling ahead, making sure the man was there, coming up with some excuse about having him sign papers for something that he'd dealt with while still at the company, but decided it was better that there not be a record of any phone calls between them. Not only that, but what if, before Michael's arrival, Len happened to mention to someone that he was expecting his former boss's assistant?

No, best to arrive unannounced.

There was a Glock in the glove compartment, but Michael wasn't sure he'd need it. There might be easier ways to dispose of Len Klay, an old man and not especially fit, even if he did cross-country ski. And there'd be no trying to change Klay's mind, like he'd tried with Gartner.

He made good time, and, with occasional consultations of the map on the seat next to him, didn't get lost. Len Klay's place was more than a cottage. It was a home. Set back from the road and nestled among the towering trees, it was a white, two-story structure on a tract of land that sloped gradually down to the water's edge. The houses along this road were spaced well apart, the neighboring buildings barely visible through the woods.

Michael had noticed few cars parked at the other residences along this stretch. He guessed that many of these places were second residences for people from Burlington or Boston or Albany, probably even Montreal, which was closer, by at least an hour, to Salisbury than Boston was.

Michael pulled into the driveway, parking behind a white Lexus SUV. He took the gun from the glove compartment and was tucking it into the pocket of his windbreaker when the back door of the house opened and Klay came striding out.

He looked puzzled at first, but when he saw who it was, he smiled and said, "Michael? What the hell are you d-d-doing up here?"

He stuck out a hand and Michael, now out of the car, took it and smiled. "How you doing, Len?"

"What a surprise!" He grinned and slapped Michael on the shoulder.

"I'm driving up to Montreal, scoping out a few motel sites, realized I'd be driving right by your place, almost. A minor detour."

"Come on in. Too early for a drink?"

"Maybe coffee, if you have some going," Michael said.

Michael followed Klay into the house. Homey, lots of wood, plush chairs and a couch with afghans scattered about. A few embers glowed in the fireplace, just enough to take off the chill. It was in the low sixties outside.

Michael walked from the back of the house to the porch that looked out over the lake. A folding camping chair and an easel sat at the end of a dock that went some thirty feet out into the water. A canvas rested on the easel. Klay was in the middle of painting the far shore.

"It's c-c-coming," Klay said when he saw where Michael was looking. "I'm no Picasso."

"Want to get a closer look," Michael said. He went out to the porch, pushed open the screen door, and walked down to the shoreline and out onto the dock. Klay followed.

Michael admired the canvas, then their surroundings. There was no wind, and the water was like glass. Not one boat out on the water to start a ripple. Michael scanned the shoreline in both directions and saw no one standing out on any of the other docks. No one sitting in a chair by the water.

Maybe it was never going to get better than this.

"It's not very good," Klay said, looking over Michael's shoulder at the work in progress. "But it's something to do." He chuckled nervously. "Keeps me out of t-t-trouble."

Still with Michael's back to him, Klay said, "You're not really on your way to Montreal, are you?"

Michael turned around slowly. "What are you talking about?"

Klay smiled sadly. "Galen sent you."

"I just wanted to stop by, say hello, see how you're doing."

Klay looked into the man's eyes, as though trying to discern the truth. "He knows."

Michael cleared his throat, gazed past Klay at the house. "It's so peaceful here."

"I know what you do for him," he said. "I can't think of any other r-r-reason you'd be here." He shook his head sadly. "What happened to you, Michael? What happened to the young man I met when he came aboard years ago?"

He's long gone, Michael thought.

"I remember your naïve optimism, thinking at the time that maybe he wouldn't break you, that maybe you had it in you to rise above it, to resist. I still recall the day you came in and handed out cigars when your son, Jack, was b-b-born. It seemed so . . . quaint. I hadn't seen any new father do that in such a long time.

I'd quit smoking years earlier, but I smoked that stogie. Did you know that? It was wonderful. How are they, by the way? Rose? And your boy?"

"Fine," Michael said. "Thank you for asking."

"Look what he does to people," Klay said. "He's like a cancer that gets inside us. I suppose I'm as much to b-b-blame as anyone. I should have left years ago. To stay was to condone, to enable, even if I never sunk to your depths."

Michael glanced down into the clear, cool water. It was only about two feet deep here, and he could make out the stones on the bottom.

"Helping the opposition, it was the only thing I could think of to get some, I don't know, pound of flesh out of the man." A sad chuckle. "Suppose I should have covered my tracks better. Should have known Galen would be w-w-watching me."

Michael had the gun, but it was so still, even with the silencer it would make a lot of noise when he fired it. Maybe there was a better way.

Klay sighed. "Do you think there's anything I can say that—"

Michael pushed him off the dock.

Klay hit the water on his back, his entire body going under for a couple of seconds. He thrashed about, found purchase on the bottom, and started to stand. But by the time he was upright, in water up to his knees, Michael was in the lake, too, pushing him under.

Why did I not bring a change of clothes? Michael thought. At least an extra pair of shoes and socks.

Klay fought back, trying to keep his head above water, gasping for air, but Michael kept shoving him back under. Klay, trying to fight back, had his arms bent, hands up by his shoulders, hoping to land a blow on Michael, but he was no match for the stronger, younger man.

Michael got hold of one wrist, then the other, squeezed hard, leveraged Klay down below the surface, and held him there. Klay stared up at him through the water, eyes wide, mouth open in a silent scream.

He continued to thrash, but there was no way he could get his head above the surface. Before long, the struggles diminished to nothing.

Michael held him there for another minute, wanting to be sure. Finally, when he was certain Klay was dead, he walked back to the shore, his waterlogged shoes squishing with every step.

Looked down at Klay's body, then at the camping chair and easel.

The man could have fallen. Tripped somehow over his chair. Taken the easel with him when he went into the drink.

Yeah, that could work.

Michael walked out onto the dock and gave the chair and easel a gentle push into the water. The canvas floated, image side up, obscuring the dead man's face for a moment.

Michael walked back to shore, then cast one last look back.

Saw his wet shoeprints on the dock.

Fuck.

Anyone coming by in the next little while would be bound to ask, how does a drowned man leave wet shoeprints on a dock?

No, it would be okay. The sun was out. The dock would be dry in a few minutes. Michael didn't have to worry about—

"*Hey!*" someone shouted.

A woman. Standing on a dock. Maybe a hundred yards down the shore.

"Hey!" she called out again. "Is everything okay over there?"

Oh, shit.

THIRTY-FIVE

Jack

"You can't be serious," I said. "You don't know where he is? You don't know where the hell my father is?"

"I don't," Gwen said, looking glum. "*We* don't."

"He just, what? Wandered off? You don't need authors to write backstories. You need babysitters."

Gwen bristled. "You want me to explain this or do you just want to mouth off?"

"Maybe both," I said. I was flabbergasted. "When you relocate someone, you check in on them, right?"

"Yes."

"I mean, everybody gets a handler or something, right? If I'm the guy, and I have a problem, like the job you got me isn't working out, or I think the people you're protecting me from have found me, or I've got some emergency that means I have to get in touch with the people I left behind, there's someone I can call, yes? One of your people picks up the phone and says what's wrong, what can we do for you?"

"Yes."

"And I'm guessing it works the other way around. Someone in your position calls me up, if I'm that guy, asks how it's going, is there anything I can do for you? And it's not like you're just being neighborly. There are rules, right? There are things I'm not supposed to do, like killing people again or knocking off a bank or just doing something stupid like running for a spot on the local school board in whatever two-bit town you've condemned me to and getting my picture in the local paper?"

"Right on all counts." She took a long breath. "But we don't do it forever. Your father was taken into the program years ago. You were nine. There's only so long we keep tabs on people. If they're adapting well to their new situation, and continue to over an entire decade or two, there's no need for us to maintain monitoring."

"But don't—I mean, *shouldn't* there be? Can't you make someone, I don't know, wear an ankle bracelet for the rest of their lives, so at least you can keep tabs on them from a central location?"

"We don't do that," Gwen said. "Tell me how someone with a new identity, trying to build a new life for himself, explains a device strapped to his ankle."

I started grasping for proverbial straws. "You inject something into their arm, like they do in the Bond movies. A tracker."

Gwen gave me a patronizing look, like I was five.

"Hey, *I'm* not the one who lost track of him. How long has he been missing?"

"They're looking into that. When I put in a status report, that prompted someone to reopen the file and initiate a contact. They didn't hear anything back."

"Jesus."

"That bumped things up to the next level. Not hearing back was not necessarily cause for alarm. Your father could have been away. Could have been on a vacation." She paused. "He could be dead."

My eyebrows went up. "*Is* he dead?"

Gwen shook her head. "We don't think so. But yes, that possibility was considered, especially considering the pandemic we've been through. And there'd be a record of that. In normal times, when a relocated witness passes on, years later, we don't necessarily hear about it. But some calls were made."

"Who did they call?"

"This takes us into an area where I can't be very specific, Jack. Your father's not only entitled to his privacy, but so are those he may or may not have built a new life with. I can't tell you who he might or might not have been living with, or where he might have been working. But we were able to make those kinds of inquiries, and it appears your father disappeared sometime in the last month."

"So that's it," I said. "You can't help me. Even if you were willing to do what I'd asked, you can't."

"You're right. I can't help you. But maybe you can help me. And your father."

"What do you mean?"

"I mean maybe you can help me find your father. Provide some kind of clue to where he might be."

"You think if I knew, I'd be asking for your help?"

"There may be things you know without realizing you know them. Or maybe your father has reached out to you over the years and you haven't been forthcoming about that."

I said nothing. I started strumming my fingers nervously on the table. Gwen, evidently as annoyed by that as by a bobbing knee, glared at my hand long enough that I stopped.

"You see, Jack, there's something about all this that you're not thinking about. The big question isn't where he might have gone."

I waited.

"The big question is *why* he's gone. Why has he disappeared? Why now?"

"Okay, I'll bite. Why?"

Gwen took a deep breath. "We don't know, but there are

a couple of possibilities. Our best guess is he believes his cover is blown, that he's at risk. And that's why he's on the run."

"If that's the case, why hasn't he gotten in touch with you guys? To set him up someplace else, with another name?"

"Good question."

I thought about that. "He doesn't trust you. I mean, not you specifically, but the people you work with."

"That's impossible. If there's someone in the program who leaked his location . . . that's unthinkable."

"If he thinks his cover is blown, and he's at risk, who's he at risk from? It can't be his boss. Galen Frohm must be dead by now."

"He is," Gwen said. "But there are others who might seek to get even with your father, even after all this time. Like the families of Abel Gartner or Len Klay. Possibly others."

I knew the names, of course.

"It's been too long," I said. "That can't be it."

Gwen took out her phone, brought up a photo, and turned the screen around so I could have a look at it. It was a man, shot from the waist up, so I couldn't guess his height. But he still looked big. Broad shoulders, thick neck, a face like a hunk of granite. Caucasian, jet-black hair, ears that stood out. About forty years old. The image was soft, slightly out of focus, as though shot from a distance with a telephoto lens.

"Who's this?"

"It might be the guy your father's on the run from. You ever seen him before?"

"No."

"We think his name is Sam. Or Stewart. Maybe Arthur. A professional. If he's who we think he is, he's a very dangerous man. And if he's looking for your father, and finds him, it won't end well."

"What do you mean, a professional? Who the fuck is he? Does my father know him? Did he piss this guy off somehow?"

"We don't think it's anything personal between them. We have reason to believe this man has simply been hired to do a job."

"By whom? Why?"

"It's not clear. Surveillance was being conducted on him for other reasons and your father's name came up unexpectedly. I can't tell you any more than that."

"Does he smoke?" I asked.

"Does he *smoke*?"

"Yeah. It's probably nothing, but there was a car parked out front of my place the other night. The driver was smoking. I could see the tip of his cigarette. It was like he was watching the place. And then, later, he was gone."

Gwen considered that. "Whoever's looking for your father might think he'd come here."

"Christ," I said.

"Cards on the table here, Jack," Gwen said. "Have you ever heard from your father since that night he was taken into the program? And if you have, do you know anything that might help us find him?"

I'd never told a soul any of this.

"What if my father's at risk because someone in the witness protection program let the information out? Telling you might be the dumbest thing I could do."

"It's your call," Gwen said. "But whatever you tell me stays with me."

I stayed silent for several seconds before Gwen said, "There's another reason why we would like to find him."

My breathing slowed while I waited.

"This is more difficult to broach with you, but you strike me as someone who would want to do the right thing. To stop something bad before it happened."

"I don't understand."

"We have to consider the possibility your father has gone back to his old ways. That he's hung out his shingle. That he's for hire. That he's doing what he did for Galen Frohm. Maybe he's gone off our radar because he's decided to do it for someone else. Maybe he needs the money. Maybe, deep down, it's the kind of work he likes to do."

"No," I said.

"Jack, whatever the reason he's disappeared, he needs to be found. Either to protect him or to protect someone else *from* him. So let me ask you again, Jack. Have you *ever* heard from your father since he went into the program?"

I thought a long time before giving her my answer.

"Yes," I said. "I have."

THIRTY-SIX

Harry Breedlove, knocking back a scotch as he gazed out the window of his Greenwich Village apartment, wondered what to do about all these messages from Jack Givins. And damn it all to hell, what was Ann Finley thinking, getting in touch with him directly? Had she not listened when he'd told her, again and again, that if you want to speak to my author, you go through me?

What a clusterfuck.

Jack was never supposed to know Ann had made an offer on the third book. The person who'd given Harry the phone had made that very clear. When Harry had asked why, no explanation was forthcoming, and his contact did not look like someone who liked to be asked twice. Harry had the sense that if he did not do what was being asked of him, he could be in a lot of trouble. While there was nothing explicit, the threat sounded real.

"It's all going to work out fine," Harry was told. "You're doing Jack a favor. Giving him a great opportunity. If I could tell you about it, I would."

Harry didn't feel good about what he'd done. He liked Jack. He liked representing him. His first novel, a touching work about a young man trying to find the father who had abandoned him and his mother years earlier, had a ring of truth to it, as though Jack was drawing on a personal experience. Not that he ever talked about it. The subsequent novels were different but drew on similar themes of loneliness and detachment. Harry had wanted Jack to publish the books under his own name, but he couldn't be persuaded.

How was Harry supposed to respond to these messages from Jack? The only thing Harry could think to do was tell him the truth. What was the worst thing that could happen? Sure, Jack would fire him, find another agent, and Harry wouldn't blame him. But he had to make this right.

Harry considered an explanatory email, but that struck him as too cowardly. But he didn't want to go all the way back to Boston, either. A phone call seemed the best way to go. He'd have another drink, and then he would—

There was a knock at the door.

Who the hell could that be?

Jack.

Had to be.

This was supposedly a secure building. You had to get buzzed up, and there'd been no buzz. So maybe Jack had hit every button in the lobby except Harry's, wanting to be able to surprise him. Someone was bound to let him in. There were Uber Eats and DoorDash people roaming the halls all the time.

Harry put down his drink, crossed the living room, and went to the door. He peered through the peephole.

"Oh, shit," he said. Raising his voice, he said, "Not a good time!"

"Open up!" someone shouted from the other side of the door.

Keeping the chain on, Harry turned the dead bolt, and opened the door a few inches.

"Seriously, this is not a good time."

A hand came up and pushed the door wide open, ripping the chain off.

"Someone would like to have a word," his visitor said.

THIRTY-SEVEN

Jack

The time had come to write my own backstory. But I wouldn't be making this one up.

Gwen had said that while the witness protection service would continue to work its own contacts in trying to find my father, it would help if I could rack my brain and think of *anything* that might offer a clue as to where Dad might have disappeared to.

Did my father have friends from his distant past that he might now turn to? Were there parts of the country he loved and might try to blend into if he believed someone was hunting for him? Were there any special skills he had (besides, you know, killing people) that he might use if he assumed yet another identity? Gwen had asked.

"Like what?" I had asked Gwen.

She had shrugged. "I don't know. Maybe he worked on a fishing boat in his youth and he's out catching lobsters or something."

"He never did anything like that."

"I'm just saying, as an example," she said, giving me that look of annoyance I was getting so used to.

I told her that if I were to sit there and *tell* her everything I could remember about my father, I'd probably miss potentially helpful details. But if I sat down and *wrote* it out, one thought would lead to another and I might have something more comprehensive.

"So do it," she said.

What seemed to make the most sense, at least for now, was to record everything I could recall about the times my father got in touch after he went into the program. There wasn't anyone else I could consult, to help me drag up details I might otherwise have forgotten, because these were stories I had never shared.

Ever.

So, that evening, after Gwen left, I got down to work.

The First Time My Father Got in Touch

I was ten. And I bawled my eyes out.

Dad had been gone about ten months. I was walking home, a backpack over my shoulder, shuffling along, looking down, trying to kick the same stone ahead of me, over and over again.

A red car passed me once, slowly. Didn't take much notice of it. And then I was vaguely aware that it must have gone around the block, because it passed me a second time. I kept working that stone, thinking about the homework I had in my bag that I would most likely never get to. Academics were not really my thing, although I was writing stories and could fill an entire notebook with one. But this obsession, if you could call it that, came at the expense of my other subjects, which I didn't really give a shit about. My teacher said to me one day, "You know, if you didn't spend so much time in your head writing stories, you'd be doing better in math."

On its third pass, the car stopped, or almost stopped. It was creeping along, matching my pace. I barely glanced over, just enough to tell that it was some model of Dodge, and that the car was in need of a good wash.

Someone called out, "Hey, pal."

I stopped and looked into the open passenger window. There, behind the wheel, was Dad. A little thinner in the face. His hair was longer, and lighter. Maybe he'd dyed it.

Dad held up a brown bag with a yellow *M* on the side. "Want to grab a late lunch?" he asked. "Got your favorite."

I took a moment to be stunned, and I was, on several levels. And then I felt this infusion of excitement.

He was back.

I burst into tears. Tears of joy, really. My dreams had come true. Prayers—not that I was big on those—had been answered. I was trembling. I was so excited I thought I'd explode.

"Whoa, sport, it's okay," Dad said. He put the car in park, got out, and ran around to the other side. He gave me a hug, pulled me in so tight that for a moment there I couldn't breathe. I was barely breathing anyway as I threw my arms around him.

He led me to the car and opened the door, hustled me into the front seat. I still remember, to this day, the smell of the fries in the brown paper bag, but at the time I was not nearly as excited about a fast-food lunch as I was about my father's decision to rejoin us.

Gleeful, I said, "Does Mom know? Does she know you've come back?"

I watched his face fall. It was the moment he realized he had totally misjudged the situation. He'd thought I would assume he was just visiting, like an inmate who has escaped prison long enough to pop in on the relatives for lunch, but still on the run nonetheless.

"Oh, no, sport, it's not—"

"She's going to be so happy!" I squealed. "Me, too! I can't believe it!"

"Listen, listen," he said. "It's not what you think."

"What do you mean?"

"I'm not . . . back. I just thought . . . I thought I'd check in on you, is all."

It was like finding out that the puppy Santa put under the Christmas tree was supposed to go to the house next door, only a million times worse.

I was speechless. I was on the edge of an emotional cliff, ready to fall off.

"But hey," he said, trying to sound encouraging and giving my leg a friendly pat, "how about this, right? Together again!"

I still said nothing. I was holding back tears of sadness. The bastard. How could he do this to me?

"We'll go someplace, park, have some lunch."

We went to the most anonymous of locations. A mall parking lot. He found a spot between two towering SUVs, as though using them for cover. He killed the engine, started bringing food out of the bag. I said nothing. I was numb.

Dad took a bite of a fry. "It's gone kinda cold. But it's still good."

He set onto my lap a package of fries and a double cheeseburger. I thought I might throw up. Finally, I found myself able to speak.

"What's your name now?"

"Well, it's still Dad to you," he said cheerfully, trying to lighten the mood. "But I can't tell you what I go by. Too risky. For me *and* for you. Someone might come and torture you to get the information." He saw something in my face and said quickly, "That's just a joke. No one's going to do that to you. I was kidding. So how's school? What are you up to? You got lots of friends?" A sly smile. "Any girlfriends, or is it too soon to ask that?"

I hadn't touched my food.

"Got you something." He reached into the back and struggled to drag a box forward between the two front seats. "It's a Nintendo 64. For games. You don't have one of these, do you?"

I shook my head.

"Well, there you go. Just don't let anyone take it from you on the way home. You got some way you can explain to your mother how you got it? Because you can't tell her you saw me, that I gave it to you. Maybe a friend got two for his birthday? Something like that? You have to promise me you won't tell her we had this little meeting."

"I won't tell," I said.

"I know. You could say you won it. In a raffle at school or something."

"She won't believe me."

He bit his lip, thinking about that.

"I could play it at your house," I said, "if you took me with you."

His head drooped. "I wish I could do that. You have no idea how much I wish I could. But it wouldn't be fair. Not to you, and not to your mom."

"Where do you live?" I asked.

"Can't tell you that, either. The less you know, the safer you and your mom are. That bastard Frohm, even in prison, has people, you know? People who will do his bidding."

"They've tried to scare us."

His jaw dropped. "What's happened?"

"Sometimes the phone rings and there's no one there. Or they leave a note on Mom's car and she starts to cry. One morning somebody slashed all her tires."

Dad's face reddened. "Those sons of bitches."

"They haven't tried to kill us or anything," I said, the same way I might have said that I hadn't failed a spelling test.

"Has your mom told the police? The FBI, anybody?"

"I think so."

"Well, I'm going to goddamn well be talking to them, too." He bit his lower lip, like he was thinking about how he might handle this. "I should just kill him," he said to himself.

"What?"

"Nothing. I just don't want anything to happen to you or your mother."

I didn't say anything. Dad fumed for another few seconds, then tried to change the mood. "Come on, eat up."

As if to encourage me, Dad took a bite out of his own burger.

"I'll find you," I said. "Someday I'll find you." I felt as though a lightbulb had gone off over my head. "I'll remember your license plate."

Dad smiled and pointed to the back seat. "Look."

I put my burger on the dash, got up on my knees, and peered into the back seat. On the floor were several license plates.

"I mix and match," he said. "Can't be too careful." His eyes softened. "Still got the wallet I gave you?"

I nodded. But I didn't have it on me. It was tucked under my socks in a chest of drawers.

"Look," he said, "I'm sorry if I got your hopes up. I just wanted to see you. I think of you every day. I miss you. I've got a job. Not the greatest, but it's okay. Working in a big hardware-type store. Wearing the little orange apron. They still keep an eye on me, you know, the government, but I gave them the slip today so I could see you. Long drive, but it was worth it, even if I only get to spend a moment—"

I grabbed my backpack, down by my feet, opened the door, and got out. I didn't even bother to close it. Left the Nintendo 64 behind, too.

"Son!" my father cried out. "Come back!"

But his voice faded fast as I ran between the cars, my eyes so filled with tears I could barely see where I was going.

Other Times My Father Got in Touch

A visit from my father became an almost annual event. He'd always show up when I least expected it, and when he was least likely to be seen by anyone else but me.

When I was eleven, I was at one end of the mall, sitting in the food court eating a sundae while my mom was at the other end looking at shoes in JCPenney, by myself at a table for four, when a man sat down across from me.

"Hey, sport," he said.

He was in what I would loosely describe as a disguise. A Red Sox cap pulled down low and an oversized pair of sunglasses.

Some ice cream dribbled onto my chin. I swiveled my head around, looking to see whether Mom was nearby.

"She's busy," Dad said. "Trying on shoes. If she's like she used to be, she'll be there for some time. Just wanted to talk to you for a minute. First thing, have the threats stopped? The phone calls, the notes on the windshield?"

"Mostly," I said, stunned to see him sitting there.

He nodded slowly. "Good. I had a word with my handlers. And the other day, they got in touch to tell me about you."

"Huh?"

"About you taking off. Your mom was so upset, she called the witsec people, who finally got to me and told me what happened. That you got on a train and went to Chicago. You can't do crazy shit like that. You could get hurt. Jesus, you could get killed. And there's all kinds of creeps out there. They see a young boy traveling alone, there's no telling what could happen. Why did you do that?"

"I thought you might be there," I said. "Because of the movie."

"You think I'm going to hang out in a train station just because I like that scene in *The Untouchables*?"

I said nothing. It had made sense to me at the time.

"Okay, look, you have to promise me you won't do that again."

I swallowed some ice cream that had melted in my mouth. "Okay," I said. Technically, I kept my word. I never went looking for him in Chicago again.

"Give me a hug before your mother shows up," he said.

I got out of my seat, came around the table, and put my arms around him. He gave me a squeeze, and when we parted, I could see that his eyes were as teary as mine.

"Gotta go," he said.

And he went.

He showed up again once when I was fifteen and walking to school one morning, and again at seventeen, when I was riding the bus and he sat down right next to me. By my mid-teens, I was always on the lookout, thinking he might appear at any time for no reason at all. After that first visit, I never again got it into my head that he was coming back. And I never told my mother about our meetings.

When I was twenty, sitting at the front of the church for my mother's funeral, I happened to turn around in the pew in time to see my father standing by the back entrance.

I was sitting next to Earl and the members of my mother's extended family who were still alive. Her parents had both died the year before, but there were a couple of cousins, and an uncle. And Mom had a fairly wide circle of friends that she'd accumulated in the years after she had married Earl and resettled in Malden. Friends and family from his side had attended, as well. The church was nearly half full, which I thought was not bad, considering.

I had happened to glance back during the minister's boilerplate remarks—Mom hadn't attended this church, and the minister performing the service wouldn't have known her from Judi Dench if she, as Mom herself would have been inclined to say, stood up naked in his soup—and saw a man I thought I recognized standing just inside the door.

Although he looked different from the last time I had seen him, I knew it was Dad.

He had a short, neatly trimmed gray beard, and had lost some weight. He was wearing a fedora-style hat, which hardly anyone wore anymore, but which I figured he had put on to make himself harder to identify.

For a millisecond, our eyes met.

I turned to look back at the minister, droning on, and briefly considered how scandalous it would be for me to get up in the middle of the service, and concluded I didn't give a shit. People would assume I'd been overcome with emotion, excuse my behavior. I was on my feet, heading for the aisle on the far right of the church, but the man with the hat was gone. By the time I was out the front doors, he was nowhere to be seen.

When I was twenty-one, I was attending Skidmore College in Saratoga Springs, across the border in New York State, majoring in English with a minor in theater. At least, those were the subjects that occupied my time when I wasn't getting drunk or trying to get laid.

A friend called out to me as I was passing through the common area of the dormitory complex where I lived. "Your dad's here," he said. "Up in your room."

At first I thought, Earl's come to visit. My coming to Skidmore had marked the end of our living under the same roof. He was selling the house he and Mom shared—he needed the money—and it was more or less understood that when school was over I'd have to find my own place to live. But he had tried to make up for that by taking on the duties a real father would, like driving me up here, and coming to get me at the end of the semester.

But this was the middle of the term, so it didn't make much sense that it would be Earl.

Sure enough, when I got to my room, it was Dad sitting there on my bed. I was slightly taken aback by his appearance. He looked thinner than when I'd caught that glimpse of him at the funeral. He'd made no attempt to disguise himself, maybe because he looked different. His skin looked gray, his eyes sunk into his forehead.

"Hey," I said.

He stood. "Jack," he said, pulling me into his arms. "It's good to see you."

"I saw you," I said. I didn't have to tell him when.

"Yeah," he said. "When you spotted me I had to take off. Would have been okay if it'd just been you, but other people might have noticed. But . . . I felt I had to pay my respects."

I nodded.

"And today, well," he said, sitting back down on the bed, "I wanted to see you while I still had the chance."

"What are you talking about?" I asked.

He put a hand to his chest. "Going in for surgery next week. They've spotted a little something on my lung. They're hoping they can get the spot without taking the whole thing. But you never know. Doctors, right?"

"I'm sorry," I said. "I hope it goes okay."

"Fingers crossed," he said. "I don't mean to be all maudlin, coming here, like it's the end. I'm sure it'll go okay." He paused, forced a smile. "How's Earl these days?"

"Pulling back."

"I gather he's kind of a fuck-up."

"He means well, I guess. But yeah." I shrugged. "He sold the house, has basically kicked me out. But he has his moments when he tries."

Dad nodded. "Well, I'm not exactly in a position to judge."

"Have you got anyone else?" I asked. "I mean, to get you through this?"

He shook his head. "No, but that's okay."

Through our infrequent visits I had learned that Dad had never settled down with anyone else, at least not for long, and if he'd fathered any more kids, he'd never mentioned it. Maybe he had and didn't want me to know.

Stuck for something to ask him, the best I could come up with was, "Still wearing the orange apron?"

He shook his head. "No. Left that job years ago. Exposed to too many people. Someone might still recognize me after all this time. Kind of bouncing around. I've been getting some work at a window factory, picking up a few hours at a printer's."

"You know," I said, "I hear you in my sleep. The conversations we had before you left. Like I'm trying to cling to that time when you were with us."

Dad looked down into his lap, maybe so I wouldn't see his face crumble. He sighed, and said, "Some advice, in case I don't get another chance. You'll be heading off into the world soon. Try to learn from my mistakes. Never let anyone manipulate you into doing something you know is wrong. Listen to that voice in your head. I allowed a man to drag me into the darkness. But Frohm didn't destroy me. I did that to myself."

"Okay."

"I should go."

He stood, gave me a light pat on the shoulder as he walked past, and whispered, "Don't be hard on Earl. We're all flawed."

He winked. "I'll be keeping my eye on ya, God willing." He left my room without another word.

And then there was the time Dad saved my life, but more about that later.

I printed out what I had and called Gwen.

"Done what I can for now," I said.

She said she would have it picked up.

All the reminiscing, at least for a while, had pushed my concerns regarding Harry Breedlove out of mind. But I still wanted to get in touch with the guy and find out what the hell was going on, and if that meant getting on a train, going to New York, and tracking him down, I was prepared to do it.

I sent him another email, texted him, tried to get him on the phone, but struck out everywhere. I felt I had given him enough opportunity to explain himself. It was time to get back to Ann, my former editor, and tell her what Harry had done.

I opted to call her directly at her editorial office.

"Oh, Jack," she said after I identified myself. "I was just going to call you."

"Sorry I didn't reply to your email right away," I said. "There's been some funny things going on with Harry."

"That's what we're all thinking," Ann said. "To take his own life. It's so sad. I mean, I suppose it could have been an accident, but it certainly doesn't look like it. He must have been very troubled. You never really know anyone, do you?"

I don't know that I heard much more. I must have zoned out. I hung up, finally, without saying another word.

THIRTY-EIGHT

June 1997

In the days following the early-morning raid at his home, Michael Donohue had a lot to think about.

They had him cold on the Len Klay murder. When that woman on the faraway dock started shouting at him, asking him if everything was okay, he got the hell out of there. Ran to his car and took off.

What he didn't know, until later, was that the woman ran from the dock to the road in time to see him race past. Even noticed the license plate number and used a stick to write it in the sand of her driveway so she wouldn't forget it.

Police found Michael's shoeprints—not wet ones on the dock, but impressions in the sand by the shoreline—and inside the house, they found his fingerprints on the screen door. Once he was arrested, and his car taken in for a forensic examination, they found sand by the brake and accelerator pedals that matched sand on the lake's shoreline.

As they dug into this case, their attention was drawn to the murder in Chicago, months earlier, of a man who had a business arrangement with Galen Frohm. Michael was unable to account for his whereabouts during that time period. They were also looking into the deaths of the manager of three dollar stores in the Milwaukee area and the child-porn enthusiast who ran some Frohm fast-food franchises in Nebraska.

Michael was in deep shit.

When Michael was arrested he'd sought help from Abner Bronklin, the top legal mind used by the Frohm organization. But it didn't take Michael long to realize that Bronklin's primary interest would be to protect Frohm, and if that somehow meant sacrificing Michael, that's exactly what he would do.

So Michael got his own lawyer.

Her name was Alicia Tarrington, and during one of her visits to prison to discuss his situation, she laid it out for him.

"They want Frohm, and they want him bad. Bad enough to cut you a deal."

"On the murders?"

"They don't have enough to charge you for what went down in Chicago. They have their suspicions, but there's no physical evidence that connects you, no witnesses. Same with Milwaukee and Nebraska. But with Klay they have more than enough. A witness, motive, that sand in your car. If you want to plead not guilty I'll give it my best shot, but I'm here to tell you your chances are about as good as the Big Dig getting done on time and under budget. You'll be an old man when you get out, if you don't end up dying in prison from something else, or some new hitter sent by Frohm. They want Frohm for the murders he sent you to commit, sure, but that's just for starters. His corporate empire is basically one huge criminal organization. They want him on blackmail, tax evasion, extortion, and a host of other things. And you're the one who can give them everything they need to put him away. You can tell them where to look, how it all went down. You were in the room, Michael."

"I have recordings," he said.

Tarrington said, "What?"

"Not for when he told me he wanted Gartner dead. But with

Klay, yeah, I had one of those mini recorders in my pocket. Thought I might need it for backup one day."

"Where the hell are these recordings?"

"Hidden. But I can tell you where to find them." He paused. "But the thing is, even if somehow you got my charge dismissed, Frohm will get me. He knows people. And so do the folks he made all those crooked deals with. They'll be going down, too. They'll all come looking for me."

"We offer them the recordings," Tarrington said, "in exchange for witness protection. When they hear you've got Frohm on tape, they'll give you anything. You might have to do some jail time. A token few months, but after that, they can give you a new identity, relocate you. Rose and your son, too."

Michael said he would have to think about it, discuss it with his wife.

Who, it turned out, wanted no part of it. Not for her, and not for their son.

And that tore Michael apart. He loved Rose, to be sure, but their marriage had been headed for a cliff for a long time. If he had to leave Rose to start a new life on her own, he could reconcile that.

But Jack. God, that was another thing altogether.

He loved his son so much. Did he love him enough to leave him behind?

So Michael had a decision to make. (1) Testify and not accept witness relocation and run the risk of getting not only himself killed, but his family, too. Or (2) don't testify, and spend much of the rest of his life in jail, without his family. Or (3) accept the offer of a new identity and go into hiding without his wife and son, provided there were assurances that they'd be safe, that Frohm and his people would know going after them would come with grave consequences.

I'll take what's behind Door Number Three, Monty.

Tough choice, but it was the only one that made sense. Did he regret betraying Galen Frohm? Definitely. But he could also see how Frohm had used him, groomed him from an early age to become a killer. Michael wasn't dismissing his own responsibility here. He wasn't whining that Frohm had made him do it. But the time had come to be pragmatic about these things.

He had to save his own ass.

The next time Alicia came to visit, Michael said, "Tell them it's a deal. And here's where you can find the key to a safe-deposit box where the tapes are."

But to make the deal happen he would have to confess to his other crimes, including the Chicago murder. It took a while to nail down the details, but there was so much multiagency interest in nailing Frohm that Michael was granted immunity for his various misdeeds.

And instead of Michael going to jail for the rest of his life, it was Frohm.

Who, as it turned out, did not die in prison, but in the hospital, having been transferred there during the early days of a raging pandemic, before scientists had a clear idea how it spread, and frontline workers were taking every precaution to make sure the uninfected stayed that way.

And so it was that Galen Frohm died alone. Didn't even live long enough to hear his loved ones, over the cell phone that a doctor held to his ear, tell him how much they loved him.

THIRTY-NINE

Jack

I went to Lana's that evening.

We hadn't seen or communicated with each other for a couple of days, and she seemed distant. Something was wrong, but I didn't know what.

"Everything okay with you?" I asked her.

"Yeah, sure," she said, her back to me. "Why wouldn't it be?"

I waited for her to ask whether everything was okay with me. When she didn't, I volunteered some information.

"Harry killed himself," I said.

Whatever it was that had been troubling Lana, whatever it was I might have done, she put it aside for the moment and said, "Oh, my God. What happened?"

I told her about the call with my editor, Ann.

"Why would he have killed himself?" Lana asked. "You have any idea?"

I shook my head. "I don't know."

"How did he die?"

"Went into the water," I said. "Hudson, East River, not sure which. But he drowned."

Lana went quiet for a moment.

"What?"

She shrugged. "Nothing. Just seems like there's a lot of that going around." She gave her head a shake, as though discarding a notion. "It's nothing."

"Like my editor said, what do we really know about each other, you know? All of us, we're dealing with some kind of shit or other, and lots of times we keep it to ourselves."

"We do, don't we?" she said pointedly, looking right at me.

"What?" I said.

"Look, I don't want to get into it. You've had a shitty day."

"No, really, what's troubling you?"

"Okay," Lana said, "I have to make a confession, to start with. I was making some work-related calls to various city and state offices and casually asked whether you'd been hired. Like, in the communications department, for example. Writing speeches. I was hoping I'd find out what you were up to and then I'd drop it on you. You know how much I hate secrets. It's like a sickness with me. I just have to know."

"Uh-huh," I said. I can't say I was surprised. It was in her nature.

"And I happened to be talking to this guy who knows a lot of the inside scoop on publishing, and—"

"That doesn't sound like your beat. How did calling someone in publishing just happen?"

She sighed. "That one was deliberate. To see whether you'd gotten, like, a ghostwriting gig or something. Anyway, I didn't get anywhere, you'll be delighted to know, but there are some rumors about you. About your past."

"Oh."

"Not something you did, but something about your family."

"And you did some more digging and you found out."

"No, I didn't," Lana said. "Not for lack of trying, though."

"So, let me see if I have this right. You're pissed with me because you did a shitload of snooping, behind my back, to find out what I've been working on, and found out I have something personal I've chosen to not share."

"It sounds bad when you put it that way," she said. "But I thought we were honest with each other."

"I have been. I've never lied to you. Have you told me every single thing about your past? Family? Past lovers?"

"That's different."

"How?"

She opened her mouth to say something, but nothing came out.

"I got nothin'," she said, finally.

We stared at each other for several seconds, as though waiting to see who would blink first. She lost, turned away, and said, "I'm sorry."

I went to the window and watched a plane land at Logan, glancing occasionally at the muted TV tuned in, as always, to the news. I could see Lana's reflection in the window. She had walked back into the kitchen area, opened a drawer, and taken something out. Seconds later, she was standing behind me.

"I bought you something," she said.

I turned around slowly and saw that she was holding a gift-wrapped package, no more than an inch thick, four inches wide, and nearly a foot long.

"What's this?" I asked.

"I'd seen this a few days ago, before I started making all those calls. Then I wasn't sure I was going to give it to you, and now I wonder if you'd consider it a peace offering." She handed it to me. I took it but made no move to tear off the paper. "Just open it, you idiot," she said.

I slowly tore off the paper, revealing a black cardboard box. I lifted off the lid and set it on the coffee table.

"When you took out your wallet the other night," she said, "I thought, Whoa, it's totally falling to pieces, so I decided you needed a new one. This is a Fendi, and I won't lie, it cost me a fucking fortune, but I just wanted to do it, so none of this 'oh, you shouldn't have' bullshit, because it's not going back."

The wallet was made of blue leather and sat in the box in the open position, displaying all its sleeves designed to accommodate credit cards and a driver's license and whatever other shit a guy might happen to be carrying around with him.

I just stared at it.

"Oh, fuck, you hate it," Lana said. "Is it the blue? Because I *could* take it back and get it in brown or something, probably."

A single tear dropped onto the wallet. I wiped it away with my thumb, then moved it onto the coffee table so as not to make a further mess of it.

"Um, it's very thoughtful, Lana. But I don't . . . thank you . . . but . . ."

"Jack, what's going on? If you don't like it, that's fine, but I get the feeling there's something happening here I don't understand."

I shook my head. "Maybe this is actually the perfect time to tell you what I've been holding back."

The story spilled out of me. At least, at first, the stuff that I felt at liberty to tell, since what happened with my father was, for the most part, a matter of public record. And once she knew even a hint of the story, she'd be able to find out the rest, between the *Star*'s files and any public library's. I told her I was born Jack Donohue, but became Jack Givins after my mother married Earl. Who my father had worked for, what he'd done, and how he had gone into the witness protection program, and why I'd had such an emotional reaction to her gift.

"I'm sorry," she said. "I had no idea."

"Of course you didn't," I said, and took the new wallet out of the box. "This *is* pretty nice."

I explained that my father's absence had haunted me since the day he'd left, that it was the pivotal moment in my life, and at the core of everything I'd written.

"And all these years, you've never heard from him at all," Lana said.

I smiled. "There's more."

She listened intently as I filled her in on all the times my father had visited me. "I have no idea where he is, except that it's probably within a day's drive. I don't see him driving here from Oklahoma just to say hello."

"You ever wonder if he's watching you and you don't even know it?"

I smiled. "Always. And once, he showed up when I needed him most."

FORTY

Earl hadn't been very successful in making Cayden—if that was even his real name—happy. His visit with Jack had not elicited the kind of information Cayden wanted.

The day after Earl's chat with Jack, a chat intended to draw out some detail about his real father, Cayden had been waiting for Earl in his parking garage. He'd parked his shitbox rental where he used to keep the Porsche and was on his way to the stairs when someone stepped out from behind a pillar and said, "Earl."

Earl spun around, saw who it was, and said, "Jesus, you gave me a heart attack."

"Well?"

Earl said, "Look, I gave it my best shot, but I don't know any more than I did before I went."

Cayden extended an arm and brushed an imaginary fleck of dust off Earl's shoulder. Jack's stepfather flinched, thinking maybe the guy was going to grab him by the neck.

"We had a deal," Cayden said. "I gave you twenty-five grand for that crap Boxster. I'd like my money back."

That was definitely going to be a problem. Earl had already spent more than half of it paying off several debts.

"Maybe there's something else I can do," Earl said.

Which explained why Earl was now sitting in his car this evening, parked half a block down the street from Jack's place.

Earl didn't feel good about what he was about to do. In fact, he felt downright shitty about it. He might not have been the best stepdad in the world, and he knew he should have given Jack a share of the proceeds when he sold his mother's house, and yeah, he had a lot of nerve asking Jack for money, but this—this crossed a line.

And while what he was about to do presented a moral challenge, at least it didn't present a physical or technical one. Breaking into Jack's place would be easy.

Almost two years ago, Jack had given Earl a key to his place. That had surprised Earl at the time, since he hadn't thought Jack trusted him all that much. But Jack led a pretty spartan existence, so there wasn't much worth taking. He'd used some of the money he still had from selling his first two books to go to Europe to do research for his third. He'd wanted to set some of the novel in Paris, and believed if he spent three weeks there he'd get a real feel for the place. Rented a small apartment in the Marais district and lived like a local. Hung out in cafés. Took long walks. People-watched.

Jack asked Earl to check his place once a week, bring in the mail, email him if there were any bills that had arrived that Jack could pay online while he was away. He might have asked Lana to do it—they were seeing a lot more of each other by this time—but he had invited her to join him on the trip. Jack, perhaps foolishly, had never thought to ask Earl to return that spare key.

So Earl was able to let himself in.

Earl tried to convince himself it wasn't Jack he was betraying, but his father, Michael. That bastard didn't deserve any special consideration. Look at the mess he'd left for Earl to deal with. Raising another man's son, or giving it his best shot, at least. That should have been Michael's role, but no, he had to run off and hide somewhere with a new name and a new life. Lucky him.

Earl didn't know whether to believe Jack when he said he

hadn't seen his father since his departure. But even if he was being truthful, it didn't mean that Michael had never been in *touch*. A birthday card, an email, a letter? Something that would offer a clue to where Michael had gone. Maybe there was some tidbit of information like that hidden somewhere in the apartment. It was worth a shot, especially if it kept Cayden from doing something that would make Earl wish he had a better medical plan.

He was waiting outside Jack's place when he saw him come out and stand on the sidewalk. Moments later, a small Toyota with an Uber logo on the windshield stopped at the curb and Jack got in.

Earl wondered how long Jack would be away. He made a call.

"Hello?"

"Hey, Jack, it's Earl."

"Hey," Jack said. He sounded underwhelmed to hear from him. "What's up?"

"I'm running an errand later in your neighborhood and wondered if you wanted to grab a bite or anything."

He hoped that didn't sound too suspicious. After going the better part of a year without getting in touch, here he was reaching out for the third time.

"Can't," Jack said. "I'm heading downtown to Lana's."

"No sweat, another time," Earl said, and ended the call.

Shit, that was too abrupt, he told himself. Should have dragged it out some, been more conversational. But Earl was so eager to get this search over and done with that once he knew Jack would be gone for a while, he wanted to get started.

He let himself into the building, climbed the steps to the second floor, and entered Jack's apartment.

Where to begin.

Earl had to give Jack some credit. His place was incredibly neat. No dirty dishes in the sink, no crumbs under the toaster, items in the refrigerator neatly arranged. In Jack's bedroom, Earl found underwear neatly folded in drawers, jeans draped over hangers, no dust bunnies under the bed.

Earl hoped what he was looking for was as simple as a piece of paper. Something with a phone number or an address scribbled on it. Maybe even in some kind of code.

Where would you hide a slip of paper?

Earl looked at the shelves that took up most of one wall in the small apartment. They were loaded with books.

Hundreds.

At first, Earl speculated that such a note, if it existed, would be tucked into a book whose title hinted at what was hidden within its pages. He scanned the spines, looking for titles that jumped out at him. When he spotted a copy of *Dad*, by William Wharton, he shouted "Aha!" and pulled it out. But leafing through the pages produced nothing. Next, he tried *Not My Father's Son*, by the actor Alan Cumming. No joy there. Maybe "father" or "dad" wasn't the right keyword. He riffled the pages of *Still Missing*, by Chevy Stevens, *Gone*, by Lisa Gardner, *Vanished*, by Joseph Finder.

Nothing.

Fuck, he thought. He was going to have to check every last one. He took the books off the shelves in lots of six or seven, depending on how thick they were, quickly leafed through them, then placed them back exactly as they were. It took the better part of an hour, and at the end he had nothing to show for it.

Kitchen drawers, he thought. People were always tucking notes and scraps of paper in there.

Another strikeout.

Next, Earl searched the bedroom. The drawer in the bedside table contained what one might expect to find. Spare change, reading glasses, lip balm for those cold Boston winters, Tylenol, condoms.

He looked through the dresser, then moved on to the bathroom. Even took off the lid of the toilet tank and checked to see whether anything had been taped underneath. He'd seen that in a movie once. No such luck.

Finally, he returned to the kitchen and looked at the two closed laptops on the table.

Why two?

Jack hadn't liked it when Earl was hovering around the laptops on his last visit. He opened them up, waited for the screens to come to life, and found they were both password-protected.

Of course they are.

Earl tried several configurations of Jack's birthday but had no success. He tried the titles of his two published novels. Another strikeout.

"I've got it!" he said aloud.

He typed OSCAR LAIDLAW. Jack's pen name.

Nothing. Tried it again in lower case, then with capitals on the *O* and *L*. Again, nothing.

His dad's name, Earl thought.

He entered variations of Michael Donohue—mdonohue, daddonohue, michaeldad—and then coupled them with the year he went into witness protection, but struck out each and every time.

"This is hopeless," he said.

He closed the laptops and sat there, scanning the room, wondering whether there were any places he had missed.

He'd searched *everything.*

Cayden would not be happy. But at least Earl would be able to accomplish one thing he'd been asked to do.

He took the small device he'd been keeping in his pocket, got on his hands and knees, and affixed it to the underside of the kitchen table.

FORTY-ONE

Jack

You hear a lot about road rage incidents. I was involved in one, not long after I'd come back from a trip to Paris to do some book research. Just about the scariest thing that, at least up until that time, had ever happened to me.

I'm willing to admit what started it was my fault. I didn't see the guy in my blind spot. I cut him off. It was completely unintentional. But sometimes lack of intent doesn't matter.

I was southbound on Broadway, somewhere around Saugus, moving from the center lane to the far right so that I'd be lined up for the exit to Essex Street. I glanced over my shoulder but somehow I missed this guy in a hulking big Ford F-150 pickup. I know, I know, how do you miss something big enough to have its own zip code, right? Somehow I did.

So I moved into the exit lane and heard the driver of the Ford lay on the horn at the same time as there was this squeal of brakes and I glanced in my mirror and saw a huge grille filling my rear window. I raised a hand and waved, which was the only thing I could think to do. A "sheesh, I'm sorry" kind of wave with no extended finger, but the driver either wasn't in a forgiving mood, or misinterpreted my gesture.

He started riding my ass for the next mile or so, coming to

within an inch or two of hitting my bumper. Hitting the horn, flashing his lights on and off.

I was scared shitless.

I tried speeding up to get away from him, but whenever I did, this asshole kept pace with me. The truck loomed so large in my mirror and rear window that I couldn't even see the windshield, or the guy behind the wheel. I flashed back, for a second, to that Spielberg movie, *Duel*, where Dennis Weaver is being pursued by the anonymous madman in an eighteen-wheeler.

The only thing I could do, I figured, was call the police. I reached for my cell, tucked into the inside pocket of my sport jacket, but as I pulled it out it slipped from my fingers and landed on the floor in front of the passenger seat.

"Shit!"

What if this nut had a gun? What if he started shooting? The only course of action was to keep driving. Maybe I'd see a cop I could flag down, or deliberately race past and encourage one to pursue me.

The truck pulled sharply into the other lane and roared past me. We were, at that moment, on a two-lane road with no oncoming traffic. As the huge truck zoomed by, I felt relieved. Okay, big man, show me how much horsepower you've got and I'll happily eat your dust if you leave me the fuck alone.

But suddenly he cut in front of me and hit the brakes, forcing me onto the shoulder. I jammed on my own brakes and steered onto the gravel, narrowly avoiding broadsiding the truck, or sliding under it, given how high it sat off the ground.

The guy was getting out. He was a Marvel superhero in street clothes. Tall, broad-shouldered, his head attached directly to his body without any discernible neck. Crew cut, shades, plaid shirt, jeans. He wasn't carrying a gun, but it didn't look as though he'd need one. He'd be able to shred me with his hands like I was made of crepe paper.

My window was already down, and I should have had the presence of mind to power it up, but instead, as he rounded the back of his truck, I put my hands up in a gesture of surrender and said, "Hey, I'm sorry, I'm an asshole, I didn't see you and—"

"You dumb fuck, where'd you get your license," he said, then reached into my car, grabbed me by my jacket, and started to pull, like he was going to drag me out right through the open window.

It all happened so fast.

There was a shadow behind my attacker. I was looking more or less into the sun, so I couldn't make him out clearly, and anyway, he was moving quickly. He had something in his hand, something long, and it whipped through the air, catching the pickup truck driver squarely in the back.

He let go of me, let out a "Fuck!" and started to spin around to see what the hell was going on, but before he'd turned all the way he took another blow, this one to the side of his head, and he went down like the sack of shit he was.

I blinked a couple of times and looked at the man who was still standing.

"Hi, son," said Dad. "Maybe you'd like to grab a coffee or something."

Fuck me," said Lana as I finished that part of the story. "How is that possible? He had to have been following you."

"He was," I said. "He'd come for another one of his occasional visits, but I was driving away from my place when he arrived, so he followed, waiting for the right moment when he could approach me. He was behind the pickup truck when I cut that guy off by accident, and he stayed on both of us. When he saw the guy force me off the road, he grabbed the baseball bat he always kept in the back of his car and saved my ass."

"What happened to the truck driver?" she asked.

"I guess he lived," I said. "There was never anything on the news about it. I drove past the spot later that afternoon and his truck was gone. Dad put him down but didn't kill him." I paused. "But that was just luck on the trucker's part. Dad wasn't even ruffled about it. I guess when you've done this sort of thing before . . ."

"Oh, my God," Lana said. "But this time, I mean, that asshole could have killed you."

I nodded. "Yeah."

"So did you go for a coffee?"

I smiled. "Something stronger."

We dragged my attacker over to his truck and propped him up against the front wheel.

"We need to call the police," I said. "He might be dead."

"He looks too big and stupid to die," Dad said.

I was less certain. "If he isn't dead, he probably needs to go to a hospital."

I glanced around, took in our surroundings. There was nothing on either side of the road but trees, and so far, there hadn't been any other cars passing by in either direction.

"Get in your car," he said. "Follow me."

Without another word, he headed back to his vehicle, parked on the shoulder about ten yards behind mine. A white Honda CR-V, one of those small crossover vehicles with, I noticed, a New Hampshire plate, the "Live Free or Die" state motto above the numbers.

I got into my car, backed up a few feet to get around the pickup, then got on the road behind Dad. I stayed on his tail, more focused on where he was going than where we actually were. Finally, after about fifteen minutes, he pulled off into a roadhouse parking lot. It was a bar and grill joint I'd never been to.

Dad was out of his car first, and was standing by my door when I got out.

"Hungry?" he said.

We went inside, took a table by the window.

"Scotch rocks," Dad said to the waitress when she came over. Before I could say anything, Dad added, "He'll have the same."

"Sure."

Dad grabbed two menus tucked behind the stainless-steel napkin dispenser and handed me one. I opened it and stared at the items without seeing them. Still numb from what had happened, I wasn't ready for food.

"It'll be okay," he said. "He was breathing when we left him. Guy like that has probably taken more hits to the head than he can remember. And when he does wake up, he's not going to call the cops because, first of all, he won't want to admit anyone got the drop on him, and second, if they ever found you, you'd tell them the guy was trying to kill you. No, he's not going to do anything. If anything, we taught him a good lesson about keeping a lid on his temper."

Dad smiled, reached over, and put his hand over mine. "Seriously."

I looked at his hand, felt its warmth. "If you say so," I said.

For the first time, I had a really good look at him. He looked well, color in his cheeks. A lot healthier-looking than when he'd visited me several years earlier at college. He'd clearly recovered nicely from that cancer operation. I asked him how he came to be in the right place at the right time.

His face softened. "Every once in a while, I have to know how you're doing. It's not complicated."

That, too, took my mind back to that college visit. His parting words had been that he'd be keeping an eye on me.

"You look good," I said.

"Never felt better."

"Where you working these days?"

He smiled coyly, like he knew I was pumping him for information. "Here and there," he said. "Get bored with one thing and try another."

"I noticed the New Hampshire plate," I said.

Dad smiled. "I'll bet you did."

He could, of course, be living elsewhere. I hadn't forgotten those extra license plates he had that first time he paid me a surprise visit.

"Any special woman in your life?" I asked.

He shook his head. "No. Once in a while, I meet someone, but things don't last. I think . . . I think if you're going to spend the rest of your life with someone, you need to be straight with them. They need to know who you really are. That's not something I want to share. You?"

"Her name's Lana."

"Nice name," he said. "Got a picture?"

I got out my phone and showed him one I had taken of her in one of the swan boats in the Public Garden.

"I remember when we used to go there," he said. "She's a pretty one. A keeper?"

"I guess we'll see."

"You told her?"

He didn't have to explain. "No," I said. "Not yet."

"It's not like with me. You didn't do anything bad, although I'd understand if there were things you felt ashamed about." His eyes seemed to dim.

When the drinks came, Dad downed his immediately and ordered another. I sipped mine. Hard liquor was never really my thing, although it did feel good going down and helped calm my nerves. We ordered some wings and fries, and when the food came we were just a guy and his dad having something to eat. Licking our fingers, trading stories.

It all felt strangely surreal. Having a meal with the man whose DNA I shared and yet I didn't know what name he went by.

When the waitress brought the check, I grabbed it before Dad could. I wondered whether I should have hesitated, waited to see whether he paid with cash or a card. If it had been the latter, I might have snatched it up to see what name was on it.

"I got this," I said. "Least I can do for saving my life."

I dug my wallet from my back pocket and set it on the table, opened it and pulled out my Visa.

"Jesus," Dad said, staring at the wallet. "Is that . . ."

I had been so used to carrying it all these years, I suppose, in that moment, I had forgotten who had given it to me and under what circumstances.

"Oh, yeah, it is," I said.

He held out a hand. "May I?"

I slid it across the table toward him, steering it around the basket of chicken-wing bones. He made a point of cleaning his fingers with the moist towelette before picking up the wallet, treating it like some rare artifact.

Dad held it between his palms, absorbing its energy. The wallet had become a talisman, empowering my father to go back to another time.

"I can't . . . I can't believe you still have it," he said, his eyes glistening. "Shit." After holding it for about fifteen seconds, he gave it back to me. "Let me buy you a new one."

"It does the job," I said offhandedly. I didn't want to get emotional here, awash in the aromas of Buffalo wings and fries.

"I hope I left you some money in it."

"Fifteen bucks," I said.

He shook his head. "Fifteen bucks. Some parting gift. God, what an asshole."

Once the bill was paid, we went back out to the parking lot and, in the moment before we parted, stood facing each other awkwardly.

"It was good to see you," he said.

"Thanks for showing up when you did. How many other times you been watching me?"

Dad smiled. "Maybe I'm always there."

I returned the smile. "Just might track you down."

"Good luck with that," he said.

"Maybe this time that plate's the real deal," I said, nodding my head toward his car. I had made a note of it, photographed it in my head.

That made him laugh. "Check it out. Be my guest."

And then he hugged me. I responded in kind. After the short embrace, he gave me another pat on the shoulder, laughed, and said, "Be sure to invite me to your wedding. Maybe this time I won't sneak out the back of the church."

He got in his car and drove away.

And now," I told Lana, "I think he's in trouble."

"How would you know?" Lana asked.

I got up from the couch and wandered over to the window again. Saw an Air Canada jet take off, climb sharply into the sky. I turned around slowly.

"You can't repeat what I'm about to tell you."

"Okay," she said, dragging out the word.

"I don't want to put you in a tough spot, given what you do for a living. It's not like I think you're going to broadcast what I'm about to say. But this *has* to be between us."

"Christ, Jack, if you're going to tell me, tell me and cut the shit."

"I'm working for the witness protection service."

Lana blinked. "Fuck me, you're not serious."

"I'm serious."

"Never saw that coming. But now, with everything else you've told me, I can see why they came to you."

"No, it's got nothing to do with my dad. They've hired me to write backstories for the people they're relocating. They didn't even know about my dad when they asked me to do this."

"You're kidding."

"No one was more surprised than my contact, Gwen. So I write these backstories. Well, back*story*. I've only done one. Someone with a new identity can't be telling their own life stories in detail because it could trip them up. I come up with a kind of character profile for them to learn and remember."

"Why you, if not because of your personal experience?"

"Some people in the program read my books, thought I'd be good at it. It's not just me, apparently. They have several writers doing this."

"No wonder you couldn't say anything."

"Seriously, you can't tell a soul about—"

She raised a hand. "Don't worry."

"But here's where it gets interesting," I said. "When I told Gwen about my dad, I asked if she could put us together. She didn't have to tell me where he is, or what his name is now, but I wanted to be able to talk to him."

"About?"

"Well, first off, I wanted to know if he was okay. What with the coronavirus, something might have happened to him. I haven't heard from him since the pandemic started."

"Okay. And why else?"

I paused for a few seconds. "Us," I said.

"Us?"

I nodded. "I wanted to tell him about you."

"Why did you want to tell him about me?"

I shrugged. "Gee, I don't know. Maybe that I love you like crazy and I want you to spend the rest of your life with me. Something along those lines. If you get my meaning."

The words hung out there for a moment. "Oh," she said.

"Sorry. That was a very roundabout way of bringing up something we haven't really talked about."

"I see."

"I was thinking maybe something more formal at a later date. But you know how sometimes you want to take someone home to meet your folks? I've got no home, and I don't have much in the way of folks, either. But he is my dad, and if I could find him, I'd like him to meet you."

Lana took a moment to gather her thoughts.

"It would seem to me," she said slowly, "that if this Gwen can set up a meeting, it might make sense for me to come along, too. Then you wouldn't have to tell him about me. *I* could tell him about me." She paused for a moment. "God, it feels sort of weird, meeting someone like your dad. I mean, you know. What he did and all."

"I know. I'd like to tell you there's more to him than that, and there is, but that's a hard climb. I get that."

"Still . . . if it could happen, yeah, I would like to go with you. I want . . . I want to know everything about you. Who you are and who *made* you what you are."

"But there's a problem."

Her eyebrows popped, as if to say *Another one?*

"He's not where he's supposed to be. He's disappeared."

"Aren't they supposed to keep track of—"

"Yeah, I know, I know. I've been through this."

I told her everything Gwen had told me. The various theories as to why my father might have disappeared, including the one that he'd gone back to doing what got him in trouble to begin with.

"So he could be dead," Lana said. "He could be on the run from someone looking to get even. He could have gone back to being a hit man."

"Yeah."

"You really want to reconnect if it's that last one?"

"I won't know till I talk to him."

"If your dad's really in trouble, if someone's *really* hunting for him, then you'll want to do what you can to help Gwen find him. But if he's gone back to being a hit man—God, I can't believe I'm even talking about this—then helping Gwen means helping to catch him."

"Yeah."

We both thought about that for a moment. Finally, Lana asked, "I don't suppose you remember that New Hampshire license plate?"

"I took a mental snapshot." I tapped my temple. "It's still up here. But he used lots of stolen plates."

Lana pursed her lips. "What if, just this once, it was the real one?"

I thought about that. "Gwen could track it."

"She doesn't *need* to. She already knows where he's *been*. She wants to know where he's *gone*. But wouldn't you like to at least know his name? Where he's been all this time? We could do a little end run around Gwen."

I smiled. "Okay."

Lana smiled. "Give me the plate. I know someone who might be able to help."

FORTY-TWO

The following morning, Lana left a message for Detective Florence Knight, asking her to call back when she had a moment. Her intentions were twofold. She wanted to know whether there had been any progress in the investigations of those two drownings, and she wanted Knight to check a New Hampshire plate number. Lana would say Knight owed her one for holding off writing a story speculating that the drownings might be homicides.

Lana had asked Jack to tell her as many details about the events surrounding his father's work for Galen Frohm as he could remember. The internet was in its infancy when his father disappeared, and his mother went to great lengths to hide newspapers that made any mention of his crimes. So it wasn't until a few years later that he was able to conduct online research on what his father had done, the names of the people whose lives he'd impacted. But some specifics had faded from his memory since then.

She also wanted to read all the material Jack had written about his father that he had passed on to Gwen. Maybe something there would jump out at her.

Around the time Michael Donohue was working for Frohm, and later cutting a deal to go into witness protection, Lana's paper was converting its files from actual clippings to a computerized library system. And in the intervening years, it had gone back, decade by decade, to bring the clipping files into the database. So all Lana had to do was get into the system and start doing searches. And reciprocal arrangements with other newspapers' systems allowed her to access their stories, too.

She started digging.

Michael Donohue had confessed to the killing of Abel Gartner, who ran a linen service that supplied all of Frohm's Sleep Tight Tonite motels in the greater Chicago area. He had been ordered to do it by Frohm. As part of his relocation deal, Donohue had admitted culpability in Gartner's death, which in turn helped build an even stronger case against Donohue's boss.

Gartner had two children. Twins, as it turned out, although not identical. A daughter, Valerie, and a son, Kyle. They were in their late teens when they lost their father, so they'd be in their early forties now.

Hmm, thought Lana.

She imagined how they must have felt at the time. The man who murdered their father wasn't given the death penalty. He wasn't sentenced to life in prison. His punishment amounted to a new, government-assigned identity and a new place to live.

How hard would that have been to swallow?

They had to be bitter about that. Sure, Frohm got what was coming to him. He ordered the hit. But still. You'd want to see something happen to the man who actually took your father's life.

Lana ran some Google searches on Valerie Gartner and Kyle Gartner. She got more results on Kyle, and she assumed it was the same Kyle, because he was the president and CEO of Gartner Linens. He'd taken over the family business. There were three business profiles on him in various trade publications over the years. Lana chuckled to herself. If Jack had gotten that job, maybe he'd have been editing *Linen Life*.

A search on Valerie Gartner brought in fewer results. But what she found was significant.

There was an op-ed piece from one of the Chicago papers, bylined Valerie Gartner, from twelve years ago. A testimonial about her personal struggle with drug addiction and alcoholism, how she'd come through dark times with the support of friends, family, Alcoholics Anonymous, and Narcotics Anonymous. And while the article did not get into the details of her father's death, it alluded to the devastation her family endured as a result of an act of violence. It was the trigger for the personal problems that had plagued her from that point on.

Then Lana came upon a more recent story, from a couple of months ago, in July, as well as an official death notice. The article on Valerie's passing highlighted her work on behalf of those struggling with addiction. Neither it nor the official obituary made any reference to how she had died. Lana bet that was because it was suicide or an overdose.

A series of possible events began to take shape in her mind that could explain why someone was seeking revenge against Jack's father after such a long time.

Kyle Gartner was grieving his twin sister. When she took her own life, he looked back at the singular event that triggered a life of addiction and depression. He knew who to blame for that.

The Gartners wouldn't be seeking revenge against Galen Frohm. He turned up in Lana's searches as one of the more famous—make that infamous—individuals who died during the pandemic.

That would leave Jack's father.

If there was anything to Lana's theory, it would have to mean Kyle had acquired details about Michael Donohue. The name he now lived under, his location. How the hell would someone get that? Lana had no idea, but she knew anything was possible. Could someone in the witness protection program have leaked it to him, figuring it was time the Gartners got justice?

And if she was right, had Kyle gone hunting for Michael Donohue himself? Hired someone to do it? Jack had told her he'd been shown a photo of a mystery man Gwen thought might be hunting his father. A big, formidable-looking guy. Online pictures of Kyle Gartner matched that description. Heavyset, thick-necked.

But seriously, was the CEO of a linen company a likely killer? It was only a theory, and maybe a weak one at that. But it was something. A place to start.

She did some more general reading about Galen Frohm and the things he'd done. The rampant tax fraud and tax evasion, blackmail and bribery, not to mention ordering hits on people. She was reading about his various convictions and the accompanying sentences that would see him spend the rest of his life behind bars when something jumped out at her. Two words.

A name.

"No fuckin' way," she whispered to herself.

FORTY-THREE

Jack

Gwen and I were on a park bench a few blocks from my apartment, Scorsese sitting behind the wheel of the black van on a nearby side street, scrolling through his phone. She was looking through the accounts of the times I had seen my father, ten pages I'd printed out for her.

"Interesting stuff," she said, taking a second scan through the pages.

"Anything there?" I asked.

We'd picked up two lattes in paper cups at a nearby café—Gwen paid—and I took a sip from mine, licking some foam off my upper lip.

Gwen sighed. "I won't lie. I was hoping for more."

"There must be something there," I said.

"If he's on the run and needs money, he's got experience from that window factory, and the printer and hardware store jobs," she mused. "He could look for work in another part of the country at places like that if he needs money." She shook her head. "Or he could rob a bank."

"He wouldn't do that."

Gwen gave me a pitying look. "He killed people, but a holdup, that's crossing a line. Can you think of anyone—*anyone*—he might seek out, other than you?"

"No. No one wants him found more than I do."

"Honestly? Maybe you're afraid we *will* find him if he's up to his old tricks."

I shook my head. "No."

"Maybe you need to approach this the way you're doing your work for us. Build a backstory for your father, drawing on what you know about him. But extrapolate. Imagine. Put things down you *feel* about your father but don't actually know for a fact. What about your father and women?"

"He didn't mention settling down with anyone."

"Doesn't have to be someone special. I'm not talking about a wife or a steady girlfriend. Maybe some friend with benefits. Come on, Jack. Your dad's got needs like any other man. Think."

"Like I said, he didn't mention anyone."

She tried a different angle. "These times your father appeared, was there any advance notice at all?"

"No, nothing. And there was never any real pattern. I think this is the longest I've gone, since he first left us, without having him show up."

"Well, if he does, hold on to him and notify us immediately. We'll set him up with another identity if need be, a new location. Assuming he's been behaving himself, of course. He's been given a pass on the crimes he committed back in the day, but not for any he might have done since."

"I get it."

"It's even possible, I suppose, that your father's not aware of any possible threat against him."

"Like from that guy in the picture."

She nodded. "Maybe your father chose to take off for some other reason, unrelated to the threat. Like he just wanted to get away. But we still need to warn him of a possible threat."

"Maybe you should go after that guy instead of worrying about where my dad is."

"There are people on that. It's not my department."

I felt exhausted and overwhelmed.

"What are you thinking?" she asked.

"I'm not big on the whole things-happen-for-a-reason bullshit. But for a while there, I was thinking you seeking me out fell into that category. That we connected so that I could see my dad again. But we're not getting anywhere."

"We just need a break, one little break," Gwen said. "Hang in there."

Shortly before I was going to order an Uber to take me to meet Lana at her latest favorite Italian restaurant in the North End—she had a new favorite about every three weeks—she called.

"Sorry. Can't make it."

Not unusual, given her job. The vice president was in town making a speech about infrastructure, and Lana had been assigned to it. The reporter who usually covered Washington-related stories was at the hospital expecting to become a father at any moment, so Lana was pressed into service.

"But look," she said, "I've found out some interesting things. They may not mean anything, but who knows, right?"

"Like?" I asked.

"We shouldn't really talk about this on the phone, am I right?"

She was right. I said, "What about after the speech? You want me to come to your place?"

"I've got an early-morning assignment, so I've only got about six hours between the time I get home and when I have to head out again, so—"

"Say no more," I said. "We'll talk tomorrow. Love—"

Lana was gone before I could say "you."

So instead of heading downtown I popped into a local sub shop and brought home a sandwich. Washed it down with a beer.

Around nine thirty, I turned on the TV and found a *Law &
Order* to put on in the background while I scrolled through various
news sites on my phone. I jumped from *HuffPost* to the *New York
Times* to the *Daily Beast* to CNN, giving anything that caught my
attention a good thirty seconds of my time.

Finally feeling the eyestrain, I tossed the phone onto the couch
next to me, settled my head back into the cushion, put my feet up
on the coffee table, and allowed myself to be entertained by the
show. I had clearly landed on one of the later seasons. Lennie was
long gone. The detectives on this night were Green and Lupo,
and they were trying to track down who'd shot someone in Central Park. Now they were interviewing a friend of the deceased,
a waiter in a SoHo restaurant.

I swung my feet off the coffee table and sat up straight, suddenly
awakened from my stupor.

"Can't be," I said.

The scene lasted no more than half a minute. The detectives had
departed the restaurant and were walking down a SoHo street.
The show wasn't streaming, and it wasn't on a DVD, so I couldn't
immediately pause it and rewind to get another look at what had
caught my attention.

I called up the guide to get more information on the episode,
found the title, then searched to see which of the countless video-
on-demand services had it in its repertoire. I found the episode
and hit play.

Then I fast-forwarded until I got to the part where the detectives
were interviewing that waiter, and froze the image.

Studied it. Looked at the actor. He seemed familiar to me.

I picked up my phone, brought up the IMDb app, which told you
everything in the world you could possibly want to know about
every movie and TV show ever made, went to *Law & Order*, and
found details about this particular episode. I scrolled down to
information about the cast, including who played all the bit parts.

I hadn't taken note of the name of the waiter, but I found a small, thumbnail headshot of the actor I thought had played him. The character's name was Del Rizzo, and he had been played by an actor named Garth Walton. I went to his page to find more pictures of him and a listing of his roles.

He hadn't done much, and he certainly hadn't done much in the last decade. One of a million actors who'd hoped that a bit part on a network show would lead to something bigger, only to have those dreams dashed. Maybe, given that the show was shot in New York, he'd had more of a stage career. Broadway and off-Broadway stuff.

I supposed there were other sites I could check to learn more, but for now I felt I had learned as much as I needed to know from online entertainment sites about Garth Walton.

Or, as I knew him, Bill.

FORTY-FOUR

The vice president's speech was a bust. Oh, she was there, and she spoke, but she didn't say anything that anyone would have expected her not to say, and she did not make herself available for questions after, but was whisked away in a bulletproof limo and escorted by about thirty cars back to her vice presidential jet, which was warming up on the tarmac at Logan. There wasn't even a respectable protest outside the venue, as one might have expected, which was either a good thing or a bad thing, Lana decided, depending on how you looked at it. A protest would at least have meant the current administration was doing something that upset some people, because when you were upsetting one constituency, you could sure as shit bet you were making a different constituency very happy. Such was the nature of politics. And not only was there no protest, the audience reaction was relatively muted. Polite applause, maybe a third of the audience on their feet. If you couldn't get people riled up, you probably couldn't get them excited about you, either.

Lana found a seat in the hotel lobby and filed a quick story to the newsroom from her laptop, then hoofed it home, since the speech was delivered at a hotel within a few blocks of her place. It was only in the moments before she fell asleep that she gave even a moment's thought to what more she might be able to learn about Jack's father.

God, and I thought my family was weird, she thought. Next to Jack's parents, her father's obsession with tinplate toys from the early 1900s and her mother's occasional manic baking episodes where she'd spend five days in the kitchen making bread and then taking it all to the park to feed pigeons seemed trivial. At least neither of her parents had killed anyone or taken on a new identity.

She was up early the next day to cover the first court appearance of a woman who had lost her daughter in a mass shooting and was charged with setting fire to a firearms retailer. Gun rights advocates wanted her jailed, while the gun control faction had turned her into a hero.

The case was getting underway when Lana sensed a vibration from her purse. She reached in for her phone and saw that Florence Knight was calling her.

"Shit," Lana said under her breath.

She discreetly slipped out of her seat and exited the courtroom, tapping the phone and whispering, "Hang on." Once the courtroom door had closed behind her, Lana was able to speak in a normal voice.

"I was in court," she explained.

Knight was not the least bit interested in why. "I ran that New Hampshire plate."

"Fantastic," Lana said.

"What's this about?"

"Just something I'm checking out."

A sigh. "We still have a deal on that other matter?"

"Yes," Lana said. "But you know how it works. If this breaks somewhere else, I've got no choice but to run with it. And I was doing some digging on another story and stumbled on something that might be a lead for you."

"I'm listening."

"Your dead judge was the one who sentenced Galen Frohm

years ago. It was a big case back in the late nineties. Big CEO type. Owned motel and fast-food chains and dollar stores. Got one of his people to commit a few murders."

"Tell me something I don't know," she said. "Willard Bentley was the judge in hundreds of high-profile cases, including a couple of terrorism ones. We're looking at those. This might be some kind of payback thing." She paused. *"That* was off the record."

"Understood," Lana said, feeling deflated. She thought she'd been onto something with the Frohm connection. "The plate?"

"It's registered to—"

Lana, without a pen in her hand, said, "Can you email it or text it—"

"Yeah, that's what I want. A digital trail of me helping you. And Lana, swear to God, if you're recording this, I will never—"

"I'm not."

"So pay attention." Knight gave her a name and an address. Once. And ended the call.

Lana didn't even have time for some mental profanity. She was repeating the information in her head, over and over. She immediately created an unaddressed email message—she'd send it to herself in a minute—and tapped out with her thumb what Knight had told her, so quickly that she made several typos. She made her corrections, looked it over, hoped she'd gotten it right, then sent the message to her own email address.

She went back into the courtroom, hoping she hadn't missed much.

FORTY-FIVE

Jack

"We need to talk," I said to Gwen when I called her on the cell she had supplied me.

"About?" she asked.

"I don't know that this is something you want me to discuss on the phone."

She paused, then said, "Give me a hint, Jack."

"It's about Bill."

"What about Bill?" She sounded very much on edge.

"I saw him on TV. A *Law & Order* episode. He was a waiter. I looked him up, found his profile online. His name is—"

"Jack. Stop."

"Okay, sorry, but—"

"Jack!" Gwen snapped. "Shut up."

I shut up.

"Where are you?" she asked.

"Home."

"Are you alone?"

"Yes, I'm alone."

"Listen carefully. Go to the window. See if there's anyone out there."

"What?"

"Be discreet about it. A peek. Don't, whatever you do, stand right in the line of fire."

"The line of—"

"Just look."

I started crossing the room, my heart starting to beat a little more quickly. "Do you want me to call you back and—"

"Now, for fuck's sake! Look *now*."

I went to the window, pulled the curtain back from the edge, and furtively checked out the street. There were several cars parked out there, all empty. A red pickup drove past going one way, an old Corvette rumbled by in the opposite direction. There was no one standing there watching my place. Certainly no one sitting in a sports car, having a smoke, keeping an eye on my window.

"I don't see anything suspicious," I told her.

"Just because you can't see them doesn't mean they're not there," she said.

I was starting to feel very nervous. "What the hell is going on?"

"I'm five minutes out. Look for a white Impala. Be watching. Until I get there, don't leave. If someone comes to the door, don't answer it. And lock your door."

"Jesus Christ, you're freaking me out."

"Good. Then maybe you won't do anything stupid. When you see me pull up out front, get in the car as quickly as you can. Understood?"

"Can you give me some kind of fucking hint what the hell is going on?"

There was a pause at the other end while Gwen debated what to tell me. For a moment, I thought maybe the call had dropped out.

But then she was back.

She said, "Bill's dead."

FORTY-SIX

"*I don't think you'll be gone forever.*"
  "*You shouldn't get your hopes up that I'll be back.*"
  "*Will you miss me?*"
"*I already miss you so much it hurts.*"
"*That's why I think you'll come back.*"
"*Go to sleep.*"
"*I'm going to dream about you coming back. Dreams can come true.*"
"*Shh.*"
"*Can't you at least come and visit?*"
"*I think they have rules against that sort of thing. But maybe you can come visit me.*"
"*Can't you just tell them you're sorry?*"
"*I wish it was that easy.*"

FORTY-SEVEN

Jack

When I saw a white Impala come to a stop on the street, I fled the apartment, running down the stairs like the place was on fire. I came tearing out of the building, glancing both ways as I ran to the car, and jumped into the passenger side.

Gwen hit the gas, tires squealing.

"What's happening?" I shouted. "Is someone after me? Am I in some kind of danger?"

She had her eyes on the road ahead, not looking my way at all as she spoke. "I don't know. I'm waiting to hear. But I wanted to get you out of there for now."

"And Bill's dead?"

She kept her foot on the gas, running through the tail end of a yellow light. She came to a stop sign, turned right, drove a few blocks, then made another right, then a left two blocks after that.

"What the fuck are you doing?"

Gwen was glancing repeatedly in her rearview mirror. "I want to be sure."

"Sure of *what*? That we're not being followed? Who the hell would follow a U.S. marshal?"

She grinned. "You'd be surprised." She eased up on the gas. "Okay, I think we're okay for now."

Gwen wheeled into a supermarket lot, drove around to the back, where the loading docks were, and parked half behind a huge dumpster. She killed the engine, got out her phone, and entered a number. She waited a few seconds, said, "We're good," to somebody, then put her phone down and, taking a few deep breaths, turned to look at me.

"You okay?" she asked.

"No!" I said. "I am not even close to fucking okay."

She raised a palm. "All right, let me try to bring you up to speed. About Bill . . ."

"He's really dead?"

Gwen nodded. "At the cabin. We had someone check in on him this morning. He wasn't answering calls or responding to texts. Wouldn't come to the door when we got there. We had to break in. Found him in the bathroom, in the tub."

I had a brief mental image of Bill—or Garth Walton, as I now knew him to be—in bloody water, having slashed his wrists.

"Killed himself?"

Gwen shook her head. "I wish."

"You *wish*?"

"Sorry, bad choice of words. But yeah, I *do* wish. Because then it would mean we hadn't fucked up. It would mean those sick bastards he testified against hadn't found him. It would mean that there's not a leak in our department, or that someone had hacked into our files. It would mean it wasn't our goddamn fault. Someone made him sit in that tub and then blew his head off."

I felt my heart in my mouth. "Fuck no." I wondered whether I was going to be sick.

"So when you called asking about him . . . have you talked to *anyone* about going to see him?"

"Of course not," I said.

Which wasn't true.

I'd told Lana. But there was no way—*no way*—that she could have let anyone know, not even inadvertently, about my going to see Bill. And besides, even if I had, and someone had been listening in, I didn't know where Bill was. I'd been blindfolded on the way there and back.

"This is a fucking nuclear bomb," she said. She took a moment to collect her thoughts, then finally turned and said to me, "So you know he was an actor."

"Garth Walton," I said.

"Yeah. He'd gotten a few acting jobs. But they were few and far between, so he turned to other ways to make money. Like drugs and stolen property, and that brought him into contact with some badass Russians. Hard to get an acting job when you're busy transporting fentanyl to Florida. You remember how much he talked about TV when we had lunch with him?"

I remembered. "Sure, yeah."

"What? Did you think there was something fishy going on because you saw him on a TV show?"

"I . . . I guess I did. But you're right. Everybody has to have done something. And he used to act. Do you think it was the Russians that got to him?"

"Most likely," Gwen said.

"Why'd you rush me out of the house? Am I being watched?"

She let out a long breath. "I hope not. I don't, as of this moment, see any way for someone to connect you to Bill, but it's better right now to play it safe. Hope for the best, prepare for the worst kind of thing. And I don't want to freak you out even further, but we need to consider that someone is very possibly looking for your father. They might be watching you, thinking maybe he'll contact you. In person. Which would actually save us all a lot of trouble, but might expose you to risk at the same time."

"Consider me freaked. Had Walton already testified, or were you keeping an eye on him until such time as he did?"

"He was done. We were sorting out the last details about where to place him."

"So they didn't kill him to stop him from telling what he knows. They killed him to make a point," I said. "A warning to others."

Gwen nodded absently. She was still thinking.

"What?" I asked.

"I'm making a list in my head. People who knew where we were keeping Bill."

"What about Scorsese?" I said.

Gwen shot me a puzzled look. "Who?" She'd forgotten that I'd referred to her driver by that name before.

"Sorry," I said. "Private joke. Your driver. He reminds me of half a dozen characters from any Martin Scorsese mob picture."

"Oh, no way," she said, waving her hand dismissively. "Cayden's totally trustworthy."

FORTY-EIGHT

Kyle Gartner was packing his bags.

"How long are you actually going to be gone?" asked his wife, Cecilia, walking into the bedroom. "You usually just do carry-on."

Shit, he thought, looking at the oversized bag he was loading with socks and underwear and shirts and an extra pair of shoes.

"There might be a couple of meetings where I need a suit," he said.

"You want some help? Anything you need me to press?"

"No," he snapped. He softened his voice. "Thank you, but no, it's okay. If I need anything touched up I can have it sent out."

"So you're back Wednesday?" she asked.

"Yes," he said. "Wednesday."

He did not expect to be back on Wednesday. Or Thursday, or Friday, not even the following Wednesday. With his back to his wife, he ran his hand inside one of the pockets in the carry-on bag. Felt the bundles of cash. The extra passport that he would use later. The other phone, which he would start using in a day or so. He'd keep using his regular one until everything was underway.

Cecilia crossed her arms and remained standing in the doorway.

"What's going on with you?" she asked.

"What are you talking about?" he said, still not looking at her.

"There's something you're not telling me."

Where would he even begin?

He took another shirt out of a dresser and set it in the larger bag. "That's ridiculous," he said.

"I know your sister's death hit you hard, that she's been on your mind," his wife said. "But this goes back to before that. You haven't been yourself."

He turned to face her and grinned. "Who have I been, then?"

She stood there, her eyes moistening. "I don't feel like I know you anymore. I talk to you and it's like you're on the moon."

"I've had a lot on my mind."

"I know you've stopped loving me."

"Stop it," he said. "Just stop it. That's crazy talk."

Not so crazy.

He crossed the room and pulled her into his arms. "You mean the world to me," he said. Cecilia's arms hung limply at her sides. Kyle stepped back, rested his hands on her shoulders. "When I get back, we'll do something special."

She looked him in the eye. "Is it another woman?"

Kyle couldn't help but laugh. "Another woman," he said, shaking his head. "Christ, where would you get a crazy idea like that?"

"These late-night calls you've been making. Hiding in your office, whispering. I know something's going on."

"I swear to you, nothing is going on. It's business. We've had some trouble with immigration officials. The less you know about that, the better. I'm protecting you."

She did not look convinced.

He glanced at his watch. "The car's coming for me." He went back to the bed, zipped up the two bags, put on his sport jacket, wheeled the bags out of the room, and carried them down the stairs.

His daughter, Cherie, was standing there.

"Two bags?" she said. "I thought you always did carry-on."

Kyle sighed. "I already went through this with your mother." He opened the front door to see whether his ride was there. A black four-door Lexus was parked at the curb. A man got out from behind the wheel, popped the trunk, and approached.

"Take your bags, sir?"

"Yeah," Kyle said offhandedly, going out onto the front step. The man grabbed the bags as Kyle gave his wife and daughter an awkward smile.

He wanted to hug them but couldn't bring himself to do it.

"So," he said.

This is it, he told himself. You get in that car and you're committed. The plan goes forward. No turning back.

"See ya, Dad," Cherie said. "Have a fun trip." She spun around and went upstairs.

Kyle gave his wife one last smile. "Goodbye," he said.

"Goodbye," she said.

FORTY-NINE

Jack

"Is it safe for me to go home?" I asked Gwen.

"Probably," she said.

That was not the answer I was looking for.

She picked up on my anxiety. "Look, we'll be keeping an eye on your place. Have the cops drive by regularly. And if you notice anything, call me. I, or someone, can be there in minutes. Just don't do anything stupid. Keep your door locked. Don't let in anyone you don't know."

She brought the car to a stop in front of my apartment building.

"I can't see that anyone has any real reason to want to hurt you, Jack. If Bill—excuse me, Garth—were still alive, someone might have come after you to try to find out where we were hiding him. But there's not much point to that now. And as far as your father goes, I don't know what to tell you. If you have some new ideas about where he might be, or if he gets in touch, you know what to do."

"Understood."

I got out of the car and went up to my apartment. Once I had the door open, I stood there, listening. What if someone was inside, waiting for me? I held my breath, and would have stopped the hammering of my heart, too, if I could have, if it meant I'd have a better chance at hearing an uninvited guest.

"Hello?" I said. "Anyone here?"

Which, of course, will always draw out a killer who's hiding in the bathroom.

Reasonably confident that I was alone, I stepped in and closed the door behind me. I did a quick check of the place, glancing in the bedroom and the closet, as well as the bathroom and behind the shower curtain.

I concluded that my apartment was assassin-free.

I grabbed a beer from the fridge and paced the apartment while I drank it. Kept going to the window, looking at everyone that walked by, studying them in a way I never had before. Was that woman jogging by a cop? Was the homeless guy begging for change actually an undercover police officer? How about that elderly man walking his French bulldog? Was he watching for my father? Would he be calling that menacing-looking guy in Gwen's phone if he saw my father turn up?

A few minutes before five I heard someone coming up the stairs. My heart started pounding. I glanced at the door to make sure I'd turned the dead bolt and put on the chain. Seconds later, there was a knock.

Why, I asked myself at that moment, had I never installed a peephole?

"Who is it?" I shouted through the door.

"It's me!"

Lana.

I turned back the dead bolt and opened the door five inches, the chain taut across the gap. It was Lana all right, balancing a pizza box on her palm and holding a bottle of red wine with her other hand, her purse slung over her shoulder.

"Let me in," she said. "I brought dinner."

I closed the door, took off the chain, and admitted her, taking the pizza and setting it on the kitchen counter.

"What's with the Fort Knox routine?" she asked.

"It's nothing," I said.

She set down the wine, quickly put her arms around me, and put her lips on mine.

"Have I got news for you," she said.

"Same," I said.

"What?"

"You go first," I said.

"Okay, but get some plates," she said. "I'm starving."

She opened the box and the wine as I went for plates and glasses. She filled two of them, handed me one, and said, "Don't overdo it. I think you might be going for a drive tonight."

"What are you talking about?"

Lana grabbed a slice, bit off a chunk from the point, and tossed it onto her plate.

"Okay, let me start with the small stuff."

"Small stuff?"

"I have a theory about who might be going after your father."

If that was the small stuff, I wondered what the big news would be.

She told me about Abel Gartner's twins. The son who now ran the linen company, and the daughter who'd recently died. Suggestions that they never got over the tragic loss of their father.

"How's that for a motive?" she asked. "He blames your father for ruining their lives."

"He *did* ruin their lives."

"And it explains why *now*, after all this time. Because the daughter died recently. He'd have had to get some intel on your dad, and I don't know how he'd have done it, but it strikes me as a possibility. I'm trying to think of some kind of angle, maybe an interview with him, a 'look back' kind of story. See what the son has to say."

"It's a possibility," I said.

"You don't look convinced."

"No, you're right, it's a possibility. Probably one of many."

She looked annoyed that I wasn't as excited as she was. "Okay, I've got more."

"Listening."

"I don't know if this means anything, but that judge who went missing and they found in the harbor? He's the one who sent Galen Frohm away, based on your dad's deal."

"That's why the name rang a bell," I said. "Willard Bentley."

"Right."

"Yeah, but if he just drowned, what does that have to do with—"

"It might not have been a simple drowning."

"How do you—"

"Later," she said, cutting me off. "Okay, so, here's the biggie."

I waited.

"I got a lead on that plate. If it's your dad's, and not a stolen one, then I've found him. Or at least found where he would have been before he disappeared."

"No way," I said.

She smiled smugly. She went for her purse and brought out a piece of paper.

"Here you go."

Written on it was this:

Frank Dutton
Trailwind Acres Unit 12
Southbend Rd.
Gilford New Hampshire

"It's a trailer park," she said. "Or a mobile home community, if you want to be politically correct."

I had my phone out and was looking to see where Gilford was. "It's about a two-hour drive."

I sat at the table and went to work on the laptop that was connected to the net. I put the name into the Google search field and got, not surprisingly, a few hundred Frank Duttons, so then I added New Hampshire, and while that thinned things out some, it didn't turn up anything useful. I checked to see whether anyone by that name, in that location, was on Facebook or any other social media sites and struck out.

"I doubt your dad would have much of an online presence," Lana said.

"True." I cleared the search history and closed the laptop.

"What are you going to do?" Lana asked. "Tell Gwen?"

I thought about that. "I could. But I don't know. I mean, if this guy is my dad, she already knows that and knows where he's supposed to be living. And she's kind of on overload at the moment."

I told her about the murder of her witness, and Gwen's urgent reaction to it.

"That explains the chain on the door," Lana said.

There was another, bigger reason for not telling Gwen I had a possible lead on my father. She'd want to know where I got it. And then she'd know I'd disclosed to Lana what I had been doing for her.

She wouldn't be very happy about that. Especially when she was worried about a possible leak.

I'd finished one slice and was reaching for another. "Is there really any point in going up there? If it's not him, it's a total waste of time. And if it is, we already know he's not there."

"I don't think you'll know that till you go. I mean, seeing where he's been living, assuming it's him, might spark some idea about where he's disappeared to."

She was right. I had to know. I was going to go to New Hampshire.

"Would you come with me?"

"I can't," Lana said. "I mean, I'm swamped. If I were actually going to *meet* him, yeah, I'd come. But this is more of an exploratory mission."

"True." I looked at my watch. If the traffic wasn't too bad, I was betting I could be in Gilford before eight o'clock. And if the whole thing turned out to be a dead end, I could turn around and come home. Be back in my bed by midnight.

But just in case . . .

"I think I'll throw a couple of things in a bag," I said. "You mind wrapping up the rest of that pizza? Think I'll eat it on the way. Oh, and—"

There was one other problem. I didn't have a car.

Lana had already taken out her pepper-spray key chain and was prying her car key off it. "Yes, you can borrow my Beemer. Just don't fuck up the gears. Have you ever even driven a stick?"

FIFTY

Cayden pulled the buds out of his ears.

This, he thought to himself, was what you called a *development*.

So Jack Givins and whoever this woman was had a possible lead on the name and an address for the man who was once known as Michael Donohue. What was so goddamn frustrating was that while it was clear they had the information, neither of them had spoken it out loud.

The woman, he surmised, had displayed the details to Givins. Maybe it was on her phone, or possibly she'd written it down on a slip of paper. Wherever the location was, Givins had said it was about a two-hour drive.

Cayden brought up a map on his computer. A two-hour drive. Well, that could be any one of a thousand places. Too bad this wasn't one of those times when he'd been staking out Givins's apartment. He could have followed him. But he didn't think he could get there before Jack departed.

Shit.

So where the hell was Jack going, and how was Cayden going to find out?

First, he had to report in. He picked up his cell and entered a number.

"I think he's found him," he said to the person who picked up.

"How?" said the voice at the other end.

"Not sure. Something to do with a license plate. Looks like his girlfriend helped piece it together."

"Girlfriend?"

"She came by, figured out some shit. And now he's heading there."

"Is the girl still at his place?"

"Didn't sound like either of them were going to be there much longer."

"You should have been watching."

"There's just one of me, in case you hadn't noticed. But I got another idea how to find out who she is, anyway."

"Do it."

The line went dead. He entered another number into the phone.

"Yes?"

"Earl?"

"Yes?"

"It's me, Earl."

A pause at the other end.

"Oh," Earl said resignedly. "What do you want?"

"That little bug you planted paid off."

"That's . . . that's great," Earl said.

"But there's something I need to know. This lady friend of your stepson. Who is she?"

"Why? Why do you have to know something like that?"

Cayden sighed. "Earl."

It was all he needed to say. After a long pause, Earl cleared his throat and spoke. "Her name's Lana. She's a reporter."

"A reporter for who?"

"The *Star*. Lana Wilshire. What do you want with her?"

"She knows something."

"Knows what?"

"Not your concern, Earl. You know where she lives?"

"No. I swear."

No problem, Cayden thought. He would find her.

FIFTY-ONE

Lana saw Jack to her car and watched as he drove off around the corner. Just before they locked up the apartment she had ordered an Uber to take her back to her place, and within half an hour she was perched on a stool at her kitchen island, looking on her laptop for more information about Kyle Gartner, son of Abel, brother of Valerie.

She reread the article Valerie had written about her addiction struggles, then the piece that came out after she had died. The stories she'd found earlier on Kyle explored the challenges he had faced in assuming the top position at the company his father had run before his murder.

She went looking for contact information for him, starting with online white page directories for Chicago and environs. Took her about ten minutes to find a Kyle Gartner in Highland Park.

There was the phone number. All she had to do was pick up the cell sitting next to the laptop and call the man.

But what the hell was she going to say?

"Good evening, Mr. Gartner. By any chance are you, or someone you've hired, hunting for Michael Donohue and planning to kill him?"

Clearly, not a productive approach.

She concluded she had to go at this not as Jack's girlfriend, but as the reporter she was, looking to write a story. A follow-up to his father's murder. The man who'd ordered it had recently died from the coronavirus. Did Galen Frohm's death have any emotional impact? Had justice finally arrived, but in the most unexpected way?

That could work. She'd start that way and see where things went. Lana didn't expect the man to confess to anything, but she might be able to discern something from his tone, from how he reacted to her questions. She picked up the cell, entered the number. One ring, then two, then three, and then—

"Hello?"

A woman's voice. A *young* woman's voice.

"Hello," Lana said. "Could I speak to Kyle Gartner, please?"

"He's not here. Can I take a message?"

"Who am I speaking to?"

"This is his daughter, Cherie."

"Hi, Cherie. My name is Lana Wilshire. I'm with the *Boston Star*, working on a story, and I was looking for a comment from your father."

"What kind of story?" she asked.

"That's something I would want to discuss with him."

"Well, like I said, he's not here."

"When are you expecting him to return?"

Cherie was slow to reply. "I'm not really sure."

"What if I called back in an hour?"

"He won't be here then, either."

From a distance, Lana heard someone ask, "Who is it?"

"Someone for Dad," Cherie said, her voice fading as she turned away from the phone.

"Take a message," instructed the other person, who Lana was guessing was the girl's mother.

"Can I take a message?" she asked Lana.

"Do you have a number where I can reach him?"

"Uh, well . . . I don't know the number of the hotel."

"So he's out of town?"

"Yeah."

"I feel it would be a disservice to your father to not include a comment from him in this story."

That did the trick. Cherie provided a cell-phone number. Lana typed it with one finger onto her computer screen, thanked Kyle Gartner's daughter, and ended the call.

She entered the new number within seconds. She wanted to catch him before the daughter phoned or texted to warn him some reporter was looking for him.

The phone rang four times before someone picked up.

"Hello?"

"Mr. Gartner?"

"Yes?"

"This is Lana Wilshire from the *Boston Star* calling. How are you doing this evening?"

"What's this about?"

"I wonder if you might have a moment to help me with a story I'm working on."

"How did you get this number?"

The man sounded very alarmed that Lana had found him.

"I called your home first and they helped me get in touch with you. I understand you're not in Chicago right now?"

Kyle said nothing.

"Mr. Gartner? Are you there?"

"I'm here."

"Are you on a business trip?"

"What's this about?" he asked again.

"Mr. Gartner, I'm doing a story on some of the people who have succumbed to the virus over the last couple of years, and—"

"We're fine," he snapped. "I had a second cousin who died, but no immediate family. And my wife's aunt, she caught it but she came through okay. And we have followed all the necessary protocols in our businesses. The rate of infection in our work-places was less than that in the general population, so I don't know why you would be—"

"As I was saying, we've been looking at a few of the more well-known people who died in the Boston area, and that list included some individuals who won't likely be missed. One of them was Galen Frohm."

Silence at the other end.

"I would imagine that's a name you haven't forgotten," Lana said.

"No. It's not." A pause. "What do you want, exactly?"

"I was wondering whether Frohm's passing, however it came about, offered any final sense of justice? I would imagine that losing your father so tragically is something one never really gets over."

"That son of a bitch," Kyle said. "God, I hope he suffered."

"I get the sense it took a toll on your sister." Lana felt herself venturing out onto thin ice.

"How could you . . . how could you know about Valerie?"

"When I was researching Frohm online, it led me to your father, and that search led to your sister. I'm sorry for your loss. It was relatively recent, I gather."

"Who did you say you were again?" he asked. Lana told him. He went quiet for a moment, and then said, "Frohm could die a hundred deaths and it still wouldn't be justice."

"Because?"

"The man who killed our father was allowed to walk away, to live his life. He never paid for what he did."

"Michael Donohue."

"Yes. If you've done your research, you know who he is."

"I do."

"What kind of justice is there when a piece of shit like that gets off? And you can put that in your fucking paper, word for word. He killed my father, and he killed my sister, too."

"I can't imagine how you deal with something like that," Lana said sympathetically. It was no act. It was sinking in, talking to this man, how much grief her boyfriend's father had caused. If this Kyle Gartner, or someone working on his behalf, was looking for Jack's dad so that he could exact revenge, could anyone blame him? Wouldn't Michael Donohue be getting what he'd always deserved?

"Yeah, it's hard to take," Kyle said.

"Do you think you'll ever get some measure of justice? And at this late date, would it even matter?"

Another long pause.

Finally, Kyle said, "I don't know. Maybe one day I'll find out."

Lana wanted to ask him flat out: Was he looking for Jack's dad? Had he already found him once in New Hampshire? Was that why Michael Donohue had disappeared? Had there already been a failed attempt on his life, and Kyle Gartner, or someone in his employ, was still in pursuit?

Was it possible Kyle was on his trail right now?

"Mr. Gartner," Lana said, "where did you say you are again?"

But Kyle Gartner was gone.

FIFTY-TWO

Jack

L ana owned a black BMW 3-series, with a manual transmission, that was more than two decades old. When Lana was in her late teens, her family had lived for three years in Berlin while her father, a banking exec, was posted over there. It was during that period that she learned to drive, and the car she'd had available to her had a stick. She hadn't owned an automatic-transmission vehicle since.

Fortunately, I, too, could drive a stick. In college, I learned on the Honda of a friend, who I often had to drive back to the dorm when he was too hammered to get behind the wheel.

I would have enjoyed the use of Lana's car more if I wasn't so preoccupied with what I might encounter in Gilford. This trip might prove pointless, but sometimes, when you have one option available to you, that's the one you go with.

Was my father Frank Dutton? Maybe. And if he was, I was hoping I might find some lead that I could pass on to Gwen, and, at that point, endure her fury at not bringing her into the loop from the beginning.

As I thought about her, it occurred to me that in my rush to hit the road, I had grabbed only my own phone, not the one Gwen had given me. At least I'd remembered to take a slice of pizza.

Whatever I might find out and want to pass on to her would have to wait until I returned.

Given this Beemer's age, it didn't have a built-in navigation system, so I used my phone for directions to Gilford generally, and the Trailwind Acres trailer park specifically. It took some time to get out of the city, but once I was on I-93 I was moving above the speed limit and watching my rearview for cops. This was a toll road that would take me through Manchester and Concord, but I figured I could save thirty minutes by not taking secondary roads.

I had more on my mind than my father. I knew telling Lana about him had been the right thing to do, but I worried whether it would change things between us. Maybe she wouldn't want to be with a guy whose father had done such terrible things. I guessed time would tell.

My phone, sitting on the seat beside me, rang. It was illegal in Massachusetts to talk on a handheld device while driving, and I was betting the same was true of New Hampshire, but what can I say? I'm a rebel. I saw the call was from Lana.

"Hey," I said.

"Just talked to Kyle Gartner."

"And?"

"And . . . I don't know. He was pretty on edge. He's not in Chicago and wouldn't tell me where he is. But he sure hasn't forgotten what your father did."

"What's your gut say?"

"My gut doesn't know, but he sure strikes me as a guy who's got a score to settle. It's not much, but I wanted to bring you up to speed."

"Thanks."

"Where are you?"

"Twenty minutes to half an hour out, I think. Only jammed the gears a couple of times."

"Don't even joke."

"I love you."

"Right back atya."

My route was going to take me around to the north side of Gilford. I found Southbend Road, a paved two-lane stretch, outside the town proper. If my phone was right, the trailer park was about a mile ahead, on the right. The houses were well spaced out, and the numbers hard to find, especially now that it was dark.

The woods opened up, and illuminated under two bright streetlights was a sign that said TRAILWIND ACRES. I hit the blinker, slowed down, and turned in.

The park consisted of one street about three hundred feet long with a broad, paved apron at the end for turning around. Lining both sides, front ends to the road, were about thirty mobile homes, all placed on an angle, with space between them for cars and covered patios. As best I could tell from the glare of the Beemer's headlights, this was a well-kept neighborhood. Many of the units were adorned with small gardens and plenty of kitschy accoutrements, like garden gnomes and pinwheels.

I drove slowly, looking for unit 12. The even-numbered residences were on the left side. I had unit 11 to my right and looked across the grassy median that ran down the center of the road and spotted a "12" under the front bay window of a trailer clad in pinkish aluminum siding. I went down to the end of the road, made the turn, then came to a stop out front of the residence of one Frank Dutton.

I felt a hammering in my chest.

The lights were on inside the trailer, and there was a light over the front door, which was, of course, as with all mobile homes, on the side.

Lights on would suggest someone was home, and not on the run. And there was a car sitting in the slot between this trailer and the next one. A silver Chevy, and attached to the back, the license plate I had seen on the car my father had been driving. If my father had changed vehicles since our last encounter, he could have taken the plate to the new one.

I got out of the car, went to the front door, and knocked. I could hear muffled footsteps inside, and then the door opened.

It was a woman. Late sixties, early seventies, I figured. Short, plump, silver-haired, and looking at me through a pair of wire-rimmed glasses.

And I thought: Shit.

If the man who lived here *was* my father, then who was this? A wife he'd never mentioned? A girlfriend? And if she was someone special to my father, how much did she know about him? Did she know what he'd done? Did she know he'd had a family that he walked away from? Did she know he had a grown son?

And was I going to have to be the one who brought her up to speed?

"Yes?" she said.

"Hi," I said. "I was—is this Frank Dutton's place?"

"Yes, it is."

"Are you . . . Mrs. Dutton?"

"Yes, I am. Can I help you with something?"

"I was wondering, is Mr. Dutton in?"

"He sure is," she said. "Who should I say is calling?"

"Uh, Jack."

"Okay, Jack. Just a second."

She left the door open an inch, took a couple of steps back into the trailer, and said, "Frank! Someone here to see you!"

The hammering in my chest persisted. I tried to calm myself. After all, there was no way this could be my father. I mean, this man was *here*. And I knew from Gwen that he wouldn't be.

I heard steps coming, and then the door opened wide.

"Can I help you?" Frank Dutton asked.

I didn't know whether to be disappointed or relieved that this man was not Dad, unless Dad had lost forty pounds, become round shouldered, and grown a mustache.

"Hi," I said. "I'm Jack. Jack Givins."

Nothing. No reaction.

And I suddenly realized I hadn't given a lot of thought to what I was going to say when this moment arrived.

I winged it.

"This is going to sound like a really strange question," I said, "but some time ago, someone dinged my car—not this one, that's my girlfriend's—and drove off, and we got a picture of the car on a security camera, and the plate on it was registered to your name."

Frank Dutton listened intently, concern growing on his face.

"But"—I pointed to the car—"while that's the plate, it was on a different car."

Dutton was slowly nodding. "Son of a bitch. That was ages ago. How long ago did your car get dinged? Who worries about something like that after all this time?"

"Yeah, I know. But it's the insurance company, trying to clear something up. You know what they can be like."

"The bloodsuckers, yeah, tell me about it. Someone did swipe my plate, but like I said, it was a long time ago. And then later it turned up again, back on the car. Whatever damage was done, it's not my fault."

I gave him a "don't worry" wave. "It's okay, I'm not looking to get reimbursed or anything."

"It was almost like someone *borrowed* it," Dutton said. "One day I looked and it was gone, and then I get up the next morning and it's back. Why the hell would someone do that?"

"Beats me," I lied.

This trip had now proved itself to be the total waste of time I'd feared it would be. My father had been telling the truth. He'd stolen, or borrowed, someone else's plate and put it on his car when he came looking for me that day.

Just being careful.

But why put it back on Dutton's car? Why go to that trouble? Was it possible Dad lived nearby? That he knew Frank Dutton?

Dutton squinted at me, then grinned.

"What?" I asked.

"Oh, nothing, just noticing a resemblance is all."

"I'm sorry?"

"You don't know anybody else here at Trailwind, do you?"

"No, sir, I don't."

"Then I guess it's a coincidence. But you look a lot like one of the other residents here. Spittin' image. You could be his son."

A chill ran the length of my spine.

"Which resident would that be?" I asked.

Dutton pointed to the end of the road, by the turnaround.

"Lives in the last one down there, on the other side. Can't miss it. Little Honda parked next to it. Kind of keeps to himself. Haven't seen him around the last few days."

FIFTY-THREE

Kyle Gartner was rattled.

He'd already been feeling on edge before getting the call from that reporter, whatever her name was, from Boston. Asking all those questions about Valerie and Frohm and Donohue. After ending the call, he'd gone to the minibar in his hotel room, taken out a tiny bottle of gin, mixed it with some tonic, and knocked it back.

He was going to need more than that to calm his nerves. Maybe head down to the bar, have a few drinks there.

Sitting on the end of the bed, the TV tuned to CNN but the sound muted, he thought about what had brought him here. Was he making a terrible mistake? Should he check out of his hotel room, head to the airport, and go home? Abandon the plan? He'd invested so much time, and money, into it. When he'd left home, he felt determined to see it through, but now, he was less sure.

There would be fallout. Repercussions.

And who the hell had given out his cell-phone number to that reporter? Cecilia? Cherie? Did it matter? He was on the cusp of getting rid of that phone, anyway. Pretty soon, no one would be able to reach him.

That reporter.

Lana Wiltshire or Wilsher or whoever she was, he began to wonder whether she was who she claimed to be. The story she was writing sounded pretty thin. Did anyone really care how he felt about Galen Frohm's passing after all this time? Was it possible she wasn't a reporter at all?

And if she wasn't, who was she? Someone checking up on him? Someone who had an inkling of what it was he planned to do?

He was feeling overwhelmed.

He looked at his cell and opened up the photo app. He scrolled through, looking for pictures of his sister. It had only occurred to him now that when he pitched this phone, he'd never be able to look at these photos again. He hadn't saved them to some cloud, hadn't printed them out.

He found a shot from a year ago of him with Valerie, his arm around her shoulder. They're both smiling, but there's a vacant look in his sister's eyes. Like she's looking at the camera without actually seeing it.

Their father's death was the asteroid that cratered their lives. The damage lasted far beyond the moment of impact for Valerie. Kyle had long ago accepted the fact that Valerie's bond with their father was stronger than his. She'd always been Daddy's Little Girl. He'd pampered her, always given her whatever she wanted. Valerie confided in him more than she did their mother. Abel Gartner was very different with his son. Kyle wasn't to be spoiled. He was to be tough. You fell down and scuffed your knee? If you were Valerie, Dad kissed it better. If you were Kyle, you were told to walk it off.

So when their father was assassinated—because that's what it was, really, an assassination—Valerie went into a deep funk from which there was no recovery. The father's love that she'd lost she sought from far too many other men. She drank too much. Then there were drugs, and depression. She'd tried to free herself from the jaws of the black dog more than once, and whenever she did, Kyle was there for her. He was *always* there for her. Getting her into rehab programs, support groups. When she started writing in her private journal about her struggles, he talked her into submitting an article to one of the Chicago papers. The reaction was amazing. Hundreds of letters and emails poured in. Valerie was persuaded to join a nonprofit that devoted itself to helping people who'd been dealing with similar issues.

For a while, Valerie found purpose in counseling the troubled. "Listen," she'd tell others, "some bastard murdered my dad, and if I can get past that, you can get past this."

But too often, they couldn't. And in all honesty, neither could Valerie.

"Maybe people can't be saved," she told her brother one night.

"They can," he said. "I've seen you save yourself. You've done it before and you can do it again. I know you can."

"I'm at the bottom of the well and I can't see the light at the top," she said in the last voice mail she left for him.

Kyle was in that well now, too. But he didn't want to be hauled back up to the world he'd left behind.

He'd had enough of it.

And now here he was in a big downtown hotel in a city on the East Coast, anonymous among millions, ready to finally take hold of his life, to do what had to be done.

Kyle put the phone onto the bed, then reached into his pocket for his second phone.

He called up a number, put the phone to his ear, and waited for someone to pick up. After three rings, someone did, but said nothing.

"All set?" he asked. "I'll meet you down in the bar."

FIFTY-FOUR

Jack

I asked Frank Dutton if I could leave my car in front of his place while I went down to check on the trailer where this neighbor who looked a lot like me lived.

"Could be my uncle," I said. "Always heard he lives up this way. Family says I got his good looks."

Dutton chuckled. "Sure, no problem."

I gave him a salute as he withdrew back into his trailer. I went back to the car and stared for several seconds at the mobile home at the end of the court. I started walking toward it.

As I got closer, I could see a dim glow coming from somewhere inside, the kind of light you might leave on if you were going away but wanted any potential intruder to think the place was occupied.

The trailer was a good sixty feet long, the front end, with its bay window, bathed in the glow of a streetlight, the back end shrouded in darkness. Near the tail end of the trailer was a parked car. I couldn't say for sure, but it looked like it could be the same Honda CR-V my dad had been driving when we'd had our last meeting.

There was a covered patio on a concrete apron next to the front door, none of it lit, although I was able to make out a name on a mailbox mounted to one of the posts holding up the patio roof: BARKER. I made my way across it, careful not to bump any of the rusted folding lawn chairs, mounted the two steps to the door, and, not seeing anything that looked like a doorbell, rapped on it with my knuckles.

Waited.

After about fifteen seconds I tried again, harder this time. Still no answer.

I took a look toward the road, glanced at the other nearby trailers to check whether anyone was looking my way. Confident that no one was watching, I tried the door.

It was unlocked.

I opened it slowly, fearing the slightest squeak would bring the entire trailer park's population down on my head. And squeak it did, but not enough to alert the cavalry. I opened the door wide and stepped inside. Then, thinking I didn't want to have someone inadvertently announce my presence, I took my phone out of my pocket long enough to mute it.

My eyes were already getting adjusted to the darkness, so between light coming in from the street and ambient light from a digital clock, I could make out my surroundings. I'd entered onto a small living room to my right, and to my left was a kitchen and a narrow hallway that led to the aft end of the trailer.

I took a few steps, turning toward the kitchen. There was a plastic microwaveable container on the counter by the sink with what looked like a bite of macaroni and cheese still in it. Aside from that, the kitchen area was neat and tidy, and as best I could tell in the minimal light, the leftover mac and cheese didn't look like it had been sitting there a long time. I touched it with my finger to see whether it was dry and cold.

Cold, but still moist.

I wiped the tip of my finger on a tissue from my pocket and opened the refrigerator, filling the kitchen with light. Not much in there. A few cans of beer, a container of half-and-half coffee creamer. I took it out, checked the expiry date, figuring that if Dad had cleared out some time ago, the cream would already be undrinkable. But the date stamped into the lid was two weeks into the future.

I put the cream back, closed the refrigerator, and peered down the long hallway that led to a couple of bedrooms and a bathroom. Did I really want to go down there? I did not. I suddenly had a very bad feeling about how this was going.

Gwen had said my father had gone missing, but had Dad's witness protection handlers actually come here to look for him? It seemed unthinkable that they wouldn't. Would they have concluded he was missing just because they'd failed to raise him by phone, text, or email? Could he be dead in the back of this trailer and no one had bothered to check?

But if Dad *had* been killed here, wouldn't there have been, well, some clue? Like a smell in the air that would make you gag? The incessant buzzing of flies? There was neither. Then again, if something had happened to him in the last few minutes, there wouldn't be any of that. *Someone* had been here recently. That mac and cheese was proof of that.

And then it hit me that just because Dutton thought I shared a passing resemblance to the man who lived here, it didn't have to mean it was my father. It was possible I was snooping through the home of a total stranger.

I ventured down the dark hallway.

At this point, I got out my phone again and brought up the flashlight app. Enough light to see where I was going, but not enough to attract much attention from the outside.

The doors ran off the right side of the hallway like berths in a first-class train. I reached the first one and shined the light in. A bedroom not much bigger than a kitchen table, but there was no bed. It served as a storage room. Banker's boxes, golf clubs, various tools. The next bedroom, same size but a mirror image, was similarly filled with junk.

Next was the bathroom. No one in there.

That left a larger bedroom at the tail end. I stepped in, waved the phone around. The bed was made, the dresser clear of clutter. If someone had left here in a hurry, they'd tidied up first.

There wasn't much else to see, unless I started opening up closets, and I wasn't up to that. I killed the flashlight app, turned around, and looked back up the length of the hallway.

My heart did a rollover.

Where the hallway ended and the kitchen began stood a dark figure. It spoke:

"Make a move and I will fucking kill you."

It wasn't my father's voice.

The man at the end of the hallway raised a hand and flicked a wall switch. Suddenly I could see him, and the handgun he was pointing at me, quite clearly.

There was something about him that was familiar. I was sure I'd seen him before, if only for a moment, but I couldn't quite place—

Fuck, no.

It was my road rage friend. The dude from the pickup truck.

FIFTY-FIVE

Once he was off the phone with Earl Givins, Cayden considered how he would go about finding Lana Wilshire. He decided to start with online phone listings. This stuff didn't have to be rocket science.

There were only two L Wilshires listed in the entire Boston area. Cayden made note of the addresses, then took a moment to consider what he was going to say should he happen to get the right person when he tried the numbers.

He called the first listing. It rang only twice before someone, an old woman by the sounds of it, picked up.

"Hello?"

"Hi. Could I speak to Lana, please?"

"Who?"

"I'm calling for Lana Wilshire."

"Wrong number."

He went to the second listing. This time, a man answered.

"Yup?"

"Hi, could I speak to Lana, please?"

A sigh. "Lana Wilshire? The reporter?"

Cayden smiled. "That's right. Could I speak to her, please?"

"For the five thousandth fucking time, this is not *that* L Wilshire. People calling here for her all the time. Gonna have to get an unlisted number. If you're pissed about something she wrote, call the goddamn paper."

The man hung up.

So, Cayden concluded, Lana Wilshire either had an unlisted number or, more likely, didn't have a landline at all.

Cayden googled her name.

Dozens of bylined stories came up, as well as her Twitter account, which featured a picture of her. He went over to the site and found that she was a frequent tweeter, usually posting links to her stories on the paper's website, and occasional comments on the news. They were generally observations, as opposed to caustic comments. Wilshire probably wanted to maintain an air of impartiality. It was clear from what Cayden had found so far that she was not an opinion columnist, but a provider of straightforward accounts of what was going on in the Boston area.

Now here was something interesting.

She'd written stories about that dead judge and that dead doctor. That shouldn't come as a surprise. She and Jack had talked about Willard Bentley. While the stories weren't speculative—no one was quoted saying the deaths were suspicious—it seemed possible Wilshire was digging into those deaths. Tacked onto the bottom of the stories was Wilshire's email address, as though she was inviting people to send her tips.

Cayden scrolled through more of the Google results, hoping he might find an address for her. She might still be at Jack Givins's place, but considering she didn't live there, it was more likely she went home after Jack left on his mission. Hadn't he heard her say something about being swamped? That she had work to do?

If Cayden couldn't figure out a way to get to her, he needed to draw her to him. He returned to the paper's website, called the main number. It was well past business hours, so he got an automated system. When he was given the option to connect to the newsroom, he took it.

"City desk," a woman said.

"Lana Wilshire," he said.

"Gone for the day."

"Oh," Cayden said, putting on his disappointed voice. "I really need to get in touch with her."

"What's this about?"

"It's something I would have to discuss with her personally."

"I'll put you through to her voice mail."

His call was transferred.

"Hello. You've reached Lana Wilshire. I check in regularly, so please leave a message."

Cayden waited for the beep, then said, in a hesitant and unthreatening tone, "Yes, hello, Ms. Wilshire? I see that you've written some stories about Judge Bentley and that doctor? Dr. Sloan? I have information that might be of interest to you. I can't . . . I really can't give you my name, but I'd be willing to meet with you in person to tell you what I know. And this might not be convenient, but I'm usually at the Marriott Long Wharf for a drink around seven, seven thirty, if you had a chance to come by later. You don't have to worry about finding me. I saw your picture on your Twitter account, so I'll be able to spot you. Anyway, I'll understand if you can't make it, but I think you'll be interested in what I have to say."

Lana kicked off her shoes and changed into a pair of silk pajamas. It wasn't even dark out yet, but it had felt like a very long day, and she was glad for it to be over. She had no night assignments and couldn't be happier.

She collapsed onto the couch, grabbed the remote and turned on the TV. Normally, she would have gone straight to CNN to see what was going on in the world, but she was on overload from all the developments in Jack's situation and needed something that would not further agitate her.

Jack's go-to was *Law & Order*. For Lana, it was *Parks and Recreation*.

She called up an episode at random and hit play. But she found it hard to focus on any of the characters' antics. She kept wondering how it was going for Jack, whether his trip to New Hampshire would be productive.

She decided she needed help to relax. Instead of opening the fridge for a bottle of wine, she opened one of the kitchen drawers and brought out a clear, snack-sized bag with what looked like jujube candies but were, in fact, cannabis-laced edibles. She didn't care much to smoke it—she didn't want to stink up her apartment—but digesting a little pot was nice for a change.

She was about to pop two into her mouth when her eyes landed on her phone that was recharging. She disconnected it from the cable, intending to take it back to the couch in case Jack texted or phoned. But first she checked for any voice mail messages that might have been left for her at the paper, something she did often.

Lana had one message.

She listened to it once, saved it, then listened to it again.

Someone with a tip on the deaths of the retired judge and the doctor? She'd made a deal with Knight to sit on the story until there were some more solid developments, but this anonymous tip, if it proved to be anything, would change the terms of that deal. If this person was willing to talk to Lana, who else might he talk to? The *Globe*? One of the local TV stations? This was not something she wanted to get beat on.

The Marriott was a short walk from her place. She looked at her phone for the time. Christ, it was already half past seven. She tossed the edibles back into the drawer and went to her bedroom to get changed back into her work clothes.

She went back to the kitchen to scoop up her phone and decided to give that message one more listen. Once she had signed in to the paper's voice mail system, she discovered she had a new one.

"Shit," she said aloud. It was probably the tipster canceling. Cold feet.

But the message was from someone else.

"Hey, Lana, you don't really know me, but this is Earl Givins? Jack's father? Well, stepfather. But listen, something has come up and it's really, really important that you get back to me." He provided a number. Said it once and repeated it. Lana wrote it down on a slip of paper.

She wondered what could be so urgent, but whatever it was, it couldn't be more important than talking to someone with information on those two drownings. She didn't have time to talk to him now, but chose to send him a quick text:

Hi Earl. Lana here. Off to a meeting at the Long Wharf. Will call you after.
And sent it.

She saw it was now 7:45 p.m. Time to get a move on.

Lana was at the Marriott in ten minutes. She spent more time waiting for, and riding down in, the elevator of her building than she did walking briskly to the hotel. By the time she got to the bar, she was out of breath.

She scanned the patrons, looking for a man having a drink alone. There were about a dozen people there. Three couples, and one party of six. Nobody on his own. Maybe her caller was part of a twosome, or in the larger group, who were all talking loudly and laughing and had probably had a few rounds already. None of the three men sitting with women looked her way. It struck Lana as unlikely that you'd arrange a surreptitious meeting with a reporter when you were hanging out with your friends.

She went up to the bar and perched herself on the edge of a stool.

"What can I get you?" the bartender asked.

Lana waved him away. "Waiting for someone."

The bartender took the dismissal without offense. Lana kept her eye on the entrance.

Her phone rang. She got it out of her purse, saw that it was Earl. She'd already told him she'd get back to him later, and turned down the call. As she tossed the phone back into her purse, she noticed that someone who'd just entered the bar was scanning the patrons. A tall man, dark hair, rugged features. When his eyes landed on Lana, he smiled awkwardly and approached.

"I recognize you from your Twitter pic," he said. "I wasn't sure you'd come."

"You got my attention."

"Listen, do you mind if we just skip the drinks?"

Lana shrugged. "I don't know. What were you—"

"There's someone who wants to have a word."

FIFTY-SIX

"Let's do this," Kyle Gartner said to himself as he came out of his hotel room.

He'd be checking out shortly, but would come back for his bags after he had been down to the hotel bar.

A sense of calm washed over him as he strode toward the elevator. He had made his decision. No more second-guessing.

In his pants pocket was the phone that kept him linked to Chicago. The one that reporter had called him on. He'd already powered it off, then smashed it several times on the corner of the desk in his room, shattering the screen. As he waited for the elevator to reach his floor, he took the phone from his pocket and slipped it into the small trash receptacle between two sets of elevator doors.

His new phone was in the pocket of his sport jacket, as was his new passport. New driver's license. New credit cards. It paid off, knowing people who could acquire bogus identification for your employees. And having the money to pay them off so they'd never tell what they did for you.

He just hoped she'd be in the bar. If he got down there and she was a no-show, then all of this work, these months of preparation, would have been for nothing.

The elevator stopped at the third floor and a teenage girl stepped in. About the same age as Cherie, Kyle thought.

He would miss her.

The elevator reached the ground floor. Kyle stepped out, crossed the lobby to the entrance to the bar.

Once inside, he scanned the room, looking for her.

There she was, perched on a stool at the bar itself, no drink in front of her. She'd been waiting to have her first one with him, he figured.

She spotted him, smiled, and slid off the stool.

"Bridget," he said breathlessly as she slipped into his arms and looked up into his eyes and allowed him to kiss her. Not some quick peck, either, but a long, lingering kiss that was filled with anticipation.

"Kyle," she whispered. "Or should I call you Glen?"

No more goddamn linen business.

No more immigration hassles.

No more boring wife and troublesome daughter.

No more grieving and no more thirsting for vengeance.

No more Kyle Gartner.

He was a new man, literally. He was going to disappear, and he was never coming back.

FIFTY-SEVEN

Jack

"It can't be," I said, looking into the face of the man at the end of the hallway.

"Do I know you?" he asked.

"We've . . . sort of met, once," I said.

"Who are you?" he asked, and not nicely, either.

"I'm Jack Givins," I said. "I was . . . I'm looking for someone."

"Who?"

Good question. I remembered the name posted outside the trailer.

"Mr. Barker," I said. "Would that . . . be you?"

"I live next door," he said. "Saw you snooping around. Better explain yourself real quick, pal."

There were a few things I wanted explained, too. Like, what the hell was the guy who ran me off the road doing living next door to my father, assuming that this trailer I was standing in *was* my father's? What were the odds of *that*?

"I think my father lives here," I said. "I've been trying to get in touch with him."

Something changed in the man's face. "Your father?"

I nodded.

He eyed me more carefully, like maybe he, too, was struggling to remember where he might have encountered me.

"Tell me," he said.

"Tell you what?"

"Where you think we met?"

"I cut you off," I said. "Didn't mean to. I didn't see you. You got pissed and chased me, cut me off. Got out of your pickup. You were coming at me."

The gun in his hand lowered ever so slightly. "Fuck me."

"And then, someone came along at the right time . . . and stopped you."

"I'll be a goddamn son of a bitch," he said, his mouth bordering on a grin. "It is you. Goddamn, I could have killed you just now. Cliff would have been so pissed with me if I'd done that."

"*Cliff,*" I said. It was barely more than a whisper.

"Should be back soon. He likes to take a walk around this time of—"

We heard a door open and close.

"Hello?" someone, who no doubt had noticed that lights had been turned on in parts of the trailer, called out. "What's going on?"

This time, it was my father's voice I recognized.

"Hey, Cliff," my road rage friend said. "Around the corner. You've got a visitor."

I heard footsteps, and then Dad appeared alongside the other man. He eyed me, jaw ever so slightly dropped.

"Jesus," he said. Dad brushed past the other man, met me halfway down the hall, and threw his arms around me. "How the hell did you find me? And what the hell are you doing here?"

"I was going to ask you the same thing," I said.

He stared at me, shaking his head, undoubtedly trying to figure out how I'd tracked him down.

"The license plate," I said. "Someone suggested I finally check whether it might actually be legit. And it wasn't, but it was close."

Dad shook his head, chiding himself. "I got sloppy. You traced it to Frank. He's such a nice guy. I hated to put him to the trouble of getting a new plate, so I only borrowed it. Well, good on ya, I suppose. See you've met Gord here. Gord, this is my son, Jack."

"Hey, Jack," Gord said. "We figured out where we know each other from."

"Oh," Dad said. He smiled sourly as he looked at me. "You probably have some questions."

"A couple," I said.

"Want a beer?"

"Sure," I said, making my way up the hallway and taking a seat at the kitchen table. Gord sat opposite me while Dad went to the fridge, brought out three cans of beer, and put them on the table.

I had my first good look at him. He was thinner than I remembered, and he'd lost that color in his cheeks that he'd regained after his health issues years back. He was gray, washed out, and he'd lost some hair.

He took a deep breath and let it out slowly. "Well," he said, glancing first at Gord and then back to me. "You want the short version or the long version?"

"The short, for now, I guess," I said.

"After our meetup, I went back looking for him, but he was gone."

"I went, too," I said.

"I woke up," Gord said. "I was pretty bad. I drove myself to the closest hospital. That's where your dad found me."

Dad nodded. "I hunted him down. Wanted to make sure I hadn't killed the son of a bitch. Found out who he was, where he lived. They had him in the hospital for about a week."

"It was the hit on the head that did it," Gord said. "Bit of brain damage." He grinned. "Not so's you could really tell the difference. I'm sorry about coming after you. I was having a bad day. Had just lost my job. Months behind on payments for my truck. My girl had just dumped me. If it hadn't been you it would have been someone else. Your dad, he kind of saved me."

I turned to my father. "What did you do?"

"After they sent Gord home, I went to visit him. Told him it was me that put him down. That he'd attacked my son and he was lucky I hadn't killed him." Dad shrugged. "Damned if we didn't kind of hit it off. Started coming down to take him to appointments with his neurologist. He wasn't supposed to drive. He didn't have a job, so I helped him out as best I could financially. When the trailer next to mine was available to rent, I persuaded him to leave his place and come here while he was on the mend."

"I'm all better now," Gord said, rolling his eyes and using a goofy voice that prompted laughs from Dad and me. "But I decided to stay."

"That's the short version," Dad said.

I looked at my father and asked, as tentatively as I could, "What does Gord . . . know?"

Dad smiled. "Enough to understand, and not enough to get him into trouble."

"Yeah," Gord said. "Your dad's got a past he hasn't told me about. That's fine with me. I know Cliff Barker's not his real name, but he answers to it, so what the fuck do I care?"

"What brings you up here, son?" Dad asked.

"Have you . . . been away?"

"Was gone for a couple of days last week. Sometimes I get in the car and just drive. Went up the Maine coast, touring around, eating lobster. Usually put the seat back down and sleep in the car. I'm retired now and have what you might call a limited income."

"I thought you'd been away for longer than that," I said.

Dad's brow furrowed. "Were you up here before, looking for me?"

"No." Something didn't seem right, but I couldn't quite put

my finger on it. "Have you always lived here? I mean, since you left Mom and me?"

"No. At the very beginning, you know, I had to serve some prison time. A few months' penance, under another name. When I got out, they placed me in Scottsdale. Didn't care for it there. People are nice, it's beautiful and all. But it's not New England. Missed the trees, especially in the fall. So they let me come back, and I've bounced around some. Vermont, New Hampshire. Spent a year or two in Maine. You took a risk, you know."

"A risk?"

"Coming here, looking for me." Another sigh. "But I guess I get it. Why, if you'd made a note of that plate, did it take you so long to check it out?"

"Something came up."

"What would that be?"

I looked at Gord. I didn't know how much to reveal. Gord got the message, pushed back his chair.

"I'll be off," he said. "Nice to meet you."

"Likewise."

He grabbed the beer. "Not leaving this behind."

As he went by Dad he gave him a friendly pat on the shoulder. Dad waited until he heard the door close before he said anything.

"So what came up?"

"Someone might be looking for you. Someone with a score to settle."

Dad laughed. "Take a number. Who is it?"

"Lana—you remember me telling you about her—thinks it might be someone from the Gartner family."

Dad's look saddened. "He had two kids. Twins. Boy and a girl. They'd be in their forties now."

"The daughter's dead. Had a history of addiction, depression."

Dad frowned. "Oh." I could see a veneer of guilt wash over him.

I said, "The working theory, at least *Lana's* working theory, is that Gartner's son is looking for you. Or has hired someone to find you. Bad as that sounds, it beats the other theory. That you'd gone back to doing what you used to do."

"Never," he said.

"But you already knew all this, right? Or had some inkling? About Gartner's son? About someone gunning for you?"

Dad raised his head. His eyebrows popped. "How the hell would I know that? Why would you think that?"

"Because that's why you took off for a few days."

"Who says I took off? I'm right here, aren't I?"

"Yeah, but no one's been able to get in touch with you."

"Like who?" he asked, reaching into his pocket and putting his cell phone on the table. "If someone needs to reach me, they call that. Where's all this coming from?"

"From someone in the witness protection agency. They hired me. To write backstories for people like you, before they get relocated."

Dad sat down. "You need to start at the beginning."

"I figured they must have picked me because I had some personal experience with the program, but that wasn't it. They just thought I was a good fit for the job. They were stunned to find out my own father'd been relocated by them years ago. So I asked a favor. Set up a meeting. You were always the one calling the shots on when we'd see each other. I wanted to turn things around for once. I wanted to know how you were doing. I was afraid maybe you got the virus. Anyway, when they tried, they couldn't find you."

Dad looked dumbfounded.

"They believed you'd taken off. That someone was hunting for you."

"This makes no fucking sense," he said. He pointed to his phone on the table. "My contact is a guy named Stan. He can call and get me any time he wants. He knows where I live. He's been here, in person, several times over the last few years."

I had a feeling I looked equally dumbfounded.

"It's a huge bureaucracy," I said. "Maybe the left hand doesn't know what the right hand is doing."

Dad shook his head. "These people are not idiots. They know what they're—and who is this *they* you keep referring to? Who have you been dealing with?"

"This woman with the U.S. Marshals Service."

"Who?"

"Gwen Kaminsky."

"Who the fuck is Gwen Kaminsky?"

FIFTY-EIGHT

"*D*ad, Daddy, can you hear me? Come on, Dad, talk to me."

"... *uhhhh* ... *uhhh* ..."

"*Daddy, I want to see you more than anything in the world. I do. But they won't let me in. I tried and they kicked me out, the bastards. You have to know that if I could be there, I would. If only they'd let you out, if they'd let you come home* ..."

"... *uhhh* ..."

"*Everything that's happened to you, it's never been fair, it's never been right. And for it all to end like this* ... *Please, just say something. There's never been a day, not one, since you had to leave us that I haven't thought about you, that I haven't wanted to see you. I love you so much.*"

"*............*"

"*Daddy, if you can hear me, just know that I'll make this right. I will. I swear, I will make this right. Christ, are you even hearing any of this? Have they got the phone to your ear? Do you even know it's me? Daddy? It's Gwen. It's Gwendoline, your good little witch, Daddy, and I love you so much.*"

FIFTY-NINE

"**S**hit," Earl said when he saw Lana's message that she would get back to him later. "Shit shit shit."

He didn't bother with the elevator and took the stairs to get down to lobby level, and then took another flight to reach the underground garage. He jumped into his rental car, feeling a pang of regret, at that moment, that he had allowed Cayden to take the Porsche from him. It was, to be sure, an older model and not in mint condition, but right now he needed something that could really move.

It took three tries, but the engine finally turned over, and he sped up the ramp in record time, the car rattling and squeaking as it bounced out onto the street. He didn't know when Lana's meeting was, and he didn't know for sure it was with the menacing Cayden, but Earl had to assume it was, and he was going to have to break every traffic law on the Massachusetts books getting to the Long Wharf as quickly as he could.

Earl didn't know what business the man might have with his stepson's girlfriend, but he couldn't imagine it was anything good. Cayden, Earl had quickly learned, was not the kind of person you said no to. If he wanted information from Lana, it was a safe bet that he was going to get it out of her.

Helping Cayden, searching Jack's place, and, lastly, planting that listening device in his apartment had been weighing heavily on Earl. He'd tried to justify it to himself by thinking it had nothing to do with Jack, and everything to do with Michael Donohue, and did Earl owe him anything? Earl's betrayal of Jack was nothing compared to what his father had done, leaving the kid behind when he was only nine years old.

But shit, now Jack's girlfriend was involved.

Earl had never met Lana Wilshire, but if she was important to Jack, that was all that mattered. There were some lines even Earl didn't feel comfortable crossing. He didn't want anything bad happening to his stepson's girlfriend. He needed to warn her.

As he sped down Boston's streets, heading for the Long Wharf, he tried calling her one more time, his eyes darting back and forth between the road and his phone. Just as he was about to tap the screen he heard a horn, glanced up, saw that he had just run a red.

"Jesus," he said to himself, no idea how close he might have come to hitting another car, or putting himself in the path of one.

He tapped the screen, put the phone to his ear.

The phone rang once, twice. And then, nothing. She'd declined it.

"Goddamn it."

Earl decided if he couldn't get Lana to answer, he'd try Jack. Warn him, and then *he* could call Lana. She'd be less likely to turn down a call from her boyfriend.

Still dividing his attention between the phone and the road, he brought up Jack's number, entered it, and put the phone to his ear.

It rang. And rang. And rang.

"Fuck!" Earl shouted.

Finally: "*Hi. You've reached Jack Givins. Please leave a message.*"

"Jack! It's me. Look, I don't have time to explain, but you have to call Lana. This Cayden guy's looking for her and he's bad news. Fucking bad news! Tell her not to meet with him, to hide out for a while. I'll explain later."

He hit the red button and tossed the phone onto the passenger seat.

The little car's engine whined in protest as Earl sped south on Congress, then made a left onto State Street, heading east, which would take him straight to the Long Wharf. The only problem was, State was a one-way street going west, and Earl was driving straight into oncoming traffic. He put on his flashers, laid on the horn, stuck his hand out the window, and waved madly as vehicles dodged out of his path.

Somehow, he managed to get to the hotel without having a head-on collision. He left the car sitting out front of the hotel, the engine coughing and sputtering even after he'd turned off the ignition and removed the key. A bellman raised his hand, ready to offer assistance, but Earl ran past him into the lobby. He stood in the center of it and did a slow turn, checking out everyone who was there.

None of them looked like Lana. Then again, what *did* she look like? Christ, how was he supposed to find someone he'd never met before?

He decided to head for the bar. That seemed the most likely place where she might meet someone. But as he was heading that way, he caught sight, in his peripheral vision, of someone leaving the hotel that he thought he recognized.

Not Lana.

Cayden.

From the back, it could be him. Tall, broad-shouldered. And he was walking with a woman, chatting with her as they exited the building.

He started to run. His knees, which he'd somehow fucked up running down his apartment stairwell so quickly, were screaming in pain, like someone had run a sword through each one of them. No matter.

Once outside, he looked to the right, back toward downtown,

301

then the left, toward the water. Where the hell had they gone so quickly? Where could they have—

Hang on.

A black van was idling about sixty feet away, the driver's side facing him. He thought he'd caught a glimpse of Cayden and the woman walking around it.

Limping speedily, he went for the van. When he came around the back of it, he saw Cayden supporting the woman, as though she were on the verge of passing out, as he helped her into the van through the side door.

"Lana?" Earl shouted. "What are you doing with her?"

Cayden got her into the van, stepped back, and turned to see Earl standing there.

"What's going on?" Earl demanded. "Where are you taking her?"

By way of an answer, Cayden reached into his jacket, brought out something dark and shiny, pointed it at Earl, and shot him straight through the forehead.

SIXTY

Jack

"I'm trying to tell you," I said. "Gwen works for the program. You wouldn't know her because she never handled your case, but it has to be a big department. Just because you don't know her doesn't mean anything."

Dad looked at his phone, picked it up, looked at it, put it back down again.

"What?" I asked.

"I'm thinking," he said. Again, he picked up the phone and put it down. "Fuck it." He picked it up, entered a number, then put the phone to his ear and waited. After about twenty seconds, he said, "It's Cliff. I need to talk to Stan."

He ended the call and put the phone back onto the table.

"Your guy," I said.

Dad nodded. "Maybe he can clear this up."

"What are you thinking?" I asked him.

He drew imaginary little circles on the table with his index finger. He watched his finger go round and round, then expanded the pattern into a figure eight.

"I don't know."

"You look worried."

"I'm trying to figure it out."

"I'd call Gwen if I could. But I forgot and left the phone in my apartment."

"You don't have a phone on you?"

"Yes. But she gave me a special one that I only use when I'm getting in touch with her."

"Did you tell her you were coming up here to look for me?"

I shook my head. "I thought about it but decided against it. She's had kind of a bad day. One of her witnesses was killed. I wanted to come up here on my own, see if that plate led me to you. Anyway, Gwen already knows you live here."

"She does?"

"Of course," I said, like my father was a little slow on the uptake. "She works for the program. She's seen your file. What she wanted my help with was trying to figure out where you might have gone. Favorite haunts, some long-lost relatives. Like that."

Dad pushed back his chair, got up and went to the kitchen window. He looked outside for a moment, then went to the front door, opened it, and stepped out. I was right behind him. I was starting to get a bad feeling.

"What do you think's going on, Dad?" I asked.

"I don't know," he said quietly. "Something about all this is not right." We both went back inside, but instead of sitting, Dad leaned up against the fridge and folded his arms. "Did you actually do any of this work for Gwen?"

"I'd only worked on one profile so far," I said slowly. "I guess I can talk about it, because the guy's dead. I knew him only as Bill, at least at first—needed a new background and I worked on it for a while without knowing him, and I didn't feel I was getting it right. So I said I wanted to have a face-to-face meeting with him."

"Gwen went for that?"

I nodded very slowly. "She did."

"She'd have been taking a risk, setting that up. She could have done it over Zoom. Or given you more details, without the face-to-face."

"It was risky," I agreed, thinking back to the meeting. "This guy had testified against some Russian mob types. I found out, totally by accident, who he really was. Saw him on TV."

"The guy was an *actor*?" Dad asked.

Our eyes met. "Yeah," I said. I was starting to feel a little queasy.

"That was something you found out on your own. Gwen never volunteered that information."

"No," I said. "She was up front about it when I mentioned it, but I can't think of any reason why she wouldn't have told me that from the outset."

Neither of us spoke. The silence between us was finally interrupted by the ringing of his cell phone. I glanced at it before Dad walked over to pick it up. On the screen it said: NO CALLER ID.

Dad put the phone to his ear.

"Yeah, hey. Listen, my son is here. Yeah, I know. It wasn't me. He found me, and I've only got myself to blame. But I want to put you on speaker. You okay with that?"

Dad listened for a few more seconds, nodded, and evidently getting a positive response, put the phone on the table.

"Okay, Stan, you're on speaker. Say hello to Jack."

"Hello, Jack." Judging by his tone, with just those two words I could tell Stan was not thrilled.

"Tell him your story, Jack," Dad said.

I told him about being recruited by Gwen to write backstories. Revealing to her, eventually, that my own father had gone into the witness protection program. How she learned that Dad was missing. Stan listened patiently and interrupted only a couple of times to get some points clarified.

When I was done, Dad said, "Would you agree, Stan, that I am not missing?"

"Yes," Stan said.

"Is this a new thing you guys are doing? Hiring novelists to imagine background stories for your witnesses?"

"I am unfamiliar with any such program," Stan said.

"Was anyone in touch with you about my case?" Dad asked.

"No."

"Is there anyone else attached to my file she might have talked to without your knowledge?"

"No."

"Any chance the program lost one of its witnesses this week?"

"If we had I would have heard about it."

I looked at Dad, then at the phone, as if I could somehow see Stan. "What the fuck have I done?" I asked.

Stan said, "Cliff, we need to bring you in. Immediately."

For half a second, I thought, who the fuck is Cliff? It was going to take some time to get used to my dad's name.

"What's your take?" Dad asked.

Stan said, very evenly, "Someone's been using Jack to find you."

I asked, "If Gwen's not with the witness protection program, then who the fuck is she?"

"Tell me everything you can about her," Stan said.

"Okay, okay," I said. "First of all, the good news is, I didn't tell her I was coming up here. She doesn't know."

"Where did you meet with her?" Stan asked.

"The first time, it was in a small office on Boylston. No big sign on the door that said 'Witness Protection.' It was Pandora Importing, something like that. A false front, I guess you'd call it."

Stan had more questions and I tried to answer them as best I could. I was feeling sick to my stomach, and it wasn't the pizza I'd eaten on the way up.

Finally, Stan said, "Cliff, we'll have to set up someplace temporarily while we sort this shit out."

Dad sighed wearily. "I was kind of liking it here, Stan."

"For now, just go. Don't pack. Find a cheap motel somewhere. I'll call you in the morning."

And then Stan was gone.

I looked at Dad, feeling the weight of what I'd done. "I'm sorry. I fucked up. I've walked right into something, haven't I? Big time. I've led them right to your door. Jesus, I can't believe it."

He shook his head. "Let's not worry about that now."

I wanted to let Lana know what was going on, but wondered whether it was smart to discuss anything on the phone. But I got it out of my pocket, anyway.

"Shit," I said. "I missed a call." I remembered that I had muted the phone when I snuck into Dad's trailer. "It's from Earl. From an hour ago."

I entered my voice mail code and put the phone to my ear.

"Jack! It's me. Look, I don't have time to explain, but you have to call Lana. This Cayden guy's looking for her and he's bad news! Fucking bad news! Tell her not to meet with him, to hide out for a while. I'll explain later."

Dad could see by my face that something was horribly wrong. "What?" he said.

"Cayden," I whispered.

"Who—"

Before Dad could say another word, I was bringing up Lana's number on my phone.

Waiting.

It rang once. Twice. Three times.

"Shit!"

Four times.

Then:

"Hello?"

"Lana?"

"Hi, Jack. I'm afraid Lana can't come to the phone right now. It's Gwen. We should talk."

SIXTY-ONE

Lana had one motherfucker of a headache.

Even before she opened her eyes, she could feel the throbbing inside her skull. In the moments before fully waking, she tried to remember what had happened to her. She recalled meeting the man in the hotel bar, walking outside with him.

There was someone, he said, who wanted to speak to her, to "have a word," as he put it. As they walked out of the Marriott, he pointed to a black van.

"This way," he'd said.

"Who are we meeting?" Lana had asked.

"She really wants to talk to you but doesn't want to be seen. She could get in a lot of trouble for telling you what she knows, what she suspects."

What was Lana going to do? Walk away *now*? Just when she might get a lead on a very important story?

They were almost to the vehicle when Lana felt something go into her neck. Something pointy and sharp in the man's hand. A needle. Within seconds she felt her legs give out beneath her, but the man caught her before she hit the pavement and shoveled her into the van.

She heard someone shout her name. And in the seconds before everything went black, a popping sound. A firecracker? A car backfiring?

Now, waking up, she went to open her eyes and realized things still were shrouded in darkness. For a second she thought she was in a room with the lights off, but then felt her eyelashes brush up against fabric.

A blindfold.

All she could hear was *tickety tickety tickety tickety tickety.* Like some kind of cheap fan.

As alertness grew, she understood she was sitting in a hard, straight-backed chair, and that she was secured to it, her arms tied behind her back. And if all that weren't bad enough, she felt a tickle in her nose, like she was going to start sneezing.

"She's waking up," a man said. She recognized the voice. It was the man who had met her in the bar, tricked her into going out to the van.

"About time," a woman said. "You gave her too much." A couple of footsteps, and when she spoke again she was much closer. Right in front of her, Lana sensed.

"How are we feeling?"

"Who are you?" Lana asked. The words came out soft around the edges, as if she'd had too much to drink. "What do you want?"

"Take her blindfold off," the woman said.

"You sure?" the man asked.

"I don't think we're going to have any problem with Ms. Wilshire here. She's going to want to cooperate, and then we'll be able to move past this. Don't you think so, Ms. Wilshire?"

Lana said nothing.

Seconds later, she could feel the fabric being unknotted at the back of her head. The blindfold fell away, and it took her eyes a moment to adjust to the light. She blinked several times and looked at the woman standing in front of her.

"Who *are* you?" she asked again.

"I'm Gwen," she said.

Lana blinked several more times, getting used to the light. "With the witness protection program," she whispered.

"Oh, so Jack's been talking. Naughty, naughty."

Shit, Lana thought. I've given it away.

But matters seemed to have progressed to a point where what might have seemed important before wasn't anymore.

"You can't kidnap people," Lana said. "Even if you are with the government."

"I suppose," Gwen said, "if I were, then this sort of thing would be highly irregular. I haven't been entirely truthful with Jack." She smiled. "We've done some quick research on you. You're a smart one. Doesn't seem much point maintaining the fiction any longer."

Fiction?

"Jack broke the rules, going off to look for his father without telling me. But there's a way to make this right. Jack doing what he did, evidently with your help, may be what brings our business to a conclusion."

"I don't know what you're talking about." Feeling that tickle in her nose again, Lana sniffed.

Gwen pointed to another chair. "Cayden, bring me that."

Cayden dragged it over and placed it in front of Lana. Gwen sat.

Tickety tickety tickety tickety tickety.

"And do we *have* to listen to that infernal racket?" Gwen asked him, looking at the fan.

"You said it was stuffy in here, so I put on the fan. Now you don't like the fan. You want it cooler in here, or quiet? Because you can't have both."

Gwen sighed defeatedly. She turned her attention back to Lana. "You've been helping Jack. You traced a license plate. Tell me about that."

Lana didn't have to ponder long how Gwen might know this.

She must have had Jack's apartment bugged. They'd been listening when she got to his place and gave him the news. So what did they need her for if they'd heard everything?

There had to be things they hadn't said out loud. She'd handed Jack a slip of paper with Frank Dutton's information on it. He'd gone onto his laptop to see where Gilford was in New Hampshire. If they'd gone to his apartment after she'd left, they wouldn't have been able to search the computer's history. They would have needed a password to open it up.

"The plate was a dead end," Lana said.

For all she knew, that might even be true. Frank Dutton didn't have to be Jack's father. If the plate was stolen, as Jack's father had claimed, Jack's trip to Gilford would prove to be a waste of time. She didn't know one way or another.

"What makes you so sure?"

"The plate I checked, it was most likely stolen. It was a long shot. A waste of time, but Jack wanted to check it out, just the same."

"Have you heard from him?"

"Yes," she said. "He called me. Before . . . before Cayden here showed up at the bar."

A lie seemed the smartest way to go. On the remote chance Jack's trip proved successful, her hunch was that it was better if these people did not know.

Gwen leaned in, her face only a few inches away from Lana's. "Why don't we check that and—"

Lana sneezed. Right in Gwen's face.

"Fuck!" Gwen shouted, recoiling, pressing her back against the chair, but at the same time, instantly, instinctively, slapping Lana across the face hard enough to leave a bright red mark on her cheek. "What's *wrong* with you?"

Lana hunched her shoulders, reminding Gwen that her hands were bound behind her back.

"Fuck," Gwen said, getting up and going to the kitchen sink to splash some water on her face. "The last thing I need is COVID," she said, grabbing a dish towel to dry off.

"It's allergies," Lana said.

That did nothing to make Gwen look happier as she tossed the towel into the sink. She came back and sat down across from Lana, but not before moving her chair back a foot. To Cayden, she said, "Get her phone."

Lana's purse was sitting on the kitchen table. Cayden rooted through it, found Lana's cell, and said, "It's locked."

Gwen looked at Lana. "Code."

Lana said nothing. There had been no call from Jack. Once they got into the phone, they would know she'd lied. Gwen sighed and said to Cayden, "I bet her thumbprint will do it."

Cayden came around behind Lana, knelt down, took Lana's right hand firmly into his and placed her thumb over the phone's home button. The screen came to life. "Here we go."

He scanned the phone's call history. "There's no recent call here from Jack, but . . . there's another call here, but not from him."

"Who?" Gwen asked. "Who is it?"

Cayden scowled. "Earl." He shook his head. "At least he's not going to be a problem anymore."

Gwen turned her attention back to Lana. "So Jack *didn't* call you. So it *wasn't* a dead end."

"I honestly don't know," Lana said, sniffing again. "Why does it matter? Why do you care so much about him looking for his father?" Lana's eyes narrowed. "It's all about Abel Gartner, isn't it?"

Gwen said, "What?"

"You're working for his son. For Kyle. For what Jack's dad did. Killing his father."

Gwen leaned back in her chair, folded her arms, and shook her head. "The misery that man wrought. The suffering he caused. The families he destroyed."

"You can blame Jack's father, but you know he was coerced into doing it by a man who was every bit as bad as him, if not a whole lot worse."

Gwen said, "Now you're getting personal."

"Personal?"

Gwen said nothing while she waited for the tumblers to fall into place for Lana, who finally said, "This has nothing to do with Abel Gartner."

"Good."

"You're . . . are you . . . was Galen Frohm . . ."

"My father? Yes. Galen Frohm was my father. I am Gwen Frohm." Gwen looked as though she was running out of patience. "Where. Did. Jack. Go?"

"I don't know."

"You're lying. A trailer park was mentioned. Where is it?"

Lana wanted to stall, but to what end? Was anyone going to find her? Was anyone even looking for her? Did Jack have any idea she was missing? She believed the moment she told Gwen where Jack had gone, she and Cayden would hop in that van and head straight to New Hampshire.

And they wouldn't have any further need for Lana.

Lana could surmise what Gwen's motives were. She wanted to kill Jack's father for betraying her own. If she found him, and if Jack was with him, she'd kill Jack, too.

"It was all bullshit, wasn't it?" Lana asked. "This whole witness protection thing. Hiring Jack to write backstories."

Gwen smiled. "It took a long time to put together."

Lana thought through what the plan must have entailed.

"You wanted to draw him in, gain his confidence, wait for him to *ask* for your help to find his father. You thought Jack might have some clues as to where he might be. Conned him into thinking his father was in danger to make finding him more urgent. If he showed up, Jack would turn him straight over to you. You made him think someone wanting revenge was hunting for him. Except the someone was you."

"His father was the one I couldn't find. The others were easy."

Others?

"And what a small world it is," Gwen said, "that you have been looking into those. Cayden tells me you wrote about them."

The judge? The doctor?

"Why . . ."

"Enough," Gwen said, and took a breath. "This is the last time I'm going to ask you. Who did that plate belong to? Where did Jack go?"

"I really . . . I really don't know."

Gwen sighed, looked at Cayden, and nodded.

He went over to a drawer, opened it, and brought out an orange-and-black-handled garden pruner. Its beak-shaped blades would cut through a thick twig as easily as they would a rubber band.

"No, please," Lana said fearfully, wondering how he intended to use the device. "I'm telling you the truth. For all I know, Jack's on his way back. He still thinks you work for the government. I won't tell him anything! I won't tell him about this! Just let me go. I'll talk to him, okay?"

Cayden approached with the pruner.

What the hell was he going to do? Cut out her tongue? Snip off an earlobe?

"*No, no, please!*"

When he came around behind her and grabbed hold of her right hand, his intentions became more clear. She wiggled her fingers wildly, trying to thwart his efforts to get the cutting tool around the base of her thumb.

Gwen glared at her. "Last chance," she said.

Cayden squeezed her right wrist hard, immobilizing it, and got the pruner in position. She felt the tiny metal jaws grip.

"Do it," Gwen said.

"*NOOOOO!!!!*"

A phone started ringing. Gwen raised a finger, a signal for Cayden to stop.

"It's her cell," Gwen said.

Cayden picked the phone back up from the table, looked at the screen, and said, "Guess who."

SIXTY-TWO

The rage had simmered for years. But it was her father's death, and the way it happened, that brought it all to a boil for Gwen Frohm.

Up until the age of eleven, she'd had a more or less traditional childhood, so long as you overlooked the fact that her millionaire father sometimes had people murdered. Gwen was an only child, the sole object of her mother and father's attention. Dare one say, somewhat spoiled. They lived in a house big enough for the von Trapps, with rooms to spare. And there was the summer place in the Berkshires.

She loved her time there. The family retreat was as spacious and beautiful as the home in Boston, but what it had over Boston was a stable, and horses. A couple of times every summer Gwen's parents would let her take a friend for a week, and they would spend almost all their time in the stables, feeding and grooming the animals when they weren't riding them. It was the most wonderful time.

It all ended so abruptly.

Galen Frohm was arrested. He wasn't taken off to jail right away. His lawyers won him release on bail while they prepared for trial. At first, he gave his daughter, who was old enough to understand what was happening and its implications, reasons for optimism. He was innocent, he told her. The charges were all trumped up by his competitors in the motel and fast-food industries. His lawyers would find a way to get him out of this.

But that all changed when Frohm learned Donohue had fired the company's top lawyer. Donohue had a new one, and he was going to tell everything he knew to prosecutors. All of Frohm's illegal business practices, the tax fraud, the blackmail.

The executions he had ordered.

"Bullshit," Frohm had said. "It's his word against mine."

"There are recordings," the lawyers told him.

So, in slightly less technical legal terms, Frohm was fucked. They had him cold on so many counts, including the murders, that he was encouraged to take a deal that wouldn't see him getting out of prison until he was an old man.

He had no choice.

Gwen and her mother visited Frohm in prison regularly. Even as Gwen grew into her teens and beyond, she never stopped visiting, never forgot her dad. Every Sunday she went, even when her mother took an occasional pass. Throughout those years, Gwen never forgot the name of the man responsible, more than any other, for her father's fate.

Michael Donohue.

Oh, sure, there were others she blamed, in particular the lawyers who failed him and especially the judge who sentenced him.

One Sunday, two weeks after Gwen had celebrated her twenty-fifth birthday, her father made a proposal to her.

"I want you to take over," he said.

"What?"

"The company. I want you to take it over. To run it. Everything."

Even with Galen behind bars, the Frohm empire had carried on. There were some rough years, to be sure. Massive fines were levied by the courts, a handful of midlevel executives who cooked the books or engaged in other illegal activities were convicted and served minor sentences, and the negative publicity turned many customers away for a year or two. But there were enough untainted people left who moved up the corporate ladder to keep the various entities operational.

Even so, there needed to be someone strong at the helm. Someone with the smarts to build on the repairs that had already taken place. Gwen, a graduate of the Harvard Business School (with, as it turned out, a strong side interest in theater), fit the bill.

She accepted her father's offer.

And every Sunday after that, she would visit her father, tell him how her week had gone, seek his advice on various issues. One Sunday she came bearing sad news. Her mother, Galen's wife, had succumbed to a six-month battle with cancer.

"But I'm here for you," she said. "I will *always* be here for you. We're a team. And I know it feels like a long time off, but one day, you'll be released, and when you are, you're coming back to the company. It's going to be a very special day. You'll move in with me and you're going to stay with me for as long as you want."

There were days, even before the news of his wife's passing, when Frohm's spirits were especially low, when the bitterness overwhelmed him.

"I wonder where he is," he would say. "Livin' the life down in Florida, I bet. Sitting by the pool, not a care in the world. That son of a bitch. He was like a son to me. I treated him like family. And then he turns around and does this. Stabs me in the fucking back."

As far as Gwen was concerned, her father could do no wrong, even when it was abundantly clear to the rest of the world that he had done *much* wrong. Maybe it was true that he'd had Michael Donohue kill people, but those individuals had betrayed her father. They'd become a threat to him. The corporate world was cutthroat. They knew what they'd signed on for. This was business, and there were consequences for those who crossed him.

Which made what Michael Donohue had done so much worse. There was nothing lower than a rat.

The good news they'd waited so long for finally came early in 2020. Galen Frohm was to be released in October. The years of waiting had now turned into months, and the months were turning into days.

In September, a month before his release date, Galen Frohm became ill.

It started with a fever and a cough. Frohm found himself without energy. He could not summon the strength to get out of his cell bed. Contagion was sweeping through the prison. Frohm's symptoms worsened. A sore throat, a headache, a rash.

Then came the shortness of breath. Frohm was going to die if he didn't get proper help.

The prison infirmary was overwhelmed with inmates who had contracted the coronavirus, and Frohm, given his age, was among the most serious. Gwen, alarmed, insisted her father be moved to an actual hospital, and authorities acceded to her demands. Frohm was moved to a hospital in Boston. Despite his frail condition, a handcuff secured him to the railing of his intensive care unit bed.

Such a humiliation. And Gwen was not allowed to see him.

The virus was everywhere. It was too risky to permit visitations. Gwen tried more than once to sneak in, even, at one point, donning a surgical gown in a bid to get past security. But every attempt was thwarted.

Dr. Marie Sloan did her best to keep Gwen updated on her father's condition. The reports were not encouraging. He was not responding to treatment. The intubation was not working. They were running out of options.

"I'm so sorry," the doctor said. "I wish the news were better."

One night, just before Gwen was going to get into bed, her cell rang. It was the doctor.

"I believe this is it," she said. "It's unlikely your father will make it to morning."

Gwen began to weep.

"I wondered if you wanted to say goodbye. Not in person, I'm afraid, but over the phone."

Gwen said yes, she would like to do that.

"I'm heading down there now," Sloan said. "I'll get back to you shortly."

Gwen waited.

When the doctor called back, she said, "Go ahead."

"Dad, Daddy, can you hear me?" Gwen said. "Come on, Dad, talk to me."

". . . uhhhh . . . uhhh . . ."

"Daddy, I want to see you more than anything in the world. I do. But they won't let me in. I tried and they kicked me out, the bastards. You have to know that if I could be there, I would. If only they'd let you out, if they'd let you come home . . ."

". . . uhhh . . ."

"Everything that's happened to you, it's never been fair, it's never been right. And for it all to end like this . . . Please, just say something. There's never been a day, not one, since you had to leave us that I haven't thought about you, that I haven't wanted to see you. I love you so much."

There was nothing.

"Daddy, if you can hear me, just know that I'll make this right. I will. I swear, I will make this right. Christ, are you even hearing any of this? Have they got the phone to your ear? Do you even know it's me? Daddy? It's Gwen. It's Gwendoline, your good little witch, Daddy, and I love you so much."

She waited, hoping for some acknowledgment that would suggest her father had heard her.

Dr. Sloan came on. "I'm sorry," she said. "Your father's gone."

Tears ran down Gwen's cheeks. "But he did hear me, right? He heard me say goodbye."

There was a pause at the other end.

"Doctor? Did he hear me say goodbye?"

Later, Gwen would think, why didn't she just lie? She could have made something up. She could have said yes, her father *had* heard her, and not only that, he had mouthed the words, "I love you, Gwen," in the moments before he passed.

Maybe, Gwen often thought later, if the doctor had told a little white lie, she'd still be around today.

If only she hadn't said, "I'm sorry, he passed before your call was finished."

Looking back, Gwen believed that was the moment when her thirst for revenge had to be quenched. That was when Gwen decided people would pay for what they had done. Three people were on her list. Two could be readily found.

It would take some planning. She did not want to rush into it. But when it came time, she wanted her punishments to be meted out in quick succession.

She would start with the judge who sentenced her father. She sent Cayden, her longtime assistant, to bring him to her one night. She wanted him to know how his actions had changed her life, devastated her family.

And then Cayden held him under the water until he was dead.

Next, the doctor.

Before Cayden drowned her, Gwen explained how she'd kept her from saying goodbye to the most important man in her life. First, by not letting her into the hospital to see him, and second, by not getting the cell phone to his ear in time.

"That will be my lasting memory of him," Gwen told the doctor. "Of blathering away to him, telling him how much I loved him, and he didn't hear a goddamn word."

Cayden waded into the water, dragging the doctor with him, gripped her by the wrists, and took her down.

That left one more. The plan to find Michael Donohue had been in the works for a while. Gwen had researched the witness protection program. She learned all she could about Jack Givins. She had ID made up in the name of Gwen Kaminsky. She'd put to use those lessons from the theater classes she took in school years ago.

To find Michael Donohue, Gwen would have to pull out all the creative stops. Set up a fake office. Staff it with some Frohm employees. She hadn't expected Jack to demand a face-to-face with the "witness," which necessitated some last-minute scrambling, but all in all, it came together.

She was almost there.

SIXTY-THREE

Jack

"Gwen," I said with forced calm, "why do you have Lana's phone?"

"Because she's right here with me, Jack."

"Put her on."

"Can't do that right now," she said.

"Jesus Christ, put her on the phone," I said, my jaw clenching.

"I told you, Jack. That's not possible."

"Have you hurt her? Have you done something to Lana?" I tried to tamp down the panic in my voice. "Who the fuck are you, *really*?"

"You've found your father, haven't you? That's why you have some doubts."

"Jack! JACK!"

Lana's scream chilled me. "Lana!"

"There," Gwen said. "Now you know she's fine."

I said nothing. I had no words. I felt helpless, terrified, in no way prepared to deal with this turn of events.

And during that moment of silence, I heard, in the background, this:

Tickety tickety tickety tickety tickety.

"You know, Jack, I should be angry with you, running off

323

without informing me. You've put our arrangement in jeopardy. Where are you?"

I said, "The witness protection program has never heard of you."

"That would seem to confirm that you've found your father. Been doing some checking."

"I have to hand it to you, Gwen. You pulled it off. I fell for it."

"It would have been easier, I suppose, to just waterboard you or pull out your fingernails to find out where your dad was, but that only would have worked if you'd actually *known* where he was. So I had to go another way. Hope you knew where he was, or even if you didn't, find a way for you to lead us to him. And it appears to have worked. You've found your father, but you didn't take me with you."

I was thinking back to events of the last few weeks that would have made me unlikely to turn down her job offer.

"You set my car on fire," I said. "You got me fired from that other job before I'd even started."

"A simple phone call to the boss," she said. "About sexual harassment allegations from a previous job."

"That's not true. He never mentioned that."

"We told him you'd deny it, so there was no point in bringing it up. But we wanted something he'd find persuasive. He said he could come up with another reason."

"And Harry?"

"Cayden told him to tell you he couldn't sell the book, but sweetened the deal with an opportunity, and that phone. Yes, I wanted you to be hungry."

"What did you do to him?"

"When you told me you were hounding him, after hearing from your editor, that was a concern." She didn't have to say any more. There was a pause, and then, "Is your father there, in the room with you?"

"Uhh . . ."

"Please put him on, Jack."

I turned and looked at Dad. "She wants to talk to you."

Dad considered the request for a moment, then held out his hand. He tapped the screen to put the phone on speaker so that I could listen in, then set it on the table.

"I'm here," he said.

"Michael," Gwen said. "Forgive me for not knowing what you call yourself these days, but when you worked for my father, you were Michael Donohue."

Dad's eyes seemed to dance for a second. He was thinking back, trying to remember her.

"You came to work with him some days," Dad said. "And I remember, when I would come to the house, I would see you sometimes." Dad looked almost wistful. "There was one day, I came to your father's office, and you were dancing for him. He called you a witch."

"Gwendoline," she said, "the good witch. You were always very . . . nice to me. You didn't suck up to me like the others, just because my dad was the boss. You talked to me like a regular person." She paused. "My father thought the world of you, you know."

"I know."

"Do you remember the day you took me for a hot dog?" Gwen asked.

Dad glanced up, as if the answer might be written on the ceiling of the trailer, as he tried to recollect. "Vaguely. Your father was to take you to lunch but he had to cancel. Asked me to take you someplace fancy. But all you wanted was a hot dog from a stand. You said your father thought hot dogs were disgusting and he never let you have one, which seemed kind of funny, given the kind of shit he sold in his fast-food outlets. But if I got you one, you said it'd be our secret."

"You're good," Gwen said. "And we had to make up a story about where you supposedly had taken me."

"What did we come up with?" Dad asked.

"Green Dragon Tavern," she said. "You knew the menu by heart, so we were able to come up with something convincing. I told my dad I had fish and chips."

"I remember."

"That's what makes this so hard, Michael," Gwen said. "Is it okay if I call you Michael, whatever your name is now? Back then, of course, it was Mr. Donohue. But we're all adults now."

"Michael is fine."

"It's hard, because I once knew you to be a good man. Before you betrayed my father."

"What would you like me to say, Gwen? After all this time? That I'm sorry? I suppose I am. Sorry that it turned out the way it did. Sorry I let your father talk me into things I never should have done. Sorry I wasn't a stronger person. Sorry I ever met Galen Frohm. I've no doubt he was a wonderful father to you, but he was the most evil person I ever knew. I understand he passed away. You have my condolences."

Gwen was silent for a moment. Then: "You took my father away from me. You robbed me of all those precious years I could have had with him. And just when he was about to be released, he got sick. He died all alone, Michael. All alone. He was treated despicably."

Dad said, "That must have been very difficult for you. I don't expect you to care, but the actions I took robbed me of years with my son and my wife. They wouldn't come with me, and if I'd stayed with them, I would have put them at risk."

"How did you spend those years?" Gwen asked. "What was the view from your prison cell like? Oh, wait. There was no prison cell, was there?"

Dad looked weary. I could tell he'd had enough of this.

"What do you want, Gwen?" he asked.

"I want you to die," she said.

"Well, that will happen eventually, but I'm guessing you'd like it to be sooner rather than later."

"Present yourself to me," she said.

Dad said, "Say again?"

"Turn yourself in, to me, and we'll let your son's girlfriend go."

Dad and I exchanged glances. I suppose we both knew this was coming. Gwen had a strong hand to play.

"Where are you?" Dad asked.

Gwen chuckled. "There's an idea. I just tell you, and then you can call the police. We'll need to work out the details. I'll get back to you. And I can't impress upon you enough that I'll kill her if I get even a hint that you've notified the authorities. Make sure Jack knows. Make sure Jack knows I'm prepared to do what I have to do."

"He understands," Dad said.

There was no reply to that. Dad picked up the phone, saw that the call had ended, and turned to me.

"She's gone?" I said.

"She's gone."

"I know where they are," I said. "I mean, I don't know *where* they are, but I think I've been there. I could hear something in the background, a ticking, like a fan. When they took me to see the witness I was writing a backstory for, there was a fan that sounded like that. But I was blindfolded. I don't know where we actually went. It was out in the country." I stopped talking and waited for him to say something. He seemed deep in thought.

I couldn't take it anymore and asked, "What the hell are we going to do?"

And I realized that my father didn't have to do anything.

Lana was a stranger who meant nothing to him. Did Gwen really believe my father would surrender himself to save someone he'd never met?

After all, hadn't he walked away once before to save his ass?

Okay, he would have argued he also did that to save my mother and me from any retribution Galen Frohm might mete out. Sure, Frohm's goons threw a few scares into us after Dad was gone, but he never went so far as to actually harm us. Frohm had to know holy hell would rain down upon him, even if he was already in prison. There were ways to make a bad situation even worse.

But this. This was different.

All Dad had to do was get into his car, find a cheap motel for the night, and come morning, Stan would find a new life for him.

And Lana would lose hers.

This was all on me. I'd been suckered and drawn Lana into this nightmare.

Dad had gone a good half minute without responding to my question. Finally, he had one for me.

"What are you thinking?" he asked.

"That the smartest thing for you is to run," I said. "Gwen knows I've found you, but she doesn't know where we are. You take off now and you're home free. You don't know Lana. You didn't get her into this."

He nodded. "True." He went to the fridge, took out another beer, opened it, and took a sip. "Show me her picture again."

Again? And then I remembered I had shown Lana's picture to him when we met in the diner after the road rage incident. I picked up my phone, found a shot of Lana I had taken one day when we were on Boston Common. She was looking into the camera, laughing.

I handed the phone to my father.

He studied the picture. "She's a lovely girl. She has a . . . a kind of sparkle in her eyes, doesn't she?"

"Yes," I said, holding my breath.

"And she means the world to you, I'm guessing."

"More than you can possibly know."

He handed the phone back to me, drew on the can, then wiped his mouth with the back of his hand.

"I guess we're going to have to go save her," Dad said.

SIXTY-FOUR

Jack

Once Dad had made the decision to help instead of run, we needed a plan.

"So you're pretty sure they're at that cabin," Dad said, "but you don't know where the cabin is."

"Yeah," I said, already feeling defeated. "The only person I can think of who might know where it is, is dead."

"Your witness," he said. "The one you interviewed."

I nodded.

"Except he wasn't a witness. Gwen's not with witness protection, so that guy really wasn't a witness. Didn't you say you saw him on TV?"

Slowly, I said, "He's an actor."

"Gwen hired him to play a part. So that you'd be convinced she was what she claimed to be. Did you see his body?"

"No."

"Did she show you a picture?"

"No." I thought about that. "So Garth Walton doesn't have to be dead." I looked at Dad. "Then why did she tell me he was?"

He gave me a look that said he had no idea.

"Wait a minute," I said. "She came up with the story that he'd been killed right after I told her I'd seen him on TV. Maybe she

330

was worried I'd start getting suspicious at that point, start putting it together. That she'd hired him for a role. So Gwen improvised. Told me he'd just been killed to put me on edge, freak me out, rattle me." I laughed morbidly. "It worked."

"If he is alive," Dad said, "and we can find him, he can lead us to that cabin."

"So long as they didn't blindfold him, too."

"No need to. He wasn't the one being scammed. You were. The blindfold was all part of the charade. Let's not waste any more time here. We head back to Boston and try to find this Garth Walton along the way."

We decided to hit the road. We opted to take Lana's Beemer instead of Dad's car. The BMW was built for speed and hugging the road, and I was grateful Lana had kept it in tip-top running condition. I got in on the passenger side because I was going to be doing research on my phone.

"Can you drive a stick?" I asked him.

"Please," he said derisively. He was about to get in on the driver's side when he stopped and said, "I need one minute."

I watched him walk over to the trailer next door and rap hard on the door. Seconds later, it opened, and Gord appeared. He stepped outside. I couldn't hear what they were saying. Dad did a lot of talking, and Gord did a lot of nodding. Then, finally, they shook hands.

Dad got back in the car, grim-faced, and said, "Let's go."

"What was that about?" I asked.

"I told him I wouldn't be coming back."

Once we were on the road, I looked in the glove box and found a notepad and a couple of pens, which was not only convenient but unsurprising, considering the car belonged to a reporter. I knew if I looked in the trunk, I'd find a bright-orange hard hat and matching vest. Lana always kept those in the trunk, along with a clipboard, because she'd learned using those items would gain you access to anything. Buildings, accident scenes, whatever. But all I needed for now was a notepad and a pen to jot down any useful information I might find online about Garth Walton.

We hadn't gone very far when Dad, after glancing down at the dash, said, "We're pretty close to running on fumes."

We spotted a station about five minutes later and Dad steered off the road and up to the pumps.

"I'll be quick," I said.

I took out my wallet, grabbed a credit card, and left the wallet on the dash, along with the notepad and the pen. I got out, hoping the pump would be one where you swiped the card and didn't have to go into the station, but no such luck. Eager to save time where I could, I only put in about half a tank.

I shouted to Dad through the open passenger window, "Gotta go inside. Be right back."

He waved okay. I ran into the station and waited behind a guy who wanted to load up on chips and dip and buy a couple of lottery tickets before settling his gas bar tab. I thought, for a moment, while he hunted through his jacket to find his wallet, that I might have to kill him, but decided that committing a homicide might delay us even further.

Dad had the Beemer in first gear before I had my right foot back in the car and took off with a squeal of the tires. The wallet slid off the dash and I had to feel around the footwell to retrieve it.

A few miles later, after I'd been looking up anything I could find on my phone about Garth Walton, Dad said, "Well?"

I'd made a few scribbles on the notepad. Walton had a website where he promoted himself as an actor and for voice work. There was a list of audiobooks he'd narrated.

"Hang on," I said. "He's in a play. In Boston."

It was a revival of *The Price*, an Arthur Miller play. I knew some of his work—*Death of a Salesman*, *The Crucible*, for example—but I had never seen this one, and didn't know much about the character of Walter, who was being played by Walton.

"Is it currently running?" Dad asked.

"Yeah," I said, and looked at the dashboard clock. It was closing in on ten. "In fact, it's on right this second. At the Citizens Bank Opera House, on Washington, a couple of blocks over from the Common."

We were about an hour out from there. I read information about the production on the ticket website.

"It runs about two and a half hours, plus an intermission," I said. "It started at eight."

"So he's there now, and should be done around eleven," Dad said. He glanced at me. "Maybe we should meet him at the stage door."

I found a picture of him, enlarged it with thumb and index finger, and turned the phone so Dad could see it.

"I know what he looks like, but you don't," I said.

Dad took a good look. "We'll take the notebook. See if we can get his autograph."

The theater was emptying out as we drove down Washington. The street was jammed with people hailing cabs and getting into their ordered Ubers.

"Not a moment too soon," Dad said.

He pulled the car up to the curb in a no-parking zone the better part of a block away. There were cars illegally stopped everywhere and no sign of police issuing tickets. No tow trucks, either. It was probably like this at the end of every show. Dad put the flashers on.

"I'll watch the front, in case he comes out that way, and you take the stage door," he said.

We both bailed from the car and ran the half block to the

theater. I scooted down the alley, hunting for where the actors would exit, leaving Dad standing amid the throngs of audience members who were leaving. When I got to the stage door, I joined half a dozen autograph seekers waiting excitedly for the performers to emerge.

When a woman finally did, she was besieged by fans. A minute later, a man in his sixties came out. He signed for a couple of people, then raised a hand and offered apologies, saying he had to meet someone for a late dinner. Two more people came out the door. Actors, production people, I had no idea. But none of them was Walton.

The autograph seekers drifted away, and I was left there alone. I decided to give it another minute.

The door opened and a short, round man came out. Definitely not the guy I was hoping to see.

"Hey," I said, "is Garth Walton coming out?"

"Oh," the man said, "I think he left right after the curtain dropped."

Shit.

I ran back up the alley to the theater entrance. There were a handful of people still milling about, waiting at the curb for rides. Most of the cabs and Ubers were gone.

Dad wasn't around, either.

I looked down the street and saw the Beemer still at the curb, lights flashing. I started running. As I got closer, I could see Dad sitting behind the wheel, alone.

I got in next to him, panting.

"I didn't see him," I said. "They said he left right away. And I didn't find anything online that would tell us where he lives."

Dad appeared unconcerned. "It's okay," he said. "He's in the trunk."

SIXTY-FIVE

L ana sniffed.

Gwen shot her an exasperated look. "I swear to God."

"If you untied me I could blow my nose," she said.

"Cayden, wipe her nose."

Cayden looked as though he'd been asked to clean up after a sick dog. "No way."

"I'm stuffed up," Lana said. "And it's worse, being out here in the woods. All kinds of pollen in the air. I have some pills and some spray in my purse."

Gwen snapped her fingers like she was getting a waiter's attention. "Cayden, find her meds."

He'd already been through the bag once to get her cell. He opened it up, started rummaging inside.

"I don't see it," he said. "There's enough shit in here to stock a Walgreens."

"I could find it if you bring it over to me," Lana said. "The pills are in a little blister pack. I might have tucked them into one of the side pockets."

Cayden carried the purse over to Gwen and dropped it in her lap. "You find it."

Gwen glanced into the bag, saw several tissues, and decided there was no way she was sticking her hand in there.

"Untie her," Gwen said, then gave Lana a menacing glare. "Don't do anything stupid."

Cayden went around the back of Lana's chair and, with the pruner he was going to use to cut off her finger, snipped the plastic zip tie around her wrists. "There," he said.

Lana brought her hands around in front of her, flexed her fingers, and rubbed her wrists, which had welts on them from the bindings. But Gwen wasn't ready to hand over the purse yet. Something she'd spotted inside had caught her interest.

"Hello, what's this?" she said.

She still wasn't about to reach in. She waved Cayden over, pointed into the bag, and said, "You see that?"

"See what?"

"That thing that looks like a key chain?"

He reached into the bag and brought out the item. It was about the size of a plastic lighter, with some kind of opening at one end.

Cayden examined it.

"It's pepper spray," he said.

Gwen made a *tsk tsk* sound.

"You're a very bad girl," Gwen said. "That's what you were going for, isn't it?"

Lana shook her head. "Keep the fucking pepper spray. I really need my meds. Let me find my pills."

Gwen held on to the purse for another moment, trying to decide whether Lana was still up to something. Slowly, she handed over the bag. Lana set it in her lap as she searched it.

"Here we go," Lana said, taking out a foil blister pack that still had a couple of tiny pills in it. She forced one out of its protective seal, then looked at Cayden.

"Could I have a glass of water?"

He couldn't have sighed more deeply if Lana had asked him to do her laundry. He tucked the pepper spray down into the front pocket of his jeans, got a glass from the cupboard, and ran some water into it. He walked back and handed Lana the glass.

"Thank you," she said, putting the pill on her tongue and washing it down with one gulp. She handed the glass back to Cayden.

Lana dropped the pills back into her bag, then reached for a tissue to wipe her nose.

"Are you quite done?" Gwen asked.

"Yeah," she said, hoping that as she withdrew her hand from the purse for the last time, Gwen would not notice that she had made a fist.

"Tie her back up," Gwen told Cayden. "And turn off that fan. I can't take it anymore."

Lana obliged by putting her arms behind the chair, her two hands still fists. Cayden cinched them together with another plastic cuff.

Neither he nor Gwen knew that there was one other self-defense tool tucked away in that purse. Something less obvious than the pepper-spray key chain. The little gadget Florence Knight had given Lana.

The lipstick knife.

SIXTY-SIX

Jack

I said, "You stuffed him in the trunk?"

Dad, putting the car in gear and hitting the gas, looked unruffled as he said, "I had a feeling he might not stay in the car, even if I asked him nicely. Good thing this is an older BMW. Doesn't have one of those emergency escape handles in the trunk. He'll be in there until we let him out."

I was speechless.

Dad said, "I spotted him coming out with the crowd. Went up to him, asked if he was Garth Walton, and he said yes, and I said he was my wife's favorite actor, which might have been pushing it a bit, because really, he's not been in all that much and he's not all that famous, but I guess actors are vain enough to fall for that kind of thing. I said my wife used a cane, and was in the car, and would he please come and say hello?"

At least he'd confirmed that it was Walton. Bad enough that he—okay, that *we*—had kidnapped someone. It would have been even worse if we'd nabbed the wrong person.

"When we got to the car and he didn't see anyone, that's when I put the gun to his gut and kindly asked him to get into the trunk." Dad held up a cell phone. "I took this off him, turned it off. Soon as I see a good place to pull over, we'll have a talk."

I hadn't even noticed that Dad had brought a gun. I was betting relocated witnesses weren't supposed to have a gun. Maybe he'd borrowed it from Gord.

Dad did a few twists and turns through downtown streets and finally found a spot that looked secluded enough that someone wouldn't observe us getting a man out of the trunk. He came to a stop, killed the engine, and the two of us got out. We went around to the back and Dad lightly rapped on the trunk lid.

"Mr. Walton, we're going to open the trunk, but I caution you against trying anything. I have no interest in hurting you, but I will if necessary. Do you understand?"

A muffled, frightened "Yes" came from inside.

Dad opened the trunk. A light came on, bright enough for us to see him clearly, curled up in the fetal position, surrounded by Lana's hard hat, safety vest, and other items. He squinted and focused on me. It took him a moment to realize that he had seen me someplace before.

"Hi," I said. "Last time we met, you were going by the name Bill."

He blinked several times. Adjusting to the light and making sure it was really me.

"Jesus, this can't be happening," he said.

"I have to say, it was a terrific performance. Not the play. Didn't have a chance to see the play. But your gig at the cabin. The whole Russian torture thing with the gas down the throat? That was a nice touch. Where'd you get that from? A James Bond movie?"

I could see he was debating what to say, wondering how much I knew. Sure, we'd blown his cover, but did we know who'd engaged his services and why? I decided to let him know.

"Gwen Frohm hired you," I said. "Told you to convince me you were the real deal. Did she tell you why? Because she was using me to try to find this man." I pointed a thumb toward Dad. "This is my father. You've met."

"You can't do this," Walton said. "This is kidnapping."

Dad nodded, glanced at me. "Astute."

"Where's that cabin?" I asked. "Where'd you put on that show?"

"I can tell you where it is," he said. "Just let me go."

"I have a better idea," I said. "Take us there." Dad was probably thinking the same thing. If we let Walton out of our sight, he might call Gwen and warn her.

"What's so important about that cabin?" he asked.

"It has a squeaky fan," I said.

Walton promised to behave if we let him out of the trunk. We put him in the back seat, and this time, it was my turn to drive. Dad, armed, sat next to Walton in case he decided to change his mind at some stoplight or grab me from behind. And just to be sure, I engaged the child-safety lock on Walton's door so that it would not open when he pulled the lever.

He directed us to take I-93 North out of the city. The cabin, he said, was off Tyngsboro Road, not far from Westford.

"Whose place is it?" Dad asked.

"Her assistant's place," Walton said. "Cayden."

"How'd she find you?" I asked, raising my voice to be heard over the seat back.

"I know her from years ago," he said. "We had a couple of classes together back in college. One of them was a theater class. I was more interested in pursuing that than she was at the time, but she was pretty good. We were kind of a thing there for a while, until it stopped working out. And then, after all this time, I hear from her."

"What was she like?" I asked. "Back in college."

"Kind of wild, you know? Not, like, in a sexual way, but her moods. They were all over the map. She could be really nice and the next minute she'd be in a rage about something. You never knew what to expect. She had this fucked-up family. Her dad was in prison. She'd talk about him all the time, how he got this raw deal, how there were a bunch of people who'd pay someday for what they did to him. It got kind of tiresome, to be honest."

"So when she asked you to do your little performance, why'd you agree to it?" I asked.

"Well, first of all, she said she'd give me ten grand, so a no-brainer," Walton said. "And Gwen's got this edge to her. You don't say no to Gwen. You want to stay on her good side."

Walton told me to take I-95 South, which actually headed in more of a westerly direction at that point, for a few miles, then head north on US-3 until we got to Westford. After we drove through Westford, I was to keep my eye open for Tyngsboro Road.

"I was only up here the once," he said, "and it was daytime, so it's going to be hard to spot. There's a mailbox with no name on it at the end of the road going in. I remember it was just past a red-and-white real estate sign."

Walton was quiet for a moment before asking, "Is it one of you guys? Or both of you? That she blames for what happened to her father?"

"That'd be me," Dad said.

"Why'd she get me to put on that performance?" he asked. "What the fuck was that all about, anyway?"

"Long story," I said. "I doubt you'd even believe it."

As we drove up Tyngsboro, I slowed down to thirty, looking for that red-and-white For Sale sign. Walton was leaning to the right, looking between the seats and beyond the windshield.

"I think we're getting close," he said.

As we crept along, I didn't have to worry about holding up traffic. It was past midnight, and we hadn't seen another car in miles.

"There," Walton said. "I see it."

The sign was on the left side of the road. Now I was driving at a crawl, looking for an opening in the trees that would indicate a driveway.

I saw one and brought the car to a stop on the shoulder.

"There?" I said to Walton.

"There," he said, his voice bordering on cheerful. "I'm sure that's it. With the mailbox with no name on it. Just a number. I remember."

My cell phone rang. On the screen: LANA. My heart did a somersault. Would this really be her? Had she somehow escaped? Or would it be Gwen?

"Hello?" I said breathlessly.

"Jack."

It was Gwen.

"Yeah," I said.

"Just an update. We do this in the morning. We'll call you at ten with further details. In the city. Same rules apply. You bring in the police and your girlfriend will die."

"I understand," I said.

"Now you can have a good night's sleep." Gwen ended the call.

"She says it goes down in the morning," I said to Dad. Looking in the rearview mirror, I could almost make out a grin on his face.

"Sooner, I'd say."

I wondered what his plan was. I figured he had to have one. He wasn't going to just walk into a trap, let Gwen kill him, in exchange for Lana's freedom. That'd be crazy. I had an inkling of what he might be up to, and I was betting it had something to do with his friend Gord. He must have given him some instructions when he'd gone to his trailer to say goodbye.

Maybe he'd been following us this whole time. Or Dad had some tracker on him that Gord was following. That had to be it. But if I was right, why hadn't Dad told me about it? He must have had his reasons.

"Okay, everybody out," Dad said. "Jack, can you pass me your phone for a second?"

I picked it up, turned in the seat, and, before handing it to him, said, "What do you want it for?"

"Want to check something," he said. "What's the pass code?"

I gave him the four-digit code. He took the phone, pocketed it, and, once I had hit a button on the driver's door to unlock the back doors, we all got out.

Dad, waving the gun at Walton, indicated that he wanted him to come around to the back of the car. He waved me over, as well.

"Shit, not again," Walton said as Dad took the keys from me.

Dad shook his head apologetically, hit the button, and the trunk lid swung open.

And then, suddenly, Dad shoved me in and slammed the lid shut.

SIXTY-SEVEN

Jack's father had both palms on the trunk lid, checking to make sure it was firmly locked.

"Sorry, son," he said, shouting to be heard.

"Let me out!" Jack shouted. "Open the fucking trunk!"

There was banging on the underside of the lid, which Michael Donohue ignored. He turned and looked at a wide-eyed Walton.

"Take a walk," Michael said.

"Seriously?" he asked.

Michael nodded. "How far down this drive is the cabin?"

"Maybe a hundred yards, give or take. Road takes a slight bend and the trees clear and the cabin's sitting right there."

Michael patted the actor's shoulder. "Thanks for your help. Hope you'll forgive the abduction. It wasn't my son's idea. I'd say, if you flag someone down in about half an hour, you could have them call the cops. Should be done by then."

"Yeah, okay," Walton said. He kept standing there, looking at the trunk, then back to Michael. Jack hadn't stopped shouting.

"*Go*," Michael said to Walton.

The actor turned and started walking in the direction they'd come from. Michael watched him until he was swallowed by darkness, then turned his attention back to the trunk. He banged it hard with his fist to get Jack to stop making noise.

"Jack," he said, just loud enough to be heard, "sit tight. I'm going to go get your girl."

Michael started walking down the drive.

Inside the cabin, Gwen, who still had Lana's phone in her hand, said, "I guess we might as well get what sleep we can."

There was one bedroom off the kitchen. Cayden said, "You take the bed, I'll take the couch."

"What about me?" asked Lana, still tied to the chair.

"No one's stopping you from closing your eyes," Gwen said.

To Cayden, she said, "We'll head back to the city around six. Get some breakfast at a drive-through. We can give her another jab so she won't cause us any trouble on the way."

Lana tried to find some small comfort in that. At least she would be alive tomorrow. Whether she would be awake, or live to see the end of it, was still in question.

The phone in Gwen's hand rang. Startled, she saw JACK on the screen, and considered declining the call. She had been about to turn it off, anyway, in the event that the phone might be used to track their location.

"What the hell," she said to herself, then tapped the screen and put the phone to her ear. "What?"

"Hello, Gwen."

Not Jack. His father.

"I told Jack I'll be in touch with instructions in the morning," she said.

"No need. Let's get this done. I'm here."

Gwen spun around, looking at the front door. "Jesus Christ," she said. She snapped at Cayden, "He's here."

He ran to the closest window and looked outside, but there was nothing but total darkness.

"Michael," she said into the phone, "how did you find us?"

"Doesn't matter. I'm here. Let's get it done."

Gwen walked to the door and opened it. "You're lying. I don't see you."

"Watch," Michael said.

In the distance, for only a second, she saw a bright face of a cell phone.

"Okay, so you're here," Gwen said. "Who's with you?"

"No one. I came with Jack, but I left him in the trunk. Wanted to handle this alone. I'm here for the trade. Lana comes out, unharmed, and I'm all yours. And in the interests of complete disclosure, I'm telling you that I'm armed. But once Lana is free, I'll toss you the gun."

She snapped her fingers at Cayden.

"Give me the gun," she said.

He met her at the door, handed her the weapon.

"Watch the girl," she said, and stepped out onto the porch.

"Show yourself," she said to Michael.

The sky was clear and peppered with stars. As her eyes adjusted, she was able to make out the shapes of trees, the gray gravel of the driveway. She could hear footsteps, and, squinting, saw a dark form about sixty feet away.

"Hold it right there," she said, and ended the call. They could chat without phones now.

"You could try shooting from there," Michael said, putting Jack's phone into his pocket, "but you'd never hit me. Not very likely I'd hit you, either. I'll wait here until Lana comes out. I'll hand her the car keys as she goes by. Once I hear the car drive off, I'll drop the gun and I'm all yours. A deal is a deal. My life for Lana's."

"You're up to something," she said.

"Your call," Michael said. "I'd rather not stand here all night. I'm not as young as I used to be. Legs get tired."

Time to roll the dice, Gwen thought. She called back into the cabin, "Cayden, send her out!"

SIXTY-EIGHT

Jack

That goddamn son of a bitch.

I should have seen it coming. Dad didn't want to risk something happening to me when he went to get Lana. I didn't know who I was more angry with: Dad or myself.

I kept banging on the trunk lid, hoping to change his mind, hoping he would let me out so that I could go with him. I didn't want him facing Gwen alone. And maybe he wouldn't be. Maybe I was right, that he had Gord waiting for him in the wings.

I'd heard him give Walton his freedom, and then the sound of his receding footsteps. He was gone, and I was on my own in the back of this fucking car with no inside emergency release. If I couldn't escape the trunk the conventional way, maybe I could get out in some other fashion.

I rolled over so that I was facing the back of the rear seats. I started pounding on them, figuring if I could get them to fold forward, I could crawl into the car's cabin and get out through one of the doors. If the rear doors were still somehow locked, I'd squeeze between the front seats and make my escape from there. And if I could manage all *that*, I'd qualify for my contortionist's certificate.

Using my elbow like a pile driver, I hit the seat back over and over again. I had felt a vertical ridge running along there in the middle, which suggested to me that the rear seats could be folded down in two pieces. So they were meant to open through to the trunk, but the releases would be atop the seats, inside the cabin.

I thought if I pounded on them long enough, whatever bracket was holding them in place would give way. But after about two dozen strikes, and an elbow that had gone numb, the seat wasn't budging.

I felt around in the trunk—Dad had my phone, so I couldn't even use the flashlight app to see what was in here—and found the hard hat and the clipboard and the fluorescent-orange vest Lana sometimes donned at accident scenes. A crowbar would have been nice.

Wait, wouldn't there be a crowbar, or something close to it, under the floor, in the compartment with the spare tire? Something with a flat, screwdriver-like end that I could use to pry open the trunk, or rip a hole in the back seat?

The trouble with that plan was that I couldn't lift the trunk floor because I was on top of it. I tried tucking myself as far forward as possible, then reaching to the back end of the trunk to get my fingers under the floor's edge. But I could only pry it up about an inch. There was no way I could get at anything that was beneath me.

I ran my hands around the inside of the trunk to see whether I could find anything else useful. I came upon something long, narrow, and cylindrical. Like a dowel, a stick of wood. Actually, it felt more like a stick of dynamite.

It was a road flare.

What the hell could I accomplish with a road flare? In the confined space of this trunk, I could undoubtedly kill myself. Road flares burned, I recalled reading, at about a thousand degrees. But if I ignited it, and aimed it at the trunk lock mechanism, could I burn my way out? Would it melt the lock? If I aimed it at the seats, would they catch on fire and attract the attention of someone passing by?

Well, there'd hardly been anyone on this road when we were coming up here. And even if some random passerby saw the flames, would they open the driver's door, hit the trunk release, and get me out, or simply call the fire department and wait for help to arrive? By that time, I'd be literal toast.

Shit.

I went back to ramming my elbow into the seat a few more times, but I wasn't getting anywhere with that. Getting onto my back, squeezing my knees to my chest, I tried pushing one more time against the trunk lid with my feet.

No luck.

I felt around again for that flare.

Lighting it would probably be the stupidest thing I could ever do. Except, maybe, for staying in this trunk and letting Gwen kill my dad.

SIXTY-NINE

ayden was on edge. Jack's dad's surprise appearance had unnerved him. He was breathing rapidly and flexing his fingers, as if preparing to take action, but he didn't know what it should be.

"Cayden, send her out!"

"Good, okay, okay," he said to himself, relieved that there was finally something for him to do. He turned to Lana and said, "Okay, sweetheart. This is it."

He grabbed the pruner from the table and moved in her direction.

Lana's mind was racing. Were they really going to make the trade? Were they really going to let her go?

No, never, not a chance.

Gwen and Cayden might go through the motions. They might make it look like they were going to keep their end of the deal. But they couldn't. There was no way.

They have to kill me, too. They have to kill Jack.

Cayden got behind the chair and knelt down. Lana's hands were still coiled into fists.

"Hang on a second here," he said, sliding the pruner over the zip tie and squeezing. The tie snapped apart. Lana brought her arms around in front of her, rubbed her right wrist with her left hand, but kept her right hand closed.

"Okay, let's go," Cayden said, coming around the chair, his back to her for about a second.

She opened her fist, moved the lipstick tube to between her thumb and index finger, and quickly removed the cap with her left hand, exposing the inch-long blade.

She bowed her head and said, "I feel a little light-headed. I don't think I can stand."

Cayden turned and leaned over to get his hands under her arms at the same moment Lana shot to her feet.

She was worried about being able to hold on to the lipstick knife. It didn't have much of a handle. A dagger this wasn't. There was no rubber grip to grasp. So she squeezed it between her thumb and two fingers as firmly as she could, fully aware that she was probably only going to get one shot at this.

She drove the knife into the underside of his throat. Hard. Cayden had started to raise his hands defensively, but he wasn't expecting it and was too slow. She felt the blade penetrate the leathery, whiskered skin under his jawbone.

She jumped back after that first strike. Cayden made a gurgling noise and slapped his hand over the wound, blood pouring out between his fingers. He lunged forward, and Lana swung, the knife catching the palm of his hand, plunging right into the center of it. She still managed to hold on to it as blood bubbled out from between his lips.

Cayden dropped to his knees, flailing at Lana with one hand while pressing down on the neck wound with the other.

Lana, panting, heart pounding, didn't want to risk getting too close to him again. The lipstick knife was great for a first strike, maybe even a second, but it was a close-contact kind of weapon, and now that Cayden understood her intentions, she needed to keep her distance.

At least for as long as he was alive.

She scanned the room, looking for something else to use as

a weapon, something to bring him down for good. Her eyes landed on the chair she'd just been tied to. She grabbed the back of it and swung it at Cayden, the legs catching him on the side of the head.

Cayden went down.

He lay writhing on the floor, blood continuing to pour out from his neck, between his lips, and his hand.

"You fruckin gunt," he said.

"Hey, Cayden!" Gwen shouted from the porch. "Let's go!"

Lana looked at the door and remembered that Gwen had the gun.

Lana didn't have much time.

She got down on her knees next to Cayden. He was too near the end to care much that she was digging into the front pocket of his jeans.

SEVENTY

Jack

I thought of a story my dad told me when I was little, maybe seven or eight years old.

We were at the park and he was pushing me on a swing. I mentioned that when I was only three or four, he used to toss me in the air and catch me. It reminded him of some parable, the origins of which remain unknown to me. He might have made it up himself.

"There was this dad and a little boy," Dad said. "The boy asked his father to pick him up and toss him into the air. The dad says okay, and picks the kid up, and is getting ready to toss him, but just before he does, the kid gets scared and asks, you're gonna catch me, right? You won't let me hit the ground? And the dad says, of course not, and he tosses the kid in the air, and makes no attempt to catch him, and the kid hits the ground hard. He starts crying and he says to his dad, you said you were going to catch me, and the dad says, let that be a lesson to you. Never trust anybody."

And here I was, locked in a trunk. I had trusted him, and he had failed to catch me.

Unless, in his mind, this was the only way to protect me.

I was thinking about all that as I ran my hand over that flare.

Did I seriously believe I could burn my way out of the trunk without killing myself? Did it make sense to light it up when I was trapped in here, no doubt right over the car's gas tank?

A few more attempts at breaking through the rear seat seemed in order before I tried anything that stupid.

I figured whatever bracket held the seats in place would be at the top, so that was where I tried to focus my efforts. I bashed it again and again and again.

"Come on, you motherfucker!" I shouted. In the cocoon of that trunk, I nearly deafened myself with my own exasperation.

I thought the seat gave way, ever so slightly.

"Yes! *Yes!*"

And with three more strikes, half of the back seat tipped forward.

"Ha!" I cried. I pushed the seat farther forward, and it flopped down onto the bottom cushion. The starlit sky provided enough illumination to make out the interior of the car.

The question now was whether I could squeeze myself through the opening. If I could get even partway, I might be able to reach the release atop the other half of the back seat. If I could drop that, things would get a little easier.

I managed to stretch my arms out above my head, attempting to narrow my body. I got my arms through the hole, gripped the front edge of the seat, my fingers rubbing up against the back of the driver's seat. I twisted onto my back, the metal framing of the opening digging into my abdomen, and reached up to find the other seat-back release. I pulled on it, and suddenly my escape hatch became twice as large.

I allowed myself no more than ten seconds to savor my victory and catch my breath before I slithered the rest of the way out of the trunk. As I'd feared, the back doors would not open, so I had to crawl through the space between the two front seats, reaching the passenger seat on my two hands. I grasped the door handle, pulled, and pushed the door wide, light filling the car from the overhead fixture as I slid headfirst out the side and onto the gravel shoulder.

The stones dug into my palms and body as I landed. I was about to get up when I heard something.

Footsteps.

Someone running up the road.

I stayed low, not wanting to be seen, but the light coming from inside the car was hindering my attempt to stay hidden.

A figure came around the back of the car, spotted me on the ground.

"Hey," said Walton. "I came back to help you get out."

I wanted to laugh. But instead, I struggled to my feet, made the instinctive gesture of dusting myself off, and said, "It's the thought that counts."

"I would have flagged down someone if anyone had gone by," he said, "but there haven't been any cars along here. But I found a house."

"A house?"

He pointed in the direction he'd come from.

"A farmhouse. Went up to the door and started banging. Some lady came to the door but wouldn't open it. I told her to call the police, to look for this car."

I reached out and patted him on the shoulder. "Great. Do you think she did it?"

"I guess we'll know soon enough."

"I'm going in," I said. "Stay here with the car, in case they do."

I started running.

SEVENTY-ONE

Michael would tell Lana, after she'd been released, to lay on the horn once she got to the car. Once he'd heard it, he'd know she was safe and on her way. Oh, and he'd give her a heads-up about who was in the trunk.

Michael didn't know whether this would work, but he didn't have a better idea. It was the right thing to do, and doing the right thing was long overdue.

Nothing left to lose, really. The clock had nearly run out.

He figured Galen Frohm's daughter was a nutcase, but you could be a nutcase and still have a legitimate grievance. Michael had done what he'd had to do back in the day, but he also knew he'd ruined her life. Just as he had the lives of those who loved Abel Gartner and Len Klay and that Milwaukee dollar store manager who was stealing from Frohm. And even that kiddie porn guy in Nebraska. There was a chance someone loved even *him*. Michael knew the list of people who never got justice was not a short one.

Did anyone *ever* really get justice?

He stood there under the stars and waited for Lana to appear.

When Gwen had shouted "Cayden, send her out!" he had expected to see her momentarily. Gwen must have, too, because a few seconds later, she called out again.

"Hey, Cayden! Let's go!"

Something was wrong.

Gwen yelled to Michael, "Stay there!" Then she turned and pushed open the door.

And screamed.

Michael ran toward the cabin. Gwen staggered inside, dropping the gun and screaming as she put her hands to her face. That was when Michael saw Lana standing there, her right arm out straight, holding something in her hand so small that he could not make out what it was. But he could guess.

Pepper spray.

Gwen tripped over a frilled carpet edge and landed on the floor. Lana sidestepped her and ran out of the cabin, at which point she saw Michael heading her way.

Although the two of them had never met one another, there were glints of recognition.

You're Jack's dad.

You're Jack's girlfriend.

And they ran, briefly, into one another's arms.

Lana, breathless, said, "I don't know how long she's blinded for."

Michael immediately noticed the blood on Lana's hand and arm. In the starry glow, it had an almost purplish hue.

"You're hurt," he said.

"No, no, it's not me!" she cried. Michael saw borderline hysteria in her eyes. If the woman wasn't already traumatized, she would be soon. "The other one! I got him! I fucking got him!"

Of all the things Michael might have thought at that moment, he wouldn't have expected it to be this: She's a keeper, this one.

He reached into his pocket and brought out a set of keys. "Your car's at the road. Jack's in the trunk. He's okay. Get him out and get the fuck out of here as fast as you can." He pushed the keys into her hand.

She started to go, then stopped and grabbed Michael by the arm. "Come on!" she said.

"No," Michael said. "Not yet."

She kept pulling on his arm. "You have to come!"

Michael raised his voice. "Go! *Go!*"

Lana hesitated for two more seconds, decided to do as ordered, and ran. Michael watched until the dark enveloped her, then made his way to the cabin.

He mounted the two steps to the porch, gun in hand, and stepped through the open doorway. Gwen was on the floor shrieking, on her side, hands on her face. The gun she had dropped had landed a couple of feet away from her associate, who lay unmoving on the floor in a broadening puddle of his own blood.

Michael said, "Hang on."

He stepped around her, and the blood, went to the kitchen sink, and tucked his gun into his jacket pocket. He found a pot in a cupboard, filled it with water from the tap, and carried it by the handle back to Gwen.

"Get onto your back and try to open your eyes," he said. "I'm going to pour water over them. Probably going to feel awful, but there you go."

"Cayden?" she said, unable to see.

Michael wasn't sure whether she was confused about who he was, or asking what had happened to him.

"Here comes the water," he said.

He poured the liquid over her eyes. She blinked furiously, her body tensed. Some water trickled into her throat and she went into a coughing fit.

"Sit up," Michael said, and got his arm under her back to raise her.

She opened her eyes long enough to get a look at him. "Why?" she asked.

"Because we had a deal," he said. "Lana's free."

Gwen turned her head, looked at Cayden. "How did she . . ."

"I don't know. She seems pretty resourceful."

"It's stinging," she said.

He poured more water over her eyes. She blinked several more times and tried to focus.

"He was dying and they wouldn't let me see him," she said. "He didn't even hear me say goodbye."

"That must have been awful," Michael said.

In the distance, the faint sound of sirens.

Gwen was now sitting without help from Michael, so he reached into his jacket and brought out his gun. Gwen's had landed too far away to reach conveniently.

"Here," he said, putting the gun into her right hand and wrapping her fingers around it. "Go ahead."

"What?"

"I don't blame you. If it gives you any comfort at all, it'll be worth it."

He guided her hand so that the barrel of the gun was touching his chest.

"I won't feel a thing," he whispered.

SEVENTY-TWO

Jack

I couldn't believe it when I saw her running toward me.

"Lana!"

Before she came into my arms I could see the tears and the blood, and my joy was immediately tempered by concern.

"Not my blood," she said before I could even ask. She hugged me so tightly I thought she might snap my spine. Her body was starting to heave with silent sobs. She was panting frantically, as if the air had suddenly been displaced.

I put some space between us and tried to get her attention.

"Lana, Lana, what's happened?"

"I tried . . . he wouldn't come . . . told me to go to the car." Several deep breaths. "You're not in the trunk."

"I got out. Whose blood is this? Dad's? Has Dad been hurt?"

She shook her head wildly. "The other one. I stabbed him, Jack. In the neck." Her eyes widened and she almost looked as though she might start laughing. She touched her own throat. "Right here. I got him here."

"Christ," I said. "What about Gwen?"

Several more deep breaths. "Pepper-sprayed her."

"What?" My face broke into a huge smile. "No shit? They're both down?"

She managed a nod.

I brought her briefly into my arms again. "Man, you are something else," I said, squeezing her. "What the hell's Dad doing then? Why didn't he come back with you?"

"I don't . . . I don't know."

I took her by the shoulders. "Go to the car. I'll be there in a minute. We found the actor."

She blinked. "Actor?"

"Just go to the car."

For the first time, I heard sirens. That lady in the farmhouse had done the right thing.

"The police are coming," I said. "Stay with Garth. He's a good guy."

Lana sniffed and said, "Hurry back."

As she headed up to the road, I started running for the cabin. I rounded a corner and there it sat in the clearing, the lights all on inside, the front door wide open.

I called out, "Dad! Dad!"

And then I heard the shot.

I poured on the speed, bounded onto the porch in one step, and came to an abrupt halt when I hit the doorway.

Took in the scene. Bedlam.

Dad lay on his side, clutching his stomach, eyes shut, his white shirt now mostly crimson. A low moan escaped his lips.

Gwen sat in the middle of the floor, legs outstretched, eyes bloodshot, her clothes and hair sopping wet, a gun in her hand. And there, to the left of her, was Cayden, facedown in a pond of blood, his arm outstretched, hand wrapped around another gun, pointed in the direction of my father.

Gwen had a bewildered expression on her face as she looked at me.

"I wasn't going to do it," she said. "He begged me, but I couldn't. But then Cayden . . . Cayden did it."

Even though Cayden appeared to have given up his last breath, I went over and pried the gun from his fingers. Then I stood over Gwen and extended my hand, inviting her to pass me the gun—I figured it was the one Dad had brought—and she did.

The sirens. They were getting so loud.

I knelt down by my father, put my hand to his neck, wondering whether I would feel a pulse.

"Dad?" I said.

His eyes fluttered open for a moment.

"Lana okay?" he asked.

"She's good," I said.

"I like her. She's a pistol."

"Yeah," I said. "Save your strength. Help's coming." I paused. "I thought you had a plan. I thought maybe Gord was coming."

"Give him my best."

"Shh," I said. "You're going to be okay."

"No, I'm not," he said.

And then he shut his eyes, and he was gone.

EPILOGUE

Jack

There were two funerals.

One for my father. And one for my other father.

I was able to work out, later, that Earl had been coerced by Gwen and Cayden to assist in the search for Michael Donohue, and that had involved working behind my back, even planting a listening device in my apartment.

But in the end, Earl tried to do the right thing. He tried to save Lana, and gave his life in the attempt, so I had to find it in my heart to forgive him.

Gwen Frohm was arrested and charged with Lana's kidnapping. That put her on ice while the authorities investigated all the other crimes she'd committed or instigated. The killings of retired judge Willard Bentley and Dr. Marie Sloan. The likely murder of my literary agent, Harry Breedlove. Although with Gwen's henchman, Cayden, dead, all three of these homicides would be harder to pin down. But there was enough to make it unlikely the daughter of Galen Frohm would ever see the outside of a prison again.

The story—no surprise here—garnered national attention for a few days. Daughter of disgraced CEO who had people killed grows up to be disgraced CEO who had people killed. What's not to love about a story like that? It had everything. As one of the players in this drama, I found myself invited to appear on Anderson Cooper's show one night but took a pass. I wanted this to all blow over as soon as possible.

Gwen had hoped to score some points for *not* killing my father, and who knows, maybe she would at some point. The way it was explained to me from those who interviewed her, my father had invited—implored—her to do it. Had her put the gun to his chest and encouraged her to pull the trigger, but for some reason she could not bring herself to do it. She was as surprised as my father must have been when Cayden, with the last ounce of life he had in him, did the job himself.

I'd really thought Dad had a plan.

When I drove up to see Gord one day—he took it kind of hard when I broke the news to him—he denied that my father had asked for his assistance.

On that same trip, Lana and I cleared out Dad's trailer and made arrangements to have it put up for sale. Inside we found autographed copies of the two books I'd written (in the name of Oscar Laidlaw, of course). That surprised me, as he'd never had me sign anything for him, in person. He would have had to make special orders from stores that had advertised having signed copies available.

Good ol' Garth didn't pursue any kidnapping charges against me. He even comped Lana and me tickets to see *The Price*.

The one I'm most worried about is Lana, although she'd tell you the one she's most worried about is me.

She's put up a brave front. She's tough, no doubt about it, and she wrote a big piece about what happened for her paper, but then allowed herself to be talked into taking a couple of weeks off. She was not charged in Cayden's death, and I can't imagine what the social media outrage might have been like had she been. But that didn't make her feel good about it. She'd done what she had to do. She'd gotten together a couple of times with her cop friend Florence, the one who, in the first place, had talked her into always keeping a few self-defense items on hand.

But underneath Lana's tough exterior was someone walking a high wire. I had moved in with her since everything happened, as much for her as for myself. We needed each other right now, although there hadn't been any talk lately about formalizing our arrangement. There was plenty of time for that.

We didn't leave her apartment much. Ordered in a lot, watched planes taking off and landing at Logan. Watched movies. Comedies, mostly, thinking they would make us laugh. Didn't work out that way.

But I believe we're going to come through the other side of this. What I'm less sure of is when.

The other morning, I got out of bed and went into the kitchen to get a pot of coffee going. On the counter was the new wallet that Lana had bought me that I had chosen, at the time, not to use.

I thought maybe the time had come.

As was my usual routine, I had left my watch and phone and wallet on the bedside table. I came into the bedroom as Lana was stirring.

"Coffee's on," I said. She saw what was in my hand.

"You're ready?"

I smiled. "I'm ready."

I sat on the edge of the bed, put the new wallet on the bedspread, and picked up my old one. Held it for a moment. It felt like something that had once been alive, but its life force was slipping away.

"You okay?" Lana asked.

"Yeah, I'm fine. It's just a wallet, right?"

I opened it up and took out my various cards from their slots. Visa, auto club, driver's license.

There was a slip of paper sticking out from under the flap that held the cards. I couldn't remember ever seeing it before. I slid it out. It was light-green stock, ruled, and I recognized it as likely coming from the notepad that had been in the glove compartment of Lana's car.

I slowly unfolded the paper. On it was a handwritten note. Done hastily. He'd obviously scribbled it in a hurry before folding it and tucking it where he figured I would find it eventually.

He must have done it when we stopped on the way back from New Hampshire for gas. I had left my wallet in the car, taking only my charge card with me. That would have given him about ninety seconds, maybe two minutes, to put his thoughts down on paper. So a few of the words took a moment to decipher, the handwriting was so bad.

But I finally figured out what it said. It read:

Jack—

   The remission period has ended. I had a good long run. Docs give me 2 months. It's all through for me. Nothing left to lose. If you find this, I hope it means we got Lana back. What are the odds a shit like me could produce a son like you? I could not be more proud. Have a great life.

Love, Dad

So there had been a plan. It was to die. To die doing something that had meaning.

I held the note in my hand, read it through three times. Lana was sitting up in bed, propped up against the headboard. I handed it to her.

As she read it, I noticed there was something else tucked into the wallet where the note had been hidden.

"What the . . ."

It took me a second to dig out what was in there.

"What is it?" Lana asked.

Two bills. A ten and a five.

"Fifteen bucks," I said, leaning over and putting my head in my hands.

Acknowledgments

I did it all on my own.

Okay, *that* is a lie if there ever was one.

So many people have played a role in bringing this book to you.

In the UK, thank you to the amazing team at HQ: Lisa Milton, Kate Mills, Claire Brett, Sarah Lundy, Alvar Jover, Georgina Green, and Anna Derkacz.

At William Morrow and HarperCollins in the United States, I am in debt to Liate Stehlik, Jennifer Hart, Tessa James, Emily Krump, Kelly Cronin, Lisa McAuliffe, Laura Brady, and Greg Villepique.

Here at home, thank you to Leo McDonald, Lauren Morocco, Neil Wadhwa, Brenann Francis, and Shamin Alli at HarperCollins Canada.

And, as always, thank you to the Marsh Agency in London and my amazing agent and friend, Helen Heller.

ONE PLACE. MANY STORIES

Bold, innovative and
empowering publishing.

FOLLOW US ON:

@HQStories